C000321193

Jack L. Chalker w
on 17 December 1
Baltimore, Maryl................ion, history and
geography all fascinated him early on, and he holds
bachelor degrees in history and English and an MLA
from the Johns Hopkins University. He taught history
and geography in Baltimore public schools between
1966 and 1978 and now makes his living as a freelance
writer. He began publishing an amateur science-
fiction journal, *Mirage*, in 1960, and has also founded
a publishing house, The Mirage Press, devoted to non-
fiction and works on science fiction and fantasy. His
hobbies include esoteric audio, travel, working on
science-fiction convention committees and guest lectur-
ing on SF to institutions like the Smithsonian. He is
also an active conservationist and National Parks sup-
porter.

He is the author of the bestselling sagas, *The Four
Lords of the Diamond* and *The Well World Saga*, both
published by Penguin. His other books include *A Jungle
of Stars*, *The Web of the Chozen* and *Dancers in the
Afterglow*. *Empires of Flux and Anchor* is the second of
the five volumes of *Soul Rider*.

**Exploring New Realms
in Science Fiction/Fantasy Adventure**

# The Soul Rider Saga
## by Jack Chalker

*Titles already published or in preparation:*

Book One: Spirits of Flux and Anchor

Book Two: Empires of Flux and Anchor

Book Three: Masters of Flux and Anchor

Book Four: The Birth of Flux and Anchor

Book Five: Children of Flux and Anchor

Cassie did not feel the Soul Rider enter her body . . . but suddenly she knew that Anchor was corrupt. Knew that the Flux beyond Anchor was no formless void, from which could issue only mutant changelings and evil wizards . . . Flux was the source of Anchor's existence! The price of her knowledge is exile – the first confrontation with the Seven Who Wait for the redemption of World . . .

—— SOUL RIDER ——

BOOK TWO
# EMPIRES OF FLUX
# & ANCHOR

## JACK L. CHALKER

**A ROC BOOK**

ROC

Published by the Penguin Group
Penguin Books Ltd, 27 Wrights Lane, London W8 5TZ, England
Penguin Books USA Inc., 375 Hudson Street, New York, New York 10014, USA
Penguin Books Australia Ltd, Ringwood, Victoria, Australia
Penguin Books Canada Ltd, 10 Alcorn Avenue, Toronto, Ontario, Canada M4V 3B2
Penguin Books (NZ) Ltd, 182–190 Wairau Road, Auckland 10, New Zealand

Penguin Books Ltd, Registered Offices: Harmondsworth, Middlesex, England

First published in the USA by Tom Doherty Associates, Inc., New York, 1984
Published simultaneously in Canada
First published in Great Britain by Penguin 1991
10 9 8 7 6 5 4 3 2 1

Copyright © Jack L. Chalker, 1984
All rights reserved

 Roc is a trademark of Penguin Books Ltd

Printed in England by Clays Ltd, St Ives plc

Except in the United States of America, this book is sold subject
to the condition that it shall not, by way of trade or otherwise, be lent,
re-sold, hired out, or otherwise circulated without the publisher's
prior consent in any form of binding or cover other than that in
which it is published and without a similar condition including this
condition being imposed on the subsequent purchaser

For Somtow Sucharitkul
a spectacle of unmitigated horror
with a dash of Bakti

# RECALCITRANT GODS

Gods do not normally expect to look out the windows of their palatial heavens and see an enemy army advancing.

Gyasiros Rex, Lord of Yalah, god and king in one, watched the forces advance and tried to think of what to do. His all-seeing eyes showed him the scope of the encirclement, despite the fact that the nearest enemy trooper was a good hundred kilometers away, but the fierce determination in the would-be attackers did not worry him. His Fluxland kingdom had an energy shield impenetrable to all except those he, as a god, might choose to admit, and it had been placed there by the sheer force of his will. Neither the troops nor their weapons could pass that shield until and unless it was broken down.

The tremendous power that Flux gave to selected individuals always seemed either to corrupt or drive the wielder of such power into some unique form of madness. Gyasiros had been born in Flux and trained as a wizard in the great magical university at Globbus, where he'd shown exceptional power in taking the raw energy that was the Flux itself and transforming it and all inside it as he willed. He was certainly a god in his own Fluxland, his power there absolute, and he loved it. Not merely political power; the very trees, rocks, animals, and even the sky were of his design and his to create, destroy, or alter as his mood moved

him. He was worshipped by his people, who knew,
too, that divine will rewarded the faithful and
punished the transgressor.

He liked things this way, and he was in no mood
to change or accommodate to anyone else's thoughts
or ideas. The rest of World concerned him not at
all, except for the necessary trade through the
stringers that brought him new toys and, occasionally, new books, which filled him with new
ideas. He knew, of course, of the seven gates to
Hell, sealed long ago, and knew that there were
those who would open them once more and end
World as he knew and liked it, but this was a
remote sort of threat that did not concern or worry
him. He knew, too, of the great Church that ruled
all twenty-eight Anchors, those places where no
Flux existed and no powers worked, but he thought
the Church welcome to such areas. Whole nations
without magic were Gyasiros' own idea of what
Hell must be.

Stringers had brought him word of a schism
within that church, led by a priestess who was
once of Anchor but now a powerful wizard in Flux,
but this, too, he tended to feel was no concern of
his. That had been far away and long ago, and
what was it to him what theology ruled outside of
Yalah and was imposed on the common masses?

And when the Reformed Church had sent emissaries to Yalah, he had not even bothered to listen
to them. Although one had been a wizard of reasonable power and had been most insistent, he had
impatiently turned them both into dogs. Later,
two more had come, both very strong wizards, and
he had been challenged somewhat. He found the
challenge amusing, but on World, where the power
of a Fluxlord was measured by the amount of
geography he or she could control and stabilize,
Gyasiros controlled one of the largest areas known.

In the end he'd changed the big man into a stately tree, and after that priestess or whatever she'd been had been forced to dance naked in the streets and then lick his feet, he'd removed her power of reason and freed her to live as an animal in his private forest.

But now, seeing the vast army besieging Yalah, he was beginning to feel annoyed.

This annoyance increased as the attack upon his shield commenced, an attack of such power and ferocity as he'd never known. The energy reserves and concentration required to stand against it caused the very ground to tremble and the reality of Yalah to shimmer and waver.

He began to get an awful headache.

Ultimately, he had to contract his shield boundaries a full ten kilometers to maintain a decent level, but this actually increased the psychic attack, as there was now less area for the enemy to concentrate upon. And as the shield withdrew, the armies advanced.

Not that he hadn't left all sorts of ugly surprises for them. The grass oozed acid that burned through clothing and armor and into flesh, while the roads became ugly tar-pits that grabbed and sucked down those who trod upon it, swallowing whole wagons. He knew that the attacking wizards must divert some power to neutralize his traps, and he waited to open his counterattack until he discerned a weakness in the attacker's will, but he sensed only a slight lessening of the attack, and that for a very brief period, and he began to grow worried. He had been attacked many times before by ambitious young wizards, some very powerful, who wanted to grab a ready-made Fluxland and, in defeating him, create instant respect and recognition, but all had failed. This, however, was different. These forces were seasoned troops, driven by some sense of mission, and there were so *many* of them! He knew that his own population, vast as it was, lacked the skill and training necessary to take them on in open battle. Oh, because he could command them, they would fight to the death and take a heavy toll, but it didn't take great wisdom to see that an army like this had faced that sort many times before—and was still here.

The headache grew far worse. He began to regret that he hadn't just sent those emissaries packing. Now, with his record, he could hardly expect them to send someone else. Mentally he cast about for his attackers, seeking the strongest wizard of the bunch. It was an easy task, although all were quite powerful. This one stood out like a beacon on a dark night, and he seized upon it. For the briefest moment he let down his guard for all save that one, and shot down its energy flow a single concept he was certain would be understood.

"It was?"

Then it all went back up, and he resumed the fight, waiting to see if the challenge would be taken. It was the simplest way out, but it would take some time after the wizard received and understood the message and invitation for word to get to the others. Now he could do nothing more than draw as much energy as possible from the Flux and wait.

The waiting was about three hours, about what he'd expected. His headache was now tremendous, but he was still holding on, after having to give up almost a quarter of Yalah.

Suddenly the attack on his shield ceased, and the relief was so great that this very cessation of hostilities almost caused him to pass out. That he did not only confirmed his own self-image and made him more confident. He was tired, true, but so were they, and so would be this one chief wizard he would have to meet and, perhaps, take on, one-on-one.

He looked out and watched as grim-faced, battle-hardened troops heard a call and divided and fell back in a mixture of awe and respect. The chief wizard, his true antagonist, was coming, as he had hoped. Still, it was difficult to believe the wizard's appearance when finally it materialized.

She was a small, thin, boyish-looking woman. She looked almost dwarfed against the backdrop of that great army. She had straight, stringy reddish-brown hair down to her waist, but wore no makeup or jewelry and looked pale and thin, her face hard and worn, aged far beyond her years. She wore only an old tattered robe that seemed two sizes too short for her and whose original color could not really be determined. She was barefoot.

Although her appearance was startling, particularly for one of such power, he did not underestimate her threat. Size, sex, age—none of that mattered in the Flux. He threw her a string—a weak energy beam that remained stable from origin to destination—and she saw it and acknowledged it with an offhanded nod to herself. Her body suddenly glowed, and then there was a bright flash and a surge of energy along the string. In an instant she was no longer so far away, but in his great hall, facing him.

Up close, she looked no different, only a bit older and more shopworn than he'd first thought. He, on the other hand, presented a more than regal appearance to her, in his flowing white robes, his golden, jewel-encrusted crown, and handsome, bearded face. He was at least two meters tall, and his body was perfectly proportioned and solid muscle.

"I am Gyasiros Rex," he told her in a melodious baritone. "Who are you that come to my domain, and for what reason?"

"I know who you are," she responded in a deep, throaty voice tinged with weariness and a trace of sarcasm. "I saw all the statues of yourself. I am Sister Kasdi, of the Reformed Church. I sent emissaries to you, not once but twice, in gestures of friendship. None of them ever returned. I come this time myself, speaking the only language I suspect you understand or respect."

"I have no interest in your church, your mission, or your emissaries," he responded, a bit irritated by her tone. He was not used to being talked to on anything like equal terms, let alone in the contemptuous tones this woman was using. "I also do not threaten you or your objectives in any way. I have what I want. I am content."

"You represent a potential threat to us that we must deal with. Many times in the past we have come upon Fluxlands that seemed no threat, only to find that they were ruled or controlled by our very enemies. We do not enforce conversation, so, if you had responded to our previous attempts, all this might have been unnecessary. It is now necessary. You have power enough that you might well be one of the Seven. That is sufficient reason to be here. If you are not, there will come a time when outside forces will make you choose a side, and your actions indicate to us that you would listen to the Seven over us. Your location is central to the routes we must take to the next Anchor cluster. You are in the way."

"And I cannot choose to be neutral?"

"You could have chosen it once. You could have chosen it twice. You have created your own situation. A neutral exists on trust. You have proven unworthy of trust. You have left yourself, and us, no choice in the matter."

He looked down at her contemptuously. "And *you* are going to do this? You think yourself a power superior to me? You, who use your power to dress in a rag and appear as ugly and worn as a middle-aged farmer's wife might after decades of fighting the land and bearing a dozen young?"

"My power may be used only to further the cause of my church and my goddess. I have willed it so."

"Then you are mad."

She sighed. "Aren't we all." It was not a question, but a statement of fact. "Still, better to become one like me than to become a thing like you."

He drew himself to his full height and roared, "You will fall down and worship me! You will kiss my feet and lick my holy ass!"

Anger rose within her at the thought of the probable fate of those who had come before. She had nothing but contempt for such hedonistic, power-mad egomaniacs as this, and no more compunction about dealing with them than she would when dealing with a poisonous snake. "Shall we see?" she asked icily, and struck.

It was one thing to have to break down a shield, a great energy construct continually reinforced from all the available energy *within* a Fluxland, but it was quite another face to face, with the quarry in sight, with the energy equally available to both and in equal amounts. Whoever could grab and direct the most of that vast yet finite energy would win any such contest.

Gyasiros felt as if every cell in his body had suddenly exploded and he screamed in mixed pain and rage. Summoning every ounce of ego and will, he beat back the tremendous energy blast, driving it from him and back towards its source. He drew in the energy around him, pushing it with his mind out towards that blaze of yellow light that represented the energy of his attacker.

She parried by the same method, their force of

wills creating a massive fireball seemingly suspended between them in the great hall, a ball that blazed and grew as more and more energy was poured into it by both sides. It did not remain still, however, creeping first one way, then the other, in small spurts. It had taken only a minute for the energy to reach critical portions in a literal sense. Whoever finally had that ball of fire forced onto their physical body could not stand against it.

The Lord of Yalah was strong indeed, but so was she—the strongest he had ever encountered—and he realized now the folly of issuing the challenge. She did not need to win, needed only to stall for however long it took for her forces, taking advantage of the collapsing shield, to move inwards towards the Fluxland's center, bringing with them wizards who at least would have had some rest. Such was his power that he might well have held half his dominion with that shield, but he could not maintain both shield and single combat.

The very realization of his mistake, and his self-acknowledgement of it, weakened his resolve. The two were barely seven meters apart, yet the ball, which had been centered for so long, now crept towards him until it was but two meters from him. And from the ball there came whispers, thoughts, insinuations that he could not shut out.

*"You are no god,"* the whispers said derisively, *"nor is your power anything like absolute. You are a mere man, a mortal man who can be killed by this woman and this thing creeping towards you, creeping, creeping. . . . Even your godlike body is a fraud, as your life is a fraud, a show, a thing not of majesty but of props and scenery, like theater. Even your power is illusion. . . ."*

He fought back the whispered doubts, knowing their origin, but he could not shut out the insults, the taunts, the claims, the—the blasphemy of it. And because he could not, he knew, in some corner of his mind, that it must be true.

The ball crept closer, millimeter by millimeter.

Summoning every ounce of divine fury and will, he lashed back at it, and when it retreated, he laughed aloud and his eyes blazed with the look of true madness, his confidence renewed as the ball retreated almost to the center once again.

Suddenly the laughter died on his lips and he looked around, momentarily confused. It was hard to breathe now. He opened his mouth to suck in air, but there seemed no air to come in. His disorientation was brief, but it was enough.

Suddenly there was air again, and he drank it in, concentration wavering. The ball suddenly rushed in upon him, enveloped him, held him in horrible pain. He had lost! But he couldn't lose! He was Gyasiros Rex, God of Yalah, a creature of perfection whose power was omnipotent! But if he could not lose, then what was this? *Transcendence!* The ball did not consume, but filled him with power beyond imagining! He drank it in, more, more. . . . *Not God of Yalah, but God of all Creation! He was now supreme!*

Kasdi broke with him and followed the string back to the lines, hoping it would be far enough.

Even now, still close to a hundred kilometers out, they saw the tremendous flash and, seconds later, heard and felt the mighty roar of the explosion.

A shaken soldier near her turned, ashen-faced, and asked, "What in the name of all that is holy was *that?*"

"Overload," she responded tiredly. "I gave him all the power of the battle and ninety percent of the remainder. He took it in, unable to control himself any longer. There is only so much energy that can be concentrated in one point. Beyond that, nothing can control it. When that point passed, he could no longer hold it nor would it be held, so it ran from the point, dispersing in all directions. It also dispersed him, of course."

"I just can't believe it could happen," he breathed.

"It was he who gave me the idea. I simply applied it literally. You see, all these powerful Fluxlords are unstable."

# DESTINY'S SAINT

It was hard being a saint, not only in being regarded as one by a large mass of people but also, quite literally, being forced to be one. It was a self-inflicted wound that had been compounded more and more over the years, but, as much as she disliked it, she believed more and more in the necessity of it.

She sat in her office in the temple of Hope. It wasn't much of an office, really. An old wooden chair whose finish was worn creaked with her every movement, although she was small and thin. Her desk was a table in barely better repair, atop which sat a battered-looking old oil lamp, various papers, and a pen and inkwell. Other than that the place was barren and quite small, totally undecorated, its stone walls and floor more reminiscent of a monastic cell than the seat of power of one of the most powerful people on World.

Although the temple and, indeed, the entire Fluxland of Hope was her creation, she spared little of that power on herself. Although there were far less spartan offices and quarters, she disdained them, and the only sop to her comfort was a small window behind her that allowed her to look out on the temple grounds and the lands beyond.

She knew as well as anyone that all this was due less to a total act of faith than to the shock and revulsion at seeing Matson fall in the battle for this place. Emotion was the trigger to the power of

17

the Flux, the raw motivator that multiplied a
wizard's energy exponentially as the intensity of it
rose. Still, she felt, *knew*, that all of it had been a
part of a divine plan and that she was the key
player anointed to carry that plan out.

The Church had been corrupted beyond any point
of redemption, that she knew. It had turned from
its holy mission of salvation to one of repression,
the alter-ego of the wizards of Flux. They had
perverted their entire faith into a massive and
effective dictatorship and had held humanity in
the grip of their corrupt power for centuries, even
rewriting Holy Scripture to support all their moves.
That had been one of her first and most important
acts—the gathering of Scripture and all other ancient and suppressed documents from the vaults of
the Church and from sanctuaries in Fluxlands, and
then the appointment of a board of the finest schol-
ars and translators to sort, evaluate, and codify all
of that material. It was a massive undertaking,
and the Codex was still years away from completion, but not from use.

Her mentor, Mervyn of Pericles, who was more
than six centuries old and one of the powerful
Nine Who Guard, called what was being done a
revolution, but it was true in only the most literal
sense. What she was doing was less revolution
than restoration, putting humanity back on the
path from which it had been diverted.

To do this, she required a true and honest clergy,
one immune to the sort of corruption the old Church
had fostered, and this had to be accomplished by
magic. Ordination was more than a commitment;
it was the acceptance of spells binding one for life
to those vows.

Because of this, she'd realized from the start
that she had to set the example, had to *be* the
saint, for it was she who imposed those lesser but
still binding restrictions on the vows. As the highest,

if she were not also the lowest, living a life that was far harsher than theirs, they could not be expected to make the sacrifices and keep to them. Her life and actions had to make their own burdens seem trivial by comparison, and it certainly did. Even Mervyn, who had taught her the one unbreakable spell that could only be imposed freely on one's self, believed she had gone too far and that the pressures of living such a life would eventually drive her mad. She had disagreed, and over the seventeen years since those first vows she had in fact added to them whenever she perceived a loophole.

The vow of poverty, of course, did not mean that the Church was poor. Far from it. It needed the tithe to spread its word, support its temples, churches, and missions, its charity and its holy works. The priestesses who did the work owned nothing, but had unlimited use of church buildings, clothing, food, and the rest. They were not living like the rich and the wizard monarchs, of course, but they were comfortable. She did not allow herself even that.

She quite literally had no possessions of any sort. No mementos of her past, no pictures or souvenirs or keepsakes. She slept, in whatever random empty monastic cell she found, on a bed of straw or, occasionally, on the stone floor. She had no aides or assistants; she cleaned out the cell every morning, using common cleaning materials from the temple stores and scrubbing on her hands and knees. She ate only the plainest of foods from the communal kitchens, along with all the others, and she even washed her own dishes. Undergarments and shoes required a special size and fit, so she had dispensed with them. She generally borrowed a comb and brush from whoever was around, high or low, and returned them cleaned, and bathed either in the river or in the communal showers

used by the acolytes, the not-yet-priestesses who
studied here. Her simple robe was a worn-out cast-
off of the temple which she washed each night.
When it wore out, she would hunt through the
trash for another that would do. Even the desk,
table, and lamp in the office she had found in
Anchor trash dumps and repaired herself as much
as she could for use.

She allowed no one to wait on her, and she
accepted no charity, although she would accept an
offer of dinner or such in Anchor or Flux if it were
truly offered in friendship and without expectations.
She did not smoke, drink, or even swear—the spell
prevented it. And her chastity was absolute, so
much so that even simple self-stimulation was
beyond her. This didn't mean she didn't feel the
need for such things—she often did, particularly in
the early days—but she had made it impossible for
her to violate her way of life. By now, though, she
hardly gave any of it a thought. It was the way it
was, the way it had been for most of her adult life,
and the way it would always be.

She had not just done this to create an example
and remove all temptation from her, though. In a
very real sense, it liberated her from all the pressures of daily life and from its temptations as well.
She desired nothing she did not already have, save
an end to these wars and the total reformation of
the Church; she had nothing at all that anyone
else might want except, perhaps, her wizard's
power, which could not be transferred in any event.
She knew that, while many might covet high
Church positions, none wanted her job—not with
the living conditions that came with it.

She took no part in the day-to-day affairs of
running the Temple or the Church as a whole. She
knew she was not temperamentally suited to be the
administrative type. Her jobs, her only jobs, were
spreading the reformation throughout World and

purifying and restoring the faith and keeping it pure.

The only time she used her powers for her own gain, other than to ward off starvation or desperate thirst, was when she went out alone across the void to Anchor. There was an inevitable tendency for people to mistake the agent for the boss; she was virtually worshipped by many as some sort of deity herself, a fact that made her uncomfortable, but which had proved impossible to stamp out completely. To go out alone, particularly on personal business, she required a disguise, and transformed herself, for that purpose only, into the guise of a low-ranking priestess of far different appearance. It allowed her a measure of temporary anonymity, although she was still bound to her lifestyle.

For she did have one thing that might be used against her if known. She had a daughter, it was true, and she had done all she could to keep that fact and her daughter's identity a deep secret. She had once considered a vow of truthfulness to match her vow of honesty, but had rejected it. That much corruption she had to allow, for a good cause. The official story was that her child had been stillborn. She could hardly hide the signs in those early days, and although she'd used her powers to eliminate the stretchmarks and other signs, it was known she'd borne a child in Anchor.

Had the child been born in Flux, it would have been a painless and effortless birth, though also one that could hardly be a seat of deception. Ironically, the lying powers of Flux would not permit an imperfect birth to a wizard; only in Anchor could the child "die" as it had to. In fact, the child had been born perfectly in any event, and those involved had voluntarily submitted to changes in their memory to conform to the official version, those changes made by Mervyn in Flux. Only four people knew that the child lived and who she was: Kasdi, of course, and her cousin Cloise, who had taken the child and raised it as her own in Anchor Logh, as well as the wizard Mervyn and the Sister General of Logh, Tamara, her oldest and closest friend.

The child had been named Spirit—it was her one conceit, and seemed inevitable. She knew that she was adopted, of course—the records of Anchor were more likely to trip them up than hide them in their scheme if they had pretended otherwise— but believed that her parents had died in the conflicts raging back at that time. Nor did Spirit look anything like either Kasdi or Matson; that had been a part of it, too, as any enemy might well look at Kasdi's native land and her large family there in its search for things to use against her.

Spirit had grown into a young woman now, and it was a shock to see her these days. Olive-skinned and curvaceous, well-built as Kasdi herself never was, with a beautiful face and long, black hair and huge, soft brown eyes, she was the heartthrob of every teen-age boy in Anchor Logh.

Sister Kasdi ached every time she thought of Spirit, which was all the time she wasn't preoccupied with matters of duty. She was proud of her daughter in every way, for Spirit was also exceptionally bright and at least shared her real mother's love for animals and nature, but there was much guilt there, too. Although Spirit had been well brought up in an atmosphere and surroundings not unlike her mother's, the girl had been raised by others. Although she had kept close track of her daughter's progress, she'd really had no input into anything not genetic in her only child's upbringing. Oh, she'd visited Spirit when she could, under the guise of a priestess who was a cousin of her late mother's, but that was about it.

She was lost in such thought when she suddenly

became aware of a throat clearing and snapped out of it for a while. Sister Karla, the administrative priestess for the level, stood there looking apologetic. "Sorry I must disturb you, Sister, but the wizard Mervyn is here to see you."

Kasdi brightened a bit. "Send him in! And don't hesitate to disturb me. It is not good when I think too much."

The priestess frowned a moment in puzzlement, then turned and walked back out the door. A moment later Mervyn entered, stopped, and looked around. He had the look of a very old man with flowing white hair and beard and a floor-length robe of cream-colored silk embroidered with gold trim. It was not a church robe, of course—only women could be priestesses—but one more in keeping with the image he liked to project. Only his bright, piercing eyes that seemed to look everywhere at once revealed the strength hidden in that baggy robe and those ancient features.

"*Hmph!* No furniture for guests yet, I see." He made a quick pass with his hand and then sat—in a comfortable, padded chair which simply appeared behind him. He studied her face for a moment. "You look lousy," he told her.

She chuckled. "Always the soul of tact, aren't you?"

"After six hundred and forty-seven years I have earned the right not to have to play silly social games. You're—what?—thirty-six, and you look half as old as I do. Your eyes and bearing look even older, and that's going some."

"It hasn't been a very easy life, as you well know. That Yalah business a week ago took a lot out of me, too. I slept for three days after that, and since that time I've been happy just living simply and routinely here."

He rose slightly and looked on the table at the paper in front of her. It was a map of World, a very simple map with a few notations written in by Kasdi. It was a record of progress and achievement unprecedented in history, but he suspected that this record wasn't what she saw in that map. Instead, it represented seventeen years of hard work and sacrifice on her part. The map was her autobiography.

The map showed the seven "clusters" of Anchors, four to a group, or cluster, each equidistant from a Hellgate in the center of the square they formed. They were quite symmetrically spaced around the perimeter of the planet, a fact that only reinforced the logic of a divine plan. A full four clusters were now under the Reformed Church, more than half the planet, with the Fluxlands between, inside, or on the stringer routes through the void that connected them, all either under the control of her partisans or in truce with them. There were still many bizarre lands there, and many mad rulers like the late, unlamented Gyasiros, but all had chosen not to challenge her power but to accommodate it.

The rest had fallen through a combination of arms and sorcery, as had Gyasiros. They had been tough at the start, with much bloodshed and wizards' contests, but there were few such these days. The word was getting around, and all save the maddest of egomaniacs found some room in their demented psyches for a compromise between the Church's wishes and their own egos. Not that the old Church and the old order had been a pushover, but not since the Battle of Balacyn, fourteen years earlier, when armies of more than a million faced off in Flux, along with some of the most powerful living wizards known—on both sides—had they tried a major offensive. Still, the next cluster would be as well-defended as any in the past, and both sides still lost bitter and bloody battles.

In fact, although much of Flux was getting easier, the Anchors were becoming harder and harder, as the opposition had plenty of time to prepare and had learned so much about its foes. Now only stringers crossed the line between old and new, and only with difficulty and much suspicion.

"I worry about how much longer we have to go," she told him wearily. "How many more years, how many more lives?"

"I'd worry about what happens when it's done," he responded.

"Huh?"

"We're the founders of a new world here. Science once again is flowering in Anchor, and a freed people are building new institutions, new ways, that we never dreamed of. Eventually there will be greatness here again—and you will have shut yourself off from ever being a part of it. In the name of moving this world forward, you've pushed yourself backward to the most primitive sort of life. Have you ever thought of that?"

"No," she answered truthfully. "There's no way to do what must be done for this new world you speak of if I think of my own future. The next problem, the next march, the next Yalah, the next threat to what we have already built—those occupy my mind." She sighed. "I suppose I shall retire when it's over. Walk World from end to end, pole to pole, seeing all that there is to see. Perhaps teach or preach or both. I don't know. It's so far off."

"Maybe, maybe not."

"But that wasn't what you came all this way to talk about, and I know it. Now—what's the real reason for all this?"

"The greater evil is on the move once more. I think at least the first part of the move will be in your direction."

Her eyebrows rose. "You mean the Seven? I

thought we must have weakened them enormously;
it's been so long since they tried anything."

He sighed. "They are not at all weakened, nor is
your statement correct. They are, in most cases,
very much in the background. Only rarely does
one like a Haldayne draw attention to himself, and
then only when it's part of the plan. Just who do
you think we've been fighting all these years?"

"Why, the old Church, of course!"

"And who exactly *is* the old Church? Doesn't
corruption on such a scale show us something right
there? I have just recently come into some information that suggests that Her Perfect Highness,
the Queen of Heaven, might in fact be Gifford
Haldayne's older sister."

That startled her. "What! I have fought them a
long time, I know, but I never thought—"

"Yes, indeed," he interrupted. "Who would? This
is not to say that the church is, as an entity, a
direct and knowing agent of the Seven. Proof of
*that* would be sufficient to win you the rest of
World without lifting a finger. But the corruption
begins at the very top. How do you suppose they
finally discovered the gate entrances inside the
temples, buried under the very foundations? They
poked and probed and experimented until it was
discovered—having access to temples."

"But—this is monstrous!"

"Indeed. However, up to now it's worked to our
advantage. The Seven now control three of the
gates through their subtle control of the church.
They are very busy making certain they lose no
more of those gates. Had we not discovered them
shortly after they discovered the temple entrances
and denied them access to at least one, they might
have fulfilled their plan without us even realizing
it was so until the hordes of Hell overran us. That's
what your Soul Rider was rushing to Anchor Logh
to prevent, and when it did, it rushed to some

other emergency. Since then, they've been very busy just trying to hold onto what they have, and with not much success. If *you* spent years fighting off an attacker and still knew you were losing, would you keep on doing the same thing?"

She considered it. "No. Of course not. I would have acted long before this, in fact."

He nodded. "I think the Queen of Heaven is the boss—or was, anyway. She kept them in line because the church was the seat of her power, and she threw everything into trying to keep it. Now, however, my agents inform me that the others have rebelled, citing her failures, and that she has been forced to go along. There was allegedly a summit meeting of all Seven, the first such known to me. At that meeting all the restraints came off. Our friend the Queen of Heaven will continue to defend in her old ways, perhaps assisted by others, but there will now be a division of forces and a new direction. The word in Flux is that they want to tackle you first, before this grand new plan is put into operation."

"You mean, call me out and face me down? I'd almost welcome that, even three or four to one."

"Don't take it lightly. They are more powerful than any other wizards known, except for yourself. It is my firm conviction that one or perhaps several of them are at least your equal. However, calling you out is simply not their way. It would bring the Nine in a flash, and they know it. They are not ready to face down all of us. They are infinitely patient, preferring to minimize risks to themselves and suffer a thousand defeats if they gain the final victory. Still, they are diabolically clever and you must be on guard." He paused a moment. "I fear that your one soft spot in your armor may be in peril."

She felt a shock go through her. "But—how could

they know? And if they did, why haven't they acted before now?"

He shrugged. "I don't know if they know or not, but as to the timing—perhaps, like the Hellgate, they just found out. As I said, they are a patient lot. And *that* brings up a rather chilling question. What would you do if they got her and offered a trade?"

She shivered at the idea. "I don't know. I honestly don't."

"You would not be permitted to do so," he warned her. "The Nine would prevent you, no matter what. You are a symbol that, right now, we cannot do without."

"But the Seven know that, too. Isn't that some form of insurance?"

He shook his head sadly. "Perhaps. But they are devious in the extreme. They have failed militarily. To gain the seven gates, they must infiltrate and, if possible, corrupt the Reformed Church. To do that, they must remove—or corrupt—you." He sighed. "We could put more of a watch on her, of course, but that alone might tip them off if they don't yet have the exact one. Or we could bring her here, to Hope. It is the best-guarded, safest place anyone could be."

She shook her head negatively at that. "What sort of life would it be for her here? She's shown no inclination towards the priesthood and much for the boys. There'd be no joy for her in Hope."

"You didn't have much inclination for the priesthood yourself at her age, and look what happened to you. But, let that pass for now. There is always Pericles, which is also as safe as they come."

"But just taking her there would point a finger at her. *Then* they would *know*, and, as you said, they are patient. She would be a prisoner there for as long as I was a threat to the Seven. That might be decades."

"Then we leave things as they are," the wizard said flatly. "I don't like it, but there it is. At least you should do one thing for her—you should tell her her true origins and parentage."

The idea frightened her. "Uh—no. Not yet. She would never understand. She would never forgive me!"

"If she is at risk, she must know it and know the reason why. She must be prepared to defend herself. If we do not remove her from harm's way, then we must give her every chance. We can't keep diverting her, nailing her into Anchor Logh. She's inquisitive, just like her mother. She wants to see the whole of World. I think it is time. You have inflicted so much sacrifice and injury upon yourself—now it is time to do it once more, this time for the sake of another."

She sighed. "I'll meditate and pray on it. That's all I'll promise right now."

"Don't think or meditate or pray too long," he warned her. "Evil is on the march once more, and the more they are set back, the more determined, devious, and dangerous they become."

Tomorrow would be a Service of Ordination at the Temple of Hope. When she was there, Kasdi liked to preside over it herself, although there were by now many other powerful wizard-priestesses capable of administering the rites. It was something she liked to do, a sort of affirmation of the rightness of her cause and the future of World to see those bright, young faces eagerly accept the vows without coercion.

Once young women were almost forced into the priesthood when they possessed some talent or ability the church needed. They were immediately ordained so they could never quit, then underwent three years of rigid indoctrination—brainwashing, she'd heard it called. She had changed all that when she'd abolished the barbaric and terrible Paring Rite that had cast her out of Anchor into Flux. Now the Flux, at least in her areas, was not such a terrible or threatening place, and population controls were managed quite easily by voluntary shifts. Those who discovered that they had some Flux power—either false, in which all their spells were illusion, or true, in which their will could truly become reality—usually opted for training and a new life in Flux anyway.

Now, at the completion of required school, young women were shown the possibilities the priesthood offered. The parish had always been the center of social life in Anchor, and the priesthood was highly respected, even more now than under the old way. If a young woman so chose, she could come to Hope, at Church expense, and spend two years as an acolyte, living a very spartan life under strict discipline while learning the intricacies of the preisthood and the faith. They were not ordained at that time, and if the spare lifestyle, the lack of comforts and modern conveniences, was too much for them, they could ask to leave and would be returned. If they found their religious training boring and their potential occupations wrong, they could also leave, and were encouraged to do so. Those that remained, about thirty percent of the women who began, could then request ordination and go on to deeper, more complex subjects and train for their life's work.

The high washout rate, both voluntarily and otherwise, had given those who remained an extra feeling of pride and accomplishment. The initial life and training was intended to be rough, and it was—but those who survived it felt closer to each other and the church than ever. They felt like something special and had pride in themselves and their work.

Tomorrow a group numbering more than eighty

would request ordination. Most would be given it without question, but a few would not, and it was those whom she wished to see that evening. These were the few that the teachers and psychologists suggested might be wrong for the job, and they required a different evaluation. Now Sister Kasdi sat in her barren Office, Mervyn's stuffed chair dematerialized back into energy, and waited for the first of the nine who had been sent for this final process.

The first girl entered, wearing only the white sheet-like garment that was all the acolytes were allowed. She looked very nervous, as was to be expected. She was a tall, gangly young woman, rather plain in appearance. She stood there, staring at the saint behind the table, a touch of awe in her face despite the situation.

"Child—tell me, why do you wish to become a priestess?" Kasdi asked pleasantly. All acolytes were referred to as "child" and "children" while here. "By that I mean, what made you choose to come here and undergo the training rather than something else someplace else?"

"Uh, Sister, I—I had no life in Anchor Chalee. I never had any close friends, and never any boyfriends. I wanted to do something *important* with my life, something that would do good and make folks look up to me. My marks were pretty good, though nothing great. This seemed like the place I had to be."

Kasdi nodded, mostly to herself. Although she was using a spell to divine the truth, she was not compelling it. The brutal honesty of the girl was refreshing, if a bit *too* honest. She clearly had very low self-esteem, and that was not good. Her motives weren't wrong in and of themselves, but they contained no dedication to the spiritual at all.

"You have been frank, so I will be, too," Kasdi responded. "The Sisters see absolutely no devotion or dedication to the Holy Mother and the spreading of Her plan. Instead, they see someone who wishes security and a sorority. What do you say to that?"

"I've had the finest experience of my life here these past two years."

"Perhaps that's true, but might it not be because here, for the first time, you were totally socially equal to the others? Still, you have stayed the entire course and even excelled in much of it. We cannot just summarily throw you out. I propose a bit of a final test for you."

The acolyte swallowed hard. "A test, Reverend Sister?"

"Yes. There is a stringer train due to go out of here tomorrow evening. It is not going back to Anchor Chalee, but over to Anchor Logh, but any Anchor will do for this. You will be given some money and a wardrobe, and you will depart with that train. Go into the Anchor and take a holiday. Return to the world. Relax. Do not check in with the Church or tell anyone you are an acolyte. Remain a minimum of two weeks, but stay as long as you wish. Only—keep the vows as you can. See if you can ward off temptation. See if, after that time there, you can bring yourself to return here."

"Yes, Reverend Sister."

Kasdi could read her thoughts in her facial expression and tone. "You think it will be easy. Don't believe it. It would be easy under normal circumstances, but this will not be normal. I have used my powers to change you. See."

A mirror appeared against the far wall, and the young woman turned and gasped. Kasdi had not turned her into a raving beauty, but she was rather cute and pleasant-looking, perhaps a hair above average. It was, however, more than enough for the acolyte, and she stared in wonder and admiration at the reflection until the mirror faded out.

"If you do not return here, you will continue to look like that. If you *do* return, you will revert to your original appearance. It is a pleasantry from the church for giving it two years of your life. It is also a test—not of faith, but of *commitment* to the church. If your true interest is service, you will return. No questions will be asked of your behavior, and your sins will be between you, your confessor, and the Holy Mother. If you return, you will be ordained. That is all."

The acolyte backed out, then turned and was quickly away. Kasdi expected she would never be seen in or near Hope again, but she had occasionally been proven wrong.

The next girl was the opposite of the first in every way. Most of the young women who volunteered for the priesthood were average, some below average, in appearance, and many just saw themselves that way. The personality quirks of the first girl would hardly have disqualified her, since most had personal goals and reasons for choosing this life, but it was her total lack of any feeling at all for the spiritual mission that had caused the problem.

This one was a mystery. Even in her white sheet, she was absolutely beautiful, totally feminine, and in anybody's book she might be called over-endowed. Her voice was as soft and as beautiful as her form. It always amazed Kasdi when somebody looking like this applied as an acolyte. Her own adolescence had been more like the first girl's, and she would have killed at one time for this one's looks. Still, she asked the same question.

"Child, why did you come here and why do you wish to join the priesthood?"

"It—it's difficult to explain, Reverend Sister."

"Try me. You've been asked this and answered this a thousand times before."

The girl sighed. "Well, all those times I've had

people just shake their heads. I'm pretty. I know it. I've always been what everybody calls beautiful. The trouble is, that's all anybody ever saw. I couldn't walk into an Anchor and open a door— men would jump to open it for me—or do much of *anything* for myself. I applied for a number of jobs, and passed all the tests, but when I was interviewed, all they saw was my looks. In some cases they just decided I had to be dumb or something, and rejected me. In others, they were more than eager to take me on, but I could see why and I knew what they were really hiring. But I'm smart, and I think I can do good things, if only people would take me for myself, not for my looks."

Kasdi thought about it. Intellectually she could understand the problem, but emotionally it was pretty tough to think of brains and beauty as anybody's curse. "But why the priesthood?"

"I got to thinking about it all after that, and walking past the temple, I suddenly got a thought. Maybe it was *supposed* to be this way. I can serve the Holy Mother, and serve humanity, too, by putting my brains to work. And if my beauty gives me an edge in attracting sinners and talking to them, then it becomes an asset, but not with sex and lust as its end-product. You see?"

Kasdi nodded, and thought about it. "The reason you're here, you know, is exactly such doubts. We don't doubt your mind, your devotion, or your reasons. I feel you would be a credit to the church. Our problem is you over the long run. The vow and binding spell of celibacy is absolute, but it does not transform you into a neuter. To do that would be to deny your womanhood and forfeit your humanity. As a result, we all still feel the same attractions, urges, and needs as all women do. Being forbidden to act on them can make the pressure inside enormous. We fear for your sanity. Have you thought about this?"

She nodded. "Yes, Reverend Mother. But if the way were easy, would it be worth traveling at all? Just because some of the others are not as pretty, do they feel those urges and physical needs any less than I do? If I cannot make that sacrifice for Her sake, and bear it, then I'm really only fit to be the brainless sex machine everybody sees. And if I have to be *that*, I really *will* go mad."

Kasdi was touched by her sincerity and eloquence. "You are absolutely positive you wish this, then? There are no doubts whatsoever in your mind?"

"None. It will set me free to do Her will."

Kasdi prayed for a moment for some guidance. Finally she said, "All right, then. We will not stand in your way, but embrace you as a sister. Come tomorrow with the rest. You will be ordained."

The girl looked overjoyed at the news. "Thank you, Reverend Sister! Oh, thank you! The Holy Mother's blessing remain with you!"

Kasdi finally excused her and went on to the next. The rest were all unique, all with their own problems, but all there with good reason. All of the acolytes actually received this sort of interview, but these were the ones passed on up the line, either by divided opinions down below or undecided ones. Now, finally, she was finished, and she got up, blew out the lamp, and walked out into the temple, then down into its depths. She neither ate nor drank, since, as the officiator, she had to fast until it was over, but that didn't bother her.

There were many empty cells—a whole floor of them—at this stage, and she had no difficulty finding one. She went back down the hall to a janitorial room and found a bucket, washboard, and some soap, then went into the now-deserted shower room. She removed her robe and then washed it, using extra bleach, then showered. She did not dry herself, preferring to let herself dry naturally. She then

spent the better part of an hour compulsively cleaning the entire shower room and lavatory. Then she
showered off again and returned with her wet robe
to her small cell. She then spent the bulk of the
night in prayer, but only some of those prayers
were for those she would ordain tomorrow. Others,
despite herself, were prayers for someone to tell
*her* what to do as wisely and as easily as she had told
the others during the night.

She, who had faced down powerful madmen,
routed a chief agent of Hell, and brought down a
church and an oligarchy, prayed for the courage to
face her own daughter.

The sacrament was a very serious and solemn
one, and Sister Kasdi always took pains to see that
it was a serious, personal occasion. Later, these
new priestesses would return briefly to their home
Anchors before assignment, and at that time, in
their local parish churches, there would be a public reaffirmation and celebration for all. This,
however, was the real thing.

They entered through the great doors to the inner temple in a processional, singing an old hymn
in praise of heaven and its works, and filed off
on either side of the center aisle, each kneeling in
turn before the altar in the middle of the aisle
before assuming her place. There were no witnesses,
and only Kasdi would officiate.

She waited for them before the altar, standing
there looking out at them resplendent in the gold-
embroidered purple robe that signified her true
office as the warrior priestess, the purple showing
her seat of power was in Flux. The robe, her original robe of ordination, was kept in the Temple
museum except on occasions like this.

The high service, said only in temples, went
smoothly, although only on ordinations was it done
solo. Usually such services had and often required

quite a crowd of officiators and assistants, and it was impressive to the newcomers to see how majestic it all sounded even when done by one lone, small woman.

Finally she turned from the altar and looked out upon them. It was time.

"In ancient times there was rebellion in Heaven," she told them, "and in the end the folk of Heaven were divided by the divine will of the Lady and Mistress whom we serve." It was a familiar story, but part of the service.

"Those who turned their backs upon Her were banished to Hell," she continued, "and the seven gates of Hell were sealed. Those who stood by Her remained in a more perfect Heaven, now purified once more. The rest were condemned as souls to World, to the place She called Forfirbasforten, which means the place of testing. Here the rest of the impure, not wholly evil but tainted by evil, were to suffer both a sample of the joys of Heaven and the torments of Hell, living life after life, as male and female, until those souls were purified to Her absolute standards or until the gates of Hell should again be unlocked and we should once again be forced to choose."

She paused for a moment, then asked, "What is the Church?"

"The Church is the guardian of all that is good and holy," responded the acolytes in unison.

"What is the mission of the Church?"

"To define good and evil, so that humanity may always choose their own test."

"Who are the priestesses?"

"Those through whom the Holy Mother acts to carry out the divine plan."

"What are the priestesses?"

"The soldiers of the Holy Mother, guardians of the Church, interpreters of the law and of divine will," they responded.

"It is not an easy road to come as far as you have," Kasdi told them. "Many believe themselves called, but when the testing is complete, only a very few remain. Those who do—you—are the best of the best, the very future of the Church and of humanity, whose souls will be in your care and will be your responsibility. All of you come of your own free will to this place today. Even now, if any among you has the slightest doubt that this is the proper and only course for your life, you should now refuse the sacrament of ordination. It will not be held against you, nor is it irrevocable—but ordination *is* irrevocable. Any who even now have the slighest doubt should stand down and leave this place."

She paused a moment, looking. Occasionally one or two actually did refuse at this point, and they all knew that such refusal would indeed be understood by all. This time, however, nobody spoke or moved.

Sister Kasdi nodded in approval. "Very well. The life of a priestess is hard. The demands are great, the rewards often not evident and always intangible. Devotion demands sacrifice. For two years you have left the type of life in which you were raised. Now you must surrender it forever." Even as she spoke the required words, she began the complex mathematical constructs that, when used in Flux by one of power, were binding and compelling spells. Those spells were upon all in the room from this point on. "Know that your responses now will blind you," she warned them, "and that there will be no exceptions in this chamber regardless of response."

In other words, it really wasn't the responses that bound them, but Sister Kasdi's wizard-shattering power. "Kneel, pray, and repeat what I say.

"I wish to be a priestess of the Holy Church. I desire no other calling, no other task. It is the highest position to which I can aspire, and the only one I desire now or forever more."

She paused after each line to get the mass response.

"I have no family but the sisters of the Church. My parents are the Holy Church, now and forever, and exclusively. All priestesses are my sisters, and I belong to no other family nor recognize any other siblings. I surrender my past utterly to the Church, as I surrender all my worldly goods. I renounce pride except in my holy office, in my accomplishments for the Church, and in the Church itself. I renounce envy in all its forms." She went through the litany of the rest of the deadly sins of humanity.

"I am the bride of the Church and can accept no other suitor. I vow absolute chastity and celibacy in all its forms for the rest of my life, so that I may never divide or betray that suitor. I renounce all worldly possessions and vow henceforth poverty, giving all I have or will have to the Church and desiring nothing material for the rest of my life, trusting in our Holy Mother to provide. All humanity are my children, my charge, and my responsibility. I vow absolute obedience to the Holy Church, its doctrines and its teachings, and obedience to those sisters whom the Holy Mother has elevated over me. My sole purpose in life is to serve humanity and the Holy Mother Church to the utmost of my talents and abilities. These things I do solemnly and freely vow, swear, and affirm in the presence of the Holy Mother and of my sisters, now and forever until death."

It was done, and the spell was a powerful one. A first-rank wizard could break it, but nothing except the self-binding spell was unbreakable. Still, none of them now would want or try to break it, so any such thing would be against their will. It was a sufficient guard against the sort of corruption the old church bred, and had proven so.

Now, one by one, they came up the aisle and removed their white robe, putting it in a container, and then went behind the altar rail and stood, totally naked, behind Kasdi. As each approached the altar and knelt once again, Kasdi pronounced a name. There was a whole department to choose the names of priestesses so that there would be no overlaps and no confusion. Henceforth, the name she gave them would be the only name they would respond to as their own or think of as theirs.

Midway through, the extremely beautiful young woman she'd talked to the night before approached, even more stunning unclothed, and Kasdi smiled and said, "Sister Marigail." She smiled back and took her place.

When they were all named, Kasdi turned to them. "Now see yourselves. All that you have, covet, or desire is what you have now." She removed her own robe and stood naked before them. "Now see all I have, covet, or desire. You are always my children, but you are now all my sisters. Through me the Holy Mother ordains you priestesses of Her Holy Mother Church. She confers upon you now the power to do work in Her name, to access the altar itself, to administer the holy services and the sacraments of the Church, all of which you may not violate no matter what the circumstances. I have given my blessing to each and every one of you. Now you may give me *your* blessing, if you wish, and depart as you came with all that you have now."

One by one they left, giving her the blessing as their first act of ordination and then walking naked through the door. Outside, the administrative people had undergarments, robes, and sandals for each, all in the yellow color of a novice priestess, and preliminary assignments to orders and training. They would also receive the basic kit, as it was called, out there—spare clothing, toiletries, a sac-

ramental set so that they could perform the sacraments and say services anywhere, and a personal
copy of the Basic Scriptures, as newly revised as
the Codex project could make them. After this,
they would be taken to the temple dining room for
the best meal they'd had in two years and then
given two weeks to a month's leave, depending on
where they were from. After that, it was back to
work.

Sister Kasdi was alone again and sighed at the
altar. Looking into their faces, thinking of her own
daughter, she had made her decision. Mervyn was
right, of course. He usually was. If Spirit was in
mortal danger, she had a right to know it and
why. She had a compromise solution to the revelation now. She was very tired and felt very, very
old right now, but she could not rest. She drew
what strength she could from the Flux and exited
the inner temple for her own office. There was no
use in putting it off and no reason to remain now.
Like those novices, she had a stringer train to
catch.

# HELL'S EARS

The stringer was a man named Gorondon—that is, that was the name he used, stringers always keeping their true names hidden so that none could ever have a hold on them. He was one of the hundreds of men and women who moved people, goods, and even ideas between Fluxland and Fluxland, Anchor and Anchor, and to all points in between. The stringer guild was a tight organization; one had to be born into it to get full stringer status, and their monopoly on commerce was jealously, even violently maintained. Still, they performed a service better and more efficiently than any other could, and so everyone tolerated them, even if they didn't quite like or trust them.

Gorondon was a huge, burly man with a full, bushy black beard, a broad, flat nose and big brown eyes. He looked much like an animated statue, chiseled from granite and given life by some magic spell.

Maintaining the train were his duggers, strange, often misshapen creatures who were once human men and women, as mad in the head as they were in form more often than not. Duggers were drawn mostly from the castoffs of conventional society; people who could not fit or were insane and had made their way into Flux, their madness made them appear like their own nightmares, but they were capable of working efficiently in the real world of the void under the direction of a stringer. They

worked hard and were fiercely loyal, afraid only of
being cast adrift with their madness once again in
Flux. Still, they were well paid and secure as em-
ployees of the train, and they herded the animals,
drove the wagons, loaded and unloaded the cargoes,
and guarded against the infrequent but still present marauding bands of robbers and savages who
roamed the Flux.

Only Gorondon had gone very far into Hope, to
transact his business and pick up messages. There
were only a few wide open Fluxlands where duggers
felt comfortable, and most stayed with the train
except for loading and unloading. Hope, in particular, was not a favorite stop, merely a necessary
one. A matriarchal theocracy offended stringer types
and made them more than a little nervous. Most
saw little difference between being the slave of a
mad Fluxland wizard and being a member of, much
less a priestess of, the Church.

Knowing he had no less than fourteen passengers for Anchor Logh, the stringer had arranged
for coaches, each of which held eight people in
equal discomfort. Although the huge wheels were
of wood and the facing bench seats inside barely
upholstered, the void was smooth and the pace of
a train was slow, so the only bumps and bounces
were from the teams of eight horses pulling each,
and even those bumps and bounces could be mini-
mized by the skill of the dugger driver.

Kasdi climbed into the first coach and, because
of her small size, soon found herself with three
other companions across, and three more facing
her. Whoever had referred to the coaches as eight-
passenger vehicles had obviously been thinking of
eight five-year-olds; even though all four on Kasdi's
side were small women, none could lift a hand
without hitting the person sitting next to them.

She was in her usual Flux disguise as a plain-
looking, studious priestess in the black robes of

the judiciary order. She had made herself smaller—
barely one hundred fifty centimeters, as opposed
to her normal height of one hundred sixty—with
shoulder-length gray-brown hair, and a long, thin,
unattractive middle-aged face that may not have
been hard to look at but you wouldn't look twice.
She had also smoothed out and raised her normally very deep voice. Nobody had ever pene-
trated the disguise, which was so complete that
there were actually records on "Sister Janise" so
complete that, if anyone checked, they would be
certain that she was indeed a separate, real person.

Janise was a useful disguise, particularly when
visiting Anchor Logh, and it was a guise known
only to a precious few who would never betray
it—Mervyn, Tamara, the Sister General of the Anchor Logh temple and her closest friend, her father,
and her cousin Cloise, who was surrogate mother
to her daughter.

Because stringers knew how uncomfortable it
might be to have to ride with a bevy of priestesses,
the dugger loadmaster had put the six sisters who
were passengers in the same coach, and the one
other had been at the school in Hope. Thus, to her
amusement, even though she expected it, she found
herself sharing a ride of several days with the new
Sister Marigail and the girl she'd denied ordination,
whose name was Mahta. Introductions and pleas-
antries were made, but conversation was minimal
inside the coach, most of the comments being about
the discomfort of the ride and the state of transpor-
tation even in this new age.

Gorondon wanted to make Anchor Logh in a bit
over three days, so he worked his crew in shifts
and planned stops only for water and meals
and horse rotation. He was behind his schedule,
planned out months ago for a half-year trip, and
trying to make up as much of that time as possible.
If he didn't make his scheduled stops before an-

other stringer, he might have business stolen out from under him.

At the meal breaks, though, there were small clusters of conversation and socializing. Mahta, in particular, seemed fascinated to talk to Sister Marigail, with whom she'd shared a dormitory these past two years. Thanks to Kasdi's spell, Mahta was actually fairly attractive, although nothing like Marigail's beauty.

"I still can't understand why anybody who looks like you would enter the priesthood," Mahta said to Marigail. "Still, that's it now, I guess. Uh—how does it feel?"

Marigail shrugged. "Not really any different. At least, I don't notice anything different. Oh, well, maybe a little. Things I thought were real important just don't seem that way anymore. Like this trip home. Even a couple of days ago it seemed the most important thing in my whole life. You know, going home a real priestess, seeing everyone, all that. Now—it's just something that must be done before I can get to work. What about you? You think you're going to come back, or is this it for you?"

"I don't know," Mahta responded. "I enjoyed it all, and I like the Church, but it just doesn't seem like my whole life. Who knows? After two years in the mines I'm just going to relax and enjoy myself a bit, just like she said. Who knows? At any rate, if you'll let me, I'll come to your public ceremony."

"I'd like that very much. It'll be in Tombar Riding, just north of the capital, the first Holy Day after I'm back. You know you'll be welcome."

Kasdi overheard, and smiled a bit to herself. Things would work out for both of them, she was sure. Later, she was amused to overhear a whispered conversation between them that was basically a less than totally complimentary impression of her. Marigail had described Kasdi as old and hard-looking, and seemed a bit disappointed at how ordinary the living patron saint of the Reformed Church seemed. It was far better and more charitable than Mahta's impression of an egomaniacal old crone. She didn't mind either impression, though. It kept her in her place and helped combat her greatest fight, the fight against her own blasphemous deification among the masses.

They pressed on through the static energy field that was the void towards Anchor Logh, following energy trails, or strings, that only stringers and wizards could see.

She was a lively, outgoing young woman. She was almost exotically pretty, a bit sexy and erotic, and she knew it. She had long, straight auburn hair almost to the waist, unusual large green eyes, a sensual mouth in an expressive face, and a trim, athletic figure that seemed put together just right. She was quite tall—one hundred eighty centimeters barefoot—but hadn't an ounce of fat nature didn't need or require. She was well aware of how attractive she was and liked to flaunt it in a teasing way.

She was also bright, if no genius, with good grades through school and a healthy curiosity about the world around her, but she preferred the outdoors to books and athletics to scholarship. She had always been spoiled as a child, and her beauty and athletic prowess had made her a center of attention as a teen as well. She had, of course, lived a sheltered and pampered life, but was not really aware that it was so. If she lacked anything, it was a sense of ambition and a sense of direction. She had graduated now, and was working on the communal farm where she'd been raised, doing odd jobs here and there, but every time her future had come up, she'd changed the subject. She didn't really like to think much of the future; she liked it too much the way it was. There were colleges she might enter, but aside from a love of the outdoors she really had no strong drive towards one field or another. Nothing she really liked excited her, and she was aware that in any given field there were far too many with better aptitude and intelligence for her to rise very far.

Still, if she did not choose more education, she would be expected to apprentice to a trade, and none of those appealed much to her either. Marriage and kids also seemed unattractive. She had lost her virginity at sixteen, a fact that would still horrify her mother and the rest of the family, but she wasn't very experienced in that department. Three times, that was all, and while she'd found the last two at least pleasurable, they certainly weren't worth the risk of pregnancy and were, in a way, disappointing when looked back upon. Still, she was fairly inhibited regarding herself. She liked playing, teasing, and, yes, *using* the lust of all the boys best. It was more of a charge knowing that you were lusted after than actually taking them up on it.

What she really wanted, she knew, was an unlimited amount of credit to go off and see all of World, doing what she wanted when she wanted, and generally having a good time. Unfortunately, real life had a way of dashing romantic fantasies. Her mom called it her "stringer blood."

If there was one thing in her life that was empty, it was her parentage. She'd been told that her father had been a stringer killed in the Flux and that her mother had been a cast-out in the days when they used to draw lots to see which young people got sent into slavery in Flux and which got to stay and lead normal lives in Anchor. It was a sweet, romantic story—cast-out girl and stringer fall in love—but it had ended unhappily, with her father dead and her mother returning with the

liberators here to Anchor Logh, only to die in an
accident when she was very young. Those were
mysteries, and mysteries she had found, after all
these years, impossible to solve or even discuss
with the few who knew anything. Nobody knew
the stringer's name, since her mother hadn't said,
or so they told her. Nobody was even positive that
her father had really been a stringer, only that this
was the story her mother had told.

As for the mother, there were no records and
lots of names on the lists of cast-outs from those
days. No pictures seemed to have been taken of
her, and the one name they gave, Helaina, appeared on no official record except a formal death
certificate. She had ▓▓▓▓ the impression that nobody wanted to talk about her mother because she
had not been formally married and had used her
body to get out of slavery instead of her brains,
but she didn't care about that. Still, she'd always
had the urge to go into Flux and at least search for
somebody who might have known, might remember and be willing to talk, as unlikely as that
might be. But as much as the Flux fascinated her
and called to her, it also frightened her. She'd seen
it more than once, from the old walls, a glittering
wall of nothingness stretching out forever, and it
had seemed cold and empty and lonesome.

She munched on an apple and walked out of the
apartment and down the dirt road through the
fields leading to the main highway. She barely
glanced at the Holy Mother above, a great, amor-
phous light banded in yellows, blues, and oranges—
the sight had always been there and would have
been unnatural only if absent. It was a warm day,
and she wore a pair of denim jeans low on her hips,
a sleeveless white shirt that came down to her navel,
and little else more, save a pair of high-heeled
riding boots, which put an extra wiggle in her
walk and added another five centimeters to her

height, and a cream-colored ranch hat, side brims
starched up.

She knew that, sooner or later, the coach from
the west gate would come by, and that Sister Janise
was aboard, and that was whom she was there to
meet. She was never comfortable with Sister
Janise—the woman was like a doting maiden aunt,
only she really never understood the relationship
the old girl had to her or her real mother. Janise
had always been a little boring and made her feel
uncomfortable, although she always thought that,
if she could ever find a way, she might learn more
from the Sister about her own origins.

The coaches were never on time, so she just
thanked the Goddess that it was such a nice, warm
day and settled down on the grass near the road to
wait.

After a while Sucha Fane rode by, spotted her,
and stopped and dismounted. He was a nice-looking
boy her age, nothing wonderful but nice enough,
and they'd shared some classes together in school.
She had never felt really attracted to him, considering her other choices, and they had never dated,
but that never stopped him from trying and it *was*
a dull day.

"Hi, Spirit. What'cha doin' sittin' here?"

"Waiting for the damned coach. My batty priestess aunt is due in for one of her interminable
visits, that's all. You?"

"Goin' in to the guild halls to see if my number's
come up, that's all. You know I got a slot as apprentice electrician."

"No! Congratulations! That's a big new field."

And it was. The reformation of the Church had
ushered in a whole new era of scientific inquiry.
Study was made of many subjects that had been
forbidden or had been restricted to the Church,
and hundreds of the brightest minds of World were
hard at work. The whole of the capital was electri-

fied now, and there was talk of extending the power grids eventually to every city, town, and farm in Anchor Logh. Her farm would be among the first, as it was one of the two or three closest to the capital. It was said that power would soon no longer be dependent on the supernatural gusher in the temple, but actually might be generated from the energy of Flux, or from units of compressed solid energy created in Flux that could be transported, stored, and used locally in Anchor.

The old books and records had yielded many suppressed miracles, including the transmission of speech by electrical energy, not just through wires but through the air. It seemed impossible, but they had all seen demonstrations of it in school and in the capital. The entire world was poised on the edge of a technological revolution that would match or exceed the impact of the Reformation.

The conversation turned, quite naturally, to the personal, and she had little trouble putting him off yet again. Still, she sometimes felt sorry for the Suchas of the world, and she felt tempted occasionally to give them a break or a thrill. Not now, though. Not today, particularly.

Crestfallen as usual from being shot down again, he sighed, got up, and remounted his horse. "Got to be gettin' in before they close," he said lamely.

"Take care and good luck," she responded. "I mean that." And she blew him a kiss.

That last really brightened his day, and he rode off at a happy gallop.

Almost on cue, the coach rumbled into sight in the distance, and she watched it approach, then got up as it slowed. The door opened, and out stepped old Sister Janise, looking the same as always.

"Hi, Sister Janise! It's been a while!" Spirit opened, trying to sound as enthusiastic as she could.

"Too long," the Sister responded, and hugged

her and gave her a peck on the cheek. The coach rumbled off, and they watched it go into the distance towards the capital.

"Everybody's waiting for you," Spirit told her. "Mom's been cooking all day."

"Well, I hope they didn't put themselves out too much for me. It will be good to see them all, but this isn't quite the usual social visit."

Spirit frowned at that, but let it pass. "Want to go see Mom?"

"In a minute. I think I'd just like to walk along the road and around the farm for a little bit. Not only have I been four days on those blasted coaches, but I like to . . . remember."

They began walking back towards the distant buildings, perhaps a kilometer in. "That's right—you *did* say you grew up around here, didn't you?"

The Sister nodded. "Yes. This very farm. It's nice to see that it's changed so little over the years, although that's probably going to end soon. Dramatic change is coming to Anchor Logh. I sometimes wonder, in ten years, if we—either one of us—will recognize this place and whether the magic of science here won't overpower the magic of Flux."

Spirit had never seen Janise in such a reflective mood. It gave her an odd sense of foreboding, particularly when coupled with the old woman's earlier cryptic remark.

Janise stopped for a moment and pointed. "Let's go over to that grove of trees. I want to talk for a moment."

They went over and sat on the grass. For a little bit the Sister was silent, but finally she said, "For a long time you've wondered about your parents, haven't you? Your natural ones, I mean."

The statement jolted her, but she repressed her excitement. "Yes, that's true."

"You're a beautiful, grown woman now. I think

it's time you were told the truth, although you will
not be able to tell it to anyone else."

Spirit felt a chill. "The truth?"

The Sister sighed. "Yes. The truth. But not because you are grown now. It was decided to tell
you because others may learn of you, others who
might wish to do you harm because of your
heritage. You must know in order to guard yourself."

"Guard myself from whom? What's this all leading to?"

"You know the story of the Reformation. That
Cass, a girl from this farm, this riding, discovered
the corruption in the temple and was exiled to
Flux. How she discovered in herself great power
and how she fell in love with a stringer, and when
that stringer died in the war against Hell, she was
transformed into the most powerful wizard World
had ever known."

"I hadn't known about the stringer part, but the
rest is taught every Holy Day."

"Well, Cass became, of course, Sister Kasdi. She
beat the evil wizard Haldayne and transformed
his evil kingdom into Hope, the seat of the Reformed Church. This you know."

She nodded. "Yeah, sure. I guess everybody does."

"And nothing so far suggests a parallel with
anything you have been told?"

She shrugged. "Except that that battle killed my
natural father, not particularly."

"Sister Kasdi had a daughter in Anchor by her
slain lover. The big secret they've always tried to
hide from you and everybody else is that you are
that daughter."

Oddly, she felt no shock at the revelation. It was
simply too ridiculous to be believed, let alone
accepted.

"She had to choose between you and the Reformation, Spirit. She chose the Reformation for the

good of everyone rather than herself, and she did everything possible to make sure that nobody would ever trace you to her. You would be the one piece of blackmail her enemies could hold on her."

"If what you say is true, I doubt if I'd be worth much. I mean, she already took the Church over me, right?" There was a heavy trace of bitterness in her tone, and it hurt.

"There was no choice," she responded defensively. "You could not be protected in Flux, and the old Church and its forces would have sought out and killed the infant Reformation and both you and her if she didn't carry it off. I *can* say you have never been far from her thoughts in all these years."

"Yeah, I'll bet. So what are you? Her personal watchdog? She sends you to bring me toys and attend my birthday parties and report to her when she's got the time?"

"That's a cruel way to put it. She *has* seen you, many times. But she is a powerful wizard, able to transform herself into just about anybody or anything, and she had to visit in deep disguise so that her enemies wouldn't know and follow her."

Spirit felt anger, not relief at all this. "So why the big story now?"

"There are rumors that her old enemies have discovered who you are. Perhaps not, but they are closing in. They suspect. No matter what you think of your mother or what you think she might do, you'd better think another way. It's not going to be *her* in the hands of Hell; it'll be *you*."

*That* was a sobering-up statement if there ever was one. She thought about it a moment, then shook her head sadly. "This is all so . . . new to me. I mean, all these years I've wondered about my real parents, and now you can tell me all this. It's pretty hard to take."

"Everyone tried to spare you all this. We worked very hard to do so. Were it not for the possible dangers, it would have continued that way. I'm very ... sorry." It was getting more and more difficult to keep up the act, the other persona, but it had to be done. It was sadly ironic that she could not come right out and tell her daughter the truth face-to-face, but if the girl was having troubles believing the truth as it was, nothing less than that would convince her that her doddering old "aunt" was truly the monumental figure familiar to all.

"I don't see why my mother couldn't do this job herself," Spirit said sourly. "She sure has a funny way of showing she cares."

"But, dear, don't you see? The only way for that to work would be for her to come as herself—and that would lead her enemies right to you. She can travel nowhere anonymously except in deep disguise. Surely you can understand that. The only safe place would be in Flux, and there, if they so much as suspected, you could not be defended or defend yourself against a concerted attack."

That logic was not what Spirit wanted to hear right now, nor was it what she was feeling. She felt a lot of resentment and bitterness churning within her, and a great deal of hurt, and yet, somehow, all of it seemed like some kind of crazy dream. Certainly none of the facts had any solidity to her, any kind of personal reality. To be orphaned and fantasize about your real parents was one thing; to discover that you were not an orphan, but that your mother was an alleged saint and the most powerful person in the world—and that she chose that path over you—was something else again. And now to find that you were in mortal danger from the enemies of the mother who didn't give a damn about you—that was just a little much to swallow right now.

\*     \*     \*

It had been three days since the revelations, and Spirit was still troubled by them. She had asked her mother—her real mother in all but the biological sense—to confirm the facts, and they had in fact been confirmed, although she still had the feeling that there were things they still wished to conceal from her. She moped around and tried to sort it all out, but it was hard.

It was far easier to look up the Cass of her own riding, though, than the mythical mother they had originally given her. She was struck both by the plainness of her photographs and the tomboy image the records and some of the older farm hands indicated. Eventually she wandered down to the blacksmith's shop. The foreman there was a familiar figure and, she'd been told, a distant relation, but now she found herself staring at the brawny, silver-haired man at the forge with different eyes.

The first thing Kasdi had done after leaving Spirit that first day was to visit her dad and tell him. He looked up at the girl just inside the wide doorways, put down his tools, wiped off his face with a rag and came over to her. "Hello, Spirit," he greeted casually.

"Hello . . . Grandfather," she responded, not at all sure of what tone to take.

He frowned. "Never say that again around here, much as I'd like you to. Come on—let's go someplace private and talk for a few moments."

They sat again under the very trees where she'd been told the truth. "I hear tell you're not very pleased at the news," he began.

"Well? Should I be?"

He shrugged. "I'm kind of proud of her myself, as you might understand. I can't say I ever understood her, but we got pretty close, you know. Even more after she took over the Church. Your momma's a little weird, but she's got brains and the guts to use 'em." He gave her a smirk. "She still hasn't got me back in the Church, though. Drives her nuts.''

Spirit laughed at that, and some of the ice melted. She hadn't known him very well before, but she liked him now, as much as she liked the irony that the father of the sainted Sister Kasdi was an unrepentant nonbeliever.

He nodded sagely. "That's better. You know, I think it drove me more crazy than your mom not to get close to you, because I saw you most every day. Still, the danger's pretty real, and for your sake and hers I kept apart. I still can't come out and claim you my granddaughter, but at least we can have a talk now and then. I can tell you're pretty troubled. Want to talk about it?''

There was something about him that inspired confidence, the same solidity that he gave to the things wrought in iron by his own hands and forge. He had a reputation for being gruff and sometimes mean and nasty, but here he seemed surprisingly gentle and compassionate. She opened up to him, and he listened attentively, never interrupting. When she had finished, he sighed and looked thoughtful.

"Your mom's a politician and a soldier, the two jobs that make more enemies than any other ten jobs combined. Me they're only mad at when something I make breaks or isn't quite right. It's never personal. Her—it's all personal. The people you beat hate you and want revenge. The people you never touched are scared of you, and to fear somebody is to be an enemy. Nobody ever agrees with the one who runs things, and everybody thinks they can do a better job. She didn't want the job, and she hates it now. She's hated it, I think, since the first. She got herself trapped into it by a bunch of slick politicians themselves who wanted what she could give 'em and suckered her into doing their dirty work. Now she's really stuck. She can't quit. Too many folks depend on her. It's kind of funny, really. Here she is, the most powerful woman on World, and she can't do anything she wants to do."

This was a different side of the image, and Spirit was fascinated. "What does she want to do, then?"

"Well, she got stuck *before* she knew she was pregnant. They could have told her—that slick old fellow Mervyn or whatever he's calling himself these days—but they needed her. So they got her in the spot where she had to make a real set of decisions before she knew. She hates this fighting, hates the responsibility. I think I would, too. She once told me that what she wanted to do most in the world was just to drop it all, disguise herself, and travel all over World, to every corner of it. See everything that could be seen, learn everything she could learn. No responsibilities, no guilt as she called it, no nothing."

Spirit had to chuckle at that. "That's what *I* want to do, too!"

He nodded. "Figures. That witch-magic gave you your good looks, but the blood's still the same. She told me not long ago that she'd love to just take you away and have the two of you get to know each other, wandering around World, poking into things, having fun."

"Well? Why can't we?"

He sighed. "Because she can't. Like I said, she's trapped. Stuck. All those vows are in her by witch-magic. You go into Flux, you get witched, and it sticks. She's been trying to get me there. Says she can ease my tired bones, make me young again. I'll join the Church before I go into that mess of stuff. Never know what'll happen to you. Look at her. She's *got* to be Sister Kasdi, live like a saint, look like Hell. You seen the pictures. She sure looks closer to the age my wife would be if she'd lived than my daughter. Flux sure did nothing for her."

"But she can disguise herself from me."

He nodded. "And only for that, she says. She's got all that power, and she's witched so she can't use any of it for herself. She's allowed to change for here only because you need it to protect you."

"Protect me from *whom? What?*

"From her enemies. She's got a million of 'em, some right here in Anchor Logh. They'd hurt you just because they know it'd hurt her."

It was Spirit's turn to sigh. "So I'm as stuck as she is. More, because they can't really touch her. I'm not powerful. They could do anything they want with me."

He nodded. "You're stuck, I agree, but not so bad. You don't have to sleep in straw and eat slop. You stay here in Anchor Logh and live the rest of your life. Thought about what you're going to do?"

She shrugged. "Thought about it, yeah—but not much more. I'm sure not ready to settle down, get married, have kids. Not now. I don't have the smarts or the patience for university, but I don't have the talent for a trade with any future. I'm just not ready yet."

"Ready for what? To grow up? You already did, no matter what. Nobody ever wants to grow up, and nobody's ever ready. In the old days you had no choice at all. You became what they told you or they threw you into slavery. You have more choice now, and slavery's only for criminals, but it's still the same. If you don't pick, they'll do the picking. What are you good at that you really like?"

She thought a moment. "Sports. Dancing. Not much else."

"Well, think about teaching gym maybe. Or maybe dancing—no, I guess that's out. You'd have to travel in Flux to be with dancers that make any money. The only kind of job like that here is on

Main Street, and *that* kind of dancing is no good
life."

She grinned. "It sure would give my mother fits,
though, wouldn't it? Both of 'em."

"You'd never get anywhere in the joints. Every
time somebody made a play for you, your grandfather would be beside 'em with a shotgun."

As much as it was irritating, the comment nonetheless warmed her. She suddenly had a real family now, and at least one who cared.

"There's no question," the woman agent told
her boss. "In fact, once you find her, everything
just falls logically into place. Even the name—
Spirit. And on the same farm, in the same family!
She's not much at concealment, is she?"

The man facing her took a swallow of beer and
shrugged. "No need. You've been too deep in cover
too long. The records were well doctored, so there
was no clue there. The people involved all had
their minds voluntarily meddled in to back up the
phony story. After that, why not put her where you
can keep an eye on her and have people around
you can trust? I mean, even if we suspected that
our enemy's child lived, which we always did—
that kid's stillbirth was just *too* convenient to
believe—we still had a world to search and thousands of suspects that right age. She's physically
matched to the family she's with and with a convincing cover. There are hundreds more with stories just like hers."

"Yes, but—"

"Hey!" he cut her off. "Look, remember—it took
us all these years. That's pretty good. These things
always look easier in hindsight. That's no longer
the problem. Tell me—how did you do it?"

"It was the Janise disguise. She was never there.
Never. But when Sister Kasdi went on retreat,
suddenly Janise was packing her bags to leave—

and always here. It was simple to follow her from that point."

"Well, we might be suspicious of Sister Janise, but she also could be any one of a lot of other unpleasant folks needing a cover. We just timed it perfectly, though, dropping that story that we were on the trail of Kasdi's daughter through that sidebar stringer stopping at Globbus just before ordination. We set the trap and watched her get the news, then were ready because she *had* to go through ordination, so the time was known. Then she did the predictable—rushed to check on her daughter as soon as she could. The same as somebody carrying a lot of money will always check their wallets and tell a good thief exactly where the wallet's hidden. You were one of many we had staked out all around, following every red herring. Now it's time to plan our next move."

"I spent two years in that hole eating shit," the agent reminded him. "Now I expect a big payoff."

He gave a low chuckle and drained his glass. "You have no Flux power," he reminded her. "You were homely and pushing fifty when we offered you this job. We made you sixteen again. That's a pretty good deal for two years you otherwise didn't have, and they even improved your looks. What other kind of payment do you expect?"

"You can't know what I went through for you!" she spat. "The humiliation, the hard conditions, the constant acting. No sex, no freedom, lousy food. Nothing you can give me would be enough payment."

"But you'll accept it anyway," he said sarcastically.

"You bet I will! I want all the things I didn't have, all the things I *never* had. I want to be *gorgeous*. I want men lusting after me. I want never to have to worry about anything again!"

He thought a moment. "And in Anchor, I presume?"

"Of course! This is no place for somebody without the power."

"O.K. I've got just the thing." He made an idle gesture with his left hand and she froze, unable to move. "You know too much and you could blow too much, but we *do* owe you for services rendered, and what you want is easy." He wove the mathematical spells idly in his mind and sent them to her as forms of binding energy. "First we'll erase the last three years from your memory completely— that'll cover all your contacts with us. We'll make life before that fairly muddy, not clear or important to you. We'll give you a face and body that every red-blooded male wants, and we'll bind your personality to total passivity, so you'll be happy to give 'em what they want. Then we'll constrict your usable I.Q. to maybe half its potential, so you'll have a one-track mind that's ruled by your body and your needs. You'll giggle a lot, but you won't think beyond the moment. And maybe a new name that won't trigger any of those old memories. 'Honey,' because it fits." He snapped his fingers and the spell was cast.

As was the case with master wizards, the effect was instantaneous. One moment the plain-looking Mahta had stood there; now a voluptuous but stupid young woman shook her head as if waking up from a dream and then looked dully around, puzzled.

"Hi!" he said pleasantly. "What's your name?"

"Honey," she answered in a very sexy voice.

"Well, hello, Honey. What do you do for a living?"

"I make men happy," she told him, cozying up. "Can I make you happy?"

"You sure can," responded cheerfully. "And when you do, I got a friend who owns a place in Anchor

Logh where you can make lots of men happy night after night."

The first problem was solved. Now go on to the next phase.

It was Holy Day, although that didn't mean very much to Spirit this time. The portrait of Sister Kasdi in the vestibule, which had always seemed so comforting, now seemed rather silly and out of place. No longer the Reformed Church, or just the Church, but "My Mother's Church," she thought a bit sourly. Still, she had gone as always, for social pressure was pretty strong in a small place like Anchor Logh and particularly on the farm and in the riding. She wondered how her grandfather had managed to escape for so many years.

There was a stranger attending services that morning who was the object of some sidelong attention. There were often strangers at services, particularly this close to the capital, but this one would stand out in any crowd. He was tall, handsome, and muscular, with a neatly trimmed, full brown beard and long brown hair touched slightly by gray at the temples and right on the chin. His clothes were casual, jeans and a red plaid shirt and well-worn boots, standing out against the formal wear of most of the locals. It was almost as if he wanted to stand out, or at least be remembered by everyone who was there.

He was so much of a standout, in fact, that the other strangers, several well-dressed but nondescript-looking men and women, went completely unnoticed. They all filed into the church together at the bell signal, paid their respects to the altar, and took seats at various points in the church. The service began right on time, and there were no variations this time. The priestess was not one who liked sermonizing, and generally she was strictly business unless there was something special to say. This, in fact, was one of the reasons why she was so popular with the locals and why out-of-towners were steered there for services.

Anchor Logh was a very peaceful place, and, as the first Anchor taken by the Reformation, it had long been far from any scenes of conflict. True, there were occasional crimes calling for a local police force, but the crimes were few and even a robbery anywhere in the Anchor was big news. As the place that spawned the Reformation and the birthplace of Sister Kasdi, it was not the place troublemakers from outside picked to pull anything illegal. There were far easier pickings both in Flux and Anchor, and even if you got away with whatever you wanted, it was a long, long route to any secure escape with Kasdi and her wizards and generals knowing and controlling all of it. As a result, no one even noticed that the strangers all sat on the aisles.

The service was almost over now, and the congregation was forward of their seats, knees on the prayer rests, while the priestess faced the altar. Suddenly, in the silence between prayer and benediction, a man's deep voice said loudly, "I think I've stood as much of this bullshit as I can."

There was a collective shock at the violation and an almost unanimous gasp echoed through the throngs of worshippers. They looked up as the priestess turned around and saw the handsome, bearded man standing in the front of the church, a pistol drawn and on the priestess. As they looked around, the congregation saw that on all sides they were covered by the strangers, all of whom had automatic weapons drawn. "O.K., Sister, you get down with your flock there," the leader ordered the priestess.

She did not move or show fear. "For what reason do you commit this sacrilege?" she demanded.

The leader smiled. "Thank you, Ma'am. Sacrilege is my chosen profession, so it's always nice to see that I'm good at it. Now, I'm gonna ask you once more to get over there, and that's that."

"This is my church, and I take no orders from scum in it," she responded haughtily.

Without further comment, the man fired his pistol. The force of the bullet struck her in the chest and hurled her back several meters, as if she'd been pushed by a giant hand. She crashed into the altar itself, which tumbled down upon her still body.

Somebody screamed, and there was a sudden panicky flurry from the congregation, but a few bursts of automatic weapons fire from the others into the ceiling of the church quieted them quickly.

"Now, everybody just sit down and shut up and nobody else has to get hurt. Anybody who makes a move, looks funny at any of us, or causes any trouble at all will join the Sister there. I won't make any more warnings. Clear?"

It was clear. The congregation sat almost like statues, although there was some sobbing. Spirit, sitting near the center, was as shocked and horrified at the violence as any of them, but even now she had no idea what it was all about. All she could think of was how completely mad these people must be to pull this in the early morning in the middle of Anchor Logh. Where could they run?

She was startled out of her thoughts when the man said, "You, there! Spirit! Stand up!"

For a moment she did nothing but look up, but the sight of the blood-soaked altar broke through her shock. "Who? Me?" she managed.

"Yes. Walk carefully out to the aisle and to the back of the church. Don't do anything funny, just move—*now*."

The tone was unmistakable, and she did as instructed. She realized now that these were the very people she'd been warned about, but she hadn't expected anything this fast, and certainly not in church on Holy Day. The sheer casualness of the violence was also somehow beyond any evil she had previously imagined.

"All right, folks, just relax. That's all there is to it, except for some business. Now, my name's Coydt, to answer your late priestess's question, and I'm one of those terrible Seven she kept warning you about." There were gasps at this, and he grinned, obviously enjoying his power. "Now, you're probably wondering why I'm telling you that, but there's a good reason. You see, your Saint Kasdi out there in her temple fortress had a daughter, and while they went to great lengths to fake that baby's death, it was a lie. Your great Kasdi lies. Me, I tell the truth. That says something about the two of us. That girl we just took out the back is her grown-up daughter."

There were more gasps and murmurings at this. Many there had known Spirit since she was a baby.

"Check it out with her Mama—the real one or the one she was abandoned to 'cause it's tough to be a saint when saddled with a brat. Now you understand what's going on here, but don't be scared. If your scared tin saint got rid of her daughter once, well, she's not about to surrender the Church or give us Anchor Logh or anything like that. It *is* a kidnapping, though, and there's a price, so you hustle on in to the temple in the capital and tell 'em Coydt will be in touch when he feels like it, and that she won't be harmed so long as nobody tries to free her or hurts me or my agents in this business. Now, aside from all the folks you've seen, outside covering the exits are two others you never saw. If you stay here for one hour, you'll never see them or us. Anybody who goes out before the hour will be killed. It's that simple. So sit and relax here, and maybe discuss why the hell if your goddess is really up in the sky like that, she allows me to do shit like this down here. Bye now."

With that, Coydt walked briskly up the aisle and out the door, followed in professional order, front to back, by the others. The door slammed behind them.

For a moment, nobody moved, then several rushed forward, jumped the altar rail, and pulled the remains of the smashed altar off the bloody body of their priestess. There was little they could do, though; a caliber that big blew a huge hole going in but an even bigger one coming out her back, and she had most certainly died instantly.

Suddenly the place was bedlam, but nobody went immediately for the doors. This was the early service, but the Vice President of the Commune Council was there and, looking pretty shaken himself, he nonetheless tried to get some order and organization. His name was Miklos Ransom, and he was well aware that his career as a professional politician was at stake here.

"All right!" he thundered. "Settle down! First things first! Now, nobody go sticking their head out the door yet!" He looked around. "Anybody here from Spirit's immediate family?"

They all looked, but there was no one. Spirit had been having some problems sleeping the past few days and she'd been up and about long before the usual family gathering. They would not be in until next scheduled service in two hours—a rather unlikely event at this stage. She had come alone, mostly to think, and that, at least, had probably saved the lives of her foster family, who would not have let her go easily.

"O.K. Now, I've been thinking this out. There *may* be nobody out there, but I wouldn't bet anyone's life on it."

"I'll chance it," one burly farmer growled, and several more voiced assent. "If I can get help fast enough, we can watch those people swing by their necks!"

"No! There's a better way!" Ransom shouted back. "You—Zida! You're the bell ringer. Get back there and ring it for all it's worth. Give the emergency alarm! Don't stop ringing for anything. That'll bring a lot of folks running. Whoever's out there won't chance shooting people coming here, or they'll never get away. They'll run when they figure what we're doing. Give it ten minutes of steady ringing, and *then* we'll chance somebody making a run for it."

The bell ringer scurried through the sacristy and back to the tower loft as quickly as possible.

Ransom looked around. There were three exits, the main one and two forward that were mainly fire exits. "Quickly—before the bells drown me out. I want one of you volunteers at each door!" He looked at his watch. "I'll signal you when to try it. Move!"

The bells began ringing.

Once Anchor Logh had been not only a country but a fortress. The huge stone wall, itself a fortress with guard stations and battlements and room for four soldiers to march abreast on top, went completely around Anchor Logh, twenty meters high, with gates only at the two outermost ends. The days when Anchor feared Flux were gone now, although few Anchor folk actually went into Flux and many, like Spirit's grandfather, still distrusted it. The gates at both ends were simple affairs now, and the guard stations were mostly tourist lookouts into the mysterious void beyond. Not only had the wall lost its purpose in the era of the Reformation, but it had shown in the earliest attacks just how ridiculously porous it was.

Coydt had fast horses, and knew his way around
Anchor Logh as he knew his way around much of
World. He was more than five hundred years old,
renewing and keeping himself young through his
own massive Flux powers, and that was a lot of
time to explore and get to know even a world.

He wanted to get into Flux quickly, where he
would be nearly invulnerable, but he knew that
his inevitable pursuers would also know this and
try to second-guess him. He had been close enough
to hear the bell ring steadily as they rode off, and
immediately guessed its purpose. He cursed himself for overlooking that detail. He did not, however,
underestimate the intelligence or will of the people of Anchor Logh. Many people that he'd known
well over his long years had died because they had
dismissed simple folk as "just farmers" or "just
grocery clerks." A bullet from a determined grocery clerk was just as deadly as one from a professional soldier.

Most of his band had scattered, changed into
different clothes, and made off along predetermined
routes to various places in Anchor Logh. Their
alibis had been easily prearranged. With him he
kept only his two closest aides and adepts, Zekah
and Yorek, and they kept close watch on Spirit.

They were riding so fast that Spirit more than
once thought of escape, perhaps by veering off and
leading them a chase through any farm or nearby
spotted town where help would be available, but
both the young adepts had submachine guns and
she knew she could be cut down the moment she
bolted—a fact they took precious time to point out
to her as they forced her to mount.

As evil and insane as these men were, she had no
wish to die like that priestess, and where there
was life, there was always the possibility of escape.

Coydt's timing and choice of exit points was
perfect. He had run a dry run on another church,

rigging an accidental-looking fire and a jammed exit, and he had a pretty good idea how long a panicked congregation took to summon help and for that help to arrive, sort things out, and take action. Then someone would have to rush back into the capital, explain the problem, and write out the notes and descriptions. These would then have to be put into capsules, attached to homing pigeons, and sent out to all the outposts around Anchor Logh. He knew the locations of those outposts, and all the back roads, and just how long it would take horsemen from those outposts, once they got the alarm, to adequately patrol their sections of the wall. Although it was an extra hour's ride, he'd picked the point he had judged most difficult to reach and had confederates waiting there. When the great wall came into view, there was no sign of any opposition force on the Anchor side.

Someone was atop the wall, flashing a short signal with some sort of lantern and mirror device, and they pulled right up to the wall, stopped, and dismounted.

From atop the wall came a large and professionally made rope ladder. Zekah scrambled up first, while Yorek covered Spirit. When the adept was atop the wall, he looked around there and on the other side and then came back to the edge. "O.K.! Let's move!" he shouted back to them.

"All right, girl—start climbing. Make it fast, or I'll break that pretty nose of yours and we'll *carry* you. Move it! Now!"

She hesitated a moment, could see no way out, and so did as instructed. Once at the top, Zekah took her arm and pointed. "Now down the other side. Better move quickly. He's in a bad mood."

She hardly had a chance to look at anything before she was on another rope ladder, this one leading down to the ground outside the wall. Only

then did she have a chance to stop and get her
wits about her. Two monstrous, horrible shapes
waited on the other side, one on either side of
her and about three meters away. They were
grotesque— caricatures of human beings with faces
that looked like the leering living dead. Surely, if
Coydt's soul showed his true self, he would look
like their brother. She shuddered, and abandoned
any hope of running right now. The idea of one of
those things even *touching* her was horrible.

She stood on the Anchor apron, a bit of solidity
that extended past the wall and in the old days
had presented a barren buffer through which an
attacking force would have to pass to get to the
wall. Beyond the apron, perhaps a hundred meters
at this point, loomed the Flux.

It looked like a solid wall of some translucent
material, somewhat of an amber shade, stretching
from the end of the apron as far up as the eye
could follow. There were no features of any sort
discernible in it, but the Flux seemed alive, somehow, with thousands of tiny firefly-like sparkles
going off at any given moment. She had gaped at
this sight from the wall as a student and again
as a visitor to a border town, but it still gave
off a cold and forbidding chill.

Coydt and Yorek came down the other side, while
Zekah continued to cover them from the top of the
wall. It had been four hours since the abduction.

Yorek ran unhesitatingly into the void and quickly
returned, leading three horses. They must have
been waiting just inside the Flux, but they had
been totally invisible until they emerged into
Anchor.

Coydt's foul, hurried mood seemed to pass quickly
now, and he visibly relaxed, looked at her, and
grinned. "You like my little creatures, I see."

"They're horrible," she muttered.

"They were normal people once, but they went

off in the void by themselves for one reason or another. Both have some Flux power—not much—and it turned on them. Alone, out there, with power, but no skill at using it, and with no wizard's protection, your own nightmares become real; you go nuts, and your outer form reflects your inner fears. You think about that as we go. Take the spotted horse there. Once inside, you'll be lost. You'll never find your way anywhere except by luck, even back here. I'll have my string on you, so you'll leave a trail I can follow no matter where you go or how you twist and turn. But if you get away, I'll leave you out there a while before I come and get you. Let you have a taste of what *they* went through. You think about that, and them. Once inside, I'm the only protection you've got."

It was not a comforting thought. Zekah had pulled in the rope ladder on the Anchor side and now was down on this one. It was unlikely that their crossover point would be undiscovered for long, but they didn't need much time now. Once in Flux, Coydt's powerful wizardry made him essentially an all-powerful god, and he was one of the best trained and most powerful wizards on World.

They mounted, and then she, and rode off towards the void. It loomed ahead of her, until it filled her entire vision, and she could not resist glancing back for one last look at Anchor Logh, its greenery barely discernible over the top of the wall. Then they were through—and into the eerie realm of the Flux and the Void.

There was literally no sound in Flux, not even from the horses' hooves, and just seconds into the sparkling energy field all sense of direction and reality seemed to vanish. The void was everywhere. Even the horses' breathing and the occasional shout of one man to another seemed oddly muffled and subdued, as if the vast, shimmering void was trying to smother all that entered it.

Coydt barked an order and they all stopped. He frowned and stared at Spirit for a minute. "Well, I'll be damned!" he exclaimed. "This complicates matters a bit, but only a bit. Looky there! See the kind of doubling aura around her? Our Spirit's got herself a Soul Rider!"

# SOUL RIDER

*It was a totally unexpected thing, unprecedented in all my long experience and in the experience of any of my brethren. We, the Spirits of Flux and Anchor that men call Soul Riders, join with and reside inside human beings, sharing what they share and seeing what they see. We have no choice as to whom we ride; that is determined by the unseen master of our fates whose identity and, indeed, very nature is shielded from us.*

*It is our mission to foil those who would open the Gates of Hell; to track down current members of the Seven Who Come Before, known also as the Seven Who Wait, and destroy them if possible. As we have no corporeal existence, our knowledge of the power of Flux and the laws of Anchor must be of use only when fed to a living being within. All of my hosts have eventually crossed paths with one or more of the Seven. How our unseen controller can know this so well in advance is incomprehensible, but it is always so.*

*It is possible that our hosts are chosen for their inherent power or intellect, since it is true that we cannot use more than what our hosts have to offer themselves and true that those hosts are then pushed or compelled, even as we, into the way of the Seven, but that is not something we can know.*

*Still, every host I have had I have stayed with for a long period of time. Usually they die, unnaturally and prematurely, but sometimes they become major*

73

*figures themselves, and I remain for decades, even after the apparent mission is accomplished, perhaps to guard the host or make certain he or she accomplishes great things.*

*Certainly I expected this with my host Cass of Anchor Logh, whose Flux power is enormous and who has become the most important figure of political and military power on World in all my long memory. And yet, for the first time, the pattern was not to repeat but to change in a most radical way, one which I am at a loss even now to understand.*

*I was irresistibly drawn to Cass when she was but eighteen and an innocent farm girl, fearing that she might be chosen to be sold to a stringer and cast out into Flux in the Church's ancient method of keeping Anchor populations stable. I was with her when she inadvertently discovered how corrupt that lottery was, and she was included in it, being thrown, naked and abandoned, into captivity in Flux. I rode her soul as the forces of Hell attacked the train and dragged her off into captivity, and because of this I was able to use her inborn Flux powers to effect an escape. Through her own impressive adaptability, intelligence, and resourcefulness, she managed to unmask the evil wizard Haldayne, one of the Seven who would open the gates of Hell, and obtain freedom and a position with Matson's stringer train. Together we participated in the attack on Persellus, which Haldayne controlled, as part of an unprecedented force of Flux and Anchor led by three of the most powerful wizards of the Nine, an attack which was difficult indeed, and together we witnessed Matson fall from his great horse, a gaping wound in his chest, her employer and only lover lost before her eyes.*

*And yet I was able to turn her shock and grief into power, unleashing the full force of her abilities against Haldayne, for strong emotion is the greatest of all amplifiers, so that she alone took on Haldayne and routed him, once again foiling Hell's plots and reveal-*

ing the safe back way to the gates through the temples of Anchor.

Emotionally powerful and with a strong sense of duty, I was in her when she joined the priesthood as the leader of a true and needed Reformation. In the ruins of Persellus she established her new Church in Flux and called the place Hope. And so revolution came to World.

But her tryst with Matson had produced one unexpected and unanticipated result, one which complicated things and produced the wonder which still awes and confuses me.

My host had a girl child in Anchor, and I underwent with her the pain and agony attending such births, although I had been through it many times before and could sublimate the most unpleasant aspects. It was different this time, as I felt the message come, the mathematical command which drove me to alter my present state. Even as the child entered the world, I was drawn to her and inside her, so that she and I were in a sense born together.

This was a totally new experience for me, and one that I still find both fascinating and chilling, for it proves as little comfort to be born as to give birth. During the boring first years I took the time to reflect on this whole unprecedented incident and to try and understand the logic of it, although I confess that I have never understood the logic of any host assigned until the crisis actually came to reveal the reason. Still, to experience the joys and pains of human childhood proved, after the first years, to be endlessly fascinating, although hauntingly familiar, as if, some time in the remote past, I, too, had been born and had grown up this way. If, indeed, we are the spirits of cleansed warriors at the temporal apex of reincarnation, then this makes some sense.

Those early years also allowed me the luxury of probing the entire body of the new host, cell by cell, even molecule by molecule. Never have I understood

76 *Jack L. Chalker*

a host so well, either physically or psychologically.
Never have I had such an opportunity to suppress
the negative and accelerate the positive where possible.
I could cleanse build-ups in the blood flow, divert
and eliminate toxins, and exercise some measure of
mental control. Not that I ran her life, or wished to,
but I could protect, inhibit some destructive behavior,
and by very mild stimulation of pleasure and pain
centers condition certain activities.

Nor, in fact, was she unaware of my presence,
although she never really thought about it. It simply
never occurred to her that everyone did not have
such a duality of spirit, an internal guardian, although she theorized that few were aware of it. She
has never resented me, but considered me a part of
her, for she has never known my lack.

Now she is in most ways a woman, young and
fresh and beautiful. We have been together these many
years, and while I suspected a guardian role, there
has been no need up to now to do anything at all. I
have no idea of her Flux potential, as she has never
been permitted out of Anchor where she was born,
but her father was a strong false wizard and her
mother has the most power I have ever seen within
one person of so normal a lifespan, so it is possible
that my host is strong indeed, if untrained. Certainly
her mother has had no more need of me, such is her
current power, that power trained and honed under
the tutelage of the master wizard Mervyn of Pericles.

Certainly the start of the true mission is at hand,
for I feel in the very air a changed energy, a tension
that builds towards a nearly unbearable point. The
ancient struggle continues, and perhaps, this time,
the answers to all my questions may lie at the end of
it.

# BLACK MAGIC

They rode for some time in silence, Coydt deep in thought. Their pace was not fast, just deliberate, and she had no more doubts that what he had spoken about the Void was true. She had no idea how far they had come or how long they had been riding, for there were no landmarks of any kind. She *was* feeling nearly starved, but hesitated to mention it, fearing that it would betray some sort of weakness to these hard, strange men of Flux. She had the idea that any weakness demonstrated would lower their opinion of the one showing weakness a good deal, not to mention please them enormously. These were people who worshipped only power and liked it, no matter how small the crumb. She resolved that, no matter what, she would give them the smallest pleasure she could in that department.

There were many romantic stories and fantasies by Anchor folk of what the Flux was like, but nobody ever thought of it as unremitting boredom. Her three captors had totally relaxed upon entering Flux and getting some distance in, and now they barely paid attention to her, but she no longer felt like attempting an escape. The idea of wandering this terrible nothingness until you died of hunger or thirst, or were driven completely insane by it, was so terrifying that such an idea was unthinkable.

She had resigned herself to this captivity, at

least for now. She didn't know what they planned, but so far she'd not been harmed or even threatened, except with the consequences of escape. Some of it still had the quality of dream, as if this really couldn't be happening to her, but she knew it was real and that these men were dangerous.

Finally they called a halt—the two adepts and she stopped and dismounted, while Coydt went on, either to check out what was ahead or to prepare something.

She looked around and saw only the nothingness. The horses looked tired and thirsty, as was she, but there were no packs, no saddlebags. Zekah, a thin young man she would have considered "cute" in another context, came over to her. "So—hungry and thirsty?"

She nodded. "No more than you or the horses."

"Watch, then," he told her, and turned away. He made a couple of hand signs and then pointed to a spot a few meters from them. A hole opened up—no, a cavity, perhaps four meters wide, and it filled very slowly and dramatically with clear water. He went over to it, knelt down, scooped up some in cupped hands, and drank. "Pretty good," he decided at last. "Yorek—bring the horses over. You, too, girl. Take a drink."

It was her first experience with Flux magic and she was impressed. She took her drink, then said, "That's pretty impressive." Maybe the aides could be buttered up a little, although she was being truthful.

"That's nothing," Zekah responded, turned back and waved his hands some more. Instantly a small table appeared with three chairs, and on the table was a veritable feast of food, hot and cold, as well as carafes of wine. She walked over to it in wonder, then hesitantly touched it. "It's *real*!"

"Sure, it's real. Come on—let's sit down and eat before the boss comes back."

It was the most bizarre dinner she'd ever had, a luxury feast in the middle of nothingness with two youthful kidnappers. Still, she ate with relish, not knowing from where and when the next meal would come.

Once satiated, the two adepts seemed in a good mood and she tried to pump them for some information. It was difficult to imagine these two as the brutal killers in the church, although it would never be possible to forget Coydt that morning.

"You just . . . wave your hand and it's done?"

"It's more complicated than that," Yorek responded. "Actually, it's all math. The better you are with math in your head and the better your memory, the more you can do. Nobody can give you the Flux power—you either have it or you don't. But if you have it, and the math skills and the memory skills, you have real power, and that's what it's all about out here."

"Money means nothing—obviously," Zekah put in. "Nothing means anything in Flux except power. The more you have and can use, the higher up you go. Now, the boss—he's got power. More than anybody, I think. If he wants a castle with servants, he just wishes them up."

She thought about it. "I would think that after a while being a god would get boring, too. I mean, what do you do after you have everything you want?"

"You've got the idea," Yorek agreed. "That's really the key to figuring the boss out. The only fun he gets is showing off his powers to others. We—we're along to learn what we can from him, but he don't think of us that way. People to the boss are just things—stick figures or cartoons drawn for his own amusement. Playthings. Even us."

"I'd think you'd be a little nervous about that."

"Not really. You see, we're the one thing he needs in the whole world. We're his audience. No use in power if you don't have people around who can appreciate it. No, the only people he might think of as people are those with as much or more power than he's got, and if he finds 'em, he takes 'em on. So far, nobody's been stronger. That's why the Flux bores him. He likes to spend most of his time in Anchor, where the power isn't in the magic but in the head. He likes to win at anything, and he almost always does. Any time he doesn't, he gets mean and nasty. Everybody's scared stiff of him, even the rest of the Seven, mostly, I think, because he doesn't believe in anything but himself."

"He doesn't believe in Hell, then? But I thought that's what the Seven were about."

Zekah smiled. "They are, and so's he. But not like them. He says there's nothing supernatural about Hell. It's just another place filled with a lot of different kinds of creatures who think. A long time ago we and they fought a war over this place, and they lost, sort of. Maybe it was a tie. Anyway, the other side's been stuck someplace, kept there by the gadgets on the Hellgates, and that someplace isn't home. We're in the way to where their home is. They want to go home now, but they can't do it without coming through here. Since they invented the Flux, they know just how to work it, so there's supposed to be a deal. Unlock the gates, let them go home, and in payment they'll show the ones who let 'em out just how to fully use the Flux on a worldwide basis. That's ultimate power."

She shivered. "Even if it's true, I don't see why anybody should trust them. If I'd been locked away in prison for thousands of years, I sure wouldn't be nice to the children of the ones who put me there."

"That's a good point," Yorek agreed, "but you got to remember that the Seven are wizards like Coydt. They're *all* tremendously old, hundreds of years, and they're *all* very bored. They figure a gamble on something new is better than living forever like this. Maybe they're right, I don't know. As soon as it's done, if they get the power, all of 'em will set out to wipe out the others and become sole god of World. That's the only reason Coydt hasn't taken *them* on. That and the fact that to unlock the gates you need a code, and each of 'em only has part of it."

It was an unreal conversation, part fairy story and part nightmare. Sitting there at a sumptuous dinner in the middle of a void, the victim and her kidnappers were having friendly, casual conversation.

"What am *I* doing in the middle of all this?" she asked them. "I don't know the math, and my mother's surely not going to ransom me for anything. My opinion of her is actually closer to your boss's."

Zekah shrugged. "They've got something big cooking. Something that's taken years to set up. Your momma is the only thing standing in their way. The boss is willing to take her on, one-on-one, but she would never be alone. It'd be ten to one, and that's suicide. Just what the whole thing's about we don't know, but you're important to it, that's for sure. Better keep this in mind, though. He uses people, that's all. He don't think much of men, but he thinks even less of women. Thinks they're kind of inferior to men. You better be ready. Best your mom would've had a boy."

She thought about it, and didn't like the implications at all.

Coydt returned just then and looked down on the scene from horseback. "Charming. I trust the boys have been keeping you amused? After all, you *are* our guest."

"I'm not your guest; I'm your prisoner," she shot back. "I don't know what your game is, but it's not going to work. My mother wouldn't do *anything* to get *me* back."

"You might be surprised. Still, it really doesn't matter if she does or she doesn't. Don't overestimate your importance either. You are not the game, nor even close to it. You are merely a diversion, some useful window dressing, nothing more. In fact, your most interesting challenge was something we didn't even suspect until we got you in Flux. Mount up. We have a short ride left to go, and then we can relax."

The news had hit Kasdi like a shot to the heart, and it brought up all the guilt to the fore. It had also triggered a massive manhunt through Flux and Anchor. Messengers, transformed into swift creatures who could fly in Flux, took the news and the descriptions to all the other Anchors and Fluxlands and even to stringer trains within the vast area under the control of the Reformed Church. Not that it would probably do much good. Coydt's powers in Flux were such that he could easily escape detection and get them all away to the relative safety of the old Church's domains or the wilds as quickly as she could spread the news.

Mervyn arrived in Anchor Logh within hours of getting the word of the kidnapping. He had much information, but no news.

"Coydt grew up in Anchor, the youngest of five children," he told her. "When his older brother was chosen in the Paring Rite, he turned on the Church and all its works with a vengeance, practically inviting expulsion himself. His parental situation is the stuff of psychology studies, but suffice it to say that he was the worst person on World to discover he had tremendous doses of Flux power and the ability to use them. He hates the Church, old or new. In fact, he hates *all* religious equally, and believes that there is nothing supernatural in

anything. He believes that women as a group are
intellectually and psychologically inferior to men
and that they should be obedient, subservient, totally passive people serving men. He is worse than
immoral, he is *amoral* in the extreme—he no more
thought about killing that poor priestess than you
would think about brushing aside a fly. He is,
unfortunately, also coldly brilliant, as witness his
plan here."

Kasdi shuddered. "He makes Haldayne sound
like a saint. And Spirit is in his hands. . . ."

He nodded. "Indeed. But there is more afoot
here than mere toying. This is the start of an organized campaign of some sort. I'm afraid we will
simply have to wait and see what this first move is
all about."

She spent the next few days with Cloise, trying
to comfort the foster mother who'd done so well
and to take some comfort from her as well, as they
waited. Messengers, as expected, brought no news,
although the attack and its aftermath was the sole
topic of conversation in Anchor Logh and made
everyone feel insecure and suspicious. Strangers of
any kind had to be restricted, and still nobody was
being allowed out, but the locals were seeing every
unfamiliar face as one of those people in the church.

Far from being a dark secret, Spirit's origin and
appearance were now as well-known as Kasdi's.
Her picture was everywhere, and it was certain
that if anyone saw her she would be instantly
identified.

Finally, word came—in a letter mailed from the
capital to Cloise at the farm. It was a handwritten
message with no identifying marks.

Dear Concerned Mothers:

Please rest assured that your daughter, Spirit,
is safe, warm, dry, and well-fed. She is unchanged,

and has not been violated or even marked. To
discuss her and our future business, please come
to the point at the Anchor apron marked on the
enclosed map tonight one hour after dark. Do
not enter Flux, but remain—on the wall, if you
like. There will be no tricks on my part, no
attempt at harming you in any way. I wish some-
time in the future to see just how good the saintly
Sister Kasdi really is in Flux, but that must be
for a later time. As a result, I will take no action
against her in Anchor, but she must see me from
Anchor only. Tell the other wizards they are to
remain at least one kilometer away in Flux from
this spot. If they do not, Spirit will suffer for it
and it will be on their heads.

    Until tonight, then, I remain,

Very sincerely yours,

        Coydt van Haaz

There would be no tricks. Kasdi insisted that
she alone go to meet him, although there would be
a squad of cops with automatic weapons posted
just in case Coydt was pulling a fast one. Mervyn
and two lesser but still potent wizards would cover
in Flux from the required distance, ready to move
if need be.

It was a warm night, but the old rock wall was
cold and damp against her bare feet. Nonetheless,
she waited there, watching darkness come and the
troops covering her lighting the torches not only
on the wall but in the apron ground as well. The
hour passed with agonizing slowness, but, right on
schedule, someone shouted, and all eyes turned to
the Flux, at this point less than twenty meters
away.

Coydt was not only punctual; he certainly knew
how to put on a show. At the appointed time the
whole huge area of Flux seemed to glow, and then

pulsate, and it was as if luminescent winds blew in all directions within the energy field. The winds then coalesced into a face—an enormous face, possibly a kilometer high, filling their field of vision. The voice, although loud, was certainly as much Coydt's as the now very familiar face.

"Glad to see you're on time," the wizard greeted her. "We can have our little chat at this point, and you needn't shout. I can hear you if you just use a normal tone of voice."

"Where is my daughter?" she demanded.

"Safe. I'm sure that everybody's got my profile by now, so you should know that I always keep my word and never lie without profit. It is rather odd, but the masses never grasp it, so that I must emphasize that point, since if someone above the law does not keep his word and play fair, he'll never get what he wants. I keep my bargains for that reason—always."

"What is it that you want?"

"I have your daughter. You have four Hellgates. I need access to them from the temples."

"You know I can't do that—even if I wanted to, they wouldn't permit it."

"A straight swap, then. You for her?"

"More tempting to me, personally. I, too, would like to try you one-on-one, Coydt. But it would be only a brief respite for my daughter, whom I could not protect, and I could not bind the Nine to any bargain *I* made. You know that."

The huge image of Coydt sighed. "Well, then, what are we to do? It seems I have a commodity with no major market value. You cannot, or will not, pay the price."

"Just let her go. I'll arrange to meet and settle our disputes."

"A wonderful idea, and part of my original hopes for this, but no longer possible," he responded. "I'm afraid we've discovered that your daughter has a Soul Rider. Neutralizing the Soul Rider has thus become an overriding preoccupation."

The news was a shock, but also something of a relief. Spirit must have gotten the Soul Rider from her, somehow. The creatures' natures were totally unknown, but they certainly protected their hosts and were on the right side in a fight. She should know. Coydt, in fact, had a series of dilemmas.

"Then you can't transform her and let her wander, because the Soul Rider would eventually make it right," she noted. "You can't try a really major spell on her, because it can probably unravel it. And you can't kill her, because then you wouldn't know where that Soul Rider was, except that it was after you."

"We've learned a lot since Haldayne's attempt on you. Very well—there is no offer *you* wish to make for her release?"

"The best I could do would be to drop all charges against you should she be returned unharmed. And agree to meet you at some point."

"Oh, we *will* meet, I promise you that. I'm looking forward to it. But not now. Very well. Here is how we will resolve this. You can't find the others who helped me pull the job, but everybody is being bottled up. I want everyone who wishes to leave Anchor Logh within the next full day to be allowed to do so without harm or prejudice. The borders will be open again, and everything will be back to normal. In exchange for this, if Spirit agrees, I will return her to Anchor Logh within three days. She may have some spells, but they will not harm her or anyone else. And, after all, you're a great wizard yourself. You can take care of those. Agreed?"

She frowned. "Agreed."

"Until we meet again, then," he responded, and the huge face shrank more and more until it was merely a point in the void and then was gone.

She shook her head in wonder and suspicion. There was more to this than what he'd said, that was for sure. Why go through all this trouble and all that risk only to settle for the getaway of some of the more minor perpetrators?

The place was called a Pocket. In many ways it resembled a Fluxland, in that it was a very substantial and substantial-looking reality designed, built, and maintained by the mind of a wizard. It differed only in size. While a Fluxland could be larger than an Anchor, a Pocket was generally small enough that one could see the Void all around from its center.

This one had a lot of trees, a stream running through it near the house, a bright whitish-gray sky, and, in the middle, on a small knoll, a rather standard-looking six-room, two-story house. It was not terribly well hidden from those who could discover it, but no strings that any but Coydt could see led to or from it, and it was well away from any stringer routes, although less than a day's ride from Anchor Logh. It seemed to stand out, but in the context of World it was smaller than the smallest needle in the largest haystack.

She had not been imprisoned here, and had full run of the place except for Coydt's own two-room complex in back of the first floor and just off the small kitchen. She had her own room, had access to a very modern shower and toilet, and except for the fact that she still had only the clothes she'd had on when kidnapped, she was quite comfortable. She had not only not been mistreated or molested; she was almost completely ignored.

Now, though, Coydt, who'd been away for a while, had returned and a knock on her door by Yorek summoned her. "The boss wants to see you," he said simply, and that was enough.

He sat in a comfortable, padded desk chair, rocking slightly and smoking a cigar. He looked over a bunch of figures on a piece of paper one last time as she entered and took a seat on a small couch two meters from him. For a moment he did not acknowledge her, but then he looked up, dismissed Yorek, sighed, and turned to her, putting the paper down.

"It's time for us to bargain," he said simply.

She was startled. "Bargain? What do I have to bargain with?"

"Just hold on a moment and listen to me. The boys told you what a Soul Rider was?"

She nodded. "I'm not sure I understand it, but I've always known it was there. Sometimes I almost think I can hear its thoughts."

"Probably because it entered at birth. It's so closely integrated with you that you and it are almost one being. That makes you dangerous."

"If it's so powerful, why am I still here?"

He chuckled. "Well, it's not human, so it doesn't think the way humans do. It knows there's a big plot going on. It knows, too, that if it takes me on, it will certainly cost your life, although possibly not its own. It's curious. That's the way they are. It won't act until it knows all the facts and is able to do the most damage. Short of your life, it won't move to protect you. For example, did you notice that while we've been talking, you have removed every single stitch of clothing you had on and are now waiting there totally naked with your legs spread apart?"

She jumped. Until that moment, she hadn't been the slightest bit aware of it. She looked down for the clothes, but for some reason just could not bring herself to reach down, pick them up, and put them back on.

"That's how simple and effortless spells are," he told her casually. "In point of fact, you don't feel the least bit embarrassed or uncomfortable, do you? You feel natural and normal that way, even though you know you shouldn't."

It was true. The idea of clothing seemed somehow unnatural, even repugnant to her, yet she knew how she should feel and even knew that she felt this way because of the man's will.

If he was trying to frighten her, he was succeeding admirably.

"I'm demonstrating power, no more," he told her. "This is absurdly simple. Child's play. If I so desired, I could make you fall madly, passionately in love with me, willing to do anything I wanted. I could make you my slave, my plaything, and you would love every moment of it." Suddenly he stood up. "On your knees before me, slave!"

She was off the couch and on her knees in front of him, head bowed, before she realized what happened. "Yes, my master," she responded. For a few minutes he put her through her paces, ordered her to do odd gymnastics and crave odd sex from him. He stopped her just short of actually performing, though, and somewhat released her. Her rationality returned, but not her control. She was a jumble of emotions, disgusted with herself, repulsed by Coydt, and terrified of his power, and yet she knew that if he ordered it, she would do it again, and more.

"That was a demonstration of the mental and emotional spells. Now, stand up. Hold out your right arm."

She did as instructed, and was horrified to see not an arm but a slithering, pulsating sucker-covered tentacle, one of a dozen. She oozed slime and filth; reeked of garbage. She wanted to scream, but nothing came out.

And, just as suddenly, she was herself again and her arm was her arm, but she was badly shaken.

"That was no mental trick. You really *were* that creature. I could do that in a moment and make you love it. I can make you old, young, male, female, human, animal, or monster. I can do anything I want with you. Do you believe that?"

She nodded, trying to stop shaking.

"I can do more than that. Little is permanent here in Flux, and your Soul Rider knows it more than any. Everything in Anchor, though, is permanent, including anything you might be when entering Anchor from Flux. Your mother and the Soul Rider aren't concerned about any spell I may cast, since they can remove it. It might take time and be a lot of trouble, but they can do it. However, I can cast a delayed spell that will make the Flux to you seem as hard and impenetrable as stone. I can cast you as I will, send you into Anchor, and you cannot get back to Flux. Without it, the spell can not be seen or analyzed, much less broken, for to take you back into Flux by force would be instant death to you. Now, how shall I send you back to your mother?"

The question was rhetorical, if terrifying, and required no response.

He sat back down in his chair and lit another cigar. "Now comes the bargain. Refuse it, and I will let my imagination run wild and then send you back—only you'll *know*. You won't be able to do anything about it, but you'll *know*. Do you want that?"

She shook her head. "No—please!"

He grinned, enjoying himself. "All right, then. The alternative is to be a part of a little experiment of mine. Human beings are animals. Some animals other than humans think, I believe. Certainly, if the Soul Rider is an animal of some sort, it thinks. I have been wondering for some time what would happen if that were *all* somebody had to work with. No tools, no artifacts. Back to the beginning, to the first people. I have devised a rather complex spell to see. The spell is of a kind rarely used, because it's unbreakable. The reason it is so is a Gordion knot of mathematics, but the basics are that it is a spell one takes voluntarily on oneself with a proviso that only the wielder can break it. And in the spell is a prohibition against doing just that. It is, in fact, the sort of spell your mother used to make sure she stayed a saint."

She had a knot in the pit of her stomach. "What . . . will it do?"

"Neither memory nor physical appearance would be changed. The mental alterations basically consist of a translation of memory and thought from one language into another. To you, there would be no change at all, but as the language is a nonvocal one, you could neither speak, understand, read, or write, although you would, of course, hear normally. Artifacts—man-made things—would be a mystery to you, even though intellectually you would recognize and know them. The basic needs would be paramount, the social inhibitions minimal. The physical part of the spell would prevent others from circumventing the rest and would adapt your body so that you could survive the elements. Do you follow me so far?"

"You'd make me some kind of animal."

"No. You'd have free will and your full memory and intellect. Flux power could be used in defense or in self-preservation, but only for that. You are a big, strong, powerful girl and you'll stay that way, forever young, athletic, and beautiful. You could defend yourself in Anchor, I suspect. And—here's the sugar. There *is* a way, and one way only, to break the spell. I won't tell you how, but it cannot be done by you. If your mother, or one of the Nine, can figure that out and is willing to pay the price, you can be freed."

"So that's it. You expect my mother to pay this price or whatever."

"Well, it'll be a clear ransom, at least. Price for

freedom. And no matter what, you'll have your
youth, beauty, and intellect and you will be free in
Flux and Anchor to go anywhere you want. An
adjunct to the spell will give you the basics—seeing
strings, finding or making basic food and water—
and they'll come to you as you need them. That's
the bargain, and it's take it or leave it. You must
see, of course, that I'm taking a chance with it. I'm
betting your ransom will not be paid, and therefore your Soul Rider is going to be stuck in a
nearly immortal body limited to the Flux powers
you can use—which are purely defensive. But if
the ransom is paid, now or in the future, that's
fine, too, for the result will make the Soul Rider's
job more difficult and mine easier. Will you accept
the spell, or shall I do my worst? It's up to you."

She sat back a moment and closed her eyes,
trying to think clearly. *O.K., Soul Rider or whoever
you are, what do you say?* But there was no answer,
only a feeling of inevitability. To be stuck forever
in Anchor as a creature, mental and physical, of
Coydt's warped imagination, or to take living like
an animal, but free, with the possibility, however
remote, of having the spell lifted. The agent of Hell
had made a terrible offer, but there was no choice.

"I'll take your 'experiment' or whatever you want
to call it," she told him. "I don't see I really have a
choice."

"I kind of hoped you'd see it that way. Oh, by
the way—one other little part of the spell is that
you will not recognize me or my helpers if you
ever see them again, unless we want you to. Forget
revenge and just see what kind of life you can live.
I'm real curious myself, not to mention curious to
see if the Soul Rider can break a spell like this if it
has to."

"When?" she asked softly.

"Now," he replied. "Just relax and put your
head back. No coercion can be used, but I can ease

it along and help you. Now, even with your eyes shut, you should see it in your mind. You don't have to understand it, just see it. Do you?"

And she *did* see, an incomprehensible spider's web of crisscrossing lines, long and short, curled and straight, in a series of knotty patterns so complex they almost, but not quite, merged into one mass.

"Now that is what *you* do in your own mind. It's simple. See it? Grasp it, then make your own pattern just like it. Just *think* it through."

It was a similar mass, but there were only a few strings in a very straightforward pattern. She concentrated on it, imagined a duplicate of it in her mind. The first faded out, leaving only hers.

"Now, if you wish this spell, just merge that little pattern of yours to the one you see and then just think, 'I freely accept this spell upon myself.' Go ahead. That's all there is to it."

It was as if two long, gnarled balls of string, one tiny and one huge, were merged together and their loose ends tied. *I freely accept this spell upon myself*, she thought, not really understanding what was happening nor fully able to grasp the reality of the situation. The two spells knotted, merged, glowed, and then seemed to flow into her. She felt suddenly terribly dizzy, as if she were falling, and she found herself confused. It was impossible to think, and she was falling. . . .

# MUTE WITNESS

She had awakened slowly and dizzily on damp grass. It took a while before her head allowed her to sit up and for her eyes to focus properly, but the more she moved, the more it all subsided. She did not know the place, but when she finally managed to get to her feet and walk a little ways, she reached a road and saw at the end of it the huge wall and the old, thick gate. It was certainly the west gate of Anchor Logh, and she was inside.

The scene confused her for a moment, but the memories crept in. She remembered the church, the shooting, the abduction and long ride, the time in the Pocket and the terrible demonstration of Coydt's power. She also remembered the bargain, but couldn't quite sort it out. Certainly she felt quite normal—in fact, quite good. Although she would have liked a reflection, what she could see of her body looked totally unchanged. Whatever the evil man had done, it didn't seem so bad. But, then, would it? She wondered about that, remembering how easily he had manipulated her mind.

There were some people working near the gate and she walked over to them calmly and boldly. Her folks must know that she was back and all right. She was halfway to them when one looked up and noticed her, then started yelling and pointing, and others also turned and looked and there was more incomprehensible jabber. They ran to her, and a man said to a woman some ridicu-

94

lous string of barking noises, and she answered in
kind. She tried to speak to them, to find out what
all the excitement was about, since she still feared
a Coydt trick, but her mouth just couldn't form
the words. All talking got her was a quick sore
throat.

The woman barked something, and then the man
nodded and threw a jacket over her for some incomprehensible reason. She screamed and tore it
off. It burned like fire, and the onlookers gaped,
amazed, at real burn-like marks where the coat
had been. The pain had been intense, although it
faded quickly. The whole thing scared and confused her and the people, but finally one of them
took charge and led her down and into the government station that was part of the entry gate itself.
She looked around, confused at the inner office,
and so just stood there as bedlam continued to
erupt around her. In the midst of all these people
she felt very confused and very much alone. The
walls seemed to close in on her, and she felt rising
panic and a shortness of breath.

"She won't stay inside, and when we tried to
put clothes on her, it burned her like a hot stove,
although the marks faded fast," said the customs
officer. "She either won't or can't talk or understand us, although we've gotten a few very basic
things over in sign language. She was pretty hungry,
but totally ignored the knife and fork and seemed
unable to pour her own water out of a pitcher into
a glass. She kept trying to stick her hand in. In all
my years this close to Flux I never saw anything
like it."

Kasdi and Mervyn both nodded gravely at this,
but were most anxious to see Spirit. She had been
recognized immediately, of course, but it was clear
from the first that she was under a ton of binding
spells. They had dispatched word immediately, and

both wizards had ridden hard all afternoon to reach the gate. Kasdi's father and Cloise had wanted to come, but these were matters best dealt with by magic, and in Flux.

"And when she had to pee—pardon, Sister—she totally ignored our bathrooms and just squatted outside and went. Messy. And we have modern toilets, too!"

They mostly ignored the little bureaucrat and made straight for the girl, who was now sitting under a tree near the gate, just out of sight of the main road.

When Spirit saw Sister Kasdi coming towards her, she felt mixed emotions. On the one hand, here at last was her true mother, looking very grave and very concerned, and even after all this it felt nice. But here, too, was a living legend and by no choice of hers the cause of her problems. The old guy she didn't recognize at all.

She stood and faced her real mother, surprised and shocked that she nearly towered over the older woman. Legends aren't supposed to be small and frail-looking. They stood there a moment, looking at each other, both unsure of what to do next. Finally, Kasdi approached, put her arms around Spirit, and hugged, and Spirit found herself crying and hugging back.

Mervyn let them have their reunion as he watched. "Interesting," he said to himself, although the little customs man was still there and thought himself addressed.

"What's interesting?"

"Huh? Oh, the clothes."

"But she isn't wearing any!"

"Well, yes, but Sister Kasdi is. You said there was a burning when the jacket was put on the girl; yet there's no effect when her mother's clothing touches her. The spell is quite specific, it seems.

This is going to be a tough one, I think. Coydt's mind is, ah, shall we say, one of a kind.''

Sign language was the only true medium of communication possible, but Spirit managed, after a dozen tries, to ask why none of the other family was there. Patiently, Kasdi tried by pointing and gestures to tell her that they were deep in Anchor and that she had to go back into Flux with them. Spirit was disappointed, but she knew that they would get word to her parents and her grandfather quickly. She realized that all the things Coydt had done to her could only be examined and possibly fixed in Flux, though, and it would be better to do it this time among people trying to help her.

Kasdi's sincere emotion at seeing her had triggered an odd response after all the resentment. The relief and love there seemed genuine, all the more so because it was spontaneous and in Anchor. She still did not feel close or kin to this strange woman, but a great deal of the anger and resentment was very suddenly gone.

It would be for the local authorities to determine how and when she had been brought here. The first business was to get into Flux and see just what in fact had been done. This would be Mervyn's job—he was the analyzer, the diagnostician, and he knew all the funny little tricks of the trade.

They brought horses, but Spirit refused to mount hers. She knew she had ridden them quite often and in fact had loved to ride, but she couldn't bring herself to do it now. They tried putting her on using a couple of big, burly guards, but she kept losing her balance and falling off, and they eventually gave up. The failure disturbed her and began to bring home just what changes Coydt had forced upon her.

So they walked, the other two leading the horses, out across the apron and into Flux, drawing many stares as they went. Spirit realized that they would take forever this way and motioned for them to mount and ride. She was was always in good condition—perhaps she could at least give them *some* lead.

She could hardly outdistance a horse, but she found a steady jogging run to be no trouble at all, and they were amazed at not only the speed she could maintain but also the fact that, fairly far out, she was barely breathing hard. Spirit, too, was surprised at the effortlessness of it all and realized that this must be part of the spell as well. It felt *good* to run.

Mervyn more than once had to stop Kasdi from halting through concern for Spirit. "Let's see just what her limits are."

"She's inhuman now," Kasdi noted.

"I know."

Finally, when they reached the first stringer water pocket and had to turn in, they found the girl barely perspiring and not the least bit winded, although she stopped when they did and went over and drank deeply of the clear water.

"That spell is a nightmare. I try and follow it and suddenly I get lost," Kasdi said. "How about you?"

"I'm beginning to see a pattern in it, but I'll need more time with her, and not on the run, to do more."

They made Hope in under three days, with short sleeps, and it was hardly a challenge for Spirit. Since she seemed unwilling to come inside buildings, no matter how open, they set her up in the park near the temple and made it off limits to unauthorized personnel. From that point on, and for the next week, Mervyn and several associates made their intensive studies, studies reinforced by being able to observe her behavior close at hand. She cooperated as fully as possible with them, knowing what they were doing and wishing devoutly that she could know and understand their conclusions. Mervyn worked tirelessly, scanning all sorts of books from the Codex project and later writings to solve the puzzle. Finally, he thought he had it all.

"You know, we often use the word 'diabolical' to talk of the works and mind of Hell, but you seldom really see the meaning of that word. *This* is diabolical."

Kasdi frowned. "O.K., give it to me. Spare nothing."

"I intend to. In one way, it's Coydt's sense of humor showing. He has taken the daughter of the First Lady of the Church and remade that daughter into the First Woman. He has, in a sense, removed her knowledge of good and evil. Not that she'll kill someone or anything like that, but all the social inhibitions are suppressed, some entirely, and the new behavior is reinforced by conditioning spells. She is naked, but she walked up to the movement workers without any attempt at concealment because she simply doesn't consider nudity odd or unusual. You might say she has no sense of shame. This is reinforced by a concrete spell that prevents others from clothing or concealing her.

"Similarly, she has full bowel control and will hardly eliminate in polite company. Nonetheless, she feels no shame at eliminating, and if it is necessary and convenient, she will do so without ever thinking of who might be watching. I believe, too, that if she were with a young man in public, and he made romantic overtures to her and she were so inclined, she would think nothing of performing sex right then and there and in public."

"But she has control? I mean, if she didn't want to, that would be that. I think the man's inhibitions will probably take care of that problem, then. Go on."

"Her body, which was always in fine shape, has been tuned to its absolute ultimate. She is, quite literally, physically perfect, at the upper limit of what her body is physically capable of. This might deteriorate slightly in Anchor, but would be restored and maintained in Flux in any case. She can run, jump, lift, and climb better than any woman alive. I watched her jump almost effortlessly to a tree limb almost *four meters* up, swing herself effortlessly onto it, and walk in that tree as if she were on flat ground. Perfect balance and coordination, absolutely flawless in every detail. She can sprint faster than any normal human, and you saw her capacity for long-distance running. She draws the energy she needs from Flux, and she could maintain it, I suspect, for weeks in Anchor. She bruises only with difficulty, and they are gone overnight. There is definite regeneration in the spells, and it's a tight spell. She will be impossible to disfigure, mar, or maim, and damned hard to kill, in Anchor or Flux. The regeneration, in fact, is so absolute that her body is nearly immortal. She will be seventeen forever."

"And the communications?"

"This is part of the diabolical portion. Somehow he's come up with a new language, a shifting mathematical abstract that serves to carry thoughts and process memories, but its basic code randomly shifts several times a minute. I would say that all of her memories and basic personality are intact, but the language is so abstract and complex that it bears no relation to ours, and since it constantly shifts, it's impossible by the present arts to decode. I would almost say it is a language better suited to machines than humans, although what machines would need languages I don't know, nor can I guess where he got it. Even duplicating the language spell won't help unless you know and start with the exact same coding as she's using at the moment—and even if you matched it up, it would require reorganizing your mind. You would be thinking in *her* language and not your own. The two are simply incompatible. Nor could you talk to her, since the language is so abstract no human throat could utter it. She can neither read, write, speak, or understand, and since her linguistic frame of reference is so different, she could not relearn ours."

"Diabolical indeed," Kasdi agreed gravely. "It would be interesting to know the source of that language. It's not the kind of thing anyone might make up."

"I agree. Much time will be spent on that question, I assure you. But his evil mind runs deeper than I've yet explained. Again, it is in the nature of the language. She simply cannot use or develop or understand the use for human artifacts. *Anything* made by humans. Nor use domestic beasts. Oh, I have no doubt she recognizes and knows these things intellectually, but she is prevented from comprehending them. It is a trigger spell that only comes into force when she is faced with the situation. In this she is less than the animals, most of whom can instinctively use certain tools or make certain constructs or at least learn some simple mechanisms. Her life is the basic human needs and no more. She is not permitted to do anything else."

"It must drive her nuts. Poor Spirit! What have they done to you?"

"Coydt's even ahead there. She sleeps a lot, and I doubt if she dwells or broods or thinks very long on any one subject. She'll sit and watch a bee or a butterfly for hours. This isn't to say that she's dumb, only that she's been totally adapted to her condition by the spells. We've already pushed the

sign language as far as we can without using
spelling, I suspect. She's a good pupil and catches
on fast. It's basic, and that's all it'll ever be. It
helps that she has such an expressive face and that
she seems now, at least, to wear her emotions like
a signpost."

"So how long will it take you now to break the
spell?"

"Never. And I mean that."

"What! But that's impossible! Even Coydt can't
be *that* good!"

"He isn't. No, if he had imposed this spell, rather
than just written it, it could be peeled off, layer by
layer, although there would be some problems,
because of the language system, and some danger.
But he didn't put it on her. She put it on herself,
with the binding spell."

Kasdi was suddenly on her feet. "What? But
how is that possible? She doesn't know enough to
use that spell!"

" You know she has your old Soul Rider."

"Yes, but—you don't mean *it* did it?"

"No, as far as I can tell, it was its usual passive
self. And since it didn't take on Coydt when it had
its chance, that means this is only the first part of
a much larger plot. In fact, it's the most downright
diabolical thing of all. You see, there *is* a way to
break the spell."

That statement was almost as great a shock to
her as Spirit's condition. "But you taught me it
was impossible!"

"There is one way, but it's a hard one, and I
think Coydt knows it. If someone of equal or superior power voluntarily takes on the spell, and if
the spell will fit the volunteer, it can be moved.
That was almost certainly the bargain. He ran her
through three days of terror using Flux power,
then offered her this way out with the chance it
could be broken. She took it. I would have, too,

under the same circumstances and with her ignorance of the limits of Flux power."

Kasdi sat back down again, looking weak and drained. "I see. And that's really what this is all about. Coydt sends her back like this, knowing it will tear me apart."

"Not to mention embarrass you through the empire," the wizard pointed out. "You can take on Fluxlords but couldn't save your own daughter. It sows nervousness and insecurity."

She nodded. "I don't really mind that, though. It'll pass. But the real kicker is that the spell will only really fit Spirit or me—right?"

"He seems to have arranged it so. Are you considering it?"

"I'm tired, Mervyn. Sick and tired. If this thing can't go on without me, it isn't worth doing at all. Don't I owe her that?"

"Perhaps. I will not argue politics with you. It is still not a solution, as Coydt well knows. It's his final joke on us, so to speak. You see, the self-binding spell is a rather simple one, as you know, and it is always the same. It is the spell or spells that attach to it that are the important ones. Should you take Spirit's binding spell, the mathematics would balance and the flow would go in both directions. You would get Spirit's binding spells—and she would get yours."

Kasdi sighed. "I see," was all she managed. It was all too clear a vision. Spirit would be bound to all the vows of the Church and to the ascetic lifestyle that Kasdi had imposed on herself. It was the sort of existence she could never imagine for Spirit, particularly without the job or any sense of commitment. She would be able to talk, and to learn to use and develop her Flux powers, but she would also not be allowed any possessions of her own, would be denied sex, would be bound to the kind of simple drudgery Kasdi now was, bound to obey all the vows, rules, and laws of the Church absolutely and to the letter; yet she would not be a priestess. She would want and feel all the things a seventeen-year-old wanted and felt, but she would be unable to attain any of them. Instead of merely condemning Spirit, he would condemn them both.

"So what can we do?" she asked him pleadingly. "What will become of her? I mean, the way you talk, she is going to be like that ten years from now, a hundred, perhaps forever."

He nodded. "I can see no other way, although we shouldn't underestimate the Soul Rider. Remember, it got you out of some impossible situations doing these things that we all were certain was against the rules. Coydt's way of dealing with that is quite interesting, but untried. Since the Soul Rider can act only through its host, he has limited her access to Flux power. She is passive, prevented from using any power or even committing any act to force her will on anyone. That's why she came along with us so readily. Her power is only available for self-defense or self-preservation on a conscious level, and while it is considerable, she has the preset spells to call upon only under those circumstances. Since the whole set of spells is integral, all must be broken to break one. He's counting on that spell holding, so that the Soul Rider, trapped in an immortal body, can not use its powers and knowledge against anyone, including them."

"Will it work?"

"We won't know until and unless the Soul Rider tries and succeeds. But the other key is in that bizarre language. If we can discover its origin and original users or intent, we might be able to mitigate the spells somehow. In the meantime, though, I would let her go."

"What?"

"I mean it. The word is already spreading. In a

few days all of World will know of the spell and its nature. She's in no danger. There is a shell over the spell that maintains it absolutely. She is as immune from Flux power as anyone could be. Let her do what you always wanted to do and what I'm told she did, too. Let her walk the length and breadth of World and see what there is to see."

"But—like *that*?"

"She must learn to live with it. People will recognize her and let her go. They will tolerate in her things they would not tolerate in themselves, for she'll be a curiosity and something of a celebrity."

"A freak, you mean."

"So? She's already restless down there. Sooner or later she's going to go away. Let her adjust and let World adjust to her. She is going to live like that for a very long time."

It was a sobering thought.

It was a bar in a Fluxland up in the north wilds called Hjinna. Like many of the Fluxlands in the wilds, away from any Anchors, it tended to be populated with people in the business of Flux— minor wizards false and true, retired stringers, and a fair number of fugitives. Powerful ex-stringers usually established the places in reality and relaxed to enjoy them rather than rule them.

The bar was Flandy's Bar, and inside tough-looking men and women were drinking and talking and showing off and even gambling, something not usually possible in Flux, but possible here under the rules of the Fluxland's proprietor, as he liked to call himself.

Through the swinging front doors stepped an enormous man, well over two meters tall and weighing, it seemed, better than two kilos. He was clearly a dugger, with a purplish complexion, a misshapen, hairless face, and a permanent, insane grin, while his skin seemed all mottled and full of discolorations. In many places he would have been the object of horrible fascination and some fear, but not in Hjinna. Lots of retired duggers and those taking a break between six-month-long stringer routes were always about. In fact, although this one was a stranger to almost all of them, only one, an elderly man who'd been drinking pretty heavily, eyed the newcomer with recognition and then growing fear. He got up and made his way quickly to the back of the bar and then stepped out into the alley behind, still clutching his bottle.

The alley seemed clear, and so he turned left—and suddenly came up against a solid wall that hadn't been there a moment before. He cried out, turned, and started the other way—and ran into another wall. In fact, he was now in a high box, the only outlet being the door back into the bar.

The door opened and a figure dressed all in black stepped out. He was a big man with a long, drooping handlebar moustache. He was dressed in stringer fashion, complete with whip and sawed-off shotgun. He was not a young man—his hair was gray and his face worn and aged, with wrinkles around the eyes—but he was in pretty good shape.

"You!" the old man croaked. "But—you're dead! A hundred saw you fall nigh on to twenty years ago!"

"Eighteen," the man responded. "Eighteen years, three months to be exact. So if I'm a ghost, Gilly, then what's that make you?"

"Hey! Wait! I always liked you!" The old man paused for a moment. "This is a trick, isn't it? Who are you—really?"

"Does it matter? I want Coydt, Gilly. I want him bad, and I want him in Anchor."

Gilly took a swig from the bottle to steady his nerves. "Coydt? You nuts? Nobody can take Coydt; you know that!"

"I'll take him, Gilly, because he won't know who's after him even when you tell him."

"I don't talk to Coydt. Oh, sure, we was cozy once, but nobody's really cozy with him for long. You wind up dead—or worse."

"You know, Gilly. You keep track. I haven't got all night either. You know where they are. You know where they *all* are. You're too scared of them not to know."

Gilly drained the bottle, but it didn't help. "He's down near Anchor Logh. Half a world from here."

"Yeah. He pulled a job down there, Gilly, and he doesn't know it yet, but he pulled the wrong one. He woke up the dead with that one, Gilly, and now I'm going to get him."

"What was that business to you?"

"She's my kin, Gilly, though I didn't even know about her until this. I can't let people do that to kin. You know the code. You put the word out. You tell any dugger along the route that's going out. It'll get to me. If it's good information, I'll make it good with you, Gilly, I really will. Cross me, and you're dead, too."

Gilly laughed. "How can I cross you? Who's gonna believe after all these years that a dead man's out stalkin' Coydt?"

"You give him the word if you want. He's so puffed up and egomaniacal that he's liable to set up a meet just to see for sure. You go ahead, Gilly. You tell him Matson's back from the grave."

# SIDEBAR STRINGING

Stringers did not usually ask for Sister Kasdi when they called on Hope, so it was with some curiosity that she decided to go down to the reception hall and see these who had. For lots of personal reasons she loved the taciturn loners who plied the trade routes between Anchors and Fluxlands, not the least of which was her envy of their freedom.

Two figures waited in the temple reception room. One was a small, thin young man barely Kasdi's height and almost as thin, although he wore the black of his profession. The other was an even shorter individual, perhaps one hundred and fifty centimeters, who was very fat, although her ample stomach was not nearly matched to her enormous breasts. She had long, thick black hair that fell down her back almost to her waist, wore unusual dark blue denim pants that seemed quite baggy, and a white tee shirt, obviously made for a very large man, but necessary to keep her enormous frontage covered.

"Suzl!" Kasdi almost screamed, and ran to the small, fat woman, hugging and kissing her. Finally, they stepped back and looked at each other.

"Cass, you look lousy," Suzl told her.

Kasdi laughed. Of all those on World, friend and foe, only Suzl refused to call her by anything but her original name—and was probably the only one who could get away with it. "You seem to have

made up for what I didn't eat," she shot back.
"You're *fat*!"

"Well, I enjoy life. Oh, uh, Cass, this is Ravi.
He's my boss, so to speak, and, well, sort of my
husband."

That caught the Sister off-guard for a moment.
"Husband?" She was well aware that, as a result
of a misfired spell long ago, Suzl was physically
female only to a point; she had a male sexual
organ and was, despite appearances and manner,
really a man.

Ravi looked a bit nervous for a stringer, but said
nothing.

"Yeah. I keep him respectable. We both have
what each other wants most, but I have two big
bonuses."

Kasdi got the drift, and wasn't sure whether to
be shocked or understanding and tolerant. Suzl
had always gone both ways sexually and was una-
shamed of the fact—even before her strange spell.
But she had been born and raised a woman and
grown up that way, and could hardly be impugned
for being attracted to men. Ravi, on the other
hand, was obviously a lifelong homosexual, and
that was a different moral problem. It was tolerated in Flux but suppressed in Anchor, and the
Church frowned on it as interfering with the prime
mission of procreation. Still, Kasdi was not one to
make preachments now. She was very glad to see
Suzl, the only person alive who could and would
tell her to her face exactly what she was thinking,
no matter how blunt or uncomplimentary it may
be.

"Come! Both of you! Sit down over here and talk
a while!" Kasdi invited, and they took chairs in a
corner of the room. "How long has it been?"

"A couple of years at least," Suzl replied. "We
were through once about ten months ago, but you
were off conquering someplace or other. Actually,

we're a little off the route here, but when we heard about the ugly business, I just *had* to come by."

Kasdi nodded, some of the euphoria fading as reality was brought up. "Yes. So it's spread through the network."

For the first time, Ravi spoke, in a thin, reedy voice that was somewhat grating. "It has spread through all of World, and not merely from this source. There is every evidence to show that Coydt's own people are also telling the tale to get maximum effect."

"He would," Kasdi said angrily. "Some day we'll meet, he and I, and he'll learn the price of his work."

"You're not the only one gunning for Coydt, Cass," Suzl told her. "Somebody else has the whole stringer network out trying to track him down."

"Oh? Who?"

"You're not gonna like this."

She felt an odd chill. "Why? What do you mean?"

"Well, those that have seen him say he looks like and claims to be Matson."

Somehow she both expected and feared those words, words she had somehow suspected to hear despite all evidence and experience for eighteen years. "You know Matson's long dead. He died in my arms from a hole in his chest the size of a grapefruit. You know. You were there, too, that day."

Suzl nodded. "I know, although I never saw him. You and lots of others *did*, though, and I don't doubt anybody. He's officially dead, that's for sure. But whoever this is has taken his form and knows all the stringer codes. Anybody with power can seem to be anybody else in Flux, you know that, but one thing's sure. Whoever he is, he has Jomo with him."

The huge, misshapen dugger came immediately to mind, so brutal and grotesque on the outside, but so very gentle and understanding on the inside. Jomo had been Matson's chief driver, the train boss, and fiercely loyal to his boss. Jomo, too, had been there that terrible day, and he had been the one to pull her off his lifeless body. She'd heard he never went back to the trains again, refusing to work for any other stringer, but had retired and gone to work in one of the old dugger communities in the wild. She had not seen him either, not in eighteen years, except in the nightmares she had off and on to this day, reliving that horrible scene.

"Jomo could explain a lot," she told them. "He always liked me, and he worshipped Matson. He'd know all the people and all the codes. If he found somebody up there with a grudge against Coydt, and they are legion, and with Flux power, it might be a way to throw Coydt off balance. Maybe— maybe he thinks he's revenging for Matson, to pay off the injury to Matson's child."

"Could be," Suzl agreed. "It's sure got old Coydt's boys running around, though. Coydt seems to feel the same way you do, and he's moving heaven and hell to find out who it is. Word is that three of his best people have already turned up dead, so I guess *they* found out."

This was getting interesting in more ways than one. "Suzl—Ravi—do you know where Coydt is now?"

"He is in Anchor, certainly," Ravi responded. "He has altered his appearance and has appeared in a number of Anchors just southwest of here, mostly under old and familiar guises and aliases. You will not catch him unawares in Flux, if that is your thinking, and people are far too frightened of him to betray him in Anchor—even to you—pardon me, but you see how it is seen elsewhere. He even kidnapped and cursed forever your own daughter."

She nodded. "I know. But he still knows I'm looking, and now he has a different enemy as well.

In a way, Jomo is doing me a great service. If Coydt fears ambush in Anchor from Jomo and his companion, whoever he really is, he will spend most of his time in Flux, where eventually he will have to come to terms with me. But if he wants no fight with me right now, and he doesn't seem to, then he has to expose himself in Anchor to an unknown assassin. I wonder if he's feeling uncomfortable for the first time in his life?"

"I would doubt it," Ravi replied. "I do not think Coydt can feel very much anymore. Do not ever believe he is afraid of you, even if he should be. If he chooses not to take you on, it is because he has other things to do. He loves only fear in others and the power it generates for him. He is quite cautious in Anchor, but he walks where he wills and when he wishes. It is for others to fear him. Nothing else is acceptable to him."

"Still, the pressure is on him, all the more if he is up to some new evil plan. If that's so, it's directed against me and the Church, and Jomo can queer his plans. If he's not afraid, he's at least being overcautious, and that's better than nothing."

Suzl decided to change the subject back to the original. "How is Spirit doing?"

"She's adjusted well, although it was very hard on her at first. She's restless, though, being trapped here. Mervyn thinks I ought to let her go into the world, but I can't see how I can in good conscience. I mean, in many ways she's like a baby. No shame, no embarrassment, and very little communication or understanding. Come—let's go out and see her, and you'll see my problem."

Her weeks in the garden had given Spirit the time to think and sort things out as the complex spell worked its way into every fabric of her and became in a very real way a part of her.

In a way, understanding was due to Coydt. His

demonstration in his office back in the Pocket had
shown her that attitudes, which are taken for
granted, were not the same as reality. Having the
time to think and reflect on her life and attitudes
before the spell and compare them both to her
behavior now and to other people's reactions to
that behavior had given her an understanding of
just what had happened to her.

Clothing was normal. People did not walk around
in the nude and it was considered immoral behavior. She knew and understood this, but could no
longer accept it. Clothing, any form of covering,
seemed immoral, unnatural, even repugnant to her
now. She knew that her beauty combined with her
nakedness would make men lustful and turn folks
on, but she didn't mind—although once she would
have. She would never again apologize or feel inhibited by anything that was normal and natural.

She slept a lot, and it seemed that every time
she awoke things seemed different to her. Small
things she'd never noticed, like the sound of a
quiet breeze in the treetops or the shapes of clouds
or the rustling of wind in the grass, were beautiful and endlessly fascinating. Nothing that other
people prized or worried about seemed the least
bit important to her anymore, not even any of
those things that used to worry and concern her.
She wasn't even sure now if she *wanted* the spell
broken. Time no longer had meaning, nor did
ambition. Her wants were simple and her needs
were few.

She found all her memories in place, but more
and more they seemed somebody else's memories,
and they did not belong to the kind of life she
could imagine living now. At first she had dwelt
on the past, but now it was becoming so unreal to
her that it was quite literally irrelevant. She ceased
to think about it, finally, and with that a psycho-

logical barrier snapped and a total change came over her.

Now, ten weeks after the change (although she didn't know it), the old Spirit was practically dead. She had come, psychologically, head-to-head with the reality of her existence and its permanence, and her mind had taken the easiest, most comfortable path of total acceptance. One day she simply awoke and thought nothing strange, unusual, or different. She was the way she was and she could no longer even think of being any other way at all. So absolute was the acceptance that she no longer even thought of herself as cursed, or as a victim, or in any way different than she should be. She no longer even missed speech or reading; forbidden forever as they were to her, she dropped the very concept. Whatever was no longer relevant or applicable she simply edited out of her very thoughts.

Her mother, of course, was both relevant and applicable. She didn't like being trapped here in the temple garden. It wasn't natural or normal, nor could she here fill her natural need for sex. She had only one particular place she wanted to go, and that briefly, but she could stand being caged only so long.

She was taking a shower under the small waterfall that was the centerpiece of the garden when they showed up—her mother and two strangers. She emerged from the waterfall and walked out of the stream and up to them, a quizzical look on her face. She felt like a giant in a land of short people; she was a head taller than the tallest of them. She realized from the man's dress that he must be a stranger, and she guessed that the fat one with the enormous tits must work for him.

"Wow! She's *gorgeous*!" Suzl exclaimed. "Hello, Spirit!"

The nude girl looked blank, and Kasdi said, "She can't understand a word, can't even read intonations. We've worked out a sign language system, but that's the best we can do. Here—I'll throw a little spell your way that will save you a lot of grief and long hours of learning."

It was simpler after that, although along with the signs a large amount of exaggerated gesturing and gyrations was necessary to convey real information. It was like doing a whole conversation in pantomime. For example, to indicate that Suzl and Kasdi were old friends required a lot of back-and-forth pointing, a hug, and a peck on the cheek by each. It sometimes took several minutes to get a simple concept across, but it worked. To Spirit, with infinite patience and no time sense, it was a conversation.

*Hello. Your mother and I are old friends. This man is my lover and my boss. We are stringers. You are attractive/sexy/pretty. We would like to be your friends.* The concept of stringer, for example, involved miming a line or rope being pulled, followed by a mock whip and ride-in-place. But the message got through.

Spirit smiled and kissed them both and returned the greeting. She turned, looked over at a nearby tree, then ran for it, leaped up and caught a branch with her hands, then pulled herself up on it with contortionist's ease. There was a small cluster of fruit there, *jabagua*, related to the banana, and she picked the stalk and jumped back to the ground, landing on her feet. She went back up to them and offered each a fruit.

Even Ravi was impressed by the display. "Anyone who can move like that can take care of herself," he commented.

"Yeah," Suzl agreed. "Look, she's gonna go nuts if she stays here and I think you know that."

"You've been talking to Mervyn," Kasdi said suspiciously.

"Sure. We saw the old boy in Globbus on the

way here. I admit it. And I agree with him—now more than ever."

"But—like *that*? What will people make of her?"

"People know of her," Suzl replied. "Everybody knows her face and what happened to her." She paused a moment. "You know more of this spell stuff than I do, even though I'm the one with a permanent spell myself. You know she should be free. That Soul Rider, or whatever the hell it is, is in there for a reason, too, and it's not to jump up into trees and eat fruit. I think maybe you're holding onto her. You never had her, and now that you do, you just don't want to let her go."

Kasdi sighed. "Maybe you're right—but my concerns are real."

Suzl thought a moment. "It's been a long time. Has she seen her family? I mean, the folks that raised her?"

"No. Most can't come; the rest won't go into Flux."

"O.K., then. That's our next destination anyway. We're sidebar stringing for Laconner through this cluster." A sidebar stringer was a junior in the trade who had not yet earned enough to have his or her own route or had not found a wizard as a client and sponsor. They ran mini-trains off the main one, allowing the stringer with business to bypass less profitable stops while still serving them. "Let us take her with us to Anchor Logh to see her folks. If it works out, fine. If it doesn't, well, at least we'll know who's right."

Kasdi considered it, and felt curiously reluctant to go along with it, although Suzl's logic was impeccable. She kept trying to come up with reasons not to permit it, but stopped after a moment. Perhaps they're right, she thought guiltily. Maybe I *am* just trying to hold on to her. "All right. But you bring her back here with a progress report before going elsewhere."

"Fair enough."

"Uh—Suzl?"

"Yeah, Cass?"

"How much is Mervyn paying Ravi to do all this?"

She chuckled. "Not much. Just a good lead on a possible sponsor for an independent train."

"I thought so. All right, then. If she's willing, go with my blessings."

Suzl turned to Spirit, who had lost interest and was studying the wrinkled skin of the fruit with absolute fascination. Suzl hesitated to interrupt her for a moment, wondering just what the girl was seeing that was so interesting, but she tapped Spirit's shoulder and the girl looked up. Suzl backed away and made out in mime, *Would you like to go with us?*

The girl's reaction was pure joy and excitement, and she even did a little dance to indicate her desire. She definitely wanted out, and the sooner the better.

Kasdi gave up. The reaction was too deep to ignore.

Ravi had to return to the train to work out his routings so that they could still make their stops and relink with the main train on schedule, but Suzl remained for a while with Kasdi.

"I can tell you're less than thrilled with Ravi," she commented.

"I'm trying not to judge. You have to live your own life."

"You've been isolated from the real world a long time, Cass. You live here with the Church, and with your powers you don't think twice about skipping along in the void. I don't *have* any Flux powers, remember. I'm just a dugger, and so if I want to travel and live my life, I need protection, and that means compromising."

"He's not a major wizard, but he has some real

power," Kasdi noted. "You know he has some personal spells on you."

Suzl shrugged. "I figured as much. He was born into the trade, and they don't believe in using Flux power to change themselves. It's against their code. Fix up, heal, yeah, but nothing more. So he was real short for a guy, and kind of frail, and he grew up worshipping those big hunks. If he didn't have the power, he couldn't be in this business. The stringers don't have much respect for guys who like guys or girls who like girls, so when we crossed paths, I was what he needed. I'm a woman who was what he wants. He's a stringer with the power and I need that. We're kind of loose. I can do most anything I want."

"It wasn't just fat that grew those unnatural breasts."

"Sure. But that power also gave me the back and muscle support, so it doesn't bother me. Same with my other self, which is also not proportional. But, you see, I *like* it this way—all of it. I'm a *dugger*, Cass, and there's a lot worse ways than mine for duggers to be that are no fun at all. So I work as his foreman and play at being his wife, and I got no worries in Flux. I'm not in love with the little wimp, but if you have to be owned by somebody, there are worse people to be owned by and not many better."

Kasdi sighed. "I suppose you're right. Perhaps I *am* too insulated from the real world. From here, surrounded by devout women and looking over maps showing the spread of the Church, it's easy to forget that so little has really changed. You really don't like to think of things that way."

"People stay people, with all the good and all the bad. Things *have* changed for the better. The Flux is safer, the Anchors better run, and there's a whole new sense of learning in both places—it's good what you did. You don't see that dull look in people's eyes so much anymore, the idea that this is what is and what will be. You gave 'em a future, a sense of change that excites 'em. But Flux is still Flux and power is still power. Short of making everybody into slaves, you're not going to change the way people are, and if you did that, then why bother?"

Sister Kasdi sighed. "Maybe you're right. It's funny—you're maybe the only one I can tell this to, but I have doubts. Lots of doubts all the time. I wonder if I'm doing the right thing. I wonder if all this is real or just some false wizardry, self-delusion. Is this really the Holy Mother's will, or am I just another Fluxlord with too big ambitions kidding myself along? I don't know. When you have this kind of power, both political and Flux, it's impossible to tell your own delusions from what's real. You know, sometimes I envy Spirit. No worries, no cares, no responsibilities. And I get the idea she knows what's true and real far better than I."

"You're better than you think you are," Suzl told her. "The old boy is right about one thing, though. You left yourself nothing but work and worry and responsibility. No fun, no vacations, no way to just let loose and relax. I couldn't have stood it this long, but if you don't figure out a way to take a breather, it'll eventually crack even you. All that's bottled up inside of you with no way to get out. If it becomes too much, it'll explode."

"I know, I know. If you think of an answer to it all, let me know. In the meantime—take good care of her, Suzl."

"That's one worry you shouldn't have."

The big, hairy, muscular man was playing cards in the Gotron Saloon in Anchor Fhaxtrod when a younger man came in and caught his eye. The big man played out his hand, and won, then excused

himself from the game and went into a back room
with the newcomer.

"Well?"

"Not much. As near as we can figure out, there
was no way that wound didn't mean nearly instant death. Nobody on the scene had any doubts
at all. Still, when the stringers sorted out their
dead, his body wasn't there. It was never found,
although that's not unusual. There was that tremendous spell from the girl and a lot of confusion
and there are always a lot of missing."

"And Jomo?"

"He showed up in Globbus a couple of weeks
later and got all the survivors together, paid 'em
off and disbanded it. Most of the other duggers
signed on with other trains, but he didn't. Stayed
in Globbus for several months, then went up north
in the wild, settled down, and got a job as a bouncer
in a saloon in Tregia, one of those dugger's haven
Fluxlands. He's real smart about some things, almost retarded in others, kind of like a good trained
animal. Real faithful to his boss, but not any boss
will do. I'm convinced, though, that he couldn't
possibly have thought up anything like this. Everybody thinks that *he* thinks it's really Matson, so
he's back on the job."

Coydt van Haaz scratched his chin a moment.
"So somebody changed themselves into Matson,
somebody who knew him well enough to imperson-
ate him eighteen years later so exactly that he can
fool even somebody close to Matson like Jomo,
then hunts up the big dugger and goes gunning for
me. I don't buy it, Yorek. It doesn't ring true. Still,
if Matson *had* somehow lived, where's he been all
these years? He's a false wizard—he has no real
powers. Can somebody like that just up and give
up the stringer trade that was his life, leave all
that credit wealth behind, and, even transformed
by somebody with power, just take up another life

and not betray himself all that time? Even if he could, he's too in touch with today. He knows the present stringer codes and exactly which people to talk to and where they are. That's not somebody even the stringers consider long dead. Either way, none of it fits.''

"Except that if it *is* Matson, his reappearance now makes sense. Spirit was his daughter, too, although he told Gilly he only learned about her when we hit. He'll live by the stringer code and try and nail you. And if he fails, another will come with two to avenge, then three—well, you know the route.''

Coydt nodded. "I can take anybody head-on in Anchor or Flux, but I don't want to get backshot by some jerk I can't even see while walking down an alley or across a street. If this operation wasn't going along, I'd lay the bait, face it down, then change into new people for Anchor, but it's important that the others be able to reach me in a hurry. This is damned inconvenient, Yorek. Old Saint Kasdi I figured on, but not some masquerading killer stalking me in Anchor. We're just going to have to tighten up our guard and keep doing it the way we planned, that's all. But the first man who works for me who botches the job and doesn't get killed protecting me will wish he *had* been killed. You spread the word. Within a year it won't matter who's stalking who.''

"You've got the best covering you. It won't be easy for him, whoever he is. In the meantime, we'll keep digging.''

"Dig him out, Yorek. If you do, we'll have our fun with him in Flux and settle this whole problem.''

# WONDROUS PATHWAYS

The experiment had worked out very well indeed for all concerned except, perhaps, Sister Kasdi. Spirit loved the excitement and animation of the stringer train, the animals and people, and they also took to her. Her picture had made her familiar to almost everyone during the kidnapping episode, and her story and her curse were also common knowledge.

At first people did treat her as something of a freak, and there was a great deal of pity as well, but it soon passed as the novelty wore off and she was simply accepted. It was tougher on the men than the women, for she was beautiful and alluring, but the few who tried to force themselves on her in Flux found that merely touching her when she didn't want to be touched could produce a painful electric shock. The more someone persisted, the more painful and prolonged the lesson. None persisted for very long.

Spirit seemed endlessly fascinated with the void as well. It looked different to her now, the continuous random sparkles of energy not only beautiful but somehow not at all the random effect that everyone else assumed. There was a structure, an order, to the whole of Flux that seemed suddenly clear to her.

She quickly learned the stringer's secret and art. The void was no void at all, she found, but an intricate network of crisscrossing lines of weak but permanent energy. Following these "strings" was like following a road, although she didn't have, and would probably never have, the stringer's knowledge and skill to be able to read exactly where she was on a string in relation to the next destination and in relation to the whole world. Still, she wondered at the fact that these strings were certainly human-made; yet she could see and understand them in apparent violation of the spell. She could even tell which ones were main strings and which led to water pockets and emergency supply caches, for these strings were coded both by color and by a mathematical structure that not only said what they were but also left a signature of sorts of their maker—and other signatures were overlaid in fascinating complexity atop the primary one.

Every time they progressed along a string, a new, very faint ghost signature was etched into the thousands, perhaps millions of others. She began to realize that in the strings was a record of all who had ever used them, all very minor and very faint but nonetheless present. One could even, on the closest of study, read the exact order in which those string echoes had been laid down and identify a pattern unique to each individual. She, too, left a slight signature as they progressed, a mathematically unique coding. With knowledge of a wizard's or stringer's symbol and the sense of time laid out mathematically in the record, she realized she could actually track someone across the void by taking only the freshest trace or retrace their path and tell from whence they had come.

In just the few days of travel to Anchor Logh, she had intuitively and deductively learned more about strings than all but a handful of people ever learned with years of teaching and experience. She could not know this, nor that even the best stringers and wizards could read and sort out only the most recent paths, the rest blending into the original pattern. It was not her degree of Flux power alone that gave her this ability to read, see, sort, interpret, and remember those millions of traces, but also the new internal language and manner in which her brain now processed information.

Anchor was different, yet in some ways the same. A blade of grass was not simply that, but a complex structure built in a specific pattern. She felt as if she could peer into its very makeup, which, in a sense, she could. Each tree, flower, leaf, even a blade of grass was unique and different and those differences were endlessly fascinating to her. Her behavior seemed often odd, unusual, and childlike to those watching her, but it was instead highly intellectual and highly complex. She was seeing in a way they could never see and understanding in a way they could never understand.

Anchor Logh was at once wondrous and painful. Here she had grown up, and here she was well-known. The pity and grief from family and friends was very hard to bear, and she longed for some way to tell them that it was all right, that she would not go back to being one of them even if she could.

She drew crowds in Anchor, of course. Lots of pity mixed with an endless fascination with the bizarre that was a part of human nature. She didn't mind it from strangers at all, and the children were wonderful, treating her as some sort of magical fairy sprite. She played silly games with them and drew out their laughter and felt well-rewarded.

And yet, the more human she was in the basics of emotion, the less she became in other areas. The psychological changes in her accelerated with the trip, and the journey home had gotten out of her system the one last link to her past. She liked people and enjoyed being with them, but she could no longer in the least understand them. Slowly but systematically, the bits and pieces of what it was like to be one of them were being erased or shut off in her mind. At Hope she had separated herself forever from their form of existence. Now, in Anchor Logh, she crossed the last mental hold to the past. She not only could no longer remember not being as she was; she could no longer even conceive of it. Once she left the farm with Suzl for the gate and Flux once more, she erased the past completely from her mind. All of the human culture into which she'd been born and raised was now irrelevant to her, and what was irrelevant did not exist.

The last link was broken with the return to Hope. The point had been made and proven. Short of her mother using her powers to force her to remain, a prisoner, she would not be contained, and she wasn't even sure if her mother had the power to restrain her. Kasdi, however, had no intention of doing so. She surrendered to the inevitable and let her daughter go.

For the next few weeks, Spirit stayed with Ravi and Suzl's stringer train, making stops at three more Fluxlands and one other Anchor that was quite different than Anchor Logh. Everything was different, everything a wonder, but still she began to feel confined. As long as she was under their wing, she was trapped, in a way, in a culture she could no longer understand.

The duggers, of course, treated her as if she were one of their own, which in a very real sense she was, but they, too, were part of a life different from hers. The old Spirit would have found most of them horrible, grotesque, bizarre—but she just found them a new series of unique wonders. Suzl was the biggest shock and wonder, though, since she didn't seem to be a true dugger at all. Yet, once, when they had set up tents and camped out for two days in a Pocket waiting for the main stringer train to rendezvous with them, she had playfully peered inside Suzl's tent (although she would never enter it) and seen her in the midst of changing clothes. She'd been bending over, displaying the largest ass Spirit had ever seen, and it was a shock to see those enormous breasts actually touching the floor of the tent. Spirit could not imagine what having that sort of frontage would feel like. Then Suzl had heard her, straightened up and turned around, and she saw the male organ so huge that it almost reached the dugger's knees. Suzl grinned at the shock on Spirit's face, and then the girl knew that this was a dugger indeed, in her own way as inhuman as the most deformed of the ones on the train.

Suzl started to reach for her special undergarments needed to manage and work with her enlarged deformities, but then stopped, winked, and came out of the tent just as she was. Ravi was off, and there were only a few duggers about who paid no attention at all. Suzl was so short without the boots that the top of her head barely came up to the nipples on Spirit's breasts, but there was something in the strange man/woman's bizarre appearance that was strangely erotic. Both were a bit surprised at what went on, but Spirit was amazed at both her own near-insatiable enjoyment and Suzl's nearly infinite capacity and variety.

For Suzl's part, she had never intended it, but found it inevitable; Spirit was so beautiful that it had seemed impossible not to lust after her. Suzl was neither sorry nor ashamed, but instead felt some of the envy Cass had evidenced. She loved men and women equally, for she was partly each, and she enjoyed being the way she was. What she had not enjoyed was the confinement of Ravi and sidebar stringing, or the necessity for all those special undergarments and all that play-acting at normalcy. She was far more of a freak than Spirit, but unlike Spirit, who never thought of herself that way, Suzl loved the very idea of it.

*I must leave*, Spirit mimed to Suzl. *I can see the strings. I am strong.*

Suzl nodded understanding, and at that point something just snapped inside her. It was hard figuring out the proper way to get her reply across, but she did. *I want out, too. But I can not see strings. I have no power. Out there I am helpless.*

Spirit was stunned to realize this. The idea that few could see as she saw or draw power from Flux, and nourishment, and all needs, just had not occurred to her before. It explained everything to her at once, and now she felt pity, not merely for Suzl but for all those at the mercy of the few. She looked at the dugger and suddenly realized that, for all her fascination with detail, she had never noticed that the strings on Suzl and the other duggers weren't their own traces but variations of Ravi's pattern. Curious, she reached out with her mind at one of the strings and touched it. It wavered and faded away.

*I have power for two*, Spirit mimed. *Do you want to come with me? You will be my speech with humans.* For, she realized, she did not want to be alone. It was not that she really needed any interpreter, nor was it really pity, either, that caused the offer. But she would be different, forever, in this world, and with no others of her own kind she badly needed a friend. This would work out well, too, for Suzl was as much a freak in human culture as she was, and far from being confining, it would be Suzl now that would depend on her rather than the other way around.

For Suzl's part, it was the kind of break with all that was secure in her life that she might not ever make if she thought about it too often. Spirit's wizardry was supposed to be restricted to self-defense only, and that wouldn't include her. But for eighteen years she'd traveled and had some laughs and a lot of hard work, though Ravi was the best of her bosses. For much of that time, too, she'd lived a lie with uncomfortable devices hiding the fact that she was not a normal human woman but really a freakish dugger, the second race of World all of whose members were unique. Now she was thirty-six and stuck with the lie more securely than ever, riding around the same old circuit as Ravi's respectability and window-dressing, going nowhere. And Spirit was going to leave regardless. Better she go with someone who knew her and whom her mother also knew. *I will go with you*, she mimed back.

Ravi returned a bit later and she was waiting for him. "Spirit's going off on her own," she began.

He nodded. "I expected that sooner or later. Frankly, it will be a relief."

"I'm going with her."

For a moment he seemed not to hear, then he finally said, "What did you say?"

"I said I'm going with her. I resign from the company."

His cool demeanor was betrayed by the nasty, bitter edge in his voice. "You are insane. You have no powers in Flux. She might be able to conjure food and drink, but not the kind you like so well. She can certainly offer no protection against other wizards' spells."

"Neither can you, for that matter. She can read strings and protect me from the usuals. Besides, I think she needs me."

"*I* need you."

"No, you need window-dressing. A cardboard woman for your business image. She doesn't need that. She needs someone to care about. She needs a friend."

Ravi's face was turning slightly purple. "If you do this, I will see that you never work for a stringer again. And in a few days or weeks, when you go mad from having no one to talk to and cannot even keep pace with that wild primitive, you will have no place left to turn. Have you considered that?"

"There's always the dugger havens up north in the wild. I've made up my mind, Ravi. I'm going."

"So you wish this, do you? You prefer her, do you? Well, let us see how well you will truly do. If you think it is so bad to pretend, then I curse you to pretend no more. If I had the knowledge, I would make you just like her, but I cannot. But this clothing business I can manage. All of your clothes are made by my magic. I withdraw that magic now." The clothing that she wore vanished. "Know now that you have a simple spell, but one that is hard to break. Like your *girlfriend*, you cannot conceal, but while she has nothing to hide, you do and will no longer be able to. I take the bit of spell from her and link it to you, so that you may wear nothing that she does not. I purchased the spells that made you as you are, and those will remain, as will you. They are tied to your curse and cannot be changed even by your Sister Kasdi."

She felt anger boiling up. "Are you finished? Or do you have a few more curses to lay on me?"

"You will not reconsider in light of this?"

"Not now. Not ever. Not after this."

"Your resignation is accepted, then, immediately. Without the special undergarments you could not ride a horse, so I will credit your account with the price. You both have ten minutes to leave."

He stalked off, and she went to find Spirit. *Come, let us go.*

Spirit was surprised that Suzl had nothing on and nothing with her, and stared a moment. She saw the spell then, linking the two of them, its stamp not Ravi's but someone strange. She realized now the depth of the sacrifice Suzl was making, and the total trust the dugger had placed in her hands. She hugged Suzl and there were a few tears in her eyes.

Suzl gestured and said, although she knew Spirit couldn't understand, "Come on. Let's blow this crummy joint before I come to my senses."

Together, with nothing, they walked off into the void.

They spent days walking in the void, following a randomly picked string. Spirit cleared all old strings from Suzl and put on her own so that, even should they get separated, she could be found anywhere in Flux. Suzl had good stamina considering her fat, but her stride was short and she could hardly keep pace with Spirit's energy. For her part, Spirit began to experiment with just what she could do with the Flux power. Up to now, she'd taken the accepted wisdom that her powers were strictly limited, but those limitations were not that precise, as her handling of the strings showed.

Any attempt to alter or change Suzl physically was a failure, although it wasn't clear whether it was Spirit's curse or Suzl's doing the blocking. She could, however, divert Flux energy from herself to Suzl by touching the dugger, such as by grasping a hand. The linkage Ravi had forged was the next experiment, and she found that she could direct the power through that linkage as easily as through a physical contact. Unknowingly, Ravi had done Suzl a favor. She found, for example, that she could alleviate the bad chafing that inevitably developed under Suzl's breasts and in her crotch, and she made a small scar on Suzl's arm vanish. She could, indeed, offer help and protection, something which relieved Suzl as much or more than it did Spirit.

Food could be materialized when needed, and although it wasn't fancy, it was filling and could be consumed by both.

For Suzl's part, she had, in the first hours away, felt very much the fool, cut off and alone, but no longer. Instead, she began to feel what she had not felt in a very long time—free. The flow of energy from Spirit to her encouraged her, and interested her as well. She became convinced that some closer links were possible, and they spent hours trying things without either quite knowing what the other was doing—or what they themselves were doing, for that matter. She sensed that Spirit was attempting some sort of link and tried to go along. For quite a while, though, the thing seemed to elude them, just out of reach. The only true non-miming communication seemed to be music, with Suzl whistling tunes and clapping time and Spirit dancing to it. Still, for all its frustrations, the dugger had not felt happier or more at ease in years.

Finally they happened on somebody's Pocket, a fairly nice little place much like a tropical garden. Whoever had made it was not at home, and it was uninhabited. Suzl suspected it was one of the Pockets developed by stringer wizards for breaks on those routes where there was far too much distance between destinations for good health, and places like this provided a break for everyone.

Because Suzl had been a dugger in Flux for so long, she did not dismiss Spirit as childlike at all. Seventeen—no, eighteen now—yes, but no child. She knew that Spirit's endless fascination with all the little things was curiosity and wonder, and the more closely she observed, the more closely she came to believe that there was real purpose in those seeming lapses. She wished hard that she could see the wonders she suspected Spirit could.

But there was a childlike quality to their existence which neither minded and both exploited.

Life was fun and games, curiosity and answers, without worries or responsibilities. Spirit awakened in the usually cynical dugger feelings long buried and assumed lost.

Inside Spirit, the Soul Rider manipulated the probabilities through Flux, establishing the proper situation.

Suzl was aware of subtle changes in her own attitudes. Before, she had always thought of herself as female, for that was how she'd been born and raised and that was the role culture dictated. Now, though, she began to think of herself more and more as a male, as Spirit's sexual opposite despite the rest of her body. Although she would never look any different, her sexual orientation was shifting firmly to the male side. She realized, suddenly, that for the first time in her life she was sincerely, deeply, and madly in love with somebody other than herself.

Spirit had never thought of herself as abnormal or unusual, always going for the handsome men, but Suzl filled a deep need in her new consciousness for solidity and companionship. What had seemed freakish and odd now seemed cute and endearing. As she could no longer imagine her old life, she could not now imagine life without Suzl, nor did she want Suzl to look or be any other way than the way she now was. The dugger who had sacrificed all to live with and like her now became the one and only important thing in her whole life. Passion replaced lust and need, and they both knew it and felt it in each other.

And the Soul Rider's equations continued to work themselves out.

They were still in the Pocket, lazing on the cool grass, lying side by side, and Suzl's hand reached out and touched Spirit's, and they squeezed. Something flowed from within to within. The love and devotion that had built up flowed from each, met, and merged into one. It was not something that was a shock or which caused sudden realization; it simply *was*. But, somehow, on a basic level, each could feel what the other felt, and, in a sense, each knew what the other was thinking. Not clear thoughts, and not specific ones, but general senses of things. Not only was miming no longer necessary, it seemed terribly slow and cumbersome—primitive. Their link did not even require looking at the other. Only their language, in which they thought, separated them. Beyond that level, they could read each other as easily as Suzl could read a sign.

Both were aware that something important, even vital, had happened that went beyond their own selves, but neither knew just what or how it applied. Somehow Suzl could now feel Spirit's wonder, and neither was afraid anymore. And so, one day, they simply decided it was time to leave and follow another string to where it led. There was a whole world to see and explore, and an infinity of wondrous paths to take.

The first Fluxland they encountered was called Galikin, a huge forest in which all the inhabitants seemed to live in trees. Not just in them, although some of the trunks were huge enough and hollow to make comfortable and spacious homes, but atop them as well, in often elaborate but just as often simple tree houses. The local Fluxlord was neither mean nor imaginative as some of them went, but did seem to have the idea that she was the queen of trees and forests. Everybody wore green outfits, and in fact, although they looked quite human, they all also had green skins. The difference was more than skin deep, however; they seemed to get all their nourishment from light, like the plants, and eagerly left their homes to be in the open every time it rained. They spent their days planting, pruning, trimming and all the rest, and the whole place seemed to Suzl to be a forest that had a manicure.

It was a good place for a first test, and it served additionally to tell the dugger just where they were in relation to every place else. They knew who Spirit was, and were properly fascinated, although Suzl made Spirit seem rather less extraordinary by her own odd appearance.

Spirit liked Galikin, although Suzl found the place rather dull. At least at night, they feared no embarrassments even in the middle of a public place.

They left after a couple of days and made their way along a route Suzl suggested but could not follow or see. She was well aware of how terribly slow their pace was because of her, and she was determined to do something about it. They ran into a stringer train at one point, and while she found that the word had been put out not to hire her on, that did not interfere with business. She had a substantial credit account, and she could use it. The stringer drove a hard bargain, but she came off with a strong, healthy young mule, a pair of saddlebags, and an extremely worn "guest saddle," as they were called in the trade. With a little help from the duggers rigging some leather straps, she was now able to ride sidesaddle, if not in speed at least in comfort. Although things still seemed very slow, the pace picked up considerably now, as Spirit could match the mule's pace with an effortless jog.

In three days they reached Anchor Kaegh, the first Anchor they had approached since going off on their own. Suzl approached it with some trepidation. Duggers, once forbidden in Anchor, were now permitted there, but permission did not mean that everybody liked or agreed with it. Duggers were feared and mistrusted, and most still believed the old teaching that their disfigurements were the curses of Heaven on blighted souls. Always before, the careful clothing had masked her as just a very fat woman. Now she could not hide her true self, and she was, naked, clearly misshapen even without the added male organ.

They entered through the high gate that was no longer sealed, and the customs man could not hide his distaste. "Names?"

"I am Suzl, a dugger of Flux, and this is Spirit of Anchor Logh."

The man softened a bit as he recognized her from the pictures and it was clear he knew the story. "Oh, yes. Fascinating." Clearly he also found lustful rewards in the seeing. He changed back to the other, more ugly tone for Suzl. "You are traveling with her?"

"Yes. Uh—I know her mother well. You understand."

The official did—sort of. At least it was true, and saved a lot of added embarrassment and questions. It was clear, however, that the official could not understand why Sister Kasdi would entrust her daughter to a dugger, particularly one with so prominent—well . . . "What do you wish in Anchor?"

"I have a dugger's account. I need a few small things from a decent market, and I would like to register the two of us at the temple to simplify things in the future." Such registration would give her documents which would prove her citizenship and secure more firmly some legal rights. With the stringers such stuff was unnecessary, but as they were to travel, perhaps to many Anchors, they would need it.

"Um, I know about *her*," the customs man commented, "but can't you, ah, put on something? It'll make life easier for you."

"It probably would," she agreed, "but I've got an involuntary spell against it. That's one of the reasons I need the registration."

They passed through and spent the first night in
a small park off the main road. They drew gawk-
ers and lots of curious stares, but had no real
problems until they passed through a town near
the end of the second day. A crowd of young toughs
cornered them and started yelling epithets, particularly at Suzl, who felt very defenseless. Spirit,
however, knew what was going on and stood between Suzl and the toughs. Three of the men started
discussing what they would like to do with the
mute girl, then rushed her. Spirit slapped the mule
and it bolted quickly down the street, then took
them on. It was half a block before Suzl could
bring the mule under control and look nervously
back, but what she saw she hadn't expected at all.

She had never seen a human being that limber
or with reflexes that fast. Spirit's physical strength
didn't show except in her hard thighs, but it was
enormous. She ran at the three, jumped, turned,
kicked one hard in the chest, a second in the groin,
and caught the third with a blow to the Adam's
apple, all seemingly in one fluid motion. This gal-
vanized the rest to converge on her, but she gave a
leap that must have been more than two meters in
the air, kicked off one attacker's back, and sprinted
towards Suzl, who needed no more encouragement.
She rode as fast as she could, which wasn't fast
but was good enough, while Spirit passed her on
the run as if she were standing still.

It was funny, but the mute girl seemed enormously pleased by all that, and as surprised at her
strength and skill as Suzl and the attackers had
been. Suzl, however, felt depressed. She cursed
her body for its inability to do much of anything.
She couldn't even get on the mule without Spirit's
help, although she always had been able to mount
a horse before. *Maybe Ravi was right,* she thought
sourly. *I can't even defend myself or help the only
person I care for. I'm weak as a baby, move like a*

*rock, and my grossness draws violence.* There would be many more incidents like that one, she knew, and one time even Spirit probably would need help.

They endured a lot more insults, but no more violence, on the way to the capital. Suzl went first to the temple to attend to business, then planned to buy what she needed and get out fast. Spirit, of course, was far too claustrophobic to enter, but remained in the square chasing and playing with the birds and drawing a crowd.

The priestess administrator, at least, seemed charitable. Suzl submitted to a full identity photo series, showing front, back, and both profiles of the whole body, and submitted to an examination. It took several hours before it was through and she received the document. She glanced down the vital statistics. Height, 144.62 cm.; weight, 108.86 kg.; sex, male. She—no, he, for now it had been made official and was in fact the way Suzl felt—stared at the weight figure gloomily, although he knew that some of that was in the special bone and muscle support supplied by Ravi's paid-for wizardry and more was for the stomach that supported the breasts and the rear that counterbalanced it. But it was still higher than it had ever been. What particularly shocked was the height. It was 6 cms lower than it had ever been. Now that he thought of it, though, his head *had* originally come up to Spirit's breast line, and now it was below. He voiced his misgivings to the priestess.

"I think you ought to see a spell doctor in Flux," she suggested. "It sounds to me like either you've got spells you don't know about or some are becoming unravelled."

They were very nice, agreeing to go out for him and get the few items he wanted, and then showing on the map a quick way out of the Anchor that would avoid major population. They understood.

The supplies consisted mostly of two boxes of cigars, a huge box of safety matches, a generalized map of World, and an octarina—a small instrument made from a specialized type of gourd. He had learned to play one on the trail and had lost it long before.

It took two more days to exit the other gate through the route the temple had suggested, but there were only minor incidents and no trouble. They headed now southwest, towards more familiar territory again. Suzl had decided that if he needed a Flux doctor, he might as well satisfy an old curiosity itch and visit Pericles, home Fluxland of the wizard Mervyn, the only publicly known member of the Nine Who Guard.

Pericles itself was off the usual beaten track and visitors were generally discouraged, although it was closer to the four-Anchor cluster in which both Suzl and Spirit had been born than to any other.

The map that Suzl had was pretty barren; it showed only some major Fluxlands and all the Anchors, but it was still something that simply would not have been permitted in the old days. The Church and the stringers had kept geography as much to themselves as possible, so much so that the amazing pattern even this bare-bones map showed was unknown to most of the population, Anchor *and* Flux.

Anchors varied in size from as small as twenty by forty kilometers to more than a hundred-and-fifty by two-hundred-and-fifty kilometers, and they varied widely in shape as well—Anchor Logh reminded most people of a shelled peanut, while Anchor Kaegh was an irregular crescent—but the twenty-eight Anchors were clustered in groups of four, all four's closest inner point being equidistant from a Hellgate. It was evidence of intelligent design that gave skeptics like Suzl pause.

The prime function of the Nine was to guard those Hellgates from any intrusions, and one lived near each cluster in a private Fluxland, although only one let it be known that he was, in fact, one of the Nine. Mervyn was the oldest and the dean of his group, as well as an instructor in Flux power both privately and in the wizards' mad university town of Globbus, where Suzl's original curse developed so many years before. Most Fluxlands were open; a few were closed off by a permanent shield of force maintained by the Fluxlord and could be entered only by permission. Pericles was one of the latter.

Because of the shield, the only thing visible to outsiders was a huge, ornate marble archway into which had been set a massive bronze set of double doors. Only this was apparent. One could walk around the gate and even see the other side of the door, but nothing else but void.

Before Suzl could even knock, though, the huge doors swung open to reveal a beautiful scene within. It was green, rolling countryside with lots of trees and what seemed like thousands of different kinds and colors of blooming flowers all around. Insects buzzed about, and the air was warm and humid, the sky a light blue with a bunch of fluffy white clouds. A creature approached them, a creature of Flux that was strange indeed, having the head and torso of a beautiful woman and the hindquarters of a spotted pony. She trotted up to them and stopped, and Spirit gaped. Suzl had seen stranger, of course.

"Welcome to Pericles," the centauress said. "I'm Melana. I'll take you to Mervyn."

"I gather we were expected," Suzl commented.

Melana smiled. "He knows whatever he wants to know, and what he doesn't know he devotes the bulk of his time to finding out. Come."

Suzl urged the mule onward, and Spirit tagged

along, keeping pace and just looking at the beauty of the land.

Here and there were columned structures of fine marble and statuary. Museums, libraries, and special collections, Melana told them. The statues and buildings were copies of things Mervyn had seen in some of his treasured ancient books.

Around and about were other centaurs, and there were half-human fish in a wide lake, sunning themselves on rocks. There were many races of strange creatures in Pericles, it seemed, most of them half human and half some animal or another. They all seemed happy and friendly and content, something which Suzl envied. They were as perfectly adapted as any human stock could be to new form; he, on the other hand, was an example of how not to put somebody together.

He had stared again and again at those four photos on the official document, and liked what he saw less and less. He couldn't understand what Spirit saw in him, and he loved her all the more for not seeing what was so evident. The profiles were particularly shocking, since the size of that belly and ass stood out along with the grossness of the breasts. It had been years since he'd been able to see down past those breasts, and he avoided mirrors. Without the stomach's support, though, those mammaries now would droop literally to his crotch, and he would be unable to stand. Recently he'd been feeling some pain in the lower back, legs, and ankles, and this helped explain it.

Mervyn met them in a pleasant open glen near one of the marble buildings. He looked old and frail and his white beard was long and scraggly, but he had tremendous power in him, a power which maintained all this for hundreds of square kilometers with lots to spare.

The usual greetings were brief but warm, and Mervyn and Suzl sent Spirit off to frolick with

some of the creatures nearby. He then materialized two stuffed chairs in the middle of the glen
for them. They looked rather comic where they
were, but Suzl sat gratefully.

After explaining the problems and worries, Suzl
poured out his heart to Mervyn, how he'd been
feeling about himself, his total sense of helplessness,
and his tremendous closeness to Spirit which by
now was close to worship. The old man listened
attentively, particularly at his account of the growing romantic feelings and the emotional bond that
created communication and his tale of the curious
linking spell.

Finally he said, "All right. While we've been
talking, I've been analyzing both your mind and
your spells. I find the rest fascinating, and hope
that the two of you will remain here a while so
that I may study your bonding. There is something
afoot here that is beyond what Coydt intended or I
or Sister Kasdi could see. But first we must ad-
dress your current problem."

"It's a spell, isn't it? Somebody threw another
whammy on old Suzl when he wasn't looking."

"Something like that. Let's start at the beginning.
You were a normal human woman, short and
pudgy, but that was all. Then you got involved in
that attempt to remove Dar's sexual spell and got
caught in the crossfire, getting his penis and a
variation of his curse. That curse is quite good and
nothing for amateurs to deal with. You knew that
at the time, and were told the possible consequences
of trying to remove it."

He nodded. "I understand the problem. Anybody who tries to remove it might wind up with
nastiness back at them. But I accepted that. I really didn't mind, after a while, although it took me
years to decide on one direction and one identity. I
can handle that. But this other . . ."

"And you really had few problems until you signed on with this Ravi a few years ago?"

"That's about it. After all those years I just got sick of being on the low rung, and when he offered me a foreman's job, I took it."

"But there was a price."

"Well, yeah, but I just figured he was doing that game with his own power to magnify what he liked. I never thought of it as permanent."

"Apparently he knew this and decided to keep a hand on you. This spell is not something he did; it's something he bought, and he also bought control of it. And you accepted it, even though you didn't know you were accepting all of it."

"Yeah, I—shit! You mean it's one of those things like Cass has?"

"Well, yes and no. Yes, it is one of those self-imposed spells. No, it isn't as absolute as hers or Spirit's because you have no Flux power, so the linkage, while voluntary, was done for you. What it did was redesign your body and give him control of it. He could change what he willed, and the spell would adjust the body to cope. What he did when you quit was simply relinquish control of the spell to you. He knew what this would do. As you had no Flux power, you could not maintain a balance in yourself, and things began to go a bit wild. It is the same sort of thing that happens to duggers lost alone in the void that turns them into unhuman and semi-human creatures. You have been, I think, sexually hyperactive, so those were the areas that were stimulated, this time beyond the spell's ability to cope. It's good you came when you did. The sexual areas are receiving all the attention, and soon you would have been immobile."

He shivered. "And my shrinkage and growing weakness?"

"There again it's you. You feel ugly, deformed, unhappy. This goes to make you more so. You feel totally powerless, while always in the past you've been aggressive and in charge of yourself. You love Spirit."

"She is the only thing of any importance in my whole life. She *is* my whole life, Mervyn. I couldn't stand life without her now."

He nodded sagely. "But to be with her, with her limitations, you must surrender yourself totally to her. She provides everything—food, water, love, protection—you see where I'm leading? You had never surrendered yourself before, but now the choice was surrender or leave her. You've placed all your needs directly in her hands. You killed your aggressiveness for this and, in the dugger way, this unconscious decision reflects in your physical self. You see yourself as weak and helpless, and so you *become* weak and helpless. In the void you would eventually become so helpless she would have to feed you."

He gave a low whistle. "So what can I do?"

"Ravi's spell is cleverly linked to your curse. At this time I would not like to remove it, but if you remained here and I could bring in others from time to time, we might eventually find a way to reverse it. I believe, after all this time, I see the internal logic of the curse and its clever traps, and I might be willing to take a crack at it. But this will have a result you might not like. It would take a massive voluntary binding spell that would supply an equal counter, and that would not only make you female once again, but would also lock that sex in permanently."

He shook his head. "A while ago I'd have jumped at it, but I am different now. Spirit's all oral."

"It would end that part of your relationship," he admitted.

"So what's the alternative? I can change into a vegetable or I can lose Spirit. I'd rather die."

"The only alternative I can see now is also a

problem. I can't say we couldn't break that add-on, but it would take a very long time before we were confident. You can leave it as it is, and I'll give you some easing spells that might slow the process down, and wait for a cure I'm sure is possible—if I can get time from the experts to work on it."

"So you're saying the same thing. A cure is *possible*, but it might take years during which time I'll get worse, and there might not be a cure at all at the end of it."

"There's certainly a cure, but, yes, it might be long before anyone will risk those traps on your curse, and there is the possibility of the cure being worse than the disease. There always is. The point is, there is hope that way."

"Big deal. Either way, I lose."

"The other alternative is a drastic one, but simple. It would involve adjusting and fine-tuning your current body for the condition you now have. But to keep your own unconscious from undoing it, it would have to be strong and voluntary. Only you could change it, and without Flux power you never could. You would be frozen in your current condition forever. And I would have to insist that you agree to some psychotherapy spells to make it work at all."

He sat there a moment, thinking. He could be a human woman again and lose Spirit. He could let his unconscious turn him from freak into monster and lose everything. Or he could submit to wizardry once more and be forever trapped an ugly freak. It was a rough choice.

He was suddenly conscious of Spirit nearby, and turned and saw the mute girl behind her chair, looking down at him and smiling, and he instantly knew the only choice he could make.

"Freeze it," he told the wizard, and Spirit took and squeezed his hand.

"Well, sit back, relax, and make your mind a

blank if you can. Be patient with me, though. This nonhuman biology is a bit complex, and you only get one chance to get it right."

The physical process, however, was not difficult to do. There was a good deal of permanent muscle to build where there should have been only fat. The trouble was, he had to work around the curses rather than changing them, so the mass he needed he had to take from elsewhere on her. Removing much of the fatty, buildup from her face restored it very much to its original, cute appearance, which helped in several ways. The legs were needed for support, so material had to be taken from her arms, which were then shortened a little. Muscle had to be placed in the breasts, so the stomach could do more counterweighting and less supporting, but those breasts, thirty centimeters long, would stick almost straight out. That allowed him to bring the stomach in and force the mass to her spine for rigidity and counterweighting. The tremendous thighs and rigid, heavy-curved spine would carry the counterweight.

Mervyn was suddenly aware that Spirit was following everything he was doing and, more interesting, seemed to understand it in detail and even, it seemed, somehow was able to suggest something here, something there. Finally, the physical part was done, and he turned to the psychological. He needed a tool to rebuild her sense of identity and self-esteem. Suzl was male in one way only, but wanted to be more. He decided to make him/her more at ease. He sensed that Spirit liked the female aspects of Suzl, and so he addressed that problem first. Suzl had been desperately trying to think of herself as a "he," when actually both were and would always be correct. He examined what made Spirit attractive physically to Suzl, and melded that image in with those areas, both physi-

cal and expressive, that would make her like that
in herself as well.

Mervyn had much experience in what was the
art of psychological adaptation. There was no sense
in turning someone into a centaur if they didn't
love to be one. His handle on the matter was Spirit,
who seemed again to understand the question. What
did Spirit see when she looked at Suzl? He took a
gamble that the unintelligible mathematical series
she sent was what he wished, and used it. If it
worked, Suzl would no longer fight battles in her
own mind over whether he was she or vice versa.
Spirit, it seemed, thought of Suzl as "she" and so
"she" it would be.

The solution was frame of reference. Suzl loved
Spirit, but now only Spirit, not Suzl or anyone
else, would be her mental frame of reference. If
her looks pleased Spirit, that was enough. If her
split sexual identity was erotic and what Spirit
thought made Suzl a unique treasure, then she
would be content with it and no longer have any
conflicts over it. It was the correct solution, and he
knew it. Her ego was now based on Spirit and
nothing else.

His only real worry about the spell was his inability to talk to or understand what Spirit thought.
It was all well and good to freeze Suzl this way,
but would Spirit always feel the same? The answer came from an astonishing quarter, and he
almost reeled from it.

*Something else* took control, something that was
from Spirit but not Spirit. Mervyn was so excited
he almost lost his whole train of thought. For the
first time, he was in a sort of direct contact with a
Soul Rider! He stared with wizard's senses at the
faint double aura around Spirit and saw it work
through her.

The mysterious and complex language Coydt had
imposed, or *thought* he had imposed, on Spirit was

the language of the Soul Riders themselves. As the Soul Rider worked, there were occasional flashes in the same language that seemed to superimpose again. At first it confused the wizard, but now he realized that, whatever it was, it was coming from yet another source. The Rider was getting, at a speed far too rapid for Mervyn to comprehend, instructions from an outside source. The strange language could handle the speed; human language could not.

The Soul Rider completed its work and seemed to sense the old wizard looking at it. He felt an eerie sense of *awareness*, and found his sense being directed to a different area of Spirit. He saw, and he understood.

The Soul Rider's plan—or its master's plan, whoever that was—would continue. Spirit was pregnant by Suzl, and had been for some time. She was so lean and trim that it was already starting to show, but it just hadn't been noticed yet. And then the contact was broken, and Suzl slept.

She slept for three full days.

# WEDDING GIFTS

Kasdi looked pale. "Even when I heard, I could hardly believe it. I mean, how often does your best friend fall in love with your daughter? And *Suzl*? She's the same age as I am!"

"You know age isn't what's bothering you," Mervyn responded accusingly. "You love Suzl, and you love duggers, but she's a dugger and a freak and she's gone and taken *your* daughter, not somebody else's."

She stared at him, but knew that he spoke true. "All right, I admit it, but Heaven help me, I can't get rid of it. I had hoped for some strong, handsome wizard. That may have been the mother talking or a girlish fantasy, but nothing in Spirit's background says this is even remotely thinkable. The list of boys she turned down is amazing, and the ones she went out with were all big, handsome, virile types."

"But her circumstance and her way of looking at things have changed. Ever see the way she looks at a flower? As if she can see right through the surface to some inner beauty and complexity? She sees everything, and everybody, that way. I think we'd all be better off if *we* could think or see others only that way."

"But Suzl's always been so impulsive and irresponsible!"

"Not now. Oh, to everyone else, yes. But not towards Spirit. After all those years and all those

148

ugly people and spells, she needed somebody badly—and she got that somebody. She always put on a big front, and she still does, but it was an act. She was miserable and she hated herself and almost everything else. She doesn't, not anymore."

"I still want to see them—right away."

Mervyn grinned. "Suzl predicted you would, and said they'd wait. Um—Kasdi. Don't muck it up. I doubt if you could, considering the nature of that spell, but don't muck it up. They're really happy."

"I just want to talk to them."

"Go then. But take care. Coydt has dropped out of sight of late, and there are rumblings that whatever those evil ones are planning is close at hand. Also, there is more to this Spirit and Suzl business than was at first apparent. It may be connected. I know that we have some divine intervention at work here, and it's working in its usual mysterious fashion."

She stared at him. "You mean the Soul Rider?"

He nodded. "It is interesting, but the new spell linking both of them is organized in much the same way as the language Coydt imposed on Spirit, but it does not bear her signature. I begin to suspect that the spell that Spirit has is only superficially the spell that Coydt designed for her. It looks right, smells right, tastes right, even to me and certainly to Coydt who must have checked the work, but I think he got took. I think that language is Soul Rider language—the pure mathematics of Flux married to the human brain, a brain in which it was designed to ride as a supplement and observer, but which now thinks just that same way. Our Soul Rider, I think, has plans for Spirit and for Suzl, too—and perhaps as well for our friend Coydt."

There was nothing to say to that, so she let it pass. "Anything new on this Matson business?"

"No. He's been effectively disposing of Coydt's

agents in Anchor, including some of the best, while keeping out of sight himself. He lets Jomo draw the flies, then traps them, milks them for information, and disposes of them. He's getting closer—or was, until Coydt dropped out of sight. Since then, our mysterious friend dropped out as well. The fact that Coydt chose to go underground rather than face down his foe is uncharacteristic. It means the evil one has something more important to do. It all begins to sound ominous.''

"Let them try their worst," she replied. "I don't fear it—I welcome it. Let's get it out in the open so we can deal with it. I respect their power and the deviousness of their minds, but I don't fear their attempts. But now, I suppose I should fly. It is not every day that your best friend takes up with your daughter and fathers her child.''

To Suzl it was like being reborn. She was happy, truly happy, and very excited about life. She didn't care what anyone else thought about the way she looked, and she liked things just fine. In fact, she'd fight the whole world and spit in its eye if it didn't like her, or Spirit, or anything else they liked or did. And that went for dear old Cass, too, who, she knew, was inevitably coming.

Wizards traveled conventionally only when it suited their needs. Otherwise, they transformed themselves into birdlike creatures and sped to places perhaps weeks of travel away in a matter of hours.

When she arrived in Pericles and reformed into her familiar self, she went immediately to where the two were. She found Suzl sitting on a rock playing a tune on the octarina as a bunch of satyrs danced. Spirit lounged lazily beside her, stroking her a bit. It was disconcerting to Kasdi to see the affection.

Suzl stopped playing and got up. "Hi, Cass. We

knew you'd be along sooner or later." The satyrs looked miffed, but stopped and wandered off.

She was somewhat shocked by Suzl's appearance. Although Mervyn had prepared her somewhat, it was not the same person she'd known. The face was more than ever the old, cute Suzl she'd known, but the body was extremely bizarre and unsettling. She was a head shorter than Kasdi now, no more than one-hundred-forty centimeters. Her arms were short and stubby and barely reached her waist—or, rather, where her waist should have been. Two enormous, impossibly firm breasts stretched out a full thirty centimeters, and while she had a short, fat stomach, it seemed as if her thighs began just below the breasts and were certainly more than half her body, and her back curved into it, giving her an almost birdlike gait. The male organ, which seemed to have grown to about fifteen centimeters, rested on a leathery forward scrotum in a state of permanent semi-erection, but it did allow her freedom to walk. Spirit seemed to have a preference for long hair, though. Both her lush auburn hair and Suzl's thick black hair reached like capes almost to their ankles.

Spirit was as lovely as ever, but her breasts were obviously enlarged and below them was an extremely prominent and obvious bulge. She looked as if she'd swallowed the world's largest melon. And she looked very content and very happy.

"Want to tell me how all this came about?"

Suzl shrugged. "It just . . . happened, that's all."

"But you're old enough to be her mother. Father, anyway," she said, repeating her lame argument that had not worked on Mervyn.

Suzl grinned. "Yeah, I'm the same age as you, but I don't look it or feel it like you do. Come on—you know the age isn't bothering you, nor even who I am. It's *what* I am that disturbs you.

Some of my best friends are freaks, but I don't like my daughter marrying one."

She started to reply, then closed her mouth, wondering if Suzl had given the comments to Mervyn or if it had been the other way around. Nevertheless, what Suzl said was still true, but she had felt forced to say it, and although she felt a little ashamed of herself, it didn't change the gut feeling of wrongness inside her, however much her vows kept her from acting on the prejudice. "All right," she said finally, "I accept that. But—do you two really love each other?"

"You can't know how much," Suzl replied, and Kasdi was both surprised and shocked to see Spirit nod and smile.

"Can she understand me now?"

"Not in the sense you and I can. Actually, not you at all, except through me. We can't talk, but we know each other better than any two people I ever heard of. Call it reading emotions or feelings or whatever, but it's got most conversation beat to Hell, I'll tell you that."

"But—what about you? Particularly in Anchor. How do they react?"

Suzl grinned. "More shocked than with any dugger I ever saw, of course. But I love it, and you know the rules. You wrote 'em. If it's the result of an involuntary spell, standards can't be applied against a Fluxer in Anchor. Not your Anchors, anyway. I actually went into a temple a while back and registered myself. I am now, legally and officially, an Anchor-born male with Flux spells and dispensation. It drove the bureaucrats nuts, but they couldn't deny the sex. I can wear clothes again, if I could ever find a fit, but I won't because Spirit doesn't want it." She paused for a moment, growing serious. "You're very upset. Am I really such a shock to you?"

She looked at the dugger and had to nod sadly.

"Yes. I'm sorry, Suzl. May Heaven forgive me, but I have to be honest, particularly with you."

"Well, this body's no fun to travel with, but it *is* the most excessive in a small area I think possible. I didn't ask for any of it. I was born short, and when my body was adjusted to carry all this, I wound up even shorter. Eighteen years of different wizards with crazy ideas and a lot of power did this to me, and if you'd stayed a dugger in Flux all those years without any Flux power, you would have wound up at least as different. What I couldn't handle, though, up here in the brain, was fixed by wizards. I don't care if I'm a monster to you, or to all of World. I'm not a monster to Spirit, or to myself, and that's all that counts. Don't you pity her or me. We pity you and your prejudices.

"All this time I've been playing at being a woman when actually I'm a man. I'm a man with a magically deformed body. All I wanted was two things— to forget the play acting and say, 'Here I am; take me as I really am,' and somebody who'd totally ignore what I looked like on the outside and see me as a human being and nothing else. Well, finally I got it all, and there's nothing more I want. I love her, Cass, more than you know, and she loves me the same despite what you see."

Kasdi was touched by Suzl's frankness and sincerity, and it was clear just by the way Spirit looked at her and stroked her body that it was in fact mutual. She would have to accept it, she knew, no matter what her inner feelings and prejudices. But she knew Suzl well, and she wondered how long all this would last.

"Suzl—this will sound funny, all things considered, and I know your feelings about religion, but—are you sincere enough in this to marry her in a binding spell in Flux?"

"In a minute," came the unhesitating response.

Kasdi thought a minute. "But how can Spirit take the vows? Or even understand them?"

"She will. If *you're* big enough, we'll do it right here and now with you performing the service. Spirit understands and goes along."

Kasdi looked at Spirit and got the odd feeling that she *did* understand all this.

"All right, then. Join hands and come forward."

The service was simple, the spell voluntary but binding. It was actually less a spell than a locking in of what was already there, and what was there was more than in ninety percent of all marriages. Spirit could not follow the service, but she accepted the spell in the same way Suzl did.

Something stirred, coming from none of the three humans. Kasdi saw and felt it, and was somewhat startled by it. The binding spell merged with the odd linking spell, absolutely freezing their emotional bond at the level it then was, which was high indeed. They would never separate of their own accord as long as they both lived.

They embraced and kissed passionately, and it was done and official.

Mervyn arrived and seemed satisfied at this resolution. He had been very nervous of Kasdi up to the bitter end.

Kasdi remained with them a while, ashamed of her own prejudices, but she knew she had to get back shortly. No one even knew where she was at this point. She explained the situation to Suzl, who nodded.

"We must be leaving, too."

Kasdi looked at Spirit. "What? Now?"

"I've given them a wedding present," Mervyn told her. "It's a small new Fluxland not on any maps, and only Spirit can see the string that leads there. I'll show you where it is, but nobody can pass the shield except Spirit, Suzl, and those whom they allow. Yet it's within your cluster and within easy reach of any of us. It's a tropical garden, with some pretty lakes and waterfalls and lots of harmless wildlife. Though not very large, about ten kilometers by ten, it will support them without need for magic or fear. It's a refuge, a home. Spirit could not create it, but Suzl was able to tell me what they both wished, and so I created it and gave it to them. Spirit most certainly *can* maintain it, and that shield is total self-protection. A few of my people, centaurs and mermaids mostly, will be there to help them with any problems, and may stay if these two wish it."

"I can ride a horse again," Suzl added, "and it's only three days. We want the child born there. It's in Flux, so there's no real danger or pain."

"I was thinking about the journey. Maybe *you* can ride, but Spirit can't. And she's certainly in no condition to run."

"She's in great shape and she can make it. Just sure and easy. Don't worry so much. You're going to be a grandma."

Suzl appreciated the special saddle that allowed her to ride normally once more. Spirit knew where they were going, somehow—she always knew, it seemed—and led them back to the main string. She was using her Flux power to compensate for her off-balance condition, but kept a steady walking pace.

Spirit was feeling wonderful these days. Suzl was her rock and link to humanity. She knew, too, that Suzl was at last at peace with herself, and that was wonderful. The dugger's bizarre and sexually provocative appearance was somehow wonderful, too. She was unique and different, as Spirit was unique and different. She loved every bit of Suzl, particularly that restored and strong self beneath that odd exterior. She felt Suzl's love and devotion and, yes, strength, and returned it in full measure. They would not just have a child; they would have a lot of children. The new life beginning inside her excited and thrilled her.

Suzl had wondered, and continued to wonder, what the child would look like. Would the genetics be Dar's, or those of her old self, or the way she was now? Mervyn had said that if it had been in Anchor the genes would be Dar's, but in Flux it could be any way at all.

They turned off the main string which was leading them to Anchor and headed directly for their new haven. Although neither realized it, within half a day they approached the huge caldera that was the Hellgate itself. Once Spirit saw it, though, she felt curiously drawn to it. Suzl, in all her years in Flux, and never seen one, so they let curiosity get the better of them.

At one point along the huge, concave dish-shaped depression there was a metal ladder. Suzl, with her short arms and prominences, did not like the idea of climbing down that ladder, and even less did she like the idea of a pregnant Spirit descending it, but Spirit was adamant and so she had no choice.

In the center was a smaller hole, with another ladder going down. Suzl feared the Guardians, fierce creatures none had ever lived to tell about, who blocked this way into the gates, but she also knew from Cass's experiences that, when you were with a Soul Rider, the guardians let you pass.

The ladder this time was very short, and when Spirit reached bottom, the whole section of tunnel glowed. Suzl could only follow and worry. As they walked, the glowing section in back of them would fade out and the one ahead would glow. Finally they reached the end of the tunnel, where they saw a whirling vortex of pure energy spiraling not inward but outward and then, to Suzl's eyes, vanishing in the tunnel. To one side was a large console with a tremendous number of buttons and controls that softly hummed.

Spirit went right up to the vortex, and Suzl feared that she would try and step inside, but she stopped just in front of it. Spirit alone saw and felt the vast amount of energy coming from that whirling fury. She saw it, felt it, and let it soak into her. Suddenly she turned and seemed, even to Suzl, to be even more beautiful, even more alluring than ever, and she was somehow glowing.

*Make love to me. Now. Here. With all your passion.*

All thoughts but that vanished from Suzl's mind. She felt the roaring energy now, but had no thoughts, only emotions.

*All that binds me, I keep. All that I have to give I give to you, freely, now and forever. Together only we are one, indivisible.*

It went on for hours and hours, until both passed out.

Suzl awoke first, sat up, and shook her head. She remembered what had happened, and where, but she could not understand why. Her first fear was for the baby, and she looked around and saw Spirit sleeping soundly on the floor of the tunnel, looking apparently unhurt. But Suzl also saw more, things she had never seen before.

Something had been done to them; something had been radically changed, and it required thought. Suzl could see the complex lines of force linking herself with Spirit and could see the massive rush of energy emerging from the vortex outward and into the very wall of the tunnel. She knew she was seeing what wizards could see, but she saw more than they usually did. Although few had ever been inside a Hellgate and even fewer had survived to tell about it, she knew the general layout. What she hadn't expected to see were four outlets arranged around the vortex between the machine and the swirl itself, one on each wall and one on the ceiling and another on the floor, each forming a unique pattern of its own. It was, she thought, something like a children's connect-the-dots puzzle. You just stood there and traced the proper pattern and . . . what? The thing opened, and it took you to Anchor.

She frowned. This was all new to her, and although she'd heard Cass tell the tale of her own entry, it had never been this clear or this obvious. She was lousy in math and had nearly flunked geometry, but she had instantly recognized and grasped the purposes of the four outlets through which the power flowed. Flowed, in fact, into the temple basements, where it was tapped and stepped down and converted into usable electricity for each of the capitals.

The machine was another story. Always the conventional wisdom and the teaching of the Church had said that those machines sealed the Hellgates to prevent the return of the evil ones—but it wasn't so. It was, in fact, obviously the vortex that prevented it. The free energy was far too violently agitated to permit any sort of passage. It would instantly atomize anything solid and scramble any energy pattern. The key to unlocking the gate, if in fact it *was* a gate and there *was* another side, was just as obviously not a combination of button and switch pushing on the machines, but something far more complex, something having to do with the vortex itself.

Part of the machine's job was to tame and route the energy that flowed from the vortex as an escape valve for its own situation, but that was only part of it. The machine blocked and directed the energy flow, but the four waveform groups were each rearranged into a complex pattern, probably the most complex type of pattern possible. And

yet—each pattern was only superficially similar.
Each was also unique.

With growing wonder, she thought she had the
answer. Anchors were not distinct from Flux; they
were a part of it. Just as wizards created Fluxlands
out of their own minds, so the four Anchors were
created by the builders of the machine and were
stabilized by it. She thought of the fear most Anchor folk had of Flux and Fluxers and of the terrible prejudice they had shown her, and she had to
chuckle. They and their world were as much a
Fluxland as, say, Pericles—only, since they were
fully determined by machine, the Anchors were
unvarying and rock-stable.

All this was new to World's knowledge, as far as
she knew, and yet it seemed so *obvious* to her,
totally new and untrained. Obvious . . .

She directed her new sense inwardly and saw
the tangled mass of spells that had been heaped
upon her, starting with that idiot curse. The intricacies had baffled the best wizards, including
Mervyn, but they were perfectly clear to her. She
formulated a complex series of strung-together
counters and sent them down, and watched the
patterns neutralize, dissolve, and vanish. As she
did, she felt a little dizzy and shook her head.
When it passed, she looked down at herself again.

There was no penis. The breasts were large, but
about the size they had been eighteen years ago.
She was chubby, just like then, but that was all.
With a feeling of horror, she realized suddenly
what she had so casually done. *All* the spells were
gone. All of them—except one. The odd linking
spell to Spirit remained, rock-solid and beyond
her newly found power and understanding to undo.
It was, in fact, still oddly familiar, and she looked
back up at the great machine before the vortex
and saw what it was.

The spell was of the same type as those being generated by the machine. Oh, infinitely simpler, but still of the same type and of the same oddly inhuman pattern. Was in fact the Soul Rider not a creature at all, but an extension of another machine somewhere?

Spirit moaned and turned slightly, bringing Suzl back to her immediate situation. She'd dissolved all the spells, and she was now, physically, an eighteen-year-old totally female female. All the physical and mental spells that had created a weird, artificial freak were gone. All that effort on Mervyn's part had been totally wasted.

Or had it? She wondered about that for a moment. She had made the choice to remain a freak forever, and that was important. Nor had she regretted it one bit. Spirit had known and understood the sacrifice. She had also forced Cass to stare at her own human weaknesses and prejudices, and to overcome them. That, too, was important.

And now Spirit had brought them both here, had drawn in and diverted a fantastic amount of power from the primary source. The Soul Rider might have determined the route, but she was absolutely certain that Spirit had understood exactly what she was doing. Suzl stared at the sleeping pregnant woman again, knowing that her love was still firm and her commitment sure. She looked inside, beyond, following the linking spell to Coydt's spell. No, it wasn't quite. Mervyn was right, although he hadn't put his finger on it. The spell was only superficially Coydt's. The evil one's work was overlaid on another spell—a machine spell. She followed Coydt's work and easily stripped it away, leaving only the actual spell in place. She examined it and saw that it was related to the others. That was why Spirit was immune to most spells. In a sense, she was as stabilized physically as an Anchor.

She realized with a sudden shock that Spirit had no Flux power. Yes, the Soul Rider was still there, its aura creating a curious double image of Spirit if looked at in a wizard's way. *All* of Spirit's power, and perhaps more considering the overload, had been transferred to her. She knew that this was impossible—it was known by all that Flux power could not be transferred, conferred, increased or decreased in an individual—but that's what had happened. And Spirit had known she was doing it, even if the Soul Rider had told her how.

Tears came to Suzl's eyes as she realized that Spirit had made the ultimate sacrifice for her, just as she had made her choice in Pericles for Spirit's sake. But the Soul Rider, too, had won and beaten Coydt's game.

It was suddenly quite clear who was feeding all this understanding to her and why she had such easy use of the power. The Soul Rider, prevented from using the power through Spirit, now could deal, by virtue of that linking spell, through Suzl.

*We are one . . . Indivisible.*

Now Suzl had the power and Spirit had the Soul Rider with the knowledge of how to use that power. Apart, the Soul Rider was powerless, and Suzl's power would be meaningless, since, as she had reflected, she was poor in those very aptitudes and skills so needed to make use of it. On a practical level, Spirit would be entirely at Suzl's mercy in Flux, while her own demonstrated physical skills would make her the boss in Anchor. Spirit would still see the things in nature and have the joys she had, and Suzl would be her connection with humanity. It was a perfect partnership, with one hitch. She no longer had the one thing that would make them opposites.

Spirit stirred, moaned a bit, then opened her eyes and looked at Suzl, who felt sudden apprehen-

sion and fear. But Spirit smiled and her face took
on the look of childlike delight. That special bond
of communication through the linking spell was
still there.

*It worked!* Spirit did not say it, nor were words
communicated, but the idea and the excitement
came through.

Suzl nodded. *Yes, but . . .*

Spirit sat up, then got unsteadily to her feet
with Suzl's assistance. The bulging stomach was
something of a problem on a rounded surface, and
they were still in a tube. *This is what you are really
like.*

Suzl nodded again.

*You are cute/attractive/erotic.* She halted for a
moment. *Did you fear I would no longer love you?*

Suzl acknowledged the fear she knew Spirit had
already sensed and understood. Somehow, the new
wizard understood, Spirit retained that ability to
look at people and things in ways no other human
could.

*You are the same inside.*

*But not outside.*

There was a slight blurring of the double imaging,
and along the linking spell floated a few more
patterns. Suzl received them, and instantly she
knew them for what they were and felt both silly
and relieved.

She had the *power.* Lots of it. If Kasdi could
change into a half-bird and if wizards could change
people into plants or substitute wheels for legs or
merge human and horse, then what was a simple
sex organ? She was back to basics, but her dual
nature was still there if she wished or needed it.
*She could be anything she needed to be*—providing
somebody, the Soul Rider or another wizard, told
her the spell. Spirit had realized this from the
start, but she had been blind to it. It *wasn't* the

same as Mervyn's neutralization, for she had the power. In point of fact, to all those with strong Flux power, sexual identity and appearance was merely a matter of personal preference, like the kind of clothing you wore or the kind of food you liked.

Suzl suddenly felt better than she ever had in her entire life. She was free, totally free, and in love, and she had the power! She wondered suddenly if power flowed both ways along that linking spell, and tried it. It did, indeed. Spirit, then, was not totally powerless after all. She could still read the strings and take what was needed—from Suzl. They needed each other more than ever.

*We should go now.*

Spirit agreed, and they made their way back along the fearsome tunnel. Suzl found it much easier to go up ladders now, and she led and got to the top and started to haul herself out when something made her stop and look around. What she saw made her duck back down, almost kicking Spirit in the face.

Up on the rim, near the far ladder, were a whole host of human figures, most on horseback. They weren't alone.

Spirit sensed the danger and quickly went back a bit in the tunnel, but Suzl decided to risk another peek. If the Soul Rider was willing, she'd like to know just what was going on up there.

She risked poking her head up and wished for some way to find out what all that was about. Not only did she want to know for curiosity's sake; she also knew that she'd left her horse tethered to that ladder up there, so they must know that someone was down here.

Energy flowed from her directly to the rim, and she found that she had limits that seemed contrary to logic. She could not make out any of the words being said, but she could see them clearly, and she saw at once that they were all wizards of great power. Two had, in fact, discovered her horse, and they were obviously discussing its implications. She hoped and prayed that they wouldn't draw the correct conclusions, and cursed her inability to make out the words.

". . . Queer saddle. Must be a strayed dugger or somethin'."

"Gotta be really monstrous to set in a get-up like that," another noted. "What d'ya think happened to him?"

"Looks like he went down and got creamed by the Guardian," yet another voice put in. "Sure isn't anywhere around here. I'd *know* if it was. I don't like it bein' here, though. I smell trouble. After all this, I'll take a look down the hole and see if we can get us a spy. It'd be just like one of those damned Soul Riders to horn in on this."

"Why not take a look now?" somebody suggested.

The man sighed. "Because my going in there is the whole point of this exercise, Stupid! Right now, just post two good riflemen up here at the ladder and have them blast away at anything they see down there."

"Sure thing, Coydt!"

Suzl felt frustration at not being able to make out the words, but she recognized the leader's face when she saw it. She began to wonder if the Soul Rider had directed them here for this purpose rather than the other. Were they really free? What terrible plot were these wizards hatching with this prince of evil? More immediately, how were they to deal with the riflemen, even if everybody else went away?

*        *        *

"All right, everybody! Listen up!" Coydt called out. "Now, you all know the plan or you wouldn't be here in the first place. This is phase two of a feasibility study. The first phase is done. All of you are top wizards, Fluxlords mostly, who've been trampled on by that little bitch in the tattered bathrobe. All of you know what'll come next, once she's beaten the last of you. Her power and the power of those who back her will be put into making this one big Holy Mother tyranny. One by one they'll wipe you out as they feel like it, and then they'll turn you and yours into scripture-quoting slaves. You all know what it's like to have great power. All you have to do is put yourselves in her place and you know what's got to be coming down the line."

It was a good argument, particularly when each of them was, in fact, the kind of person who'd act just as he said.

"Now, I'm gonna show you how it's done. She preaches revolution, so let's give *her* a taste of revolution. All of you have Fluxlands and those Fluxlands have limited borders. Why? That's all you can protect, defend, and hold. Now, *she's* taken so much of World that there is no way in Heaven or Hell that she can protect, defend, and hold it all. Break her in pieces, scurry all those forces and wizards all about as you strike and run, and you demoralize her whole empire. Soldiers won't keep marching hundreds of kilometers to fight when they know their own homes might be overrun. Wizards can't keep you in line while they're rushing around defending first this place, then that. And any church that can't stop all hell from literally breaking loose in its own backyard isn't gonna have many converts or keep the faithful in line. So that'll provoke her into repression right off and, in turn, swell our own armies."

"We know all this," somebody shouted. "But we still doubt it's possible."

Coydt chuckled. "Oh, it's possible, all right. Now, first I went into her own home Anchor and snatched her kid in broad daylight, then turned her into a nature fairy. They couldn't stop me and none of my people even got a splinter. That sowed doubt and also took her mind off empire and towards revenge. She hasn't taken a new place since. Next we recruited all over Anchor and Flux. We have a real *army* ready and willing at my signal to converge on the target. They're mean, nasty, and full of hate. None of them could resist the idea of being able to loot an entire Anchor at will.

"Now, for my next trick, I'm going to demonstrate to you how to get in and out undetected. A selected sample of you will remain here. I'm going in that big hole over there and I'm coming back out by way of Anchor. I'm not going to be electrocuted or ripped to pieces or anything else either. And I'm taking two of you with me to show you how easy it is. Now, you're welcome to try it yourself, but don't kid yourselves. The Guardian is real and it's deadly. Without me, all the Flux power in the world won't save you. That's why *we'll* be able to get to *them*, and get out, at any time we want, but *they* won't be able to get *us*. When I return here, you'll know the whole plan will work. Then we can set a date and a target."

Suzl watched as two Fluxlords dismounted and walked forward to Coydt. She recognized one of them—Darien, Lord of Kalgash, supposedly a friend and ally of Cass. She closely examined some of the others and picked out more than two dozen that she knew. She didn't know the details of the betrayal Coydt had discussed with them, but she certainly had the general idea—and the names and faces. If she could get to Cass, she could finger a number of those damned traitors. One of them would talk and spill the details she could not make out.

She watched as Coydt and the other two grinned and flexed their Flux power. Where the three had stood now stood apparently three middle-level priestesses in temple robes. She really didn't like the implications of that. It meant that Coydt and the other two were actually going to come in the Hellgate! And since all Hellgates exited in the temple basements in Anchor, they'd need disguises to escape detection. But how was it possible for Coydt to pass through the gate? Was this gate Guardian somehow destroyed? That, too, was important news, but it didn't solve the immediate problem. She scampered back down the ladder to Spirit, who read her fear and concern.

*They are coming. We must exit to Anchor.*

Quickly they made their way back along the tube to the vortex and the four energy patterns. The gates were easy enough to operate—but which ones went where? That was an important question for several reasons, not the least of which was that all of the entryways were supposed to have been sealed with almost a full meter of crushed rock and cement at Cass's order. Obviously one wasn't if Coydt was going to try it—but which one? She reached out to the Soul Rider for help, but it was conspicuously silent.

There was a clanging sound at the far end of the tunnel that reverberated through to them. They were coming. *The hell with it*, Suzl decided. *Let's just pick one and trust the Soul Rider to pull us out of it.* She traced the pattern nearest them on the right wall, grabbed Spirit's arm, and stepped into what still seemed like a solid wall.

They were suddenly in complete darkness, and for a moment Suzl feared they would end up stuck in the concrete or rock. She still had hold of

Spirit's hand, and she calmed down as she realized she could breathe. She felt Spirit starting to panic at the closed-in darkness, and didn't feel very reassuring, but she kept hold of the hand and began to probe. She wished violently to see.

Suddenly the place was bathed in an eerie, unnatural light. Suzl realized then that they were still on the gate, which was in the floor on this side, and that that gate was still, technically, Flux. The light she was seeing was being created by the energy around her.

She looked around frantically, fearing that Coydt and his buddies would be through behind them in a second, and saw a trap door in the ceiling which was not two meters above them. Of course! They had to have some way to get that concrete in!

She stared at it and pushed with her Flux power. It budged, then moved up and out of the way. They went for it, and suddenly the only light was the faint electric light from the opening above. Spirit reached down and, with difficulty, picked Suzl up and pushed her through the opening and to the floor above. Then Suzl strained to pull Spirit up enough to get both elbows on the flooring and hoist herself up. It was an ordeal, with the swollen abdomen, in Anchor.

They caught their breath for a moment, but Suzl could feel Spirit's claustrophobia returning. They had to find somebody somewhere in this temple. There was not only a lot of news to tell, but somebody also ought to know that it didn't matter how much junk you heaped on top of that Flux entry—it ignored it.

Coydt had known, she realized.

One of Kasdi's innovations had been the installation of arrow exit-pointers in every corridor and stairway in every temple. Her whole life had been changed because she'd got lost in a temple once, and she'd never forgotten it. Suzl, therefore, was able to just follow the glowing green arrows, thanking heaven that Spirit had not been alone in trying this. The arrows would have meant nothing to her.

They were only part way up when they ran into a priestess in an administrative robe who was far more shocked to bump into them than the other way around. Suzl, in fact, thought she'd lost her mind, because she kept shrieking and making all sorts of weird noises.

She tried to tell the woman who they were and ask where they were, but found she couldn't. Her mouth just wouldn't form the words. *Now I know how Spirit feels*, she grumped, then straightened in shock. It was *exactly* how Spirit was. And now, as other priestesses scurried up to them, all making nonsense sounds, she realized that there had been a price to pay for all that Flux power.

The Soul Rider knew that it had to communicate directly with her in order to provide what was needed. Not residing in her body, it could not access her thoughts directly and feed what was needed. So they needed a common, transmittable language. Spirit's nonverbal language. The language of the Soul Rider and the big machine.

That was why she was able to recognize so clearly those machine spells and identities, although none other ever had. That was why she could see the pitiful human attempts at mocking the language commands, commands they called "spells." That was why the nonverbal link with Spirit was so clear it was almost thought-to-thought, but she'd been unable to understand Coydt and his men.

She had no spells on her but the Soul Rider's, and she was not limited as Spirit was. Spirit's spell had to outwardly mimic Coydt's or else he would never have freed her. So Suzl had no fear of artifacts, no confusion as to signs and tools, any more than any other human. But her mind had been converted to the language of the machines, and that made speaking, understanding, reading, and writing impossible.

She had all that news, all that information, and no way to impart it to anyone. She was *not* back the way she used to be, but still very much a freak in the human world.

# KILLING HEROES

By the time help arrived, Suzl was ready to commit mass murder or even suicide. Her temper was calmed only by Spirit, and even she had problems containing her emotional partner.

First they'd tried to keep them in the temple while Spirit was going nuts. Then somebody recognized Spirit and understood *that* problem, but they all got worried and overly solicitous of the pregnant girl. Then they had problems with Suzl. Word had come of Spirit's attachment to a stranger dugger, but here was a perfectly normal-looking young woman, totally nude, who didn't seem able to speak or understand any more than Spirit.

At that point there was sudden fear of an epidemic, as if Suzl was proof that whatever was wrong with Spirit was catching. So they wound up sticking them in a livestock pen that wasn't private and had been recently used by cows as it was intended to, delivering food to them on trays attached to long sticks.

After a little of that, some wiser heads in the Church decided that it would be a bit hard to explain this sort of condition should Sister Kasdi show up, and they were moved out of town to a small pasture which had few trees but some room. It wasn't great, but it beat the livestock pen.

She did have time to reflect on the earlier situation, though, and realized that her present form was useful in at least one way. The saddlebag on her horse had contained her registration document and photos as well as all her vitals as a dugger. All of that showed, of course, a deformed creature with massive sexual abnormalities. She was very different looking now, so at least Coydt's people would be looking for someone who no longer existed. Unfortunately, they would also tie that creature and that name to Spirit, and they were sitting ducks out there if word got around that Spirit was in fact there.

"There" was Anchor Nanzee; that much was clear. It was the easternmost of the cluster that contained Anchor Logh, and Suzl had been there many times with Ravi on the route. It was hard rock and rolling country, with some rugged-looking, tree-covered hills, and it was here that some of the new scientific generation were actually talking of getting electricity from water. How that was possible when water even put out a match Suzl never understood, but after half her life in Flux she didn't disbelieve *anything* anymore.

Suzl was also getting more and more frustrated by her inability to communicate and almost envied Spirit's blithe acceptance. Not long ago she had been the most grotesque of freaks, but fully able to communicate. Now she found that even simple and obvious sign language would tend to bring less understanding than smiles. She thought being a physical freak was in some ways easier to take. Nobody necessarily confused deformity with stupidity, since it was so easily disproved, but mutes, it seemed, were always assumed to be childish or retarded.

Most distressing of all was that Spirit, being in Anchor, now was suffering the pains and discomforts of pregnancy, problems Suzl could sense and almost feel herself, but that she could do nothing about.

It was a real relief when, after four days, Sister

Kasdi showed up. By that point they were both very glad to see anybody, but Kasdi was more shocked at Suzl's appearance now than she had been in Pericles.

*Oh, Goddess forgive me!* she thought. *I've given my own daughter to a lesbian relationship and sanctified it with a church marriage!* And nobody looking at Spirit could say it wasn't consummated either. Of all the Suzls, she felt least comfortable with this one. The fat dugger woman pushing middle age was consistent with her own view of herself and her generation; the spell-deformed creature was horrible, but there was a certain acceptance of it. But here was Suzl, looking like she had looked back in school in Anchor Logh, all cute and chubby and very much all-woman—and apparently nearly worshipped even now by her beautiful and pregnant daughter.

Clearly, something very strange had happened to them on their way to their new home, and it wasn't anything she could handle there or even at Hope. She got them washed off and cleaned up, then headed for Flux. She decided she could use the huge bird form and somehow carry both of them on her back, so she worked the spell. Suzl watched, saw the spell, made several improvements on it, then did it herself. She knew that Spirit could never ride on her mother's back, but she might permit herself to be picked up and held by Suzl's clawlike legs.

When Suzl worked her transformation, Kasdi was even more shocked. Somehow Suzl had Flux power now and the ability to use it. She almost oozed it, in fact—and this was inexplicable. Bowing to the inevitable, she took off and headed back for Pericles.

Suzl found flying tremendous fun, and she was fascinated to see at last the stringer trails she'd followed blindly for so long. From up high they looked like a series of crisscrossing, multicolored carnival lights stretching off in all directions. Somewhere down there was Ravi, she thought mischievously. One day she'd like to meet up with the little wimp again and pay him back for his parting shots at her. How pleasant it would feel to leave him with no sexual organ at all and a tremendous sex urge.

The wizard was quite surprised to see them again, and seemed a bit annoyed and preoccupied, but he couldn't eliminate his fascination for this new thing. There were certain rules for both Anchor and Flux, and between Kasdi's earlier experiences and now Suzl's strange transformation quite a number had been broken. The old man's world had been turned upside-down within a generation, and it both bothered and stimulated him.

Pericles was a far busier place than the one they had left. It seemed as if human riders and wizard-transformed messengers were coming and going with incredible frequency, and even the creatures of the Fluxland could not be found playing as usual, although once or twice they would be glimpsed going from one of the marble structures to another with businesslike efficiency and worried looks. Still, Mervyn took time out from whatever was going on to see them and quickly came to the same conclusion that Suzl had—that the Soul Rider had indeed finally found the loophole in Coydt's trap.

"Suzl is not like Spirit," he assured Kasdi. "The mere act of the transformation proved that, not to mention her unsettling ability to materialize lit cigars in her mouth that she developed just this afternoon. She'd been trying to communicate with me all through this, though, and going slightly crazy with frustration. I wish I knew just what she was trying to tell us."

"Knowing Suzl, the mere fact that she can't

shoot off her big mouth is the problem. The fact that the old Suzl is back at all worries me more."

Mervyn chuckled dryly. "I know your feelings, and understand them, if I do not agree with them. Take heart in the fact that the host of a Soul Rider is not the master or mistress of his or her own fate. You of all people should know that. Spirit was lonely and had a desperate need for close companionship. Suzl was disaffected and attracted to Spirit. The Soul Rider closed that gap, filled both needs, and magnified the emotional kernels, having found someone it could trust to put its plan into action."

"You mean the Soul Rider caused them to fall in love?"

"In a way. The seeds were there, or it would never have worked, but once the seeds were there, it did the rest—which might or might not otherwise have happened. Spirit was turned on by Suzl's sexual grossness and liked it that way. It was sincere. But that was necessary to the Soul Rider because at the time it could do nothing about it. When conditions were right and the Soul Rider's spells perfected linking the two so that the power could be transferred, that was no longer necessary. Again, the seeds were there. Suzl felt weak and powerless and it almost destroyed her. Now she's neither—and is happy except for the language barrier. Spirit sensed Suzl's unhappiness and reacted badly to my major attempt to compensate. She realized, I think, just what Suzl really was going through and knew that the new Suzl, while content, was a lie I constructed. She took the appropriate actions. In many ways it was an expression of love, since Suzl's other form suited Spirit a bit more."

"Yes, but what do we do now?"

"Why, nothing, I would suspect. Suzl has no training and can not receive any, yet she is able to manage spells that I would be hesitant to try. That means the Soul Rider is feeding them to her as she needs them. It's one very powerful wizard in two bodies, both necessary for the magic. Together, they are no more in danger than you or I. Let them go to their Fluxland and be happy."

She didn't like it, but had no alternatives at the time, so she changed the subject. "What's all the comings and goings around here?"

"Come into the map room over there and I'll show you."

Suzl had been standing there, knowing that she was being discussed, unable to follow it at all. Still, she had hopes of getting through to one or the other of these two, so she tagged along. Spirit remained in the meadow, just relaxing. The period and strain in Anchor had taken a toll on her, and she was feeling neither totally well nor in any way ambitious.

Spread out on a round table in the center of a comfortably appointed room just inside the marble building were all sorts of papers and documents. A centaur and two nymphs were over to one side, working on some of those documents and correlating them.

Mervyn picked up a huge bound volume and opened it. On each of its large pages was pasted a picture or drawing of an individual man or woman, along with a lot of handwritten information about them.

"A rogue's gallery of World," he told Kasdi. "These are Fluxlords of great power, one and all. Every one of them tinged with some form of madness, as it must be."

Kasdi grinned. "Are *you* in there?"

He nodded. "Yes, indeed, although the file is rather less than objective, I'm afraid. And you, too. See?" He turned to a place about three-quarters of the way back in the volume, and there she saw her picture and vital statistics, and in between what looked like dozens of scribbled pages.

The last thing Suzl needed was a library, but she watched from the background, and when Kasdi's picture showed, she suddenly got very interested. To the dismay of the other two, who were hardly even aware she'd followed them, Suzl leafed through the book until she found a number of familiar faces and guessed what it must be about.

Kasdi moved to pull her away, but Mervyn stopped her. "Wait. We may be on to something here."

Stringers and duggers knew Fluxlords well. They'd better, for they had to deal with them regularly. From the series of familiar faces in the book, Suzl knew what it must contain and searched frantically for one in particular. Finally Darien's page came up, and she stopped, pointed to it, then made a motion with her index finger as if she were slitting her own throat.

"Darien!" Kasdi explained. "What can she mean? That Darien's dead?"

Suzl realized from the expressions that the message was incomplete, and so again pointed to Darien, then made the same slit motion—this time across Kasdi's neck.

"I think she's accusing Darien of a plot against you," the wizard suggested.

Kasdi's look of shock and surprise told Suzl she'd scored one. She leafed back through the book, stopping every once in a while at a face she'd seen in that mob at the Hellgate and going through the same motions.

Mervyn frowned. "A wizard's revolt. This sounds ill. But where could she have learned this in so short a time?" He rustled through a pile of papers and came up with a map of the cluster. "Their route from here would be mostly like . . . so." He began to trace with his finger, and when it came

close to the Hellgate Suzl reached out, grabbed his
wrist, and put it directly on top.

"At the Hellgate!" Kasdi exclaimed. "So they
were going to their wedding gift by a route that
took them by the Hellgate, and there they saw all
these wizards gathered." She stopped. "Why at
the Hellgate? And how? None of those Fluxlords
could even stand to be in the same land at the
same time, let alone gather and cooperate on
something. It explains how those two wound up in
the temple, though. I thought we'd sealed those
internal entries. I wonder now if they *can* be
sealed?"

Again Suzl was leafing through the picture book,
but did not find who she was looking for. She
looked up, shook her head from side to side, then
pointed at the shelves around.

Mervyn frowned. "More Fluxlord pictures? Or
. . . not a Fluxlord, perhaps? Ah!" He walked over
to a shelf, took down another book, brought it over
to Suzl and opened it. There were, perhaps, a hundred more faces covered, but she didn't have to go
far. The face of a handsome, bearded man smiling
back at the observer was enough.

"Coydt van Haaz. I should have known," Kasdi
sighed.

But Suzl continued to flip through and found a
few more pictures as well.

"These are the prime enemy," Mervyn told the
Sister. "The Seven and all those of a strong power
that we know of who work with them. She has
picked out a number of strong-arm wizards who
work this side of World, and also Varishnikar
Stomsk and Zelligman Ivan, two more of the Seven.
Put them all together with the Fluxlords she picked
out and you have a concentration of power that
could level a Fluxland. Put that together with what
*we* have learned and it spells disaster."

Kasdi looked up at the old man. "What have you learned, then?"

"A number of people who work directly or indirectly for Coydt and others of the Seven have been recruiting in both Flux and Anchor. They are looking for killers, the kind of people who have a grudge against the Church, the system, or life in general. One by one, these people have been vanishing from their usual haunts. Not just a few, or even a dozen, but hundreds. The Seven are recruiting an army."

She looked worried. "And no sign of where they are?"

"We've tried very hard to infiltrate that group, but once in Flux and with the power of the Seven we've been unable to fool them. Oh, a few we've never heard from again, but those I suspect were caught by one of high power and are now unrecognizable."

She nodded. "Do any of them have Flux power?"

"Inconsequential. A lot of false wizards, few with anything worth mentioning. What is also interesting and ties in with Suzl's information is that, despite a wonderfully vicious rogue's gallery of females, all of them have been male. That immediately puts the Coydt signature on them."

"He hates women?"

"No, not at all. He believes women to be the inferior sex, far too emotional and mentally different to be worth trusting. It gives you an idea of World ruled by Coydt. Women as the servants, slaves, and baby rearers, with no power or decision-making abilities."

"It would never work. Nobody has ever said men and women weren't different—if they weren't, they wouldn't be attracted to each other. But World has always been run with an equal partnership, with different occupations certainly, but in sum an equal sharing of power and authority. The old

Church rotted when it began to make itself dominant."

"Coydt has little love for the Church or scripture. He does, however, have access to writings lost to the rest of us. His ideas are both radical and unthinkable, but I suspect they are not new ones."

She shivered. The very idea of a world totally dominated by the male ego was frightening. "And what will he do with this army now that he has it?"

Mervyn frowned. "I had suspected an attack on an Anchor, but with Suzl's information it seems likely to be a bolder plan. Considering all this, he might be thinking of attacking Hope itself. After all, an attack on Anchor would only be a temporary victory after which all the participants would be exposed. And what good would Fluxlords be in Anchor?"

"Then I'd better get back there at once."

"Yes, perhaps you should. But that leaves open the question of why he called a meeting at a Hellgate. Most of these Fluxlords would hardly look forward to opening the gates, as much as they fear the empire. It would be like risking the removal of one's heart in order to cure a badly bruised knee."

"Well, we'll soon know. I think perhaps I will pay a call on our friend Darien. He's close and I know his limits."

"You do that. I'll see to Spirit and Suzl. Save your worries for the fight that's coming. The way this is shaping up, it's an all-out attempt to stop you out of sheer desperation."

"Another Balacyn," she sighed. She remembered Balacyn. She'd still been young and idealistic then. Her whole future had been turned by the shock of seeing Matson fall in the rather minor battle for Persellus. She had been revolted by combat then, and she still had not any idea of what the old guard could do.

Balacyn taught them. All of the Seven and their cohorts were there, as well as the best wizards of the old Church, and she and the Nine and all the best on their side faced them over an obscure and meaningless little Fluxland. It had gone on for three weeks of sheer horror, and after all of the tremendous powers of wizardry were employed, it was finally decided not by magic but by sheer body count. Over a quarter of a million people had died in that terrible battle, and on the magic front, in fact, the reformed Church barely held against a terrible psychic onslaught. But they could not hold; they had to advance and crush the spreading rebellion, and so they had sent their armies in as the revolutionaries had been pushed back by magic, and Kasdi's troops, filled with the fires of revolution, had fought like wild beasts, killing the other side at a ratio of six or seven to one. Wizards, too, had died both in the battle and from the stress of it.

The old order held most of World that day, but they had to fall back, losing too much to sustain an offensive. Many wars had been fought since Balacyn, but never on such a scale again. Both sides knew that such a fight a second time would cost at least as many, and World had barely forty million people, even counting those inhabitants of all the Fluxlands. The cream of both sides had been lost at Balacyn; the next one would take a million lives and probably be just as indecisive. Both sides recognized this and had limited their actions after, for neither wanted to inherit the shell of a destroyed World.

But the old order had been losing those smaller battles and suffering more and more desertions from their sides, as the powerful and the opportunistic had perceived an eventual winner.

Were they, then, about to risk all-out war? They

certainly had the wizardry for it, if Suzl was to be believed. The power, yes—but not the men. An army of even a few thousand madmen would not be nearly enough.

She went out to find Spirit and say good-bye, still brooding on these dark matters, then stopped. It was an odd feeling, unlike any she had ever felt before, a sense of something not quite right, something very close by.

Suzl, now satisfied that the message had gotten across, had been following Kasdi out when she saw the robed figure suddenly stop and look around curiously, disturbed expression on her face, then abruptly begin walking, not towards Spirit, but down a walkway and towards another of the marble buildings across the field and partially masked by some tall trees. *Now what the hell?* Suzl wondered. *It must be the power, but I've got the power and I don't see anything.* Now very curious, she followed the small figure along the path. Suzl did not worry about Spirit; she would know in a minute if she was wanted or needed.

Kasdi approached the strange building, the sense of strangeness and foreboding building inside her, but she stopped at the last of the trees and stepped off the walk and into partial concealment. The building was marble, like the rest, and had a series of stone steps leading up to a high porch, the roof over the porch supported by thick marble columns. There was no door as such, just a large squared cavity leading into the white stone block, but as she watched, a figure came out of that opening and looked around, yawned, and stretched. She recognized him in a minute—as would anyone who'd ever met him. She stepped out and continued to walk to the building, then up the steps to the porch area, hurrying now.

The figure hardly paid her any attention at first, but then looked at her again as she approached.

Huge brown eyes that seemed to be ready to pop out of a massive, deformed head opened even wider, and he moved to step back into the building. She saw it and shouted, "Oh, no, Jomo! You stay right where you are!"

Suzl, too, recognized that figure from their common past.

Jomo hesitated, trying to decide what to do, then turned and waited for her. When she reached him, he broke into a grin that looked so fierce and grotesque it would scare most people half to death. "Hi, Missy Cass. Been a long, long time."

So great was his bulk and so slight was she that the sight reminded Suzl of a cat trying to figure out a cow.

"Don't give me that, Jomo!" Kasdi responded sharply. "If you were glad to see me, you wouldn't have hidden out over here. How long have you been in Pericles?"

The huge dugger shrugged. "Not long."

"You know you can't lie to a wizard, Jomo. More like months, isn't it? You've been using this as your base and your hideout." And that, of course, meant that Mervyn knew a whole lot more about this business than he'd let her believe.

The big man nodded. "O.K., long time, then. Mister Mervyn, he need me."

"Where is he, Jomo?" she said firmly, but with a dread she could not conceal.

"He in the Map Room, last I know."

"Not Mervyn. You know who I mean."

"I'll take you off the hook, Jomo," said a voice from within the darkened entrance. "It's about time we got this all out anyway." With that the man walked out onto the porch and into the full light.

"Matson," she breathed.

\*       \*       \*

He had changed a little in eighteen years, but
not nearly so much as she had. Age had been good
to Matson, making him, if anything, more rug-
gedly handsome than ever. Oh, his face was lined,
and his hair and long, drooping moustache, which
he'd just been starting to grow back then, were
now partly gray, but he was trim, weathered, and
in obviously excellent shape for a man who was
certainly pushing the mid-fifties—and in superior
shape for a man who'd died in her arms on a
battlefield more than eighteen years before. He
wore the all-black stringer outfit and gun belt, but
was hatless and unarmed.

Kasdi swallowed hard, everything coming back
in a rush. She started feeling dizzy and swayed a
bit, and both Matson and Jomo ran over and stead-
ied her and lay her down on the stone porch. She
opened her eyes and saw his face looking down at
her, and tears came to her eyes. "Take it easy,
girl!" he said sharply, but with a real sense of
concern in his tone. "I know I'm a shock, but I
never thought this moment would come."

He understood what she was going through, but
only slightly. Matson had taken her into slavery
and then gotten her out of it. Matson had been the
only man she'd ever made love to, the only man
she had ever loved. And she still loved him, even
after all these years, still loved him and wanted
him desperately, as if all those years had never
happened. Every feeling she had suppressed all
those years welled up inside her so painfully she
wondered if she could stand it.

And she was a Sister of the Church, bound by
vow and spell not to act on any such feelings or in
any way find release.

*"You died in my arms,"* she wailed, choking back
the tears.

"No, my little Cass," he responded, brushing
back her tears. "Oh, I was good as dead, that's for

sure. Nothing, no amount of magic, could have saved me in time—but you did."

"Me?" she sniffled.

*He sat upon his horse, directing the artillery fire, when she'd come up. He remembered talking to her, then turning back, and then there was a tremendous explosion in his chest and he felt himself falling, and that was all. There was no pain; the shock was too great for that. There was only darkness and a curious sense of fading out, although his mind was strangely clear and he knew he was dying.*

*And then, suddenly, her voice had come to him in the nothingness. "No more," it said. "No more . . ." And he found the moment suspended, himself commanded not to die.*

"Jomo refused to give up on me and dragged me back to one of the wizards supporting the batteries," he told her. "I didn't know any of it, of course, until later. Much later. They put a sustaining spell on me and dumped me in a wagon, or so I later learned. Jomo took the wagon and found a stringer he knew in the back. The stringer, whose name we never got, guided Jomo all the way to Globbus, where they again decided I was beyond saving. But I didn't die—I couldn't—and they finally bowed to Jomo's persistence and worked on me. When I finally came to again, it was three weeks after the battle; I was recovering, and the bill wiped out half my assets."

"You could have come back. Told me."

"What good would that do? By that time you'd taken all your vows. I was *still* going to come back, if only to let you see, but Mervyn came and visited me and convinced me not to."

"Mervyn!" For the first time in her life she said that name with bitterness.

"You were organizing your new church, starting your revolution, and beginning to put together the new empire. Mervyn pointed out that you'd already taken your vows and were bound to them. He said if I didn't stay dead, it would destroy you and the whole thing would collapse. I think he was right. Look at you now—you're shaking like a leaf."

She pulled herself unsteadily to a sitting position, then turned and looked not at Matson but at the beauty of Pericles. "It was a lie all along," she whispered. "All of it has been a stinking *lie!*"

She remembered the commitment she'd made so long ago in Hope, a commitment to Mervyn. At that time he'd asked her if Matson's still being alive would change things, hinting at a possible survival, but she had been so sure of his death and still in a state of emotional shock that she'd said it wouldn't make any difference. She realized now that the wizard was testing her out in more than a theoretical way. He had the leader of the revolution he and his colleagues had wanted so much, and he had only one threat to that leader, that symbol, on which they would build their empire.

Such potential leaders come very rarely in human civilization, and even more rarely are they in the position to act to change history forever. Mervyn had known that, had understood that there was no one else who could rally a revolution and keep its fires burning. And when she had assured him that she was committed, that Matson's survival would not change her, he'd known it was a lie, even if she herself did not at the time.

*You can't lie to a wizard. . . .*

But a wizard can lie to a wizard.

"Where have you been for all these years?" she asked him, still staring out at the beauty of the Fluxland.

"I retired from the business, basically. I didn't want to go back to it on the other side of World under some phony name and face. I didn't really want to go back at all. I'd really survived in that game longer than most and I figured that hole in my chest was telling me that I'd used up the last of my luck. I have to admit that having a pack of powerful wizards anxious to retire me was part of it, too. I got the real strong feeling that they'd be real nice to me if I went along, but that it would be nothing at all to make me really dead if I didn't. I went up to Strongford, a nice Fluxland up north that's full of retired stringers and folks who were either dead or missing for one reason or another. Jomo declared me dead, then paid off the rest and came up to a dugger's haven near Strongford. Got a job and a fat account."

Strongford was very exclusive, and by design. The shield, maintained by powerful retired stringers in concert, was incredibly strong and selective. It admitted everyone, with the exception that it kept out any wizards who were not members of the stringer's guild, but you could leave only by special permission. A lot of people with a lot of ill-gotten gains took advantage of that, and the place had a lot of money and was something of a pleasant, benign pleasure palace where no questions were asked—and a rake-off of the enormous profits went to the guild. Matson described himself as "in the hotel business," but since a place you couldn't leave except to be thrown out to the wolves hardly needed a hotel, it was pretty obvious that the place was not the usual sort of rental hotel. He was also a deputy there, helping to keep things right and peaceful and to teach newcomers the rules.

"Why did you come back, then?" she asked him.

"You know why. We got word of the snatch, and it was pretty easy to put two and two together. I mean, you didn't have time for Spirit to have been anybody else's kid, although she was something the wizards in Globbus sort of forgot to mention in all this. She's my daughter as much as yours, and I couldn't stand by and let that bastard get away

with this, even if I'd never seen her. Old man
Stankovitch—the head stringer wizard in Strongford—agreed with me, and I put on the old outfit,
picked up Jomo, and we headed south. I didn't
want to cross old Merv, though, so I got in touch
with him, and he's been my protection."

*And mine, too,* Kasdi thought, growing more
bitter. He knew he couldn't keep word of the reappearance of Jomo and Matson from her, so he
diverted her. No wonder he was so annoyed to see
her here now, when Matson was here, but because
of the emergency with Spirit and Suzl, he couldn't
deny her entry. No wonder he was so anxious to
get rid of her!

And now, here he was, coming up the stairs to
them, looking resigned. He stopped and faced her.
"So now it's out in the open. In a way, I'm almost
glad. It's been quite a burden for me to carry."

"You hypocrite!" she snapped. "You spout plati-
tudes about the purity of the Church while you live
in this echo of some pagan fantasy. You lie whenever it suits you. You don't believe in the Church
or its teachings one bit. You're just a more subtle
version of Coydt and Haldayne and the rest. You
want power. You wanted more power than you
could get on your own, all nine of you, so when I
came along, I was your perfect patsy. And I trotted
off and gave you your empire."

Mervyn looked genuinely stung by the remarks.
"I wish things truly were as simple and as cut-and-
dried as you see everything. After all this time, you
still see the world through a little girl's eyes. In
one way that's a help, because it's allowed you to
bear your burdens, but in a situation like this it
serves you ill. No one is all evil or all good. That
has never been the nature of the conflict with the
Seven. Not Coydt, certainly—the man is truly evil
by any definition. But the rest are as sincere in
what they believe as we are in opposing them. But

it is not necessary to be evil to be wrong. They are wrong, and you are wrong now. We had a dying civilization and a dying race. You revived it. You made it live again."

*"You stole my life!"*

"Nobody asked you to be a saint; we wanted merely a leader. You imposed all those conditions on yourself—against my will, if you'll remember. That little girl side of you couldn't deal with anything other than absolutes. You looked at yourself and you saw the face of Diastephanos, the Sister General who'd gone over to the other side. *You* stole your life, because you were so afraid to be human."

"You gave me no choice, no chance to grow up! You manipulated me from the start, and you manipulated Matson, too, for that matter. I am exactly what you wanted most. *I am your ultimate lie!*

"You're worse than that. Because of all this, you stole Spirit's life, too. She should be training for a trade, romancing the boys, facing a solid future and a normal marriage and life. Now she's a pregnant mental cripple worshipfully married to a thirty-seven-year-old woman who's always been a social and sexual deviate. Coydt didn't do that because she was Cassie and Matson's daughter. He did it because she was the daughter of a monument you created, something she didn't even know until almost when it happened! You robbed me of her all the way along, you know. *I never even was able to say one word to her without pretending to be somebody else!* You took my daughter, my chance for love and a normal life, *everything*—and gave me what in return? A chance to wear a rag, to age fifty years in eighteen, to sleep on stone and straw, unable to even keep a lock of my daughter's hair or ever be loved by anyone except as some kind of

angel or demigod. It's more than my life! You took
mine and Spirit's *humanity*!"

Jomo looked down at her sadly, and there seemed
to be a tear in one of his bulging eyes. Matson
leaned back against a pillar and lit a cigar, looking
a little sad. Down below, Suzl watched the thing
play out, not understanding the words but totally
understanding them all the same. Her first look at
Matson, alive and well, had told her just what was
coming. She didn't need to know the words, for
she knew the situation and she knew Cass.

*Poor Cassie*, she thought sadly. *All that power, all
that influence, all that force—and it's nothing. Welcome to the real world, Cass. I'm sorry you had to
finally make the trip.*

"Are you finished?" Mervyn asked her.

"I'm only starting," she snapped. "It's the only
thing I *can* do and you know it. I can't live any
other way. I can't kill myself, because I can't violate my vows. But I'll fight no more for you, old
man. I'll make no more pious speeches. I'm no
good to you in any way anymore—no good to
anybody. I'm a priestess, and I will remain one,
even if my faith is weak and I feel like I've been
raped. But I resign my sainthood. The Church and
the empire sink or swim without Sister Kasdi. I've
retired. I will do no more killing for you. Do it
yourself from now on."

"You've paid a big price, Cass," Matson said
finally, "but it hasn't been a waste. The old boy's
right in one thing. We're moving again. Thinking
again. The change I saw in the people during this
business, going through those Anchors, was amazing.
But I can't really talk about this. After all, *I* didn't
have to pay the bill."

Mervyn sighed. "Well, if you will fight no more
for empire, even to protect it, will you fight for
personal reasons?"

"Huh? What do you mean?"

"I came here not just because I received word that you two had met. I came here primarily because the three of you were here. Word has come that Coydt has made his move. He has taken Anchor Logh, and we are powerless to do anything about it."

"What!"

"Somehow—I don't know how, and won't until I get there, I suspect—there is a wizard's shield of tremendous force around the entirety of Anchor Logh. No one has been able to penetrate it. And Coydt and at least fifteen hundred insane killers are inside that shield right now, doing whatever they wish."

# EXPLORATORY MISSION

"Why Anchor Logh?" Kasdi asked them as they studied the situation in the map room. "There are twenty-eight Anchors. Why is it always Anchor Logh?"

"It isn't, really," Mervyn replied. "There have been attacks on many Anchors, and our forces had to fight street-to-street taking some of them. It boils down in this case, I'm afraid, to you again. Coydt is feeling the pressure and he doesn't like it. Obviously he planned this operation carefully with the rest of the Seven. If they can get away with it once, here, they need take not twenty-eight Anchors but only seven to access the gates from within. If they can take, and hold, a single Anchor for a matter of days, or weeks, or whatever, it will show that it can be done. Then they will only have to solve the communications problem to unlock all the gates within the requisite one minute period. Considering the other obstacles, they will solve that one, too."

"So this is their demonstration," she said sourly. "To the others and to me. He knows that all the people I hold dear are there. He knows I will have to come to him."

Mervyn nodded. "Yes. And he'll have you in Anchor, where his might will overwhelm your power. He wants you, too, Matson. He doesn't know who or what you are, but you've cost him the

192

heart of his own personal organization. He'll meet you in Anchor, but on turf he totally controls."

"First," the old stringer commented practically, "we have to figure out how to get the hell in."

It was agreed that Mervyn and Kasdi would fly to Anchor Logh and assess the situation. Others of the Nine and some of the top wizards on the side of the empire were already flocking to the border, and troops had been mobilized and were moving in. Should the shield lift, Anchor Logh would be instantly under a siege more powerful than any force seen since Balacyn.

The whole of Anchor was invisible to those not blessed or cursed with the wizards' Flux power. There was only an indistinct grayness, a solidification of the void into a barrier none could pass.

The big names in wizardry were already there. Here now was Tatalane, the green, elfin wizard only one meter tall with the shell-like ears and piercing emerald eyes. Here, too, was Krupe, the fat, balding wizard who was never far from his wine. Also present were the beautiful wizard MacDonna, all two-hundred-fifteen centimeters of her, with flaming red hair and piercing blue eyes, and the tiny, dark-skinned Kyubioshi, her shaved head and quiet presence making her seem almost a life-sized statue. Five of the Nine, then, were present here, the other four holding back lest this terror be but a diversion for some other less obvious plot.

"The shield is multilayered and extremely thick," Tatalane told them gravely. "This is no work of some major sorcerer; it is most certainly the combined and practiced work of an entire team of enormous power."

Kasdi shook her head in wonder. "But how can they do it? Anchors can't have shields. The magic doesn't work there!"

"The shield isn't *in* Anchor," Krupe explained.

"It's so simple I'm surprised no one ever thought of it before. It is by our measurements exactly five meters into Flux around the entire Anchor boundary."

"It's simple why it was never tried before," Mervyn put in. "Nobody has ever been able to make, let alone sustain, a shield that is roughly three hundred kilometers by one hundred around. I'll hand this to Coydt—he's the first man in the history of World to get so much power to cooperate for so long."

Kasdi stepped back and looked thoughtfully at the shield. "What I want to know is how they expect to get back *out*. They can't sustain this indefinitely."

"I suspect we couldn't stop the wizards," Krupe noted. "The shield doesn't need a top, nor could it have one. It's too high up for us to get over it, of course, but they could pick any point up there at a reasonable altitude and simply fly out. As for the others, it's unknown, but I'm sure they have something planned. If *I* were they, I'd simply have a good stock of uniforms like we use, put up some resistance, then fade and join our own troops. We'd never know if they were good at it. We have too many soldiers to sort them out. We'll work on covering that angle, of course—it'd be a simple matter to vary our own uniforms—but that is not the problem now. We have a battalion and some very good wizards covering the Hellgate in case they want to use the back door, by the way. Pity we can't use it."

"Years ago I could have, with the Soul Rider inside me," Kasdi noted. "But even if we could, only a few could go and there would surely be a nasty reception committee waiting at the other end."

"We could take care of that to a point," Matson said. "Send in a few good concussion and shrapnel bombs ahead of us. It'd clear the corridors and probably blow the power plant as well. Everybody would be equally in the dark. Then come up with automatic fire to establish ourselves. From that point, anybody who knew the temple could probably give 'em a good run for their money—providing they didn't stumble in the dark and kill themselves. I may be wrong, but I don't remember ever seeing a window in one of those things."

"You're right on that," Kasdi told him, "but the dark wouldn't necessarily be a problem. There are some easy spells for adjusting your eyes to the dark. I doubt if many of them would have the same ability, since it makes you oversensitive to light. And they wouldn't have a wizard to correct it, since they'd be in Anchor." She sighed. "But what's the use? We can't get in to begin with."

"Yes, we can," Mervyn replied softly.

She stared at him and immediately guessed what he was thinking. "Oh, no! That is definitely out! In the name of Heaven, she's so with child that it could come at any moment! You've got her and you've got me! Do you want to kill my unborn grandchild as well? What is *enough*?" She turned to Matson. "You can't go along with this!"

He stroked his chin thoughtfully. "I want Coydt in Anchor. If I could get in, I'd go. But Anchor Logh's nothing to me. I'll get him, sooner or later. If there's a way in, I'm going. But I'm not anxious to get at him now at anybody else's expense."

Kasdi turned back to Mervyn. "See? We absolutely forbid it!"

"Kasdi—your father's in there," Mervyn reminded her. "And so are your three sisters, five nephews, and three nieces. Not to mention Cloise and Drunyon, who raised Spirit, and all those other relations, as well as Sister Tamara and the rest of the Church personnel. They may be undergoing unspeakable tortures now."

"Or they might all be dead," she responded, "in which case, what you suggest will wipe out the whole line. Won't the Seven be pleased *then*!"

"We only need her to bypass the Guardian and reach the end of the tunnel," the old wizard reminded her. "Once we're through, she can return. The risk is there, true, but it's relatively small."

"So two or three of us get in. What good will *that* do?"

Matson was considering the problem. "In tactics they call it a beachhead, for reasons I've never understood. It seems to me that the problem's easy to state. We can't break this shield from outside, but we've got to break it. We can't get enough troops in that little hole to fight our way to the walls. But if some good fighters can get into that temple with some knowledge of it and decent weapons, we can secure it long enough to bring some top class wizards through. Then we get out to the countryside. A small number. Make it to a predetermined place on the border. Our wizards and our guns take out those holding that section, and a small part of the shield collapses. We come in and *they* are bottled up, and that's the end of that."

The wizards nodded. All of them were concerned with Flux power and politics; none were truly military people, and none had any real feel for the soldier on the ground with a weapon, although that was who always had to take the ground after they blasted a path. Now it was the opposite problem. Now they needed the soldiers to blast a path to the shield.

"General Hawney had something like that in mind," Krupe told them, "but it might not work. It's entirely possible that the temple part of that passage is so well booby-trapped that no one could survive. And if they did, there aren't very many ways out of that temple."

"If you have the right equipment, you can always make your own exit," Matson replied.

"Yes, and bring every one of the enemy in the capital running to you. Then it would be a cross-country trip with nobody you could be certain was a friend and with the whole pack on your heels. Finally, the wizards' positions just inside Flux will be well protected and well defended, and none of those wizards will be pushovers either. There is simply too much that can go wrong. It's impossible!"

"What other suggestion do you have, Mister Krupe?" Matson asked him. "Wait here until they get tired and come out? Well, I'm here to tell you that they don't *ever* have to come out. You as much as admitted that you can't stop the wizards if they want to get out. The rest of 'em are false wizards, duggers, and Fluxers with no power at all out here to speak of. This here is their own Fluxland, sort of, under their rules. I lived these past years in a place where almost nobody could get out and nobody particularly wanted to."

That was sobering. It had never occurred to them to think of this as a permanent condition, but it would certainly have occurred to Coydt.

"These wizards will never sit still for it indefinitely. They'll want something more," Kasdi argued.

It was Tatalane who spoke now. "True, but whether it is a matter of days or weeks, they can be reinforced and replaced as need be. What is certain is that nothing will stop the Seven from doing this in the next cluster, and then the next, while holding here. They can spare many wizards if we must divide our forces in half, or thirds, or more. The longer they hold out here, the greater that danger will be. And when we are divided enough, and weakened enough, *then* the old order strikes full with its armies. Not just the empire will fall, but civilizations as well. The communications problem, if they have not yet solved it, can then be attacked at leisure. We *must* break this— now!"

Kasdi felt very little love for their empire or even human civilization at that point. But what kind of a world would her grandchild grow up in? Who in fact could stand against such evil totally triumphant?

And yet World was a big place, and there were many places to hide with no real chance of discovery. Flux wizards like she and Suzl could create their own impenetrable Fluxland in the wild north far from Anchor. The Seven would not pursue. Their goal was Anchor.

Their goal was to open the Hellgates.

"Only as far as the vortex," she said at last. "And then only if you can first somehow communicate the problem to her and if she is willing to help."

Getting the situation across to Suzl proved relatively easy in Flux, where images could be conjured up at will. The total lack of meaningful communication with Spirit had been due to the other parts of her spell and her mental state. It was Suzl's job to get that message across, and this she resolutely refused to do.

It wasn't that Suzl was unsympathetic to their plight, only that she had no more ties to Anchor Logh and it was a remote place filled mostly with faceless, nameless people. Kasdi had come home a hero; Suzl had come home half male and half female, had been called names, had been disowned by her own family and friends. The hurt she'd suffered then remained with her for her entire adult life, and she simply could not find it in herself to do for them what, in reverse circumstances, they would never do for her.

Spirit and the baby were a different matter. She

insisted that no action be taken that would endanger them until the child came, and as they had no luck getting the situation over directly to Spirit, they finally had to gnaw and gnash their teeth and do it Suzl's way.

Attempts to break the shield were being made all the time, but so far it had weakened only slightly for short periods of total attack and then firmed up again. Coydt's skillful alliance forged with the Fluxlords had sustained itself over a period far longer than anyone would have guessed, and it showed no signs of abating.

They whiled away the time planning the expedition, knowing that every day's delay meant their chances were slimmer and slimmer. Only Matson, who knew Coydt from the old days, thought otherwise. "The longer time passed, the more secure they'll all feel. If we'd come through that hole right away, we might not have had a chance. Now I'll bet there's maybe two bored guards, both of whom are bein' punished for something."

Nobody knew how many people the Guardian would allow in with a Soul Rider, but it had to be few even for physical reasons, and with equipment and Suzl along at least as far as the vortex, that meant a small group indeed.

Matson would go, but Jomo could not. His great size would make him stand out anywhere, and he was instantly recognizable and certainly on Coydt's shoot-on-sight list. Kasdi would go, although she, too, had many liabilities and no real fighting will. She wanted Coydt in Flux as much as Matson wanted him in Anchor. She would go, she realized, because her family was there, because Matson was going and she could not bear to send him off again, and because she knew both the temple byways and the Anchor better than just about anyone else they had.

Matson chose two tough career soldiers, Captain

Macree and Sergeant Zlidon, because both had fought in campaigns in Anchor. Macree was an explosives expert, and Zlidon was good at organizing and at automatic weapons. Both had been born and raised in Anchor Logh. But Kasdi was the only true wizard—Matson was a false wizard, good only at illusions, convincing though they were. Mervyn forbade any of the Nine from going; the wizards inside would certainly be of lesser caliber, except for Coydt and perhaps one or two others at the gates, and he simply didn't want to risk losing them to a bullet before they even had a chance to use their stuff. They finally found a number of powerful volunteers both from the Sisterhood and from the staffs of the major wizards.

It would be Matson's and the soldiers' job to get them into the temple. It would be Kasdi's job to get them positioned and moving through the temple so that they could command it. Little by little, then, more and more good soldiers would be ferried in a few at a time, and they would fortify the temple against the outside. At the same time, small teams of wizards led by Anchor Logh natives would move out and attempt to reach and breach the wall and the shield.

On the twelfth day everyone held their breath as Spirit delivered a 368.5-gram healthy-looking baby boy. The delivery was not effortless, but it was painless, thanks to the wizard powers of Flux. The child looked quite normal and human in every way, to the relief of all, but didn't really seem to look like either Spirit or Suzl—or Kasdi or Matson. He *was* cute, though, and both grandparents were pleased. As both parents were mute and illiterate, Kasdi, with Matson's shrugging permission, named him Jeffron, a diminutive form of her own father's name, and so it was recorded by Mervyn in the official registers.

Suzl was a bit put off when it turned out to be a

boy. She had so expected a girl that the idea that it might not be hadn't even entered her mind. She was, however, relieved that it was over and that mother and baby were doing fine, and also relieved, as were Mervyn and Kasdi, that the Soul Rider this time had remained with the mother.

"Maybe it only likes or favors women," Kasdi theorized. "How do we know?"

Suzl warmed quickly to the child, however, particularly when she discovered that she could breast-feed as well as Spirit. Duty now called, however, and it was time for her to make good on her end of the bargain.

*How much do you remember of your past?* she asked Spirit. It was sometimes unsettling to discover the lack of frames of reference when talking to the woman who had, after all, grown up normally.

But Spirit had put almost her entire past so far out of her mind that it might as well not exist. What was there was sometimes hard to dig out. With that last visit to Anchor Logh, Spirit, by spell or by psychology, had literally buried all that she had been.

Slowly, Suzl began to draw from her a present state of mind. She could not remember much, and what she *did* remember was impossible to grab hold of or build upon. To Spirit, it seemed, there was only the present, and her practical memory seemed to go back only to the time when she gave Suzl her powers to use. She could not remember life without Suzl, nor could she remember what Suzl had looked like before. She did, however, remember her mother—her real one—as her mother and a kindly, middle-aged man who she seemed to think might have been her father. Suzl recognized the vision as not her father, but her maternal grandfather, who apparently had made quite an impression on her. She did not remember Coydt.

Still, Suzl was able to put across the idea that a

lot of people, perhaps the kindly man, were in trouble from evil others, and that she was needed to guide some rescuers to the place where she had surrendered her powers. She agreed to help, simply by following Suzl's lead and doing what was asked of her, whether or not she understood what she was doing.

Anchor Logh had been in the grip of the enemy for sixteen days when they returned to the Hellgate, hidden behind a shield that had revealed none of its secrets.

Spirit led Suzl, Kasdi, Matson, Zlidon, and Macree down the ladder to the long tube. Jomo took command of the caldera itself, to make sure that nothing went wrong at this end.

Tatalane had come up with a reasonable compromise on the lighting situation, and all now looked slightly inhuman with their eyes adjusted. All now had eyes like those of a cat, eyes that adjusted for any available light and would be fine in all but total darkness. Texture, contrast, and distance ability were all quite good, although the laws of physics, which had to be obeyed for an Anchor situation, had rendered them colorblind, and there was a focusing problem they had to get used to. Either they could see far away or very close up, but not both at the same time.

It was the first time in a fearsome Hellgate for the three men, and the first time in many years for Kasdi, but while there seemed to be a flickering of some bright, ghostly spiderlike thing here and there in the tunnels, they were allowed to progress to the vortex.

Suzl could see the patterns clearly, and it was with some amazement that she realized that Kasdi could not. But the priestess had never forgotten the pattern needed to open that way, and she did not now. Matson reached into a pack on Zlidon's back and removed three small devices, which he proceeded to set. "Now, when I tell you, you open that thing and these three things go through. I don't think they'll be expecting anything. We'll give it a count of twenty, then I'll go through and check to see what else is needed."

"No," Kasdi told him. "I will go. There will still be some Flux power on the emergence spot. You would not be able to draw the pattern and get back in time. I will be able to shield myself."

He stared at her a minute, then nodded. "O.K. In, look around, and back. If all's clear, we all go through. If not, we'll give them a lot worse than these three, then go right in after. You're sure Suzl understands her part?"

"I think so. She's better."

"O.K., as soon as we're in, it's back for the next group. When we get a minimum of a dozen or so, we'll start to move out and explore the place. Now— let's do it!"

Kasdi traced the combination, hoping that the devices would go through without a human attached. As far as she knew, it had never been tried this way. Matson tossed in the devices, and all held their breaths, hoping that they would not hit the wall and bounce back into the chamber. They went through, and Kasdi started counting down from thirty aloud. At "five" she traced the pattern again, and then held her breath and jumped in at "zero." Jeffron, in Spirit's arms, was crying, the sound reverberating up and down the tube. Instantly the sound was cut off and replaced with a far different one.

The room had been sealed except for a trap door at the top. The grenades had blown right through the floor and had also blown the trap door right out, sending it far into the hallway. The bloody bodies of three men, who'd obviously been sitting almost on top of the explosives playing cards, were about in heaps, as were the remains of their deck and their chips. The lights in the immediate area had been blown out, but the generator was still humming at the far end of the hall. She ducked back on the spot and traced the design. Jeffron's cries suddenly picked up where they'd left off.

"Three men dead, big hole!" she shouted over the baby's din. "Lights are smashed, but the power's still on!"

Matson nodded. "Let's go," he said coolly.

She traced the pattern, and they all went in except Suzl and Spirit and the baby, of course. Suzl watched them vanish, then nodded to Spirit and they made their way back along the tunnel. There was a fair number of people to get through yet. After that, she'd sit up with Jomo at the top of the caldera and, with the big dugger, worry herself sick.

They all made it through safely and quickly heaved themselves through the hole in the ceiling. There were some shouts down the corridor, and the sound of a few people running. Somebody yelled, "Get some lights down here!"

They took their postions, and Matson handed Kasdi a semiautomatic rifle that seemed to weigh a ton. She took it anyway, getting a gun belt from Zlidon's pack filled with ready clips. She wasn't much of a shot, and killing this way wasn't exactly her field, but she was prepared to do it.

"Want us to blow the generator?" Macree whispered.

"No," the stringer responded. "Let's see if we can keep it intact. If the power stays on, nobody will come running except those in the temple itself. Maybe we can take it as it is."

"If they don't have five hundred men in here," Zlidon added worriedly.

There were some torches with the fire equipment on each level, and somebody finally thought of them. Two torches flared down the hallway, and after adjusting to the new light, they could see four or five men coming down the hallway. All wore pistols, but none had their pistols drawn. Clearly they were thinking less of an attack than of an accident, which meant they either had relaxed too much or weren't that bright. Either way, it was a break.

They let the newcomers come all the way down, until they actually passed Matson and Macree. They saw the bodies of the three men and the huge hole in the floor, and hands went to their guns—but too late. They were mowed down so easily there wasn't any challenge to it at all.

Matson waited for the noise to abate, then stamped out the torches. They held their breath, listening, but heard nothing more. Finally Matson said, "Dump the bodies down the hole. I don't care if the next group *does* have to climb through them!" He and Macree quickly managed the feat and also threw the dead torches down. "Now let's see who comes looking for *them*," the stringer said.

But another five soldiers were in and there still was no sign of any newcomers. The bodies had given them something of a start, since the instant fear was that those were the bodies of Matson's group, but Matson was able to detect movement and whisper the password before they started throwing nasty explosive things.

When the next five also arrived without incident, Matson began to feel secure. "Cass, you want to go back and give them the situation? I think I'm going to take a small party exploring here."

"Why me? This is *my* temple, remember. I know my way around it better than anyone."

"And you spent several days drilling it into us. You're not a soldier, Cass; you're a wizard. We need you later."

"I'm coming along," she said firmly.

"All right. Soldier—you know the route back.

You don't need the girl to get out. Tell 'em to bring 'em through as quick as possible. We're going to sweep this level, then return and get more people to go up."

And with that, the four who'd been there first started along the corridor. Cass passed the secret passage to the Sister General's quarters and said, "We ought to put somebody on this." Matson nodded, but he had no one to spare right now.

The whole area was mostly filled with old and stored furniture and other such material as they expected to find in the temple. Here and there a rat would scuttle by, and there were a record number of bugs, but no more people. They finally reached the far stairway, and Matson ducked in and listened, then returned. "Don't hear anything, but even if nobody comes to investigate why those guys are missing, somebody's bound to be down to relieve the watch."

They made their way back along the corridor to the waiting soldiers. Now they were twenty-four. He formed a second five-person squad and sent them ahead. "Floor by floor, nice and quiet," he told them. "If that security system is still on, they'll know when you get one floor up. Throw a bomb if you have to, but when you're discovered and can't wipe them out, make enough noise to reach anywhere in the temple. At that point, you men use those explosives there and blow the power plant." He turned back to Kasdi. "Now let's go see who or what's in the Sister General's apartment."

It bothered him, and the rest as well, that it had been so easy so far. Had complacency set in this quickly? "Consider the quality of the material he used," Kasdi noted, but she was only hoping.

They climbed the dusty back stairs of the passageway single-file, rifles at the ready. Carefully, Matson pushed at the panel that opened into the large walk-in closet in the Sister General's bedroom.

Matson listened, peered out, then walked out and into the bedroom, the rest following. He stopped there. The stench in the room was nearly unbearable.

There were five dead women in the room, and none had died a nice or quick death. All had been stripped, tied to objects, then slowly and brutally tortured. Butchered was a better word for it; butchered alive. Blood was everywhere.

One of them had been tied to the bed with some kind of wire, arms and legs bound spread-eagle. The expression frozen on her face was one of unforgettable horror. All of the bodies were in an advanced state of decomposition.

"Oh, Goddess!" Kasdi sobbed. "It's Sister Tamara!" Matson barely recognized the strong-looking woman who'd died so horribly, but he remembered being told that the Sister General here was formerly one of the group from that last, fatal stringer train.

"Leave her!" he said curtly. "I don't want any signs we were here until we're ready to take this place. They may not have ever found out about that secret passage." Kasdi gave him a terrible look, but it left him unmoved. "You wanted to come," he reminded her.

The office had been ransacked, with papers all over the place, pictures torn from the walls, and furniture overturned and smashed. All of the religious objects of any value were gone.

They had blown in the security doors and apparently moved with lightning speed against the helpless women occupants. The walls showed a wavy line of bullet holes at about waist level, so they'd come in shooting.

Macree was thinking. "We're two levels up, right? Then our other team has to be just below us, heading from the front back down this way. Offices on that level, if I remember your diagram, Sister."

She nodded absently, hardly hearing, her face cold and immobile. *Damn Suzl!* she couldn't help thinking. *This might have been prevented if we had moved earlier!* It was an irrational thought; the temple had to have been hit quickly and early, and certainly for the first two days it had been heavily defended, including down below. It might not have been possible before this to get this far. And she, too, had opposed using Spirit earlier. Those things were convenient to forget, for somebody had to be blamed.

The rifle suddenly seemed far lighter than it had, and friendlier. She just wanted to find them. Find them and kill them all.

They went carefully down the stairs and advanced up the hallway, checking each office as they did so. All showed signs of being ransacked and looted and there was much senseless vandalism, but little else. With a shock Kasdi recognized the very room where she'd gotten lost and blundered into the old Sister General fixing the Paring Rite with her priestess lover. The records were still kept there, but all of the equipment was smashed now. Matson, however, made an interesting comment. "This room doesn't have all the papers spread around."

"All the records were on film," she told him.

"Yeah—for everybody in the Anchor. Where's all that film now?"

She saw what he meant. Cabinet after cabinet had been overturned, but all were empty. "Every man, woman, and child living in Anchor Logh or who had ever lived here were in those records," she noted.

"Nice," he commented. "If they have a film reader somewhere, and I suppose they do, they have everything they need. Who owns what, who's married to whom, whose kids are whose, who knows how to run or fix this or that—everything."

"But why?"

"We'll know when we can ask them," he replied.

Shortly they met with the first squad. So far—nothing. Some shot up and badly decomposing bodies were in some of the offices, but nothing alive.

"Send one of your people back and get guard posts set up all along the access to this level," he ordered. "Start wiring explosives all along as well. We'll try the next level the same way."

The next level was a chamber of horrors. Offices and small chapels, even cells, had been used to stack dead bodies, hundreds of them. The smell was sickening, and they could hardly stand it. Some sort of masks would be needed just to clean the level up, and the flies and maggots were well at work. They wanted off that level as quickly as possible, but the next level was the one below the inner temple itself and the street entrance. On the next level were street-level front and rear entrances and exits. Matson backed them off a level. The new soldiers were already establishing themselves, and it looked like they now had a fair force in there. Matson sent them up in squads to the deadly level above, so they would know just what kind of people they were dealing with. The point was well-made.

Progress was going very well, and that worried Matson more than a fight. "It isn't like Coydt to leave his back door open. He knows the rules as well as we do. That opposition barely qualifies as token. The time to stop us was before we got established, not now. I don't like it. We're still bottled up in this one big building, and there's always the possibility he's just waiting to get the most of us with one big bang."

"You mean blow up the temple?" Kasdi was appalled at the idea. "But—that would certainly block the Hellgate for him, too."

"Yeah, and us. We'll have the troops check for it.

If it's here, it's got to be real big or it wouldn't dent a solid joint like this."

They prepared for the assault on the ground level. This time there *was* opposition—a lot of it, but it was disorganized. Men yelled and screamed, explosions went off, and the hallways were criss-crossed in automatic weapons fire. They finally managed to clear the hallways, but then it was room-to-room combat, with Matson's men tossing in explosive grenades as they went. It took the better part of an hour to secure the level, at the cost of twelve dead or seriously wounded. The kicker was when somebody got word below, and the temple was suddenly plunged into darkness. The soldiers with their specially adapted eyes had the run of the place.

Kasdi had fired at the men in the corridors with the others, and although she had a sore hip from bracing the weapon and firing it, she felt much better.

The front and back entrances were well covered. Barricades and even some artillery had been brought up by the invaders, and weapons were trained on the front street-level entrance from temple square. The back exit opened on a narrow street, though, and all they could do was seal off the street and put firepower at both ends.

They examined the remains of some of the rooms on the street level and were surprised to see them pretty much outfitted as rooms with beds. They had taken no chances and gone after anything that moved, and some innocent had been killed with the invaders. They *did* find a few people alive, although none in any condition to talk, and took them back on a series of litters to the gateway and to Flux, where they could be treated and interrogated.

Some of the men had been in a state of undress, and there had been women in the rooms as well.

They turned over and examined the body of one young woman, killed by a grenade. The concussion had done it; her body was definitely lifeless, but seemingly unmarked. She was wearing heavy makeup, had been as heavily perfumed, and was naked from the waist up. From the waist down she wore some sort of fishnet-like pantyhose that concealed nothing and ended at the ankles, and she had on very high-heeled shoes.

"They turned this temple into a combination charnel house and whorehouse," she said disgustedly. "This Coydt is beyond mere insanity. Look—what's that on her behind, there?"

Macree pulled down the fishnetting, which was secured by elastic. "It's a number and a word in purple. It's a tattoo, like they used to have in the old days of the Paring Rite."

It was, in fact, the same sort of tattoo, and after all these years Kasdi could still feel the sting of getting hers in this very temple and remember how she hadn't felt truly free until her own sorcery had wiped it away. "She's too young for that, and that would imply they were bringing in people from Flux. No, the number's wrong. It's not a Paring Rite number. By the angels! It's a registry number!"

"Huh?"

"It's the file system used for the master records in the temple. See? That's the code for native born to Anchor Logh. You wouldn't recognize it because it's strictly temple code and confidential. And under is her name, see? Johbee 19. That would be her riding number in the files."

Matson had gone off, but now he returned and listened to the conversation. Finally he said, "Well, we got over to the gym on the other side. It was pretty well guarded, too, but not inside. We finally have some live prisoners in good shape, but I'm not sure we're gonna get anything useful from them."

They followed him around and through a back hall to the other side where the huge gymnasium was. In the old days, this was where you got processed after being picked and enslaved in the Paring Rite, and now it was what it usually was in any era—a place to play and relax for temple personnel.

It was now filled with bedding and at least a hundred women, all made up and dressed in the same fashion as was Johbee, but these were very much alive. "Bear with me," Matson whispered to Kasdi, then looked over at one of the closest women. "You! Come here!"

The woman smiled and walked very sexily over to him on her high heels. "Yes, sir?"

"What's your name?"

"I am called Tabby, sir."

"Well, Tabby, what is it you do? What's your job?"

"To serve men, sir, and minister to their needs. We live only to serve as the Lord commands us."

He nodded. "Which lord is that?"

"Why, the Lord High God who created World, sir." She spotted Kasdi standing there. "You are dressed in a blasphemous manner, my sister."

Matson turned. "Look around at them. Look at their faces." She looked around, not quite understanding where he was going with this and feeling as sickened by this as she had from the dead bodies below. Suddenly she saw one face and gasped. It was an absolutely beautiful face, attached to a supernaturally gorgeous body. Matson saw Kasdi's reaction and called the woman over. She was so beautiful that it was almost impossible to keep his mind on business, but his job and his discipline won out. "They won't answer to you, so—what's your name, girl?"

She smiled and bowed her head slightly. "I am called Marigail, my lord."

"Sister Marigail! Don't you recognize me?" Kasdi cried out, but in response she only got, "You blaspheme in that rag, old woman."

Matson turned to Kasdi. "Get it? These are all the priestesses in the temple who survived the initial attack. And they still are, in a way. It's just that their definitions have been changed."

Kasdi frowned and shivered. "Drugs?"

"I doubt it. They're too knowledgeable, too alert for that. And, frankly, they're uniformly better built than they should be. Besides, their vows were bound by spell in their minds. Even a drug would have trouble overcoming that. Those spells had to be broken or rewritten."

"Marigail always looked this good, but I see what you mean. Flux, then. But how?"

"Well, as a guess, I'd say they marched each one down to the hole and did it in the Hellgate one at a time. It's a lot weaker, of course, but they didn't need much. A better guess is that they trucked the whole batch out to the Flux apron and had a job done on 'em *en masse* by a wizard in the space between the end of Anchor and the shield."

"It's disgusting!"

He felt a little ashamed of himself, but he had mixed feelings on that looking at Marigail. Still, it worried him. "You see what it means? First they march in and quickly secure each riding as a military district. Then they take the capital and chop up each little bit of resistance. The rest of them, mostly farmers and townspeople with no weapons and no real experience in this, give in and go along for now. Maybe they torture and exhibit the bodies of some of the smart mouths and rebels to give 'em a reminder. That was the first stage, and while it might still be going on in some places, it was probably mostly done in the first ten days. Now, little by little, using the records they got from the temple, they're taking the people out into Flux where they're being remade to order. Pretty soon the first riding's all done, and they can move all their forces to the next. I've seen the pattern used when a young wizard took over an old wizard's Fluxland."

"And they're turning everybody into—this?"

"Not hardly. If they plan to stay, they'll need folks who know how to grow things, how to make things, and so forth. No, you won't have to do it to everybody, just enough to create a real example. The rest of the folks will fall into line and fall all over themselves doing whatever they're told to do. You forget these folks' fear of Flux. They have all the records, too. They can hold husbands, wives, kids' lives over 'em. No, they'll go along because they'll be afraid not to. And the longer the new way stays, the more normal it'll feel. Folks don't like to be different than everybody else, especially when it's not healthy."

The standoff outside continued, with the forces of the invaders sealing off the temple while not firing into it. They could blow the doors, but they'd still have to attack across open areas. Their artillery would do little to break down the tremendously thick and tough material from which the temples were made, a material that had not been duplicated, even in Flux, for there was no way to break off a piece and get it to Flux.

A sweep of the temple got some more prisoners, both transformed priestesses and even a few of the invaders, now rather meek and pretty scared in the dark, not daring to light torches. From them, and from those sent back to Flux, the story of the invasion of Anchor Logh emerged.

# FEASIBILITY STUDY

There had been no warning. The entire thing had been carefully planned out to the last detail, with Coydt directly in charge. It was, he told his followers, a scientific exercise, a "feasibility study" of several new theories and techniques in war and political control, as well as social theories he wished to test out and demonstrate. Most of the men who joined with him didn't really understand or care about all that, and he knew it. He promised them their own private Fluxland, all to themselves, and a safe haven for as long as they wanted it.

Whether he was mad or whether there was true method to it, he told each group he needed what they wanted to hear. He promised the Fluxlords that he would break the back of the Church, pull it back not only from expansion but even from their own domains, and show it demoralized and impotent. Their fears of the Reformation were far greater than their lifelong enmity towards one another. If Coydt could deliver, they did not want to be left out.

There were a bit more than a million people in Anchor Logh, divided into fifty-seven political subdivisions called "ridings," each with a population of about eighteen thousand. This included the concentration around the capital, which was a riding all its own. Firearms, and even bows and arrows, were strictly illegal in Anchor Logh. Almost no one, except perhaps a few stringers and others trapped with the general population, would be armed or have access to arms beyond the rather weak border patrol.

The number of his forces had been underestimated by Mervyn and the rest; they failed to take into account the contributions of population from the participating Fluxlords, which swelled his ranks to perhaps ten thousand. All were extremely well trained and well drilled in secret camps in Flux, and the attack was perfectly planned and timed. At the same moment that soldiers were being introduced into the temple basement in the same manner as Matson and Kasdi had reclaimed it, both gates were hit and specific points in the old wall were blown completely out. Within the first hour, all of the arsenals were taken, and there was only scattered border guard resistance. The shields went up at that point, coordinated by the Fluxlords. The mass of them maintained the shields only for the first few days, though; they were replaced later by something new. They weren't sure exactly what, but they had the idea that the shield was now being maintained by only a token force of powerful wizards and a lot of very strange machines.

The temple was taken in less than two hours, most of that time consumed in getting enough men into it to handle it all without the general population becoming alarmed. Small teams then went after the police, all of whom were unarmed except for "billy clubs" in the Anchor tradition. The small arsenal and almost all the police arms were taken with few shots being fired. All electrical power was cut off.

The forces divided along well thought-out lines, occupying riding centers, while a strong force rode in on the capital from both directions. They quickly took control of the waterworks and major buildings.

There was resistance. A number of invaders were literally beaten to death by an enraged mob that surprised and jumped them, but quick examples had been made, along with assurances. Those who showed any opposition were summarily shot. For every invader killed, ten people were picked at random and mowed down in the temple square. The rest were warned that the next time it would be a hundred for a life. However, everyone was also assured that cooperation and obedience to what were called "martial law liberation forces" would result in the people's homes and families being safe-guarded. There were even apologies made for the brutality, and excuses that it was necessary to avoid greater bloodshed.

Huge numbers of people tried to bolt out of Anchor Logh, but were stopped at the wall or at the shield itself. Again, examples were made.

It took Coydt and his ten thousand less than two days to secure full control over Anchor Logh. Local civil servants cooperated with them, knowing the alternative. All public roads were declared military, and anyone on them without a letter of permission from the local commandant would be tortured and then shot or hung. A dusk-to-dawn curfew was established, not just in the cities and towns but everywhere, and ruthlessly enforced. Within five days, all people of Anchor Logh were required to report to their local churches. There they were matched with records from the temple, churches, and government, were photographed and fingerprinted and given identity cards. They were also, to their indignation, tattooed, with machines not seen since the days of the Paring Rite. Women were tattooed on their left thigh or rump, men on their left arms. Resisters were simply forced to do it. Objectors were taken away and not seen again.

Local watch groups were established through-out the whole of Anchor Logh as a part of the processing. People in positions in every commune, town, and apartment were told that they would be held directly responsible for anything traced to their local area, and all of them were married and most had small children. By the tenth day, enough examples had been made that everyone was afraid to speak of anything but work or the weather.

By the end of the second week, hope for a quick rescue had faded, in some cases into bitterness. An astonishing number of officials and merchants began to cooperate openly, even enthusiastically with the invaders. Also, the new rules were being enforced.

These struck at the very social balance of Anchor Logh and most Anchors. The Church was dissolved as an institution. Priestesses, those who survived, had vanished early in the invasion, but were now back and being paraded out as "ministering angels." Women in supervisory positions were removed, and it became illegal for a man to work for a woman. Women were restricted to their homes and work places only, unless escorted by a man at all times. Worse, women were forbidden to wear anything above the waist, something which caused much embarrassment and much protesting— which was dealt with in the usual manner. Reminders were made that a sufficient amount of Flux remained to remake anybody into anything the new rulers wished, and again examples were made.

Men were only marginally better off. They bore direct responsibility for everything, and they were accountable for it, including a woman in their company mouthing off or protesting. One of the invaders remarked that a man was probably asked for his I.D. four times just going to a public bathroom.

More, and nastier, changes were coming, that was for sure. There were already reports of a riding commandant freeing political prisoners, who were naked and dyed red, into a forest, then hunting them like animals. The killings had slowed to a trickle, as resistance had, but there were tales of torture, Fluxchanging, and other horrors all over. Tales of mass orgies by the occupying troops were rampant, and the ridings nearest the border were reported to be model and faithful citizens of the "New Empire" to a frightening degree. There were rumors that soon an emperor and lesser royalty would be established.

Coydt's hang-ups over women were obvious in the plan and also his methods. He was showing how an Anchor could be taken and totally transformed into something else. He was proving that the kind of control exercised by Fluxlords could be done in Anchor and that the same kind of mad empires could be established there, based on fear and physical power rather than magical abilities. True, he was using Flux, but sparingly and as a weapon. The odds were that the "social" part of his experiment would result in greater absurdities on both men and women, of which the nothing-above-the-waist rule was just a taste. He would, in fact, see just how insane the rules could be that a population not bound by Flux magic would swallow. He was going to push them to the breaking point, and find out if there was one.

The rest of his "feasibility study" was more mechanical. He had machines that could draw upon and use Flux power. Where had he learned how to build them, and how had he done so? These machines were a threat to Flux as well, for they could create an impenetrable shield anywhere, as much bottling up perpetrators as keeping enemies away.

Finally, there was the temple takeover itself. Somehow, Coydt had managed to do the impossible —to walk into a Hellgate and come out unscathed, without aid of a Soul Rider. How? And if *he* could, then why couldn't the others of the Seven? Was communications strictly the problem? Or, in fact, did Coydt feel so secure with his new discoveries that he really didn't want to open those gates after all—and hadn't told the others how he did it?

Coydt was emerging as more and more of an enigma, although a very dangerous one—on the surface, a brutal psychopath who viewed people as things to be used and objects of his curiosity as well as his odd social and sexual hangups; yet below, a coldly brilliant, analytical mind capable of finding out what others could not and understanding and applying principles others hadn't even dreamed of. The two were not necessarily incompatible, and there was the tragedy for World and its people.

The temple was supposed to have been consistently well guarded, but Coydt had been away for more than five days—where, nobody knew—and in that time things had gone lax, as the best officers were concerned with putting all Anchor Logh under their control and the top brains were concerned with Flux and the shield. A good officer had been in command at the temple, but the quality of his troops was low. He had tried to keep them in shape and in line, and had become the early victim of an "accident." Things had been much more fun after that, and that explained the ease of entry. Unfortunately, the military commander of the capital was neither lax nor incompetent. The empire had the temple, but they were totally sealed off.

Matson, Kasdi, and the generals fumed at the standoff, but whatever they tried seemed to fail. The old stringer's glib assurance that they could blow an opening through the temple proved wishful thinking; while there was a thick inner layer of wood and then masonry, the outer walls, of that strange substance, would yield to no power. That left only the three exits, and those were death traps, as attempt after attempt failed. The only thing the empire had accomplished by all this was the denial of electricity to the city. Another maddening week passed, with no way to even get news.

The former priestesses had been passed back to Flux and examined by top wizards. The spells were consistent and insidious, clearly bearing Coydt's personal handiwork. Stripping those spells off, layer by layer, brought them back, but at a great price. The memories, the horrors, of the first day of the invasion and the rape and perversion worked on them would drive most people mad; in addition, all of it had been done against their vows and binding spells—a mental conflict they simply could not resolve. No one had ever discovered a magical way to selectively erase memories. They could be suppressed, of course, but then they still were there and caused problems; or there could be wholesale erasure and replacement, but to bring them back to the point just before the invasion was beyond anyone's power.

The generals began to worry about their backs. There were fifteen other Anchors to guard against a similar invasion, and nobody knew the whereabouts of Coydt or any of the other of the Seven. With at least one Guardian neutralized somehow, the other three Hellgates also had to be defended, and that took powerful wizardry as well as troops. They had a quarter of a million troops and reserves they could count on and about a thousand wizards powerful enough to matter. Concentrated around Anchor Logh and its Hellgate, they were the greatest power on World. Divided up into twenty divisions, each guarding an Anchor or Hellgate in the empire, they amounted to fifty wizards and twelve thousand five hundred soldiers per location. The enemy alone could easily put a hundred thousand soldiers and three hundred top wizards against any one of those locations, and the math, when put in those terms, was pretty grim.

Kasdi, in particular, was amazed at the situation. "How can we have so much power, so much population, so much of World and still be scared of the dark?"

Suzl couldn't follow all the fine points, but all she needed were her eyes to see that things had gone nowhere. She itched to see what the situation in the temple was like, but Spirit was not anxious to enter a building she couldn't get out of. She was aware of Suzl's itch, though, and finally indicated to her that she could stand Suzl's absence if she were careful and not away too long.

Nobody could stop Suzl, of course. She had the combinations and the codes. She traced the pattern as Spirit nervously watched, then stepped through. She had done it before with Spirit to Anchor Nanzee via this same Hellgate, and she knew that transmission was instantaneous, probably at the speed of light. She found the entryway lit and an actual stairway built up to the reinforced floor. There were military emplacements and lots of equipment, and quite a number of uniformed men and women who were less than thrilled to see the nude mute around poking into things.

Suzl had no intention of getting in the way; she'd seen the grim bodies pulled from here back to Flux through the gate, and she had recognized Nadya, who had become Sister Tamara. She had no idea why she thought she could do anything, but just sitting around that big hole was driving her nuts.

She spent the better part of an hour just exploring the place and saw nothing she didn't expect. They did not let her near the doors, of course, but she was pretty sure that anybody who peeked out of those would peek no more. Finally, she walked back down, thinking about it all and trying to find a way around the problem. She knew she was

kidding herself that she could come up with something the pros could not, and even if she did, she
might never be able to get the plan across, but she
had to try.

She walked back down the steps to the place
now sketched in chalk and stepped on it, but she
didn't trace the pattern right away. Instead, she
drew in the weaker Flux power emanating from it
and tried to find out where it went. She had no
idea why she thought of this, but it seemed an
interesting line of thought. *Let's see,* she thought.
*From the vortex to the entry gate, and from the entry
gate to here.* No, that wasn't quite right. There was
a tremendous amount of energy going *in* from the
vortex and an incredibly weak amount coming out
at this end. One of the immutable laws everybody
knew in both Anchor and Flux was that there was
just so much of everything, and that energy and
matter might be transformed, even into each other,
but not created where there wasn't any—or destroyed. Where was the extra power going?

Well, she didn't know much about electricity,
but she knew that such power needed a transformer to make it weak enough to use in the capital by the electrical generators. She looked down,
found signs of the flow going *past* the entry port
and coming up just over from it. The stone and
cement filler had buried both the point at which
that energy came out and the transformer or other
device used to capture it, but the thick cables
emerged and then were routed through the floor
to the power plant that took up most of the rest of
the basement. The power flow going through that
cable was very different from the pure Flux power,
but she could still follow it and sense its amount.
It was more than that which existed at the trans-
fer gate, but the total was still only a small fraction of what was going in.

She cast mentally down to the original flooring

and below it, trying to find the actual entry point for the pure power of the vortex. It wasn't difficult to sense, nor the point at which it divided—perhaps through some sort of transformer built into the temple structure itself? There was the gate, and there was the electrical power line—no, it couldn't be. The line did not come from the junction point as the gate's did; it came from someplace else, someplace even further down. *Down!* That's where most of the power was going! That's why it hadn't really been noticed before. She tried to follow it with her mind, seeing as a wizard saw, and suddenly found herself suspended in darkness.

There was no up, no down, no forward or back. No light at all showed anywhere, nor in fact were there any of the sensations—no sound, touch, smell, taste—nothing.

But she was not alone.

Something touched her mind, something at once very frightening and very powerful; yet it seemed more curious than threatening. For a moment she feared that she'd gone the wrong way and touched those in Hell itself, but she was powerless to do anything about it. Little probes seemed to tingle all over her mind, unlocking memories and sensations long dormant or unused, and she knew that whatever it was, it was finding all it needed to know, but she had no way to talk to it or to even ask any questions. She had the distinct impression that it could not have answered her if she'd had that ability. This was something new, something totally alien.

Suddenly there was a blaze of light, and she knew she was back in the temple once again, yet not quite a part of it. She seemed to float above the floor and was not conscious of having any physical form at all, but that seemed irrelevant as she had no control over her movements anyway. She entered the generating system and flowed with it forward, until she *was* the electrical system of the entire temple. Power had been restored inside when experts had figured out a way to decouple the temple's power from the city's, and everywhere that energy flowed Suzl was, sensing all of the great building and its contents at one time. Despite being very frightened by it all, she still thought the whole thing was neat.

In one room, Cass was sound asleep over a bunch of papers. There was one of the temple intercoms nearby, and suddenly it began to buzz irritatingly, awakening the sleeper. She reached up groggily and flipped the switch. "Yes?"

"Exactly this time tomorrow night I will turn off the sector known as Temple Square," said an eerie, electronic voice that was somehow still familiar. "This condition can be tolerated for only one minute exactly or the structure of Anchor itself will be endangered."

"Who are you?" Kasdi shouted back, flipping the switch. "Who is this?"

"This sector condition will resemble what you call the void, but it will not be. It will be raw energy. All in the square will have to be suspended, and I will retain control. Because of the intricacy of the action, I can sustain no more than four of you. Move from this center straight forward until you reach Anchor as quickly as possible, for when sector stability is restored, all will be as it was, but none in the square will be aware that any time at all has passed. This is the best I can do without endangering the lives of everyone in my district."

The voice was strange, oddly distorted, but she suddenly realized why it was familiar. "Suzl?" she asked wonderingly.

"The remote operative, which you call the Soul Rider, will be needed to fully act against the shield. It must be along. Destroy any one of the devices or its operator to create a necessary thinness. The

translator will give you the necessary formulae.
Remember, exactly this time tomorrow on my
mark."

She frantically flipped the switch over to "talk."

"Wait! Tell me who or what you are!"

"My mark is—*now.* Farewell." And the intercom
went dead.

Suzl found herself withdrawing from the omni-
science of the temple as if she were water flowing
down a drain. She had understood every word
said in both directions, but she hadn't uttered any
of them.

The creature, or whatever it was, withdrew, and
suddenly she found herself standing back on the
chalked-in gate once again. She looked down at
herself and saw that she *glowed* with a faint energy.
She frowned and went back over to the stairs. Her
body crackled when it walked, but it was undeni-
ably hers again and it tingled, or itched, like crazy.
She touched the metal handrail and got a real
shock that stunned her and flung her back. "Yow!
Damn it!" she screamed in pain, bringing several
of the soldiers running.

"It's the mute," one of them called. "Something
happened. I thought she was long gone."

"Mute, my ass!" Suzl screamed back, then sat
up, feeling numb. Suddenly she looked up at them
and frowned. "Hey! I can talk again! How *about*
that! Hot damn!" She paused a moment. "I need a
drink and a good cigar."

The message had been heard through all the
intercoms in the temple, although only Kasdi's
could talk back, and it wasn't until she had answered that it had spoken. A fair number of higher-
ups, including Matson, had already gathered in
the refurbished gym to discuss it when Suzl was
brought in.

She told them her story, sparing nothing. "I

don't know what it was," she concluded, "but, damn it, Cass, it *lives* in here. I think it always has. It lives down deep, under the temple. Hmmm . . . Do you think I just had a religious experience?"

"Not you," Kasdi assured her. "We've already sent for Mervyn and some of the other experts. Let's try and sort it out."

The old wizard was totally fascinated by the account. "The best I can guess, and it's only a guess, is that you are the first person to meet the Guardian face to face, as it were, and survive."

"I almost didn't. That was a *hell* of a shock," Suzl grumped.

Using a lot of witnesses, they put the message back together and were reasonably satisfied that they had it right. Fortunately, the military mind being what it was, quite a number of people had checked the exact time on their chronometers at the "mark" statement. All but three of them said 2209. That was sufficient to order those three to check their chronographs.

"This fits with what I saw in the tunnel," Suzl told them. "This and the other three Anchors are nothing more than Fluxlands stabilized by that gadget down there instead of by a wizard's mind. You figure this Guardian is the mind behind it?"

Mervyn shook his head negatively. "I seriously doubt if a being like you describe would build a machine. *Use* one, perhaps, but not build one. You know, this brings back memories of Kasdi years ago. She was turned into a bird and imprisoned in this very temple, and she somehow got out and was transformed into a Flux creature with Flux powers. Remember?"

Kasdi nodded. "I remember nothing from being turned into that bird until I emerged as that flyer."

"I suspect our Guardian was responsible there as well. It fits. We will have a lot of work ahead to consider all the implications of this."

"But now is not the time for that," Matson put in. "At 2209 tomorrow, this thing claims it'll sort of turn off the whole square and all that firepower. Four of us will have exactly one minute to dash across to the other side and then be on our own. If we can believe it, the forces out there won't know anything happened. Do you think we can trust that?"

Mervyn nodded. "We have no reason not to. And, of course, if it doesn't happen, nobody has to make the dash. The real problem is who must make it. The Soul Rider would be necessary to neutralize Coydt's machines, the thing said. Suzl, you know what that means."

"Hey! Spirit would be screwed in this kind of set-up! And we got a month-old baby!"

"Nevertheless, she must come. And so must you. You are obviously the translator it spoke about. Can you still remember the language Spirit and the Soul Rider use?"

She thought a moment, then mentally shifted gears, using the linking spell as a guide—and found she couldn't speak or understand the rest of them again. She thought consciously and hard and willed herself "back"—and suddenly she could understand the comments once again. "Yeah. But it's total. One or the other, not both at once."

"It is sufficient. The Soul Rider knows the complex spells needed to punch the hole, but obviously must first see what it's up against to devise them. It will then feed them to you and any other wizards along, and you will use them."

She shrugged. "I'm game, but, damn it, Spirit will never go for it. And what's gonna happen the first time she stands up in plain view to follow a butterfly, even if she did?"

"You must convince her—and keep her under control. Otherwise, we must give this place, and eventually this world, over to Coydt and the others."

"*She-it,*" Suzl grumbled.

\*    \*    \*

Suzl had no choice in convincing Spirit but to trust to the Soul Rider. She took Spirit off where they could be alone, leaving little Jeffron with a nurse, and after the predictable failure to really explain the situation to her, she sat back and decided that what worked accidentally for the Guardian might work for the Soul Rider as well. Both were certainly kin, and both were apparently living, thinking creatures of pure energy, as hard as that was to grasp. They were not the same, certainly, but both could communicate with humans and understand them far better than humans could communicate with them.

She tried sending the story, the impressions, of her experience using what she called "Spirit language" to the Soul Rider through the linking spell, but didn't seem to get anywhere. Finally she decided on a last measure, and together they walked into the Hellgate, which Suzl had requested be cleared temporarily of any traffic.

Bathed in the flow of massive energy emerging from the vortex, Suzl took hold of Spirit and fed that energy into the both of them. No one else could do this, she'd found, but the Spirit language was the key to it all. Suzl executed the spell that the Soul Rider had sent her that first day, the one she knew would have the desired result. She metamorphosized, changed back into what she had been, a creature of gross deformity, but a creature with what was necessary.

Emotion was the key, and intense emotion was the medium. Strong, overriding emotions blocked rational thought, concentrated all on one specific to the exclusion of all others, and, if strong enough, they blocked thought altogether while maintaining a direction—like love, or passion, or whatever focused the participants excusively on each other. Hate was also an equally strong focus, as were the other emotions taken to extreme. This, however, was the easiest and the most pleasurable route.

They joined physically, but also, thanks to the language, amplified by the proximity to the direct full flow of the gate vortex, they joined mentally as well on all the levels it was possible to join. The Soul Rider understood, and used that, as Suzl had hoped it would.

And then another joined them there in the Hellgate itself, a creature that looked as if it were an unbearable ball of light out of which fiery tentacles of pure, crackling energy whirled. The two humans did not see, nor were they now permitted to.

For all its history, which was the history of World, the Soul Rider had seen a Guardian only once before, when, riding the body of Cass, it had been plucked from imprisonment in Anchor by the creature. At the time it had acted but had not communicated. Now it reached out again, hoping against hope not only for communication but also to discover if this creature were the unknown source of its directives and commands.

*"You have failed, remote,"* the Guardian sent. *"The fall of Anchor is the worst of all sins."*

The Soul Rider felt elation at the communication, coupled with disappointment that the creature was certainly not its unseen master, unless in total disguise.

*"My mission is to seek out those who would open the Gates and destroy them,"* the Rider responded. *"I would assume the safety of Anchor was your responsibility."*

*"No, only its stability, a condition I am now commanded to jeopardize."*

*"You allowed one of the Seven to pass into Anchor. Had you not, this might not be necessary,"* the Rider pointed out.

*"The one you mention knows the pass codes as you do. I was without power to stop him. Where and*

*from whom he learned this I do not know, but he is one of great power."*

*"He is in the employ of Hell. I am charged to stop him."*

*"Then you must allow the host to pass to Anchor."*

*"Her mind is not like other human minds,"* the Rider pointed out. *"The same one I now seek has put her somewhat beyond my reach."*

*"Then I will render the matrix inoperable. My jurisdiction is entirely within this chamber and Anchor, so it will be inoperable only so long as she is within my sphere of influence. Should she pass out of it, the matrix will be restored as permanently as before."*

*"That will help, but it will not undo the damage to her mind."*

*"You have been with her since she was made operational. I am willing to aid you in common goals, remote, but I will not do your job for you, nor can I."*

*"I will do what I can,"* the Soul Rider promised, *"but you have given me very little time."*

*"If it is not sufficient, you are defective and should be replaced. There. It is undone. I leave you now to your own task."*

*"Wait!"* the Soul Rider cried out. *"Remain a moment! Tell me what you are, and what I am, and who commands the both of us!"*

*"We are not supposed to know,"* the Guardian replied, and faded out.

The Soul Rider, feeling the press of time, went to work. It couldn't help but note and appreciate the Guardian's methods. The binding spell was still there, but it was diverted from her by a thin addition that linked it, somehow, to that great machine over to one side. The machine took in the power from the vortex and changed and split it, stabilizing the four Anchors and, in fact, the Hellgate itself. So long as Spirit remained in areas under the control of that machine, the spell would be drawn off, diverted to it and rendered harmless. It was a tenuous thread, however. Once back in Flux, the small link would be broken, and it would take the Guardian again to restore it. Somehow it doubted that the creature who operated the machine would be so inclined.

Because the Soul Rider had lived inside Spirit since birth, it had its own duplicate set of memories and impressions. These could be read back in, but selectively, and subtly altered. It did not wish to withdraw the power from Suzl, as Suzl was clearly better temperamentally suited to it and would continue to have a direct link with the language of the Soul Rider itself. Spirit, then, must remain with Suzl, and Suzl needed to retain her own personal anchor. That meant fabricating a set of false memories and impressions that would take Spirit logically to the emotional, passionate love and commitment to Suzl and away from her heterosexual base. It was rather easy to do to someone you had already made fall in love with the same person anyway and made keep that love when that person had become a grossly distorted creature.

It was also necessary, and only fair, to convey the ground rules as much as possible to both of them. That was far more difficult. It longed for the Guardian's powers of communication, but had to content itself with what it had. The Guardian, after all, had never experienced the joys and pains of living human lives as had the Soul Rider. On balance, it decided that the Guardian was more deprived.

It was done now, as much as it could be done, and the Soul Rider was content. Minor adjustments could be made, but only slightly out of Flux. It would have to do.

It allowed Suzl to awaken first, but time was running on.

# SHATTERED HOME

Suzl sat in the tunnel and tried to sort it all out. Certainly her scheme had worked, but the information she seemed to have from somewhere was a little unnerving. She could see the tiny diversionary spell trailing off from Spirit to the machine, and that confirmed the truth of what she knew.

When Spirit woke up, she would be free of the spell—so long as she went to Anchor Logh and remained there. Only Suzl would retain the machine language ability; Spirit would be back among the humans once again, and that worried Suzl no end. How would Spirit feel? Towards her and everything else? Quickly Suzl changed back to her human form.

Spirit moaned, rolled over, and opened her eyes. For a moment she seemed unable to focus or even grasp where she was, and she looked puzzled. Then she sat up, looked over at Suzl, and shook her head slowly. "What a strange, strange dream," she rasped, and the shock of hearing her speak, of hearing her voice for the first time, was great, even though Suzl had expected it. "My throat hurts."

"If you feel up to it, we can go into Anchor and get you some water and some clothes," Suzl responded hesitantly.

She shook her head slightly from side to side. "No, darling, just let me sort it all out first."

Suzl felt an electric shock. *Darling!* She reached out for a small spell, got it, and materialized a

233

canteen of water, which she handed to Spirit, who took it and swallowed cautiously.

Slowly, everything came out. Spirit seemed to remember her past pretty well, even after Coydt put the spell on her, but after she saw her family in Anchor Logh that last time, things seemed to get fuzzy and less distinct. She remembered feeling lost, alone, confused—adrift, somehow, until Suzl had gone away with her. Every moment after that seemed to focus on Suzl—and the baby. She had no real sense of time or events beyond her personal, basic experiences, nor did she quite understand why she was back—and how.

Somehow, in her memories of earlier times in Anchor, she seemed to believe that she always found women attractive, but had fought and suppressed the tendency, perhaps overcompensating for fear of what family and friends might think. "I don't care what anybody thinks anymore, though. I love you, and I'd tell all of World."

Together they went back into Anchor, where they caused as much commotion and excitement as Suzl had, perhaps more. The obvious romantic bond between the tall, lovely young woman and the short, chubby Suzl put many people off now that both were "normal," although they hadn't even thought about it in Flux with all the spells. Several things emerged, though, that were certainly different from the Spirit known of old. She deferred almost entirely to Suzl, who was clearly the dominant personality in the relationship, and she seemed rather shy and very passive. She did, however, seem to clearly enjoy being part of human culture once again, to be able to talk and be understood, and, most of all, to understand and use common objects. She seemed deathly afraid that this period of renewed normalcy would abruptly end.

She wanted to see her baby, and they brought

the child through to her in the temple. With the child, however, came Sister Kasdi, who wasn't quite sure how to react to all this. On the one hand, she wanted desperately to talk, for the first time in their lives, as mother and daughter. On the other, the relationship between Spirit and Suzl made her feel almost ill. When Spirit and Kasdi finally faced each other, there seemed nothing really to say. Kasdi just stood there for a while, staring at her.

Matson entered, looked at Spirit, and grinned. "Welcome back to the almost-living," he said good-naturedly. "I'm your dad."

That took a lot of explaining as well, with Suzl acting as intermediary as best she could. No family reunion on World had ever had such confusion and hostility mixed together. Matson, sensing this the most, got down to business. "Suzl has explained to you what's going on?"

Spirit nodded. "I think so. The same evil that got me now has all of Anchor Logh."

He nodded. "I know we're asking a lot, but we need you. The odds are it'll be very dangerous, and the odds are against us ever really doing what needs to be done, but we have to try. No matter what you think of me or your mother, it's got to be tried."

Spirit looked down at little Jeffron, sound asleep in her lap. "I understand. I have to be honest, too. I want to stay here and look after our son. I don't want to go, and I hate the idea of all the death and destruction, but of course I'll go with you. Suzl tells me that if I leave Anchor, I'll go back to being like I was—probably for good. I can't raise him in a fortress. And out there are all the other people I really care about, all at the mercy of that madman. I have no choice. I can walk back out and become what I was, or I can go with you and try and end it all. Of course we'll go."

They found shirts, pants, and shoes for the two
women, but while the clothing was all right, if
itchy and somewhat abrasive, the shoes proved
impossible. Both had been barefoot too long, and
it was decided that they didn't have the time to
get used to shoes again. Nurses and provisions,
should they not return, for little Jeffron were found
or fixed, and Suzl, Spirit, and even Kasdi had
their hair cut very short so it would not get in the
way. Spirit refused all weapons, but did take on a
pack as large as the one Matson was going to
wear. Matson, too, clipped on his old stringer's
bullwhip and sawed-off shotgun to his belt, while
Kasdi and Suzl, whose builds were unsuited for
packs, still managed two ammunition belts, strapped
X-shaped across their chests, and small, effective
semiautomatic rifles. They managed to find Kasdi
a black stringer-like uniform to replace her tattered robe, and her spell, which compensated for
necessity in the interest of others, accepted it.

Matson looked her over. "You know, if you'd put
on a little weight and exercised a little, you'd look
almost like you did eighteen years ago," he noted.

She smiled, thrilled at the compliment, although
she knew she looked old and tired. Matson didn't
know, and could never know, the sheer torture she
had been undergoing the past month. She was as
insanely, passionately in love with him now as she
had ever been, and she wanted him desperately.
Just to be near him was agony, all the more so
because she knew that he *would* give her at least
physical release if she asked him—but she couldn't
ask him, nor accept his offer if he were to make
one. She had always had an extremely low voice
for a woman and somewhat mannish features and
mannerisms, so much so that those who knew her
in the old days would not have been surprised if
*she* had taken up with a Suzl, but those were
surface items only. She was very much a heterosex-

ual woman in love with a strong, handsome man, and yet her mannishness intensified and her voice, if anything, seemed even deeper, with all traces of femininity in her vanishing as things had gone on.

It was the binding spell, of course, forcing her to do and be just the opposite of what she so desperately wanted to do and be. The trouble was, while she could turn off Matson, she could hardly turn off herself.

Finally, they were ready, and with very little time to spare. The forces outside would be stationed in two equal groups outside the shield. Normally, a shield was supported from a single center point which represented the wizard. This shield, however, was enormous, and supported at least partially by machines, and so there were a number of power points identifiable from outside. Assuming these had to be machine locations, they picked two about fifty kilometers apart along the northern border. This would allow them the luxury of a choice of targets, while still keeping the empire's forces close enough to support one another and shift positions as necessary. Suzl and Matson knew the city and countryside the least—it had been a long time since they'd been in Anchor Logh, and things had changed, even there—but Suzl was a tough veteran of Flux, and Matson was an expert at military affairs. It was agreed that it would be Matson's game until they reached the Flux. Wizards tended to forget what it was like not to have or depend on the magic.

"You've been briefed on what it's likely to be like out there?" Matson asked Spirit.

She nodded. "I have met our Mr. Coydt before. I'm sure I can't imagine the surprises his mind has come up with."

Matson returned the nod. "What's he like these days? He was always the real nervy man's man, anything for a thrill, the riskier the better. And he always got away with it."

"Still that way the last I saw him," she replied. "I just can't imagine how someone so handsome and so brilliant can become so evil."

"Word always was that something happened back in his childhood. Something that warped him sexually, although he has quite a reputation with some of the ladies and he's certainly no man-lover. He's always been a cold-blooded killer and a sadistic wizard, but he has the odd reputation, too, for always keeping his word. If he promises something, he'll always deliver, whether good or bad. We never knew how he got into some of the Anchors, but he always liked Anchors better than Flux. Flux was too easy for him. No thrill, no risk. He liked to gamble on cards and was pretty good in the joints, but he was as good a loser as he was a winner. I doubt if anybody's ever figured Coydt out, but if anybody ever did, he'd probably kill 'em." He looked at his chronograph. "Whoops! Ready, everybody! One minute!"

Kasdi had been standing there, going slowly mad. It wasn't from what they were going to attempt so much as it was her emotions, and not just for Matson. For the first time she was with her daughter as herself, with no blinders and no spells and no other funny stuff, and she hadn't been able to find any kind of break or opening at all. She felt as sealed off from Spirit as she did from Matson.

All that was pushed into the background now, though, as the timers ticked down. They were going out the front street-level entrance, to avoid having to run down those interminable steps, and they were going right into the face of a machine gun battery and light artillery aimed straight at them.

Matson went to the door. "At minus two I'm going to throw it open. If it doesn't take, be prepared to duck and scatter fast. If it's go, then you, soldier, better slam this door behind us, and fast."

He looked again at his watch. "Minus ten . . . nine . . . eight . . . seven . . . six . . . five . . . four . . . three . . . *two!* . . ." The door came open, and almost immediately the machine guns began to open up.

And stopped.

Outside, very suddenly, was nothing but a gray fog. It wasn't even the void—it was *nothing.* "Go!" Matson shouted, and they all took off on the run into the blankness, running as fast as they could straight ahead. The surface under their feet seemed hard, almost like rock or cement, but there were no signs of anything at all around them.

The total distance they had to traverse in the minute was a little short of eighty-four meters, a considerable run. Spirit kept hold of Suzl's hand and literally yanked her along. Kasdi and Matson lagged behind, she feeling the strain the worst, although she'd done a spell in Flux to strengthen her legs. Matson was in good shape, but he was quickly being reminded by his lungs and his muscles that he was not a young man.

The square re-exploded into life around them, with machine guns rattling in back of them, but even though Kasdi and Matson hadn't quite reached cover, it was a dark night, and there were no lights in the buildings and no electric lights in the square, which was still without power. There were no observers in the rear part of the square either—all attention was focused on the temple.

They went down a street that led to the main shopping district and ducked into an alley, where they found Spirit and Suzl waiting. Matson began coughing and braced himself against the wall for a moment, while Kasdi joined a collapsed Suzl in gasping for breath. Spirit was hardly breathing heavily, and she'd run with a full pack.

Before the rest felt themselves ready, they prepared to move, knowing that the curfew was on, that it was shoot on sight, and that their only chance was to clear the capital and make it to open country as quickly as possible. From this point, they were in Matson's hands, and they followed his lead, moving down darkened streets pressed against buildings, crossing from deep shadow to deep shadow.

At one point they stopped next to a large poster, and Kasdi took the opportunity to read it.

"PROCLAMATION #10562, MILITARY GOVERNMENT OF THE FREE KINGDOM OF ANCHOR LOGH," it read. "1. All girls between the age of puberty and the age of 45 shall henceforth be considered indecent unless they appear in public wearing proper makeup, including but not limited to lipstick, rouge, eye shadow, nail polish, body scent, etc.

"2. Proper attire in public shall include jewelry, such as necklaces, earrings, bracelets, pendants, etc., and shoes with heels of at least 7.5 cm.

"3. Proper attire outside of home, farm, commune, etc. for all girls shall consist only of clothing secured from and approved by the Kingdom.

"4. As no handbags or other carryables are permitted, nor the possession or use of cash or commodities for trade (see Proclamations #3126 and 4164), all employers and public places shall have available such items as might be needed for girls to continue to comply with this proclamation on a request basis.

"This regulation will take effect at the end of the curfew on 08-22-02 and will be strictly enforced. Physical punishment is authorized on the spot for all violators."

Suzl, who'd snuck in and read it as well, gave a low whistle. "Well, I guess we're all immoral now. Aren't we, *girls?*"

"That is the most incredible thing I have ever read," Kasdi added disgustedly. "That date was three days ago."

"Well, that's Coydt all right," Matson told them. "Still, there's even a method in this shit. There must be a lot of ex-priestesses and the like around who know all the facts and where to cause the most trouble. This keeps 'em all bottled up."

They kept snaking their way through the city, often dodging mounted patrols and occasional foot patrolman and having several close calls. The city was well patrolled, but it was not absolute. All of the police/soldiers carried small automatic weapons, though. They would take no chances, that was for sure, and an occasional distant or even nearby burst of gunfire punctuated that point.

There were also some fixed positions on the rooftops, but these were less of a problem once the quartet discovered they were there. It was harder and more nerve-wracking to move through the shadows with the knowledge that any sound might trigger a blast from above, but it was easy to avoid being seen. Cutting the electricity to the city had been the best idea they'd had.

Finally they made it to the edge, only to find that a tall wire fence, with what looked like cowbells all along the top, had been erected around the whole town. It was simple and clever. Suzl looked at it glumly and asked, "What'll we do now? It'll be light in an hour or so."

"We dig," Matson replied, getting a small shovel out of Spirit's pack. "We dig fast."

After the top layer was gingerly removed, it proved relatively easy in the moist earth. Matson was largest, so he tried it first, barely slipping under. Suzl was next, and actually jiggled the fence slightly, but no one came running. Next came Kasdi, and then Spirit found she had to deepen the hole a bit to push the packs through. Finally, she, too, was under, just as the sky was starting to lighten.

They decided against the roads and took a cross-country route through pastureland designed more to keep cows and horses in than people out. The area just southeast of the city was heavily wooded, and they headed there as fast as possible. Once in the relative safety of the trees, they relaxed as day broke gray and gloomy.

"Unless you women want to put on high heels and sexy panties, I'd say we rest all day," Matson said. "I don't much like stopping this close to town, since somebody's gonna find that hole, but I don't see any choice. At least right now there's nothing to trace that hole to us."

Spirit thought for a moment. "We could go down towards the farm. I think I can get us there without taking us out of the woods, and it'll give us a clear view of the road."

"Let's do it, then," he decided. "But slow and easy."

This country just south of the capital was where all three women had grown up. It was not quite as easy as they'd expected, for they ran into countless nasty little booby traps and trip alarms planted in the woods, and Spirit got caught in a snare net and was left hanging there until the others climbed up and freed her. Matson was adamant that they not cut her free, and after she was out he reset the trap very professionally.

"These traps mean they run regular patrols through these woods," he warned them. "We'll have to be on guard every moment."

Finally, though, before midday, they made it to the thick grove overlooking the road which had been the start of both Kasdi's and Spirit's lives, as well as providing a view out to the main road about a kilometer away.

Matson unclipped his binoculars and studied the

scene. "Well, we know that some of the men aren't getting off too well either," he said softly. "See those poles set up along the edge of the farm road and the main one? They've got bodies stuck on 'em. Men's bodies."

"Oh, Goddess! My father!" Kasdi gasped, and reached for the glasses.

"You won't tell anything from this distance about 'em," Matson assured her. "Even up close they'd be pretty tough to identify now. They've been there for some time, I think."

"Those vermin!" she hissed. "When we get through with them and I have the survivors in Flux, the living will envy the dead! Those men will find out what us 'girls' can do when *we* have all the power!"

"Take it easy," Matson cautioned her. "Remember, *I'm* a man, and so's your dad, your grandson, and all those poor devils out there."

She sighed. "You're right, of course. But if this is an example of the male ego in charge, I want none of it."

"Let's get some sleep," Matson suggested. "I'll take first watch, and anybody who snores even a peep gets second."

Even at a distance and through binoculars, watching the new order go by proved to be quite an education. The main road was regularly patrolled at randomly timed intervals, although the longest gap was under fifteen minutes. There was, however, little other traffic, and all of the common folks seemed to be either walking or in open wagons. Only a few women were glimpsed on the road, always bare from the waist up, always walking a step or two behind a man.

More sights, sounds, and smells were closer at hand. The smell of cooked food wafting into their hideout was maddening as they munched their concentrated rations, but crews checked and replenished the cow troughs in the same old way, and there were sounds of work from the smithy and of horses being exercised in the corral. Every once in a while people could be seen walking between the farm buildings as well. This was strictly the livestock side, so it was far less populated than the administrative area several kilometers west, and farmers working in cultivated fields were also elsewhere. From the few closeups they saw, it appeared that men were being required to wear hats outside, for some reason, and all seemed to be growing beards.

"I have to know about my parents," Spirit told them. "I have to tell them that I'm whole again and see that they're not on posts somewhere."

Kasdi felt a jealous pang, considering both her real parents were there, but she understood, too. Matson tried hard to talk her out of it, but on this she wouldn't budge. Finally he said, "All right, but not all of us. If anything happens, we most likely won't be able to pull you out of there, and the less they know of who and how many we are, the better it'll be."

"I'll go," Kasdi said. "Alone. I'll deliver your message, Spirit, and give you a complete report. But there's no use in risking two when one will go, and right now I'm the most expendable of the bunch."

There was some argument, but finally it was agreed. Matson cautioned her again that they would leave on the first sound of trouble, and added, "We're southwest. Let's agree that if nothing happens on this journey to blow our cover, we head for the nearest one. If anybody gets separated, any time, for any reason, we'll rendezvous at the closest place of concealment near the secondary target. Got it?"

They nodded, and Kasdi kissed them all and

left. It felt very odd to be an armed individual
sneaking into such a familiar and friendly place
with the knowledge that discovery might mean
death, but she took nothing and no one for granted.
Darkness had fallen but the cloud cover had not
lifted, so there was an extra measure of darkness
for her, although a slight and slippery drizzle had
also begun.

A mounted patrolman turned off the main road
and came down all the way to the buildings
themselves. He was pretty relaxed, and he rode
past the blacksmith's and right past Kasdi, stopping near the large cow barn. A figure there greeted
the patrolman and walked out of the barn carrying a rifle. They talked and exchanged a few laughing comments, and then the patrolman turned on
his horse and rode back. Kasdi was grateful for
him; she would have missed the man in the barn
without him.

Keeping to the shadows, she made her way to
the apartment complex, a structure of cubes on
top of cubes, each slightly offset from the row
below, where those who worked on this side of the
farm lived. She thanked heaven that Cloise and
Dannon lived on the ground level. She stopped,
facing the building while still hidden, and saw
lights inside just about every apartment. It was
particularly bright because, it seemed, they had
had to take their front curtains down allowing
anyone to peer inside at least the living room. She
could see people moving about, although most
seemed to have abandoned the living room as a
usual place for very obvious reasons. It was a good
thing, she thought, that the one-room studios were
on the top—the sixth—level.

She saw no one, but did an extra-careful check,
even tossing a few stones in different directions to
see if there was any reaction. There was not, and
she decided to chance it, although she hated being

illuminated so well. Perhaps, she thought, my looks
will get me confused for a man in the dark. It
didn't matter. If she was going, she had to go now,
and there was no back door.

She approached the steps to the porch from the
side and ducked low beneath the open windows.
Finally she reached the familiar door and stood,
peering in the window. She knocked softly, and in
a moment Cloise came and opened the door. When
she saw who it was, she gasped, pulled Kasdi inside,
and shut the door fast. "Quick! Into the back bedroom before the patrolman sees you!" she hissed,
and they went back.

Once there, they both relaxed a bit, although
Cloise looked nervous. More than nervous. Also
pretty odd in full makeup, ring-type earrings, bare
to the waist, and below it wearing a very tight-
fitting green body stocking that was see-through
close-up.

"What are you *doing* here?" Cloise wanted to
know.

"Delivering the mail, mostly," Kasdi told her.
"Boy! You look like one of the women on Main
Street minus the bra."

"It's easy when everybody has to do it. They
confiscated all our clothes and issued new ones.
You don't know what it's *like*. You *can't!*"

"I got an idea from some of the people we cap-
tured and some of the proclamations we read."

"We?"

She nodded. "Spirit's here. And she's well. She
can speak and wear clothes and is almost back to
normal." She decided not to mention Suzl. It might
be one shock too many for the poor woman.

Cloise sat down in a chair. "Well, thank somebody for that! But I wish it were anyplace but
here." She paused a moment. "Uh—you know about
your father?"

Kasdi's stomach did a turn. "No. Tell me. I have to know."

"When they . . . came . . . not everybody just sat back. Your father and a number of others formed a group, jumped some of them, and stole their weapons. It didn't do any good. They got them all pretty quickly and made examples out of them."

Her heart sank. "Then one of those bodies out there is . . . him?"

She nodded, and named a long string of other men's names, many familiar. Her fury, which she didn't think could get worse, grew, but she remained calm. "Where's Dannon, or is he . . . ?"

"Oh, no. In fact, he's been promoted to chief mechanic. He has special permission to be out late on the farm to check on things. You had better be gone when he gets back."

She frowned. "You sound like you're cooperating with these butchers."

"A fat lot you understand the situation! They have complete control. The government officials they didn't kill or who didn't see it their way were taken off and came back in uniforms as dedicated soldiers of the Kingdom. The enforcers carry a kind of whip that is terribly painful and hurts for days but doesn't leave a mark on you. They use it for the least infraction. But they reward cooperation handsomely. Everything is tightly rationed, but those who cooperate get more. People are seeing the light. They're going along."

"But—*you*? And *Dannon*?"

"Who are you to judge us? You brought this on Anchor Logh, but you don't have to live with it. They've started classes now, separate ones for men and women. It's a fast question and answer, and hesitation can cost you the lash. Pretty soon you realize that the only way to always answer correctly is to start thinking their way. It doesn't take long, and it's *easier* that way."

Kasdi was appalled. This soon? This close? She was more than happy now that Spirit had not come.

"You're going to cause trouble here, aren't you?" Cloise asked her.

"We hope more than trouble. There's a whole army waiting for the door to be unlocked."

"Kasdi—don't. Haven't you hurt Anchor Logh enough?"

"What do you mean?"

"First the war, then Spirit, then this takeover. We're peaceful people. We can't stand another war, Kasdi. Particularly not of this kind. These men will fight to the last and will take us with them. You may win, but you'll kill us all. If you just knocked out that guard out there—you didn't, did you?—ten of us in this complex would be picked at random and shot. I don't know how you got in, but please go the same way and quickly. I'll not report this, even though Dannon would be tortured for it if they find out."

"You would rather live with women reduced to slaves? Live out your whole life this way or worse?"

"Rather do it than what? Mass killing? Mass destruction? Total devastation? Yes! And you'll find that almost all of Anchor Logh will agree with me. They won't aid your army—they'll fight it. We all want to *live*." Cloise suddenly looked very tired. "Please don't bring in your army. Things are levelling out now, easing up. People are getting used to the new ways. You destroyed so many lives. Don't destroy us all. Now—go!"

Cloise went into the living room and pretended to be straightening up. She then turned out the light, as if she were going to bed, to allow Kasdi some exit darkness. As she slipped out of the door, she heard Cloise whisper, "Don't come back, Kasdi."

The drizzle had turned into a chilly rain, which matched her dark mood.

The others were still waiting for her, and as briefly as she could, she filled them in on the conversation as well.

"I can't believe they would do it!" Spirit responded. "I just can't believe it!" She wanted to go down there, but Suzl believed it and dissuaded her.

Matson thought things over a moment. "Trouble is, she's probably right. This is a new angle, folks. One we better think about before going further. These guys have done a lot of meanness here. Cass, you yourself said what would happen to them when you got hold of them. They know it, too. In the time it takes us to march, they'll blow the buildings, burn the fields and forests, and machine-gun all the people they can. And while we're trying to pick up the pieces, the bulk of 'em will drop all shields and run like hell in all directions. They got no other choice. And Coydt wouldn't care if he did make this place a burnt-out ruin. That alone would collapse the empire, and you know it, and it would maybe take the Church with it."

Kasdi wished she hadn't vowed never to curse. "I don't care about the empire *or* the Church. They're not mine. The real rulers just used me all these years. I thought I grew up when I found that out, but I was wrong. I just grew up now. I'm forced to make a choice between wiping out perhaps a million people and the land of my birth, or leaving it to an insane system where women are slaves and all men are like they're in the army." She looked strickenly at Matson, Suzl, and Spirit in turn. "What do I do?"

# DEMON PRINCE

*when* Coydt had kidnapped Spirit from the farm and made away with her into Flux in under five hours. Unfortunately, that meant he knew all the best getaways and had compensated for them. With individual horse use also restricted to specific farm use except for officials, even stealing four horses would only have raised a sign telling everyone where they were. So, two hours after Kasdi's return, they were still threading their way southwest through the woods. On foot, through well-patrolled and booby-trapped country on a rainy night, the one thing they were not making was time. They did, however, continue to agonize over the choice they had not yet been forced to face.

"My feeling is, Coydt's won no matter how it turns out," Matson said as they made their way over rough, rocky ground about twelve kilometers from their destination. "By relegating women to property and forcing them into accepting public humiliation, he's totally undercut the social and moral fabric that was supposedly divine law and broken the heart of the faith. Now, if we don't invade, he and his apparently very smart officers here will have this new system so well dug-in that they can make it a base and demonstration for every half-baked crackpot with a grudge against the system as a better way of doing things back home. He'll control the shield machines, and so he'll control them as well."

"Then they must be crushed regardless of the cost? Is that what you're saying?" Kasdi asked him.

"That's the trouble. If we manage to punch a hole from this side and establish our beachhead, they'll have plenty of time before we can overrun the place from such a small entry. These officers and men are committed. There's nothing for them in Flux. They'll fight to the last man, just like your cousin said they would. They'll burn the fields and the forests and blow up the buildings. They'll machine-gun the population, if only to make it tougher on us. It won't be easy going either, since faced with total destruction, the people of Anchor Logh will fight us, too. And if we win, along with enormous casualties we'll inherit a ruined and brunt-out land with maybe sixty to seventy percent of its people dead. Coydt won't care. He and his wizards will be long gone to do it somewhere else and leave the horror of Anchor Logh for everybody to look at as a warning. He wins."

"But we can't leave them to this insane system," Suzl protested. "I mean, women suppressed and owned by man, while the men are all sort of like in the army, expected to obey every order no matter how nutty. It's a horror."

"Nevertheless, if this Cloise is typical—and from what we've seen so far sneaking around, it looks like she is—these people would rather live under a tyrant than lose their land and children and their very lives. People always were that way in Flux; I don't understand why it's such a shock to see it in Anchor, where folks are, pardon me, even more naive. That's why we haven't even been able to risk any contact at all. Most of them would turn us in in a minute."

"Then you would leave them to this?" Kasdi asked, appalled.

"In quarantine. The knowledge of what happened

here must be limited to a very few. Nobody will
believe Coydt's claims; they'll be dismissed as out-
rageous and unbelievable. The empire will invent
a good excuse for the quarantine. Empires are good
at getting people to swallow what they want. But
you won't get a quarantine with Coydt and the
wizards running the show."

"Huh? I'm losing where you're going."

"I know this place is being run like the heads
should all be locked up as crazy, and that's probably true. But if you sat back, you'd see that all
systems are crazy, some just slightly more crazy
than others. In the empire, old or new, for example,
the sexes are still divided. Men and women don't
dress for utility; they dress in totally different
clothes. Oh, the underwear's different because
different places need to be supported, but why
dresses for one and not the other? Why is a lot of
makeup terrible on a man but flattering on a
woman? Why are women well qualified for government and administration prevented from going into
those areas? Why are men who are sincerely religious and want to serve through the Church forbidden to do so? Why does a woman, to have real
power and authority, have to give up sex and
property? Why does society consider the man the
primary bread winner under the law, even if his
wife earns more? To an outsider, it's *all* insane."

"And you're an outsider," Suzl remarked dryly.

"Yes," he agreed. "I am. Men and women dress
alike for utility in the guild. Position, power,
prestige, money—they're all based on your own
intelligence, quick wit, and talents, and nobody
cares whether you're male or female on the job. In
stringing, everybody's equal until *they* prove *themselves* different."

"And you have to be born into that guild and
have the sight to see the strings," Suzl retorted.
"What works for a small, inbred family monopoly

wouldn't be practical on a big scale. It gets too complicated too quickly. You still need the power to really get anywhere, too."

"I have very little power and I rode string for fifteen years," he pointed out. "Power doesn't mean that you're smarter or quicker or cleverer than the one without it. It's true, though, that anybody who struck at one stringer would bring all the stringers and stringer wizards down on them—if that strike were in the line of duty. We look after our own."

"You've got something cooking in that brain of yours about this problem," Kasdi said. "Let's hear it completely."

"We have to break this, or it's good-bye to everything we know. World will be in continual revolution, and deaths will be massive, while the new systems the new rulers will cook up will make this one or a Fluxland look tame. We're looking at the breakdown of society all over the planet here. Hell even with the gates closed. That's why the stringers themselves participate in putting down these kind of things. So it has to be stopped, to prevent its spread. But you can't invade and wipe it out, because you'll also destroy an Anchor and its people and have all the other Anchors selfishly closing up and going into self-defense, and so you lose your empire anyway. So we deal. We punch our hole, establish our beachhead, and stop. We deal with the bosses here. They will be allowed to keep what they have and run it the way they want, but they will be technically within the empire. Everybody stays out, and they stay in, but their sovereignty is assured. They'll go for it. They'll fight to the death if we invade—remember, Cass, what you said you'd do to them? But they don't want to die. They'll buy it."

"That's easy for you to say. You're a man," Suzl noted. "Spirit can't go back to Flux. Are you suggesting we apply for our tattoos and tights and find ourselves a good man to own us?"

"No, but you're not that limited if I understood you right. There are four Anchors in the cluster, and it applies to all of them. Go back through the gate, but don't enter Flux; go out to one of the other three."

"I'm interested in this," Kasdi put in. "What sort of terms do you think they'd accept?"

"Anything that guarantees their safety and positions. We'll still dictate the other terms. We want those machines and we want control of them. The empire itself will keep them going. We will also control the temple as a garrison to protect the Hellgate access, but won't otherwise interfere. Experts from all over, all of them approved by empire security, will study what happens here."

"And Coydt will go for this?" Spirit asked, joining in herself.

He shook his head. "No. Co-opting this revolution here will be the one thing he won't buy. Nor will the other wizards, but they're only being held together by Coydt. To make it work, Coydt is going to have to be eliminated permanently."

"Then we must face Coydt *before* we open the shield," Kasdi said. "How do you propose to do that? Nobody even knows where he is."

"Oh, he's here, someplace. I can feel him. Smell him. His odor permeates Anchor Logh. How we're going to draw him out, though, is the real problem. I—"

Suddenly all were frozen as the sounds of many horsemen approached. Soldiers on horseback, carrying torches, seemed suddenly everywhere around them, officers and noncoms shouting instructions.

"Free ride's over," Matson whispered. "Looks like they know we're here. We're going to have to fight our way through from this point."

"Remember," they heard an officer shout, "no

firing unless fired upon! We want them alive if possible!" They were spreading out forward, and the foursome could hear the sounds of more coming on foot through the woods in back.

Matson thought furiously as the human net formed. "We're going to have to split in two sections. One will bulldoze its way through with all it's got, drawing the rest. Then the other can slip through the hole."

Suzl looked over at him. "Who takes the heat?"

"Cass and I will. It's more important to get that Soul Rider to the border than either of us, but we'll have a chance, too. Don't you fire at all unless you're seen and in danger of being taken. Give us half a minute after the shooting starts, then break for the best route."

The two women nodded grimly but said nothing. Matson looked at Cass, who unshouldered her weapon, and they slipped off to the left and were soon lost to the woods.

As soon as they were well away of the others, Matson looked to pick his spot. He saw it and almost didn't believe it. There were two mounted officers and four troopers walking in, all nicely illuminated by small burning torches that sizzled as the light rain hit. He looked at Kasdi. "You take the ones on foot; I'll take the two horsemen. As soon as everybody falls, you run like hell through that opening. If those horses don't bolt, we'll take them, too."

She nodded and readied her weapon. She felt only the normal tension; she had faced down great wizards in their own lairs many times. The only difference this time was that she really *wanted* to shoot some of those men, wanted to see them die, for the first time in her life.

"Now!" Matson shouted, and both stood and opened fire on their respective targets. Matson shot high, the force of the slugs knocking the two mounted men off their horses. The horses neighed and bolted forward a bit, but seemed confused and didn't run off. Kasdi opened up on the four infantrymen, and they seemed to simply fold and collapse like pricked balloons as more than sixty large caliber slugs fanned out in their direction in the space of less than a second.

And then they were running towards the horses. Both were experienced riders and mounted almost simultaneously; they were away as the others were just reacting to the sounds of the shooting. Scattered shots were fired after them, but they were wild and not in large numbers. The soldiers were unsure if their orders not to kill except in self-defense applied here, and most opted to chase rather than shoot.

After the firing began, the men nearest Suzl and Spirit turned and began to run towards the spot where everything was happening. They took the opportunity and ran out and across to the next grouping of trees, then continued to thread their way along the edge of the woods. Men were yelling and running about, some shooting wildly, and more horsemen roared into the gap and began shouting orders. Four horsemen took off after the already vanished pair, but at least one of the officers was taking no chances and started fanning out the infantry up and down the opposite side of the woods. Foot soldiers began to go into the woods where Spirit and Suzl were, forcing them deeper into the extremely dark and damp vegetation. The soldiers were coming in fast, and they began to run.

Suddenly Spirit tripped on a vine and went sprawling. Suzl, behind her, avoided the vine and ran to help her up. She started to get up, then grimaced in pain. "I've twisted the ankle, damn it!"

"Then get down in the brush!" Suzl hissed. "I'll try and lead them away and circle back!"

She started off again, but did not go far before stopping and checking. It had been a vain hope anyway that they would overrun Spirit, and she saw a bunch of grim-faced men pointing rifles down at the woman.

"You in the woods!" somebody shouted. "You have five seconds to come back here unarmed, hands in the air, or I'll shoot your pretty friend through the head here and now."

Suzl quickly tried to assess her chances of shooting all of them, but realized that with Spirit's ankle it would just bring the rest down on them firing to kill. She removed her rifle and let it drop, then shouted, "All right! Don't shoot! I'm coming out!"

They were taken back, manacled, to the communal farm of their birth, but to the other side where the administration building was, and then they were taken inside. A doctor or some kind of medic gave Spirit a shot in her lower calf that numbed it below, allowing her to walk on it with great difficulty. It was only a mild sprain, though, not a break, and they weren't very concerned by it.

Once in the building, they were taken separately into a small room where a man in the mud-brown uniform of the conquerors checked their faces and prints against a film reader record. Then they were stripped, given showers, and taken into another room where Suzl found a device she hadn't seen in almost nineteen years. Then, having been chosen for the Paring Rite, she'd been seated in a chair much like that one—perhaps that very one, from the look of it—and a technician had dialed in something on a small control panel just like now. The tattooing hurt more this time; she wasn't drugged now.

She was ordered to stand and they examined it. She could see in a full-length mirror what they'd done, and it was very large. A long number, her temple registration most likely, and underneath, SUZLETTE-C-04. Area C, Riding 4—here.

She was then issued a pair of skimpy underwear, what looked to be a pair of thin, brown pantyhose so transparent the tattoo was easily read through them, and a pair of ridiculous-looking sandal-like shoes with thick heels easily fifteen centimeters high. Then they pierced her ears and actually soldered large rings to close the earrings permanently. She would later discover that whatever man "claimed" her would attach two small charms that would bear his I.D. on one and his rank in society on the other. She felt like she was back in the Paring Rite for real.

Suzl was not one to go along meekly with things, but she was a streetwise survivor who could count the odds. There was simply no purpose to do or say anything antagonistic at this point. Waiting for an opening was the first guiding principle in the survivor's handbook.

Finally they took her to one of the smaller rooms on the top floor of the administration building. Records and valuables had always been stored here, on the theory that it was difficult for a thief to make six stories of a sheer building. As a result, there were barred gates at both the fifth and sixth floor stairwells which required different keys, and the only windows were high-up slits, not large enough to let a bird through but just enough for ventilation. Lighting was by gas from an external tank, so it was quite bright in the hallway. Finally they reached a door, unlocked it, and told her to go inside.

The room surprised her. There was a comfortable real bed and clean bedding, a pillow, a table and chair with a large vanity mirror, and a pull-out portable potty. The guard asked, "Can you read, girl?"

She swallowed hard and resisted the put-down response she wanted to make. "Yes, sir."

"There is a manual of rules and regulations over there. Read them through. An interrogator will be here tomorrow. Failure to comply with any of the regulations will be painfully punished." And, with that, he closed and locked the door.

Suzl had never put much stock in makeup or other fancy stuff, and she was so out of practice that she might as well have never used them at all. Still, she examined the vanity and began reading the manual. It was worse than she'd imagined, and it contained not only the basic regulations but also the theory of this new kingdom.

She had called it a military state, and it was one in fact. The leaders of Anchor Logh, it seemed, were all former military men both from Anchor and Flux. There was much about the value of "perfect discipline" and "natural order and superiority" in it. In Flux, nature determined who had the power and how much one had. In Anchor, it argued, nature had been perverted by the growth of the Church. The argument seemed to run something like: men were on the average larger and stronger than women, and were the sexual aggressors. Women on the average were weaker and smaller, but were specifically designed for sexual pleasure and for child-bearing and rearing, something men could not do. Therefore, Anchor nature determined that men should dominate, and their job was to protect and provide for women and children. The woman, being basically passive and maternal, had created a culture through the Church which was basically passive, and therefore stagnant, and had tended to treat all citizens as children. They were restoring a male aggressive society based on natural power and natural sexual roles, as they saw it.

This, then, was Coydt's basic outlook on society and the sexes, and he had chosen his administrators well for their experience and compatibility with his views.

The state, which would be the most powerful men around with a will to rule, owned everything. The ranking of men in society was quasi-military, with a series of "grades" going from "OO" for basic unskilled labor to "50" which was, of course, the head of state. Life would be grim for the lower grades, even the men, who were expected to think as little as possible and follow orders to the letter. All necessities, including food, were rationed and the amount of your ration depended on rank, from food to living quarters. Polygamy was allowed, again based on rank, and unattached women were basically cared for by the state and regularly put on "parade," as it was called, where men could come, look them over, and "claim" them. Women who were unclaimed for a long period or who failed to "socially adjust to nature," were taken to Flux and "readjusted" there for a "useful social role." She had seen the former temple priestesses and guessed what that phrase meant.

They fed her a good, hot meal about an hour later in the cell, and she wolfed it down appreciatively. It was the best meal she'd had in quite some time. Then she settled back on the bed and tried not to think about the future. She could only wonder where Spirit was, who'd never undergone anything like this before, and whether Cass and Matson were punching through the wall or dead in some lonely grove of trees.

After breakfast in the morning, they brought in a woman dressed in a bright green version of what Suzl had been given, bare from the waist up, but wearing lots of makeup and jewelry. "I am Jerane," she said, "and I have been asked to prepare you for the interrogation." Suzl noted that Jerane had little tags on her earrings.

The preparation consisted partly of doing Suzl's hair, teaching her makeup, and an interminable session walking up and down the hall in those shoes. Suzl found the shoes an amazing fit, considering how long she'd gone barefoot, and also found the art of walking on heels came back rather fast. She had always used boots with heels on the trail to increase her height. What she didn't like were the critiques, and she was ready to blow up if she heard "Wiggle, don't waddle" one more time.

Still, when she looked at herself in the mirror, she was amazed at the difference. She really *was* kind of cute and sexy, she decided.

Jerane was something of a mine of information as well. The killing had all but stopped, except for the major offenses you'd expect. Rape, however, was no longer a crime if the woman was unaccompanied by a man. The bodies were being taken down and buried; the economy was starting to improve again, and the rules were no longer being changed every day. The invaders were settling in, marrying local women, and actually helping in the clean-up and spruce-up work that had to be done. People knew who was what now, and they were memorizing posted chains of command.

On the dark side, all education for women had ceased. Block captains, who were local residents and not invaders—she used the term "liberators"— checked daily to see that each dwelling and work place, inside and out, was cared for. They were quite strict, and the wives of workers at various places were brought in as a team to clean and polish everything there as well. For those women who just couldn't be "re-educated" properly, there was, in addition to the lash, a new device worn like a necklace. Patrolmen all had little boxes that could activate them. If you were close to them, say no more than two meters, they would deliver an agonizingly painful shock that would do no real damage. It had done wonders, she said.

Yes, virtually everyone she knew now accepted the system. It was dangerous to voice any negative comments, since anyone could turn you in for extra ration coupons, but negative comments were fewer and fewer these days. Jerane had been an inventory clerk on the farm, but was now a housewife and part-time cleaner for the administration building, and she was trying desperately to get pregnant. Suzl asked her whether she missed her job and career and was told, "It is no longer relevant to my life or future. I no longer have any real pressure, and I have the time and the duty to have children. For a while I resented it, but accepting it and living it is just so much *easier.*"

It was always easier not to think but to obey, Suzl thought glumly. At first she'd been repulsed by the woman's meek acceptance, but then she'd thought of her own life. Kicked as a slave into Flux by the Paring Rite, she hadn't even tried to resist. She'd lucked into freedom on Cass's coattails, but it was an illusory freedom. As a dugger with no Flux power, she'd done nothing but take orders and compromise all those years. Ravi seemed the ultimate compromise, considering what he wanted from her for protecting her.

Of course, she'd kidded herself that it was nothing personal; there were two kinds of people in Flux, those with the power and those without, and she'd been one of the "withouts" through no choice of her own. Now she had Flux power, but no real knowledge of how to use it, and here she was in Anchor, a woman in a society that decreed that women were the ones "without." She seemed destined to always be in the right place on the wrong side.

Sooner or later there *had* to be a way out, a way to escape, but, until then, she decided that it was

Ravi time once more and she had to be a good little girl.

The interrogator, who identified himself as Captain Weiz, was a young, handsome man with striking blond hair and beard. She walked into the interrogation room wiggling, not waddling, and he smiled, got up, and offered her a chair.

"We need to know the answers to some questions," he told her. "Are you willing to cooperate?"

"As much as I can, sir," she responded.

He nodded, liking having his ideology reinforced. "Now, you came in from Flux. We know that. Did you exit through the temple?"

She nodded. There was no use denying it now. "Yes, sir. There was a one-time condition that was induced to let us pass."

"How many people emerged?"

She considered that but knew that hesitation was loss. "Three. Myself, Spirit, and Cass." None of them had ever seen Matson, and there was a slight chance they didn't know about him. It was a chance worth taking.

Weiz nodded. "This 'Cass' is also known as Sister Kasdi?"

She nodded again. "Yes, sir. But we grew up together and I never could think of her any other way except as Cass."

"I see. And what was your objective?"

"Several, sir. First, if possible, we were to destroy whatever or whoever was maintaining the shield in any one spot and create an opening. Second, we were to get out and report on conditions here. Finally, if the opportunity arose, we were to find and kill Coydt van Haaz."

Weiz seemed pleased with the answers. "You are the same Suzl who was once a somewhat male dugger in Flux?"

She nodded. "Yes, sir. It was a curse that finally got lifted."

"You prefer being female, then?"

Loaded question in this rulebook! "Yes, sir, I do. That's why, when it was finally learned how to dissolve the curse, I opted for my current form."

"And what would you wish for your future life?"

Another loaded one! The fellow was good at his job. "Sir, I would be lying if I didn't say I would rather return to Flux."

"And if that was impossible?"

"Then I would accept life here, sir. I'm a survivor. I had no power in Flux, so I went by others' rules. This is no different. I would only like to be near enough to Spirit to see her regularly. We are very close."

"Spirit was claimed by her legal father this morning, as is his right. He has been promoted to Chief Riding Mechanic in Trobovar, near the east gate, and they left immediately. Would it shock you to know that her parents are the ones who told us about you?"

"I kind of figured that out, sir."

"They don't *want* a hole punched in the shield," he told her. "Not even our critics in Anchor wish that. It would be the end of us all, and everyone knows it and believes it because it is true. I say this because I want you to know that there's no help for you here now and no help in the future. If you adapt to this life, there are rewards. Enough of Flux is ours so that the *best* citizens, male or female, need never grow old or lose their looks. If you live by the rules, punishment won't exist and only rewards will flow. You adjusted to Flux; you must adjust here."

She nodded, herself finding the logic easy and seductive. She wondered, though, what they would do with the excess population—or was that the Fluxlords' payment? They went through lives like water and had lost their endless supply with the ending of the Paring Rite. Their power had been weakening from slow attrition. It made sense.

For the next few days she underwent "re-education" and it was no fun at all. Again, the methods were simple but seductive. They would have you do things, memorize things, then surprise you with all sorts of unexpected situations. If you hesitated, gave the wrong answer, or didn't do it exactly right, you got a shock from the little collar. In an amazingly short time, you found it much easier to go along with it and found your mind concentrating only on what you were expected to do or say in any given circumstance. She knew that if it went on for too long, even a few weeks, she would be doing it so automatically that it would be impossible to resist. She'd seen the technique in Flux, but never thought it could be applied to Anchor.

The sessions were long and punctuated by uneven breaks. Food and sleep periods did not come with any regularity, and it was quickly easy to lose all track of time. She knew they were giving her hormones or something in her food; she felt constantly turned on, and her breasts gave milk, and she was ready for anything, man or woman. Hopes for rescue faded with time, and thinking of Spirit and the baby only made it worse.

She was awakened and told to "prepare herself," and so she washed, got herself done up right, and dressed, then reported to the main office. She was no longer even surprised at herself for ogling men and checking out their asses. She'd always swung both ways, depending on the person, and would always have hopes of eventually reuniting with Spirit, but she was always the practical survivor, too, always adaptable to whatever conditions came along.

She was surprised to see Captain Weiz waiting.

She approached him and stood silently, waiting for him to speak.

"You've made excellent progress, Suzlette," he told her. They insisted on full names, and she'd decided it made sense to use it for this new personality to keep confusion down, although she'd never used it before.

"Thank you, sir," she responded.

"A question I forgot before. Just which point in the shield were you to attack?"

"The one nearest Lamoine, sir, if separated," she heard herself replying without thinking. It took that to realize how far they'd taken her.

He reached into his pocket and took out two small charms and reached up and clipped them so they hung from their circular earrings. "Let us go back to your room," he said, and they walked back, she keeping deferentially slightly behind him.

When they got there, he closed the door and smiled. "I have just claimed you, Suzlette. What do you think of that?"

She was shocked. "I'm honored, sir."

He put her through all her paces, including the sexual. She was very, very horny and so was very, very good. It helped that he was attractive, but it was remarkably easy. You just turned off your mind. . . .

Nor, in fact, was he that bad either.

They relaxed after, and she felt very good, even though a back corner of her mind said that she should not. Clearly, linking spells did not work in Anchor.

"I was attracted to you from the start," he told her. "I was in Flux, too, most of my life. Most of the women here are terribly inexperienced. We can go far together, you know. You can supplement and help me with my job."

She began to grow suspicious. This was for a purpose.

"Get dressed and come with me now. We're going to take a long ride up to Lamoine."

He had an open surrey on order and drove it himself. It was a bright, pleasant day, and quite warm, and it felt good to be outdoors once more. He didn't take a direct route but a number of back roads, stopping often in small towns and at farms. He seemed genuinely affectionate, and she played the servile game, all the time wondering what this was about. Clearly, he was showing her off conspicuously, but that might be to show her conversion. Everybody would know who she was.

They reached the small farming village of Lamoine in about four leisurely hours. The wall, and Flux, was only a kilometer away, but trees had been cleverly planted to block the view of it from the town. He made all the courtesy calls in town, and she was beginning to get used to being called Suzlette Weiz and even identified herself once as Madame Hamir Weiz. She was taken to a small kitchen and told to prepare a good picnic dinner for two. This surprised her even more, but she did as instructed.

She had found the whole experience and the day rather educational. She found herself critiquing other women's hair and makeup, and found herself feeling quite comfortable looking and acting as she was—which was how all the other women in town were acting. It was a vaguely disquieting feeling. As the woman had said, it was so *easy* to conform.

They rode out past the trees and the wall came into view, a huge stone structure that looked impenetrable, although it was never more than a psychological joke to ones wanting to sneak in and out. A wooden superstructure had been built and the road had been extended to it. A bevy of armed guards and a machine gun outpost were set up there. The shield, not the wall, sealed them in, and they were there not to protect the wall but that machine that sustained the shield.

They ate in the shadow of the wall—a very nice picnic lunch, which she served. During the whole time Weiz had talked about inconsequentials, even some of his past, but never about what this was all about. Now, all packed up, he said, "Walk with me to the wall. I want to show you something."

She followed him, and they mounted the stairs to the top. The defensive positions, which looked both in and out, were formidable in appearance. She reflected, though, that if anybody could get close enough to the wall and had the arm for it, it wouldn't take more than two big grenades to wipe the post out. As a good wife, she kept her opinion to herself.

She looked out at the apron, fairly short in this area, and to the void beyond. Usually the scene was a total sameness, but not now. Out there, so close to Anchor it could be dimly made out, was . . . something. She stared at it and frowned.

"The machine you and your friends sought to destroy," Weiz told her, seeing her fascination. "Come. Walk down the other side and we will take a look at it. As you can see, it is still very much intact."

They walked out onto the apron and across the area bounding Flux and Anchor. It was odd to be going into Flux, and her wizard's senses switched on in an instant.

The machine was basically a cube, with an operator's cab on one side. It had never been moved here; it had obviously been built, or more likely created, in Flux.

"It is an amplifier," Weiz told her. "It magnifies the power of the wizard in the chair a thousand-fold." She saw the enormous Flux energy flowing into it on all sides and saw, too, the massive concentration that radiated outward from it.

Another figure, a man, walked up to them. She turned and looked at him and knew him in an instant. That handsome face, those bulging muscles, that light, gray-tinged hair and beard she had seen only once, other than in pictures and accounts, but she knew who it was.

"Suzlette, Meet Prince Coydt," Weiz said amiably.

Prince of Darkness, Prince of Evil. Demon Prince. What did you say to such a man as this?

"Hello, sir," she managed.

# SHADOW PLAY

Coydt van Haaz stood there dressed in a loose
flannel shirt, blue denim work pants, and boots; a
slight smile played on his face. "You may go now,
Captain. Remain on the wall. I may need you later."

Weiz looked nervous, but he responded crisply,
"Yes, sir," and departed, leaving Coydt and Suzl
alone in Flux. She stared at him, feeling the
tremendous energy inside him and also real fear
inside her.

"The captain really *is* fond of you," Coydt told
her. "He's quite smitten, in fact. What about you?
Is he the idea you had of the kind of men who took
this Anchor?"

"No," she responded, adding "sir" almost as an
afterthought. "I *do* like him."

"That's nice. One wizard to another, open, honest.
I like that."

"I'm no wizard," she responded.

"How very astute of you to realize that. One
without power in Flux is a victim who finds a way
to survive, to accommodate to power. But one
with Flux power who has no knowledge or training in its use is in far greater danger from a real
wizard, for only those with the power can take the
binding spell."

She nodded slightly but did not respond. All she
could think of was that he was going to do something awful to her and she needed to buy time, any
kind of time, if only to think of something to do.

"Take me, for example. Did you ever wonder how I wound up this way? What colored my attitudes, drove me on?"

"I've often wondered how anyone could wind up like you."

"It was over four hundred years ago, in a place very much like that one back there," Coydt began. "I was pretty wild as a kid, the youngest of eleven and always out to prove myself. Even then I liked the thrill of things, the danger, the risks. I'd take any bet, and, of course, boys being boys, they were always egging me on. One day, after getting a scolding from the local priestess for some minor mischief, the gang dared me to get back at the Church. I was fifteen, and I was clever. The appeal of sneaking into an all-women's domain and stealing something was irresistible. I resolved to sneak into the temple itself and steal a personal artifact from some high-up temple priestess."

"I can see you weren't bothered by religion even then."

"About as much as you or even old Mervyn is. I broke into the local laundry in the city where the temple robes were done, and I stole one that fitted. Then I appropriated a pretty good wig and some sandals that basically fitted from one of my sisters. And, one day, I just walked right into that temple and back to the living quarters. None of them gave me a second glance. In fact, my only mistake was that I really had no way of knowing where was where in there. I wound up in some office I shouldn't have been in and got challenged. My falsetto was not all that convincing, I'm afraid, and close-up the deception was quickly unmasked. I almost didn't mind getting caught then, because of the shock on their faces. I expected to be sent to the local jail, where they'd either cover it up to save embarrassment or make me a local hero to my peers. Instead, I was hauled up before a religious court in the temple that was strictly for priestesses and was presided over by the Sister General herself. I was charged with heresy."

"Go on," she encouraged him, interested in spite of herself.

Coydt seemed to enjoy telling the story, as if it was something bottled up inside him that needed to come out. "They were faced with an unprecedented situation, and they resolved it as best their little minds could. They could think of only one way to sponge out the heresy, and they did it. They took me to the temple clinic, filled me with all sorts of chemicals, and then performed agonizingly painful surgery on me. They castrated me, then used the scrotum to create a vagina. By more surgery and drugs, they smoothed my skin, changed my muscle tone, raised my voice half an octave— well, you get the picture. When they finished, months later, I was still very much a man inside, but outside I was an overly large, lunkish woman. Now the temple had not been violated, you see?" His tone grew suddenly bitter and seemed tinged with an insane anger. *"I was fifteen years old!"*

"I didn't even know such a thing was possible in Anchor," Suzl admitted.

"My parents were told, of course," he went on, not really hearing her. "My mother said it was divine punishment. My father thought it was funny. *Funny!"* He struggled to retain control of himself, and finally got it. When he continued his tale, his voice was calm and rational once more, but his story was not.

"Using various hormones and hypnotics, they kept me around for a couple of years as the temple slave. I was property, and that was that. I was still masculine enough to be a pretend man to the horny bitches, too. But the old Sister General retired, and the new one was a real moral type. She told me that it was over, that I had the choice of joining the priesthood or being sold to Flux. Three guesses which one I gladly took, even though I had no idea what was out there. After what they'd done to me, what did I have to fear?''

"Believe it or not, I understand. I've had some sexual identity problems myself.''

"When they found out I had some of the power, they sold me to a wizard in Globbus who needed an assistant. He was a rather unpleasant fellow named Voryer, and he heard of my condition and thought it was very funny, too. The first spell he taught me was the binding spell. He said he liked his first lesson to be one his pupils never forgot.''

Slowly, all of Coydt's clothing faded. He reached up to the side of his face and drew his finger down the side of his beard, and it and the moustache peeled away and fell to the ground. In most ways, his body was male and muscular. He had a tight ass and the sort of hip and other bone structure one would expect. In many ways, he reminded her of Dar, a huge farm boy who'd had a female organ, thanks to a spell, but there was a bit more to Coydt. The breasts were clearly breasts, although they were sized well enough that under a shirt they would just resemble overly large pectorals. Except for his hair, eyebrows, and pubic hair, he had less body hair than did Suzl or Spirit. Suddenly the carefully tailored clothing faded back in, and the false but very convincing beard and moustache jumped up, reformed, and reattached to his face. He looked now quite the normal, handsome man again.

"The voice broke and the breasts shrank when the hormones ran down and the male ones dominated,'' he told her. "But you can see what I had become. I learned all I could from the old wizard, and when I had more power than he did, I killed him. For years I plunged into spell research, learning all I could and getting ever stronger. I tried to find a

274 Jack L. Chalker

way to break that spell, and I couldn't. I was a
man who felt like a man and loved pretty women,
but I couldn't make love to them. Oh, I could
make them *think* they had a good time, but *I*
couldn't have it. I hid my problem with cheap love
spells, building a reputation as a hot lover. I worked
so hard building up my muscles that I became
very strong, and I liked to pick fights. I studied
with the masters of every physical fighting form,
and I mastered every weapon of Anchor and Flux.

"When I was ready, I hired on with a stringer
who needed big-time protection, so I could get
back into my old home Anchor. I strangled my
mother, then cornered and beat the hell out of
my father. When he was down and out, I took a
knife and made him like me, only a little messier.
When he didn't laugh, I cut out his tongue and
blinded him and left him there to bleed to death.
One by one, I tracked down every priestess that
had been at that temple during those times. All of
'em, including many who'd moved on or retired,
who were still alive. Each one of them I could get
into Flux I made into obedient whores. Those I
couldn't died, but they all died begging and on
their knees. The authorities couldn't catch me. Oh,
not that I wasn't collared now and then, but they
couldn't *hold* me. Now I had only this spell to
break, and I went looking through all of Flux for
the key.

"Eventually I signed on with a wizard named
Grymphin, who had one hell of a library from the
old days. He was also, it turned out, one of the
Seven of that time. He was one hell of a math
whiz, though, and he was devoting his life to
breaking the codes used by the Hellgates and to
stabilize Anchors. We didn't know about the temple entrances then, not until less than twenty years
ago, but he was determined to just walk into a
Hellgate, right past the Guardian. Got so fired up

convinced he had it one day that he tried it himself.''

"I take it he was wrong.''

"No, he was right. Only I changed one little number in a string that seemed five kilometers long. He got zapped; I won the resulting power struggle. And that's how I got my present job.''

"But you never found the way to break it.''

"No. But *you* did. You or somebody. I figured by using that language on Spirit, considering who she was, they'd bend heaven and hell to figure it out. The basic spell is the same. I want to know how it was done. Tell me, and you'll be fine and so will she. Come on—you don't owe Saint Bitch anything, either one of you.''

"As a woman in *your* idea of Anchor?''

"Was it so terrible? Truthfully, now—could you see yourself as Madame Weiz?''

She thought about it, and the horrible truth was that she could. She made no direct reply, though.

"I thought as much. You don't like to admit it, but my little demonstration was quite effective. Come, now—never mind the philosophical or ideological objections. What is your personal objection to living that way? Just yours?''

She thought a moment. "It's demeaning.''

"Oh, come. Being the consort to a homosexual stringer is not demeaning? Looking like a bloated sexual nightmare wasn't demeaning? Only a handful of people are ever truly free in any society, and that's as much accident as design, even in my case. You're a survivor, which is a valuable thing to be, but you are not a leader. Being his wife, the mother of his children, a ranking woman because of that and a privileged one as well—you'll live a better, more satisfying life than you have ever lived. Tell me—have you ever been truly free?''

She thought about it. "Yes. Once. With Spirit after I got the power.''

Coydt laughed. "Don't be absurd! The Soul Rider used you, cast its spell upon both of you, to bind you together, and not because it was a romantic soul either. It needed you to work the power it can command in Flux. I have dampened the spell chemically in Anchor, and now I remove it entirely. You may still love her, but you don't *need* her."

And it was true. She *did* love Spirit, and always would, but she did not crave her. More education. "Uh—Spirit. What have you done with her?"

"The same as with you, only more intensive. And we gave her a goal, something to strive for. We showed her a baby that looks *exactly* like hers. It didn't originally, but that was no trouble. She is convinced it's hers. She's not really a survivor like you, you know. She actually needs other people. Her conditioning will proceed well because of the baby. It is an incentive and a threat. I cannot bring her into Flux without giving the Soul Rider opportunities, but perhaps in time I will risk even that, since she has no power. She will continue to love you, if it suits the Soul Rider, but she will love that child more. She will be a good wife to someone. Which brings us back to the big question. How did my binding spell get dissolved?"

"It didn't," she told him. "You've lost again, for all your power. Her spell is diverted to the Hellgate machine by the Guardian only if she stays in Anchor. *You* seem able to talk to the Guardian. Why not command it to do the same thing?"

"And be stuck in Anchor as well?" Coydt sighed. "I feared as much, I might as well tell you. All my science, all my research, all of it says that there is only one way to break a binding spell, and that's to have someone of equal or greater power take it voluntarily in Flux. I have never found anyone my equal in power, not even those assholes that are the rest of the Seven. Perhaps I will, after all, have to teach them the machine language so we can open the Gates. If they don't kill us, they will be able to do anything."

She stared at him. "You *know* what's behind those Hellgates, don't you? You really do!"

"I know . . . some . . . of it. There are many gaps. I'm still not sure what the Soul Riders are, for example, or exactly how we came to be in this situation. But I know much. More than anyone else, certainly. I found it, in little bits and pieces over the centuries, from sorcerers I knew and some that I killed. Bit by bit I put the pieces together. I suspect that what I do not know, I lack the frame of reference to know." He sighed. "But I've talked and dallied enough. Back to business."

"What do you plan for me now?" she asked, terrified of the answer.

"Choices. I give you choices, that's all. Despite all our efforts, your sainted friend is still at large in Anchor."

She gasped. Where had they hid all this time?

"I've been sneaking around and eavesdropping on the empire outside," he told her. "There were so many wizards that nobody noticed one more. The fools were bemoaning the fact that there was no way to selectively alter memory and personality in Flux. That *is* true, because of a little thing called the subconscious. But it is not true for those with the power. Not those who can accept the binding spell."

She saw where he was leading. "What would be in this binding spell?"

"Very little. You would simply remember things, but differently. I stole the idea from a Soul Rider spell, in fact. You would remember Flux, and emphasize its bad points on your life. You would not remember Spirit, or the child, or how you came to be here, but you would simply never even ask that of yourself. The conditioning you underwent would be reinforced. The events leading up to it would

seem irrelevant. You would be madly in love with
Captain Weiz, bear and raise his children, and
support him utterly. You would be a model wife."

She thought about it. He was certainly leaving a
few things out, of course. Illiteracy, perhaps, and a
mathematical ability to count using fingers. Un-
questioned obedience to Weiz and servility towards
all other males went without saying. She tried to
imagine herself compulsively worrying over lint
on the carpet and the shine on her dishes and
trading recipes. On the other hand, she'd have
rank, thanks to Weiz's status, she'd have a nice
place to live with all the luxuries and amenities
and, alluringly, a feeling of total security for the
first time in her life. She began to realize that a
search for security had been the most important,
perhaps the only, objective in her life the past ten
years or so. She'd had adventure, travel, thrills,
danger—and what did she have to show for it?
Still, there was that insolent playful spirit in her,
too. . . . Or was that just a mask for what she
desperately wanted and never had?

"And the alternative?"

She saw the enormous, complex spell coming,
but could not dodge it or deflect it. She simply
didn't know how. In an instant, it had her.

"You remember that little picture of your old
self that you forgot when we accidentally met
before? Well, I found it, saved it, and dreamed up
several improvements on it."

She was still her one hundred fifty centimeters
in height, but her ample breasts were now blown
to huge proportions, each as thick as her thigh and
going out for a full meter. Additionally, she knew
she again had a male organ, but this one was
impossibly fat, like a banana, and went out from
her an impossible thirty centimeters. She should
have fallen over, but while the breasts and penis
acted as if gravity was pulling them down, it was

a sidewards pull. She felt an enormous, insatiable sexual urge.

"I do so love playing with what Anchor thinks of as natural laws like gravity," Coydt told her. "Also, I've redesigned the bottom so that there's not a scrotum in the way. It's elsewhere. You have a vagina to match the rest, and that organ is virtually prehensile, moving up and out of the way if need be. You can be like that, and I'll just leave you to wander this little area of Flux or return to Anchor with your memories. Any man who wants you, you will submit to. Any woman alone will be powerless against you. You'll eat garbage and love it, and you'll be so conspicuous that you'll never get near Spirit or the temple. Once you're in Anchor, we'll find some drugs and burn out your mind. A pet freak, an example for Anchor.

"Which do you choose? A happy life—or *this?* I have little patience left. Here is the binding spell I spoke of. Take it, embrace it, and join your husband. Or refuse it, and stay that way until hunger forces you in."

She saw the binding spell clearly in her mind, in Spirit language, but it was far too mathematically compex for her to follow. Why not take it? she asked herself. What choice do I have?

Matson and Kasdi jumped off the horses not too far from where they had gotten them and, slapping them on the rump, rolled into the brush. The pursuers, following the hoofbeats, rode right on by as fast as they could.

Matson had been forced to discard his pack, but Kasdi still had her rifle and gun belts, and Matson still had shotgun, whip, and knife. Water would be no problem, but food would.

They made their way cautiously overland to the southwest, on the lookout for more searchers. But the searchers, it seemed, had lost the trail.

"What now?" she asked him.

For a while he didn't answer, because he didn't know, but soon they reached a respectable stream flowing in the direction of their travel. He stopped and thought a minute. "If this thing goes all the way to the wall, it'll either have to empty into Flux or flood. Any big lakes in Anchor Logh?"

She thought a moment. "Not that I know of."

"Then we'll follow along here as best we can, all the way to the wall. If *it* can get through, then we might be able to. There must be hundreds of drain outlets. It's how many people sneaked in and out of Anchor in the old days."

"Well, say we can get out. What then? We can't escape."

"We can get into Flux, no matter how little. And in Flux you can conjure up what we need to survive. You can change into a bird—a little one, this time, like Haldayne does—and scout our positions. Even a few square meters of Flux will give us some kind of breather and help."

More than ever, she realized how a man with almost no Flux power had survived and prospered in a world of mad wizards for so long.

There were occasional patrols, but because the search was now over a far wider and less well-defined area, it was easy to avoid them and keep to the river. They reached the wall before daylight and saw that the water flowed through a series of huge drain pipes. There seemed to be no obstacle to passage, but they knew that could be deceptive. The great concrete pipes were all filled with a constant flow of water to almost eighty percent of their area. They studied the problem, noting the lack of guards on the wall at this point, and worried.

"I'm willing to chance it," Kasdi told him. "I can't see how they could have screens or mesh down there without all three pipes clogging up with silt and debris. But that water is fast and deep and that's a long tunnel. Can you swim?"

"I can, as a matter of fact. You?"

She shook her head slowly from side to side. "There was never any place or reason to learn."

"It won't matter," he assured her. "That current's so fast that it'll have you through before you can drown. Most of the drains I've seen from the other side are pretty level, often at ground level and rarely more than a meter's drop. The trouble is, the water will spread on the apron, so it might be shallow and tricky, and there might just be a canyon worn into it with a river this fast. That could make the drop really nasty."

"What choice have we got?" she asked him. "I mean, do we climb the wall? Surely that'll bring people running. We aren't all *that* far from one of the strong points of the shield."

"I'd say we jump in, take our chances, and let you dry us and our powder out in Flux, not to mention fixing us up."

She swallowed hard. "If I'm in any condition to do it. O.K. What do I do?"

"Take a breath, hold it, and jump in as close to the pipes as you can. Then hang on for dear life, and if you hit the sides, kick away." With that he looked for signs of life, found none, and ran into the open towards the drain and jumped in. Kasdi waited a moment, summoned up her courage, and followed.

It was a nightmare that lasted only twenty seconds or so, but it seemed an eternity. Carried along, she was surrounded by endless water and total darkness and flung at high speed against a wall of the drain. She was totally at the mercy of the flow, but, suddenly, she was plunged back into outside air and then fell into a roaring pool. She panicked, but then felt strong arms around her and let herself be pulled by them. She assumed it was Matson, but right then she didn't care who it might be.

And then, quite suddenly, the roar and the wetness stopped and they were flung and dropped onto a spongy surface. The water itself struck the Flux barrier and crackled, and was converted into energy itself and added to the void. Wracked with pain, she passed out.

When she awoke to the same formless void, it seemed almost a familiar friend. She tried to move, and found every single part of her body felt broken. She must have called out, because Matson heard and came over to her. The sight of him was almost unbearable, as he'd removed all his clothes and laid them out on the ground to dry.

"You all right?" he asked, concerned. "You had a pretty bad time in there. I got sort of banged-up myself, but not like that."

She saw that there were huge bruises on his arms and on the right side of his chest. He also had a nasty swollen place over his right eye.

"I think you got several broken bones," he told her. "You've been out a while. We're in Flux, though, so you've got your power back."

"Yeah, Flux," she responded weakly. "But the pain's tremendous! I need to do a thorough self-examination and construct—*agh!*—the proper . . . formulae and con . . . centrate. The pain . . . makes it . . . hard to . . . concentrate."

He nodded. "Take it slow and easy and one step at a time. Those forces out there got no place else to go, and I don't think anybody knows we're here." He paused a moment. "Just don't die on me, Cass."

She smiled, and drifted back into sleep. It was a turbulent, nightmarish sleep in which she was back in that roaring tunnel once again, only this time not alone. Suzl and Spirit were there, and they were drowning and she couldn't save them; the whole of Hope opened before her, but all the priestesses turned away from her and began worshipping statues, laughing statues, of Mervyn, and Krupe, and the rest of the Nine, and of Coydt and Haldayne as well. Matson was there, too; she kept trying to reach him for help, but the closer she got to him, the more out of reach he became.

She awoke again, and the pain was worse, but her mind was clearer. She looked around and didn't see Matson, but that was all right. She remembered the horror of the dream and feared she might have been calling out things best left unspoken. She tried doing a diagnostic on herself and found that she was in fact in pretty bad shape. Some of her internal injuries were serious enough that she might well have died from them, and would, if they were not corrected.

She took self-repair in slow stages, shutting off all pain from any but the area she was working on. After a few tries, she realized she just wasn't going to be able to do a piecemeal approach. She brought up and constructed a spell for a whole new body based on the old, a spell that was tremendously intricate and difficult. She almost passed out several times in doing it, but finally managed and put the spell into effect. She felt relief flow through her and lay there for a while luxuriating in that feeling.

Matson returned. He'd put on his pants, but little else, and they were still slightly wet. "I assume that's still you in there," he said after a while.

She sat up and smiled. "Yes, it's me. It's a body I designed for visiting Spirit in secret. The only one I could manage on short notice. It'll give me time to concentrate on reforming me as myself."

He nodded. "Well, it's not all that flattering, but if it lets you conjure up something to eat and a way to dry everything out, that's fine with me."

With no references, time had little meaning in

the void, but they got their food and drink and
dried not only the clothes but the weapons and
ammunition as well, and she managed to get back
somewhat to a normal appearance. Well, not quite
normal. She had felt herself eighteen again, out
here in the void with just Matson, and somehow
she had come out looking eighteen in spite of her
vows or herself. She could not have him the way
she wanted him, but they were together now, alone,
in Flux, and for the moment that was enough.

In a while, they decided to risk forays into Anchor to see what was going on. Borrowing a trick
from Haldayne, one of the Seven she'd bested
before, she turned herself into a normal-looking
bird and flew out and over the wall. Matson, too,
could and did become transformed by her power,
and together they scouted the area.

It would have been easy if she had been able to
change *back* in Anchor, but she could not, nor
could she be some human-sized flying beast, for
that would require either too much wing to remain inconspicuous or too much weight to stay
aloft and remain in touch with the required physics.
Still, they were able to map out the terrain and
get a look at the guard post and the Flux machine
itself. That had been the one risky point, since the
wizard operating it might well have sensed her
power, and any observer who saw two birds fly
into the void would be instantly suspicious of them.

Both became intimately familiar with the town
of Lamoine and the military post on the wall. The
town disgusted her. The natives there had dis-
carded ways and attitudes of generations very
easily, and both men and women seemed to be
acting under the new rules automatically and without threat or supervision. She had expected *some*
laxity, particularly among women off by themselves,
but she'd seen none. Of course, their proximity to
Flux and a wizard would tend to make them model

citizens, she reasoned. Otherwise, model citizens could be *made*. Her opinion of the human race in general took something of a beating.

There were some large, predatory species of birds in the area that had been imported from some far-off Anchor generations ago to control a rodent infestation. These had strength and speed, and she used their form to perch right on the wall near the emplacements. They used this not only to steal some more palatable food by snatching it with strong claws, but to snatch items occasionally from the emplacement as well. They didn't need much; once in Flux with one of them, she didn't have to know what it was to duplicate it.

Still, they kept planning and putting off any real attack. For one thing, they hoped for some time that Suzl and Spirit would eventually show up, and they undertook long searches for them to no avail. When they didn't appear, and had to be assumed captive, another problem arose.

"The Guardian said we needed the Soul Rider to knock out the machine," she reminded him. "It obviously amplifies Flux power. How can we do anything without Spirit?"

"I've been thinking about that," he replied, "and I feel we have to try. I keep going over that Guardian's message again and again."

"It said we needed the Soul Rider to knock out the machine and its operator," she recalled.

"Uh-huh. I know we've been over this a hundred times, but I *knew* there was something not right about that, and when you said it, it just hit me. It didn't say the machine and its operator. It said the machine *or* its operator."

"So?"

"If we knock out that guard post, the guy in Flux won't know it right off. The sound's dampened, as you know. I looked over that machine again and again, and that open operator's cab is only a little over one meter into Flux."

"So?"

"If I can get my back cleared, I can take him. He's like most all the wizards; he doesn't think that anything can hurt him in Flux without being in Flux, and maybe he's right. But I got a trick I pulled over twenty years ago on the border of a Fluxland called Rakarah that might just work here."

But it would take two to work it all, and she was still undecided as to what to do. She simply did not want the specter of her homeland devastated, and she certainly didn't want it on her head. It was so nice and comfortable being here, just she and Matson, no stress, no responsibility, and nowhere to go. He was getting restless, yes, but he understood her agony and was willing to wait a while.

And then, flying over Lamoine, they'd spotted a carriage coming into town with some brown-uniformed officer and his lady driving. A close, curious inspection sparked some familiarity in that woman, and when the pair picnicked near the wall, she was able to get a closer and more positive view.

*It was definitely Suzl!* Suzl, decked out like all the others, and acting just like they did, and seemingly not minding a bit. She watched as they packed up and walked up to the gate, then to the wall, then down the other side, and then saw, as they approached Flux and the big machine, another figure, casually dressed and in no uniform, come out of the small temporary guard station on the wall and descend to the apron.

She and Matson returned to their Flux base and became human. "I've decided," she said. "We have to pull her out of there. She's already half gone, maybe with drugs or something. Now they're taking her into Flux without Spirit, and she'll be lost forever.''

He nodded, but said, "Are you sure about this? It seems kind of funny that they'd bring her here and parade her around and then Coydt shows up. I think they know we're around. Suzl's bait to get you out in the open for Coydt, Cass. It's a trap."

"Then it's a trap we take. You've been itching to move. Let's move now or forget it."

Their weapons had been well prepared in advance and needed no more done to them. Practice was impossible; either it worked or it didn't. Matson set the detonators; then Kasdi changed them into the great birds again and used her power to make the packs fit correctly. They could take off with them in Flux, but whether or not they would be able to handle the weight in Anchor had yet to be proven.

They flew in formation, one close behind the other, right down the roadway atop the wall. Matson gave a quick glance towards Lamoine and saw no massed troops and made the final decision. They swooped down on the emplacement and let go their loads, then quickly gained altitude and headed for Flux.

Captain Weiz had waited nervously for a bit at the emplacement, then decided he wanted to smoke. Rather than go further down the wall, he decided to go down into Anchor and see to the horse and carriage. He had barely reached the horse when suddenly the world exploded behind him. He turned and was knocked over by the blast and almost trampled by the panicked animals, but he was the only one able to see what had happened.

One set of high explosives had struck near the barrels where oil for the night torches and lamps was stored; the other fell on the other side of the small makeshift hut, near the ammunition. When the birds came in, there were only curious stares,

but when they dropped loads that clanked metalli-
cally on the stone, they leaped into action, some
starting to aim at the fast-fleeing birds, others
jumping for what was dropped. All too late. Matson
had perfect timing.

Suzl's initial estimate of their vulnerability had
been right. The two containers exploded within a
fraction of a second of each other, one blowing the
oil barrels and sending flaming liquid everywhere; the other blew up the concentrated boxes
of ammunition. The whole post was bathed in a
massive fireball; then individual explosives began
to go off in all directions. Weiz, on the ground
below, could only keep low and try and make
himself as small a target as possible. One thing
was sure—the wooden stairway was also aflame,
and he could not reach the top now even if he
wanted to. He looked up when the explosions di-
minished and made a run for it away from the
wall and towards Lamoine. Coydt's trap had been
sprung, but in a way he hadn't expected.

Kasdi quickly restored Matson in Flux, then
kissed him. "Good luck!"

"You, too," he responded softly, giving her a
hug.

Both reentered Anchor east of the machine and
saw the remains of their work. Kasdi quickly ran
down well past the machine to where they'd seen
Suzl and Coydt enter Flux; Matson gave one brief
check of the wall to make sure that anybody alive
wasn't going to shoot him, then stood on the apron
looking directly at the machine, barely visible despite being so close.

The machine had its own protection against Flux
magic, but he had no Flux magic. He had studied
this problem over and over again, and he knew
he'd better be right.

Carefully, he uncoiled and tested his four meter
bullwhip, then walked right up to the Flux bound-

ary and stuck his head in. He saw the wizard sitting there, relaxed in a comfortable chair, reading something. "Hey!" he shouted. "Trouble on the wall! We're under attack!"

The wizard jumped up, revealing the two small probes on his head, and looked puzzled for a moment.

The whip cracked out, wrapped around the wizard's neck, and as it did so Matson pulled and was back in Anchor, still pulling. The action was so quick and unexpected that the wizard literally flew off the machine's cab deck and landed, with a pull, in Anchor.

Matson cooly walked up to him, leveled his shotgun, and blew the wizard's head off.

He unclipped two timed explosive charges, walked into Flux and attached one to the cab area of the machine and another to a random spot on the smooth cube of the basic machine itself. Then he ran back for Anchor, unsure of just what the hell was going to happen when they and that thing blew.

Kasdi entered Flux and immediately saw Suzl, grotesquely deformed, frozen there about five meters from Coydt. The evil wizard was talking to Suzl.

"Which do you choose? A happy life—or *this*? I have little patience left. Here is the binding spell I spoke of. Take it, embrace it, and join your husband. Or refuse it, and stay that way until hunger forces you in."

*That spell! Suzl was going to accept it!* "Suzl! Wait! Don't do it!" Kasdi screamed.

Coydt looked over at her, turned, and smiled. "How melodramatic," he commented softly. "Friend saved in the nick of time from a fate worse than death by the timely arrival of—Sister Kasdi, is it not?"

"I am Sister Kasdi. And you are Coydt. I have

290 Jack L. Chalker

been looking forward to this for a very long time now."

He grinned. "That is certainly mutual. Would you care to step over here a bit? I wouldn't like to get out of range of our audience here, but I wouldn't like to injure her either."

# SAINT DEVIL

"Cass! Watch out for his hate!" Suzl called to her. "He was castrated by the old Church and stuck with it in a binding spell! Power's the only thing he's got and hate's his only fuel!"

"She's right, you know," Coydt told her. "In a way, we have things in common, you and I. Both of us were abused by the system, and both of us are trapped in binding spells that leave power as the only outlet. Power for its own sake."

"Yes, we're probably a pair made for each other, but you've become so foul that it's impossible. What you have done to me and mine cannot be excused."

"Excused?" He laughed. "I don't ask to be excused! It amused me to do it. It proved out many of the theories I've read in the old books and fragments, the old records. Power needs no excuse! Power exists, and those who have it make the rules! Look what I've made them swallow in Anchor Logh! Your birthplace, the start of everything you've done—and the ending of it. The end of your empire, and the beginning of a new one, one based on reality. They were sheep under the old Church, willingly sending off their children to slavery and death! Actually *thanking* the Church for its tyranny! Then they followed *you*, built monuments to you, called you a liberator and denounced the old ways, not ever once thinking that by doing so they were denouncing themselves.

"And all they had done was changed mistresses, substituting one rule for another. *You* were the Fluxlord to whom they gladly sent their daughters, and you bound those daughters to absolute obedience, and then you sent them back to unquestionably enforce whatever rules you and your empire thought up."

"I gave them their freedom," Kasdi responded.

*"What* freedom? To happily send the best of their young off to die in distant wars for a cause *you* decided? And how did you free them, make their life better? Was it really different in any way?"

"Science is once again open to them."

"Ah! Science! And I thank you for that. As long and hard as our research teams worked to develop the amplifier machines, it wasn't until your own bright ones came up with the new transformers capable of handling an Anchor's power and the internal electronics needed to feed them that we had the answers. The scientists thought they were working on a means of inter-Anchor communication, which is what attracted us in the first place. Perhaps they *will* invent that, but mine is of more immediate practicality. Science is always a two-edged sword like that. That's why it was suppressed and feared by the old Church."

"You've killed thousands in Anchor Logh," she accused. "You killed my father."

"Oh? I hadn't known. But, no matter, it will simply add spice to your attack. And how many have *you* killed, or caused to be killed, I wonder? Ever add it up? I'll bet you've got me beaten by at least hundreds of thousands. And for what?"

"To keep scum like you from opening the Hellgates! To save World!"

"I would open the Hellgates only as a last resort. The rest are, in their own way, self-deluded fanatics like yourself. They, too, are idealists; only they will go to any length for those ideals. Me, now, I know that there's nothing mystical about it and that the chances of *your* vision of Hell on World is about even with *theirs*. If you were caught and trapped for over twenty-five hundred years in a terrible place, cut off from your own and from any life at all, would you be grateful to those who released you? Or would that hate be so refined as to destroy all human life? Perhaps, one day, I'll be bored enough or disgusted enough to find out. Right now I would rather not take the bet, and they can't do it without me. You see? I'm the best friend either Church has!"

She thought for a moment. "Suppose *I* took your binding spell? I have already, in a sense, castrated myself. Being superficially male wouldn't bother me. What would you do then?"

He chuckled. "I'd hardly reform and start praising the Goddess, but it would be worth a great deal to me. It would be worth Anchor Logh and the researches I and my teams have compiled over the centuries. It would be worth the truth about World and Hell. It doesn't really matter what I offer. Eternal slavery. Anything. You see, it can only be assumed by one of equal or greater power than myself. That's the real curse, don't you see? There *is* no one equal to me."

"You seem pretty sure of that. Want me to try?"

He shrugged. "What have I to lose?"

She reached out and found the binding spell. It was absurdly simple and direct, in no strange language and with no traps for the unwary. How it must have frustrated him, galled him, all these years to have godlike power unlike almost any other and yet not be able to break this one simple little spell! She was quite sincere in her offer, and she reached out and voluntarily seized it, took hold of it, and reached to bring it to her.

The spell remained in Coydt.

He laughed, but it was a strange laugh, half

triumphant and half sad. "Not even close," he told her. "I've had it hurt. You have a great deal of power, but I have more. You have much training and experience, but I have more, for I know what it is and what it is for. I will not kill you, if it can be avoided. No, I will take you into Anchor as my bride, and you shall serve me gladly, worshipfully. Your binding spells are easily accommodated by ones I will place upon you. Sex, needless to say, I will not require. With you as my servile slave, I will own your empire."

Tremendous energy emerged from his body and lashed out at her. She quickly brought up her own personal shields and drew upon Flux to push it away. Both of their bodies and the three meters separating them crackled with raw electrical energy so clear and blinding it could have been seen and felt even by one without the power.

She strained against his massive onslaught, and perspiration broke out all over her body. She held him in check, but barely, and she could not hold his thoughts.

*"Do you know what you've been worshipping all these years? A giant bag of poisonous gasses! A world, just like this world, but so huge it keeps us in its gravity as a natural captive. A world so foul and poisonous nothing could live there. The stars are but other worlds, more distant than our own."*

She had already lost her faith, but there was underneath still a bedrock that sustained her, told her she knew her place in the universe. The empire had been a device for powerful men to rule indirectly what they could not directly have. They had wanted Anchor, and she had delivered the Church to them while sacrificing all. Now Coydt was saying that even the faith had been a lie, that there was nothing out there but science and nature. The thought of the Soul Rider came to her.

*"But I have seen the supernatural, had it in my body, had it guide me here to this place!"*

He was unmoved. *"Machines and unnatural and artificial life, or life perhaps left over from the time before men were here! There are no gods and goddesses except those here on World! Those with the power are the gods! There is nothing else!"*

The energy from him intensified, and she found it more and more difficult to counter it. She thought fast, knowing that she could not sustain it long, that her defense now was being sustained only by her contempt for him and for what he had done to her family. She reached out to Suzl, who sent her the power, and for a moment the combined assault staggered him.

But only for a moment. Suzl's power was raw, untrained, unformed. A shard of crackling yellow-white light came from his side and joined the link with Suzl, then traveled up it, overwhelming it. Suzl cried out in sudden pain, and the link was diverted. Now her power, despite all her efforts, was flowing not to Kasdi but to Coydt. He burned with a new fury, a new sense of triumph, and he attacked with renewed force and vigor. *"I am the way, the truth, the light!"* he trumpeted. *"On your knees before me and worship me!"*

A tremendous force, like a giant's hand, pressed on her, and she fell to her knees. *"This is the man who crippled Spirit and killed my father!"* she kept repeating to herself over and over, trying to drown out his force and his will. Her clothing burned away from her, and the force pushed against her head, bowing it down.

*"It is meaningless to resist further,"* he argued. *"I am the god of World, and my name is Power. I can grant any wish, or visit any calamity, when, where, and how I choose and on whomever I choose! Fight me no more! Surrender control of your power to me, and be the priestess of my Church! You shall have*

*your daughter and grandson and friends, and you
will have no worries, no cares, no pressures upon
you. I will take away those things and give you
peace. Otherwise you shall die, and as you truly
know in your heart, you will be dead forever."*

The vision of her father, bleeding, rotting, hanging from a pole came to her, and she summoned
enough strength to raise her head and look him in
the eye. It was, she realized, the last thing she had
to throw at him. Already his visions of her as she
would be were creeping into her mind, looking
desirable, alluring, and she was having more and
more trouble casting them out. Her head drooped
again, and she felt so tired, so sick of it all. . . .
"No!" she cried. "No!" And drew her last ounce of
strength.

There was a loud explosion, and suddenly Coydt
cried out and fell forward. She barely had the
strength to move out of his way, but she saw in his
back an enormous hole, a tremendous outpouring
of blood, and she heard him scream and moan as
she felt the power weaken as he withdrew it into
himself.

He almost won it back by her confusion and
hesitancy, but she saw his bloody back and drew
on what reserves she couldn't possibly know or
guess that she had. He screamed again, but the
pain and damage were so great, the shock and loss
of blood so severe, that he could sustain his life or
fight off her attack.

A tall, dark figure behind her lowered his shotgun and broke it, inserting two more shells. Coydt
managed to turn himself over onto his side and see
the man standing there. "Matson," he croaked,
blood running from his mouth. "Why?"

"You shouldn't have done that to the girl, Coydt.
She was kin."

Kasdi had not the strength to attack or to do
much of anything, but she had enough to keep

Coydt from coming up with any kind of repair spell. But he wasn't through yet, and he managed to chuckle, coughing up blood and phlegm as he did so.

"Done in by a man with the power of a shotgun. My own fault. First time I got careless in four hundred years." He coughed again, as his life poured onto the spongy Flux surface. He still had enough strength to stem the flow, but he knew that too much of his insides were messed up. He had the power to heal himself, but if he took the concentration and time to do the spell, Kasdi would have a free hand to do with him as she willed. He knew it, and he made his decision.

"You think you've killed me, but you haven't. You haven't begun to kill me yet. You must kill a million before you kill me. I've still got your empire. All you have done is guarantee that at some point in the future the Hellgates will be opened." He coughed some more and seemed to fade for a moment, but Kasdi was on guard and knew he was still alive. Any less powerful man, in Flux or Anchor, would be gone long before.

He opened his eyes and managed a smile. "And now I will make you mine," he said softly. She realized what he was doing, but he put so much force of will into it and she was so weakened she couldn't stop it.

Coydt took upon himself *her* binding spells. His body twitched and shimmered, and lying there was a mannish-looking woman, still big and powerful, and still dying. And he/she started laughing, then laughing and choking. There was a sudden convulsion of the whole body, and then the life force simply went out of it.

Coydt van Haaz was dead.

A dull explosion was heard, followed by a second, and then off to the south the whole of Flux seemed to flare into blinding power, but only for a brief instant.

The power was distributed in all directions, but was more intense because it was limited by and deflected from the Anchor boundary. They all felt a brief burning sensation, and then it was gone. With a start, Kasdi realized that her skin had turned a deep brown.

"I guess I put the things where they should've gone," Matson said dryly. She turned and looked up at him, and saw that he was burned, too, on his face and hands. She had neither his clothing nor facial hair, and had taken it evenly all over. She looked back down at Coydt's dead body.

"He finally found the way to break his binding spell," she said softly.

# HARD CHOICES

Cass made her way over to Suzl, who hadn't moved much in the whole affair. The gross malformation was the worst Suzl had ever been and among the worst that Cass had ever seen. The woman was unnaturally balanced and grossly obscene.

"Let's see what we can do for you, Suzl," Cass said, and started examining the spell. She frowned. This was no spur-of-the-moment spell; it had been prepared in advance and custom-tailored to Suzl. It was in Spirit language and monstrously complicated.

"Don't fool with it, Cass," Suzl warned. "I may not understand a spell from a bill of lading, but I know curses when I see them. This thing has a million traps in it for anyone trying to take it out, and you don't know this language. I do. I've been looking at it this way and that for a little while."

Cass sighed. "Well, Mervyn and the others should be here soon. They might have better luck."

Suzl chuckled mirthlessly. "Yeah, he'll have a lot of nice psychology spells that will make me think this is just *wonderful* to be this way. He couldn't even lick the old curse, and that was child's play compared to this one. Coydt had everything planned out from the start. Everything but Matson's shotgun. At least I owed him that. He never knew Matson was here, and that was his only mistake."

"Perhaps if you can link with the Soul Rider—"

"Fat chance. Even if I could, it would revert Spirit. And Coydt knew the Soul Rider's langauge, too. I'll bet that somewhere in this spell there's a nasty little thing that would add on to Spirit's curse. She has enough trouble in Flux without turning into a thing like I am."

Cass sighed. "But what's the alternative?"

"Cass, Coydt had a very evil mind. I doubt if I have ever known anybody more totally evil and yet so damned smart. Whatever he touched he corrupted, and that's still true. I have a way out that he gave to me. I think it's the only way out for many, many years."

Cass was shocked. "Not that binding spell! Suzl! It would turn you into a different *kind* of thing, one just as unpleasant."

Suzl sighed. "I'm tired, Cass. Real tired. All my life I've been owned by somebody and took orders. Every time Flux touched me, it was to turn me into something more strange, more grotesque. I was owned by the Church, then owned by stringers, then owned by the Soul Rider. None of 'em ever gave a damn about me. Even Spirit was a lie, just the Soul Rider hyping both of us up because it needed somebody to do its dirty work for it."

"I'm tired, too, Suzl. I've been as much a victim and a pawn as you have, but I didn't really realize it until just a little while ago. Now I'm free, for the first time. I don't know why he did it, but he freed me."

"You really think so, Cass? I think *I* know why he did it, and I think Matson does, too. Tell me, Cass—could you take back on yourself all those binding spells and restrictions right now?"

"No. Never again. Even if there was a real need. Even if life depended on it. I could *never* bring myself to do it."

"Then he's got you, too, just like me. He's undermined the whole Church with what he did to Anchor Logh so quickly and easily. But the Church, and the empire, could stand that. You see, he's also taken away its foundation, the rock on which your Church and revolution sit. They won't march off to fight any more if their own homes are in such mortal danger, and they don't have the symbol, the example, to lean against and be inspired by. They don't have you anymore."

"I made my sacrifices! I deserve some reward!"

"Yeah, you have and you do. But that's not the way it'll be seen by others. They'll march for a saint, Cass, but not for a Fluxlord. And with nothing to keep your power, your temper, your wants and your needs down, that power will corrupt you just like it did all of them, Coydt included. He trapped you just as sure as he trapped me."

"Suzl—promise me you won't do anything rash until the wizards get here and I can sort this out. Will you at least do that?"

She nodded. "For a little while."

Relieved, Cass looked around. "Where's Matson?"

A fairly strong force had been waiting on standby north of Lamoine, but Coydt had ordered them well back and it had taken some time for Weiz to make it back to the town and then send a runner with the news. Now they rode forward to the wall. The fires were out, but it was still a smoking ruin up there.

General Shabir, chief administrator of the riding, looked disgusted. "I *told* him that it was a pushover. You know what he said? 'I *want* a pushover, but a convincing one.'"

Weiz nodded. The steps were in ruins, but were still serviceable for about three quarters of the distance. It wasn't easy, but a crew managed to get up with hooks and ropes and lower down netting for the troopers to climb up. One of the first to survey the apron from the top turned and shouted back, "Sir! There's a lone civilian standing there just below us! Looks like a stringer! He says he wants to talk to you!"

"Don't shoot!" Shabir ordered. "Tell him I'm coming up. Keep him covered, but that's all!" He turned to Weiz. "Want to come with me?"

The captain nodded.

The stairs on the side leading to the apron had been blown out about a meter, but they had somehow escaped catching fire. They were singed, but serviceable, and were easily drawn back and secured with hooks. With a hundred guns trained on him, Matson stood calmly and waited for the brass to show up.

The military men approached him cautiously but correctly. He had dropped his weapons belt and was clearly unarmed. "My name is Matson," he told them, not offering his hand. "Coydt van Haas is dead. Your wizard is dead over there, and I've blown up your pretty machine. If we can't come to some agreement fast, in an hour or so an awful lot of power is going to burst right through that area right there."

The military men swallowed hard at the news. Dimly, in the void, they could see where the machine should have been, and there was nothing.

"One of you wouldn't happen to have a cigar on you, would you?" the stringer asked. "I'm dying for a smoke."

One of the infantrymen looked to the officers, who nodded, then handed Matson a cigar and a safety match. He lit it and seemed much more content.

"If what you say is true," the general said slowly, "then it is the end of Anchor Logh. Many of my men are scum, I freely admit, but they've been made that way. They've marched and died on command in other people's armies for nothing. The Fluxlord I once served, and deserted for this, is a particularly nasty sort. The military leadership here is experienced and superior. They were given a chance to take their own land, and they did it. They will not return to the way they were, and they will leave this place a costly hell."

The stringer nodded. "I figured as much. That's why we have to take this time to make a deal. We have to keep all this quiet from the rest of Anchor Logh, or the other wizards will panic and let the shields drop as they run, and everybody will be primed for the last stand. Then it might be too late."

The general frowned. "Too late for what?"

"A deal. Suppose there was no invasion outside of this small area? Suppose we let you keep Anchor Logh and run it without any interference? What would you say then?"

Both officer's mouths fell open in surprise. Finally, the general recovered. "At what price?"

"The empire controls the machines, and the temple becomes a sort of embassy. We need to insure that it's not a free and easy passage to the Hellgate. Beyond the temple, no one leaves or enters without the permission of your government and the empire's. The stringer guild will deal with you at east and west gate. I've seen a thousand Fluxlands, General, and so have most of the others. We'll keep your trade open, and we'll be the intermediaries between the empire and your people. It makes no sense to cost a million lives and make this a wasteland. No sense at all, for either side. They want to keep this contained. If you're here, running the place, they can do so. They do it by co-opting you into the empire. Making it legitimate. Anchor Logh is restored, but has total internal self-government. Everybody benefits and nobody else dies."

"If we could only trust the empire on that,"

Weiz put in. "But it's a theocracy. How can we trust it?"

"Guarantees can be worked out. You and the Church have both been working with an illusion. The empire isn't the Church; the Church serves the empire. Nine wizards set policy and control everything that it does, and none of them are in the least bit committed to the Church. The war has bled off the surplus population so far, but that won't last forever. Flux will absorb the surplus, though, as it always has in one way or another. The ones with the power, the Nine Who Guard, are really mostly concerned with securing those Hellgates. Secondarily, they went as far as they could in learning. They needed a mechanism to break the control of the wizards, each of whom had some piece of old knowledge that usually meant nothing to them until fitted into the whole. They needed a way to pry the ancient stuff out, and they needed Anchors, with fixed laws, to experiment with what they learned. I think they can spare Anchor Logh."

"It seems reasonable to me," Weiz noted. "But it'll have to be sold to higher-ups, in secret, while everything is contained here."

"Just keep your men on the wall. I'll stop them and explain the conditions there, too. I think the head of the Nine will be among the first through. You sell it to your side; I'll sell it to mine."

"It's a tough job," the general noted. "Still, I agree, for what that's worth, and I'll cooperate so long as there are no tricks. But no empire forces are to cross the wall or extend more than a kilometer in either direction. If they do, it's all off."

"These are hard choices you're handing both sides, Matson," Weiz noted. "You're the only one free and clear in all this. You don't give a damn."

"Life is all hard choices, Captain," the stringer replied. "I've had more than my share. But most folks never get any choices at all, and hard as they are, I'd rather be the one making the decisions."

Weiz stirred. "Did you see a woman in Flux? Short, chubby, kind of cute?"

"Yeah, Suzl's alive. Why? What's she to you?"

"I . . . sort of married her."

Matson chuckled. "On orders, of course."

"Well, yes, on orders. But I find her a little special."

"You can hardly even know her!"

Weiz shrugged. "I'm a gambler."

"Well, we'll see if she is. Do your job first, Captain. The rest is academic if we fail."

It had been kind of imposing, even threatening, to stand in front of a point in Flux and try to talk an invading force into not going into Anchor. Fortunately, the initial shield opening was quite small, and there were few soldiers to work with—and a wizard. The wizard had contained the assault and sent for Mervyn.

Weiz was a glib talker, and it had been a surprisingly easy sell on the Anchor side, although, of course, it would be years before the military government felt safe enough to relax and remove its martial law organization designed mostly to fight a tough war. On the empire's side, there was almost a feeling of relief at Matson's offer. Many of them were appalled at legitimizing such a terrible and repressive sexist regime, but when you had the Fluxlands for an example, the bizarre could be made palatable and the unthinkable allowed. The people of Anchor Logh knew the hard choice. All-out war to the death or the system they had now. Most hardly liked the system, but they were terrified of the alternative. They consoled themselves that such a rigid system would have to bend someday, and slowly reforms would return. They would wait, making a characteristically human decision that none not in their place could comprehend.

They had seen the burned-out and desolate future, and they had decided *no more, no more*. They would accept the system, with faith that it would eventually change from within, if not in their lifetimes, then in their descendants'. Slavery and repression, in the end, only ever existed with the consent of the slaves and the repressed, who preferred their condition to death. On a mass basis, there was no other way for such systems to survive.

Mervyn had called in a whole crew of top wizards to examine the spell on Suzl and found it fully lived up to her expectations. Its traps were based on her own Flux power; automatic spells that would trigger when the one before was touched. Such was the way of curses. They could see the traps, but there were so many of them, and all of them so subtle, that there was no way to disarm them without exploding them, to the detriment of any wizard—and innocent bystander—who tried. Coydt had made good use, too, of the linking spell between Suzl and Spirit, now inoperative. Through that, Coydt had engineered a system which would backfire on Suzl when she disabled the spell, sending it along via the linking spell to Spirit and attaching it to the binding spell. To free Suzl would send the curse intact to Spirit, making her curse even more grotesque.

There was always a chance, of course, that the Soul Rider could work it out, but they wouldn't know until it was tried. As far as the Soul Rider was concerned, Suzl was convinced that her part in all this was done. The Soul Rider had stuck with Spirit. It would not risk her, particularly when Suzl could still use the power through the Soul Rider's spells. From the Soul Rider's point of view, Suzl, as translator and spell receptor, was still just fine the way she now was.

"And the binding spell Coydt handed me?" she asked the spell doctors. "What would it do?"

"He was as good as his word," they replied. "You would remember, but your perspective will have changed. You would see your previous life as a waste, a miserable emptiness. You would see this system of theirs as perhaps not right for others, but just what you've always wanted and needed. Once in place, you would consider it natural and normal. You would know all the rules, and you would embrace them. It would dampen your aggressive streak, and pump up your hormones, and freeze your sexual orientation, and focus your interests on what your new life demanded. There would be no regrets."

"And the body?"

"Physically and emotionally, you would be seventeen or eighteen again and would be somewhat frozen there."

"So it's *this* forever or *that* forever."

"Perhaps not. When we get to really understand the power amplifiers, we can perhaps reform and refocus them. Technology and our knowledge will advance. What one person created, another can surely uncreate one day."

"One day."

Cass was appalled that she was even considering the binding spell. "For whom? A guy who was ordered to marry you and parade you around to draw me in? A man you've known for maybe a day?"

"Or somebody else. What does it matter, Cass? I told you a while back that you just can't relate to what kind of life I've had."

"But you've always been the clever one, the big mouth who'd always point out the truth. You figured out how to reach the Guardian and made it all possible! You've always been the independent free spirit!"

"It was an act, Cass. An act to convince everybody, even myself, that I wasn't a freak, wasn't owned, wasn't property. But I was. The only time I felt really genuine, really free—with Spirit—turns out to be phony as well. My absolute master was the Soul Rider. My mind's been messed with by the wizards of Globbus, by Ravi, by Mervyn, and by the Soul Rider. I'm not even sure what's really *me* anymore."

"But that life back there—treating women as *objects!* Even *you* made fun of it! It's repulsive!"

"Why? Because it's only women and not both who are objects? Who are you kidding, Cass? You're arguing ideology. A place where they oppress and degrade women is bad, but a place where they oppress and degrade *both* men and women, like ninety percent of the Fluxlands, is O.K. or at least acceptable. Sure, I know it's stupid to oppress and retard half the human race, but it's just as stupid to oppress and retard *all* the human race. You know what I've got, Cass? The same old thing I've had ever since they threw me out of Anchor Logh. Never mind the principles and the masses—all I've got is my choice of oppressors."

"Suzl—*live* with it a while. There's a beautiful and private Fluxland waiting for you that you've never seen, and there's a child out there as well, one who now has no parents."

"I'm going to be just *great* raising a child like this. Just *look* at me, Cass!" She paused for a moment. "Are you ready to prove your commitment?"

"Huh? What do you mean?"

"Make love to me, Cass. Right here and now. I'm totally turned on, and I'm having to repress the urge to leap on you."

Cass was suddenly taken aback. She looked at the gross breasts, the enormous male organ, the whole sexually misshapen body, and she was revolted. As

much as she wanted to prove her points, she knew
that there was no way she could possibly do what
was asked. No way at all. No spell prevented her,
nor any moral qualms—it would have been moral,
in a sense, to shut her eyes and allow it for Suzl's
sake—but she just couldn't. She just wasn't a self-
sacrificing saint anymore, and all she could do
was turn, run, and cry it out.

She did not, however, cease her assault on the
kind of agreement they were sealing. Finally Mervyn
lost his temper and angrily snapped, "What's all
right one way is wrong the other, huh?"

She was puzzled. "What do you mean?"

"Coydt recruited his men mostly from Fluxlands
ruled by female Fluxlords. Crazy, nasty Fluxlords.
Matriarchies, and worse. *They* were the objects
there, fighting when told, prevented from any real
authority or position, doing the heavy, dirty work.
Coydt freed them and fed their lifelong resentments.
His system reversed the roles and fed their egos.
Some of those Fluxlands—most, in fact—are within
the empire. Lands you allowed to continue."

"If it was wrong for it to have been done to
them, and it was, then it's just as wrong the other
way."

"Human nature seldom operates like that. Even
its loftiest principles tend to become excuses for
doing what the powerful want to do. In Anchor,
crippled and deformed male babies were put to
death by the priestesses. Female counterparts were
taken to Flux with the aid of stringers, made whole,
and returned. They were good children, model
students, and virtually all of them went into the
priesthood. The argument went that those girls
didn't increase the population and they filled the
need for priestesses painlessly. Most everyone knew
about this and accepted it. Since the mothers of
killed male children were convinced the births were
stillbirths or that the causes were natural, they

took it hard but accepted it. World is a rotten place, but it's what we made it, and we can hardly judge them and not ourselves."

Slowly, Cass was losing whatever faith she had left in human nature and whatever hope she had for the future. It seemed like blow after blow was coming down on her, and she was powerless to change it.

She went to find Matson and found him preparing to leave.

"Where are you going?"

"Home," he answered. "It's all done now, Cass. I beat the odds again, and that's that."

She felt sudden emotional turbulence. "What about me?"

He sighed. "Cass, so long as you were a priestess, it wasn't worth the telling, but I been married more than fifteen years to the same woman, a tough ex-stringer like me. We got three kids of our own, and it looks like my oldest daughter, who's fourteen, is leaning to both the power and to stringing."

She felt shocked, hurt, even somehow *betrayed* by that. She began to tremble with anger and emotion.

He looked at her. "What'd you think? That I was sitting up there pining for you? You made your choice to go one way, and it looked permanent to both of us. You're a good woman, Cass. You'd have made a hell of a stringer and there's no bigger compliment I can give. But I love my wife and I love my kids and they're probably all in a panic that I'm lyin' dead someplace. I have to go back."

It suddenly all burst out in a fury. "I'll *make* you stay!" she screamed at him. "I'm a wizard and I can make you love me and forget all about them!"

He tensed, but kept his self-control. "Yeah, sure. You could make me your pet lover and slave. You been goin' all over this camp telling people how

*lousy* it is what they're doin' to women in Anchor
Logh. How *immoral* it is. But it isn't immoral if
*you* do it to *me*, is it? No, because Coydt was right,
and those guys in Anchor are right, aren't they? If
you have the power and you want something, you
just *take* it and the hell with the others! I could be
the star of a whole Fluxland of men worshipping
you, couldn't I? It'd be O.K. because it'd be *you* on
top and *me* on the bottom, and the hell with me,
right? The hell with my family, right? Go ahead—
use your damn Flux spells to make me what you
want. Then you'll be just like all the rest of 'em,
and you'll have no kick coming. Do it now, 'cause
if you don't I'm gettin' on that horse over there,
picking up Jomo, and goin' home!''

The spells needed came easily to her mind in her
hurt and anger. And somewhere, off in a corner of
her mind, she heard Coydt's voice whisper, *"Go
on! Do it! You got the* power *and that's all you need.
I'm not dead. I'll never die. Go on and take him . . .
and I'll be* you *next time around."*

Matson checked his packs, got on his horse, and
rode slowly away into the void.

And now she had nothing at all. *That* had been
Coydt's intent and his revenge upon her. He had
removed the spells and the way of life that had
insulated her from truth and allowed her to use
them as a convenient excuse to hold on to her
fantasies. He had stripped all that protection away,
protection she realized now she'd put on herself to
protect those fantasies. Coydt's final, cynical lesson was that power meant nothing to the wielder
unless it was used on other people and at their
expense.

Mervyn found her, sulking and alone, the evidence of many angry fits and many tears abounding.
"They're bringing Spirit to the apron," he told
her. "We're bringing Jeffron."

She did not look at him or change her facial

expression. "She'll probably stay in Anchor Logh with him," she sighed. "And I might as well stick on tights and heels and go with them. I don't want to live in this ugly world any more."

"She might surprise you. She's stronger than you think, considering how much she went through with no preparation and how well she came out of it. Her idealistic world has collapsed, too, you know."

She turned and looked at him. "She's with her Mom and Dad. She can't have Suzl, although I suspect the Soul Rider has already begun readjusting her from that. It still has power in her, and it'll protect its host if it doesn't conflict with its own objectives."

Mervyn scratched his beard. "Let's see. Oh, by the way, that bronze color is a sort of skin tan ~~form~~ FROM the radiation given off when the amplifier exploded. It looks good on you. Perhaps you should make it even and keep it, perhaps lightening your hair."

She gave a dry laugh. "For whom?"

"Who knows? You're alive, you're powerful, and you're one of the very few people now who are completely free." He paused and said, gently. "It wasn't a waste, Cass. We contained a great evil, and we made a better life possible for those who can do nothing for themselves. It's not perfect, but it's better. That's an accomplishment worth some pride."

She just stared after him as he walked away.

"I've come to say goodbye, Cass," Suzl told her. "I'm going to do it."

She nodded. "I can't ever understand living in that place as it is now, but I think at least I can understand why you have no choice."

"No, you can't. I doubt if you ever will. You're strong by nature. A leader type, Coydt called it.

I've been strong by necessity. You retired, and now I'm ready to retire. Good-bye, Cass. I hope you find what you're looking for."

"I—I hope you do, too, Suzl."

The great, misshapen creature that was Suzl was helped by duggers, many as strange and grotesque as herself, into a wagon and she rode off. They rode down to the end of the perimeter and lifted her off, then drove away. She looked around the void, and there were tears in her eyes, not just for herself, but for Cass and Spirit and the others as well. None of them really understood, but, oddly, Coydt would have. She was a terrible freak with the power. If she remained this way, she could survive and even learn to use that power. Eventually she would dominate and make others like herself, and others like she wanted to be would be forced to worship her. She would be yet another child of Coydt's, and she knew it. World had too many Coydts now. Hard choices. No more hard choices. . . .

She engaged the spell. She felt momentarily dizzy and lost her balance, but her mind cleared quickly. She sat up and looked down at herself. She was normal again! If anything, a little slimmer, a little shapelier. It was odd. She didn't *feel* any different. She remembered everything clearly, the good and the bad. Mostly bad, though, she knew. A depressed, unhappy, unnatural and abnormal life that had accomplished very little. Flux had been cruel to her, and she hated it. Still, she had the power, and, interestingly, she now knew a couple of spells. She got up and gestured at the void, and a shining mirror appeared. No taller, but she *was* shapelier, sexier, better proportioned. The breasts were still big and sensual, but after what she'd been cursed with, they were just fine. Big and sexy—not deformed.

She made her hair longer, so that it came down

on both sides of her face and, pushed forward, kind of hung down sexy-like over the breasts. She gave the image a sensual kiss. Big eyes and sexy lips. She liked what she saw there. The earrings with the tags had returned, but nothing else. She used the power instead. Rosy lips, shadow, eyebrows . . . everything. She created clothing by using very fine black mesh that hugged tight and hid nothing, not even the tattoo. To this she added open-toed shiny black shoes with thin eighteen-centimeter heels, very high, but they made her seem taller and gave her *such* a walk!

Lengthen and paint the fingernails and color the toenails to match; set things for no unwanted body hair—and she decided she was ready. It was, she thought, the first and only positive help the power had been.

Suzl ~~She~~ turned and faced the Anchor border, and something inside her whispered that, even now, she could turn around. Some ghostly link, perhaps with the Soul Rider or the Guardian, or some corner of her mind the spell had missed? She knew she could, realized that there was a certain chance here at freedom, but if she walked back into Anchor, it was for keeps.

She walked into Anchor with a strut and a wiggle that was worthy of any Main Street entertainer. There was a new temporary set of stairs there and two soldiers standing guard at it. Their eyes looked at all of her in a way she had never been looked at before, and she found she loved it. She walked up to them and waited.

"What do you wish, lady?" one of them asked.

"Sir, my husband, Captain Weiz, is somewhere in this area. I would appreciate it ever so much if you could take me to him," she said in a voice that was high, yet soft and sexy, and rather helpless-sounding.

"We've been told to expect you," one of the soldiers replied. "Allow me to help you up the walk-way here."

She allowed it, even enjoyed it. She had seen other women do this and be treated this way, but she had never been. The trick, she decided, was in never letting men know what suckers they were for this sort of thing. *This is what I've always wanted*, she realized, and didn't even trouble herself about whether it was the spell or her real self thinking. Whichever, it was true, and she neither looked back at the void nor had any regrets.

Dannon and Cloise brought Spirit to the apron with them. Cass watched them come, and still she felt nothing but contempt for the pair she'd en-trusted Spirit to all those years. Dannon was wear-ing a military-style uniform with second lieutenant's bars sewn on. Cloise walked behind him, looking just as ridiculous in her hooker's outfit as she had before, but also looking very strong-willed and confident. Behind them was Spirit, on whom the same sort of outfit looked absolutely stunning. She, however, did not look happy about the whole thing.

Cass had taken Mervyn's advice, with the advice and help of a few others. She had filled herself out a bit, trimmed off those boyish edges and flattened chest, kept the smooth bronze color on her skin, and made her hair a light brown streaked with blond. She wore a light tan pullover shirt, blue work pants, and a pair of riding boots. She had smoothed her faced and skin a bit as well, and made herself look attractive but thirtyish. She wanted to give the onlookers, particularly those on that wall, a look at a strong, independent woman who was in every way their match. It was the only blow she had left to strike.

They came up to her and stopped. "Hello, Sister Kasdi," Dannon said, clearly not happy to be there. "You look quite different now."

"Not Sister Kasdi, just Cass," she responded coolly. "I no longer represent the Church or the empire. I'm here as a concerned mother and grandmother." She paused for a moment then looked at Spirit. "No drugs or hypnos, and she's been told the truth?"

They both nodded.

"Spirit, how do you feel?" Cass asked her.

"Sick," the woman replied, and Cloise and Dannon both looked startled.

A man came out of the void behind Cass with Jeffron in his arms. That, too, had been a little rub in the noses of the onlookers. The boy wasn't crying, just sucking his thumb and looking around wide-eyed.

"Here is your son, Spirit," Cass told her, taking the baby from the man and walking up to her daughter, whose height, with the shoes, was towering in proportion. "My grandson. The *real* one."

She took the boy and held him close. Then she said, "They told me Suzl was dead. Is that the truth?"

She thought a moment. "Yes."

Spirit looked around at all of them. "What am I to do now?"

"Choose," Cass told her. "Remain here if you wish. Or we will arrange to take you through the temple and into one of the other three Anchors and get you and the boy settled in."

She stepped forward and looked at the two whom she'd loved and thought of as her parents almost all her life. "You make me sick," she told them, and they both looked shocked. "Most of the people I can understand, but not you. I *loved* you and you betrayed us! Out there in Flux I thought how nice it would be to be back in normal, loving Anchor Logh. I felt cut off, lonely, insecure. But not *nearly* as cut off, lonely, and insecure as I felt this past two weeks. There's more love out there than in all of Anchor Logh." She handed the baby back to a startled Cass, kicked off her shoes and removed the rest of her clothing. She was *still* a lot taller than Cass. "Coming, Mother?" she asked the woman with the child.

All of a sudden they all realized what she was going to do, and all for reasons of their own yelled out, "Spirit! Wait! Don't!"

Cass looked at her, feeling not a little pride and admiration for her courage, but she wasn't sure if the result was right. "You don't have to. There are three other Anchors. It'll hurt them, certainly, but it's for keeps. They'll recover. You won't."

"I've been there before," Spirit replied. "The first time I wasn't prepared for it, mentally or emotionally. I am now. Hard as I'll try, I won't be able to forget what happened this time. But, you know, maybe I'm better off not understanding what you people are saying and doing. Maybe it'd be a lot nicer if everybody saw the beauty in a butterfly's wing or the wonderful patterns in a blade of grass and if everybody spent a lot more time on love and had no more time for fear and hatred."

"I could lift that spell, you know," Cass told her. "I could take it on myself. It would be far better than what I had all those years."

"No. Jeffey's got to know both worlds. He needs a wizard's protection, and he needs experience and guidance I can't give."

"There'll be no men in that little Fluxland, you know."

"Oh, World's full of men, just as nice and just as rotten as the ones we've known so far. If we need them, either of us, I'm sure we can find them."

Cass felt everything drain away to be replaced by new and far different emotions. She wanted to hug Spirit, but couldn't because of the baby. Well, there would be plenty of time for hugging later.

Dannon and Cloise still seemed in a state of

shock. They could no more conceive of Spirit's choice than she could of theirs. Cass grinned at them and looked back at Spirit. "If you ever want out, just let me know, somehow, and I'll switch with you. I owe you that."

Spirit smiled back at her. "You just want *in*," she replied, took little Jeffron and stepped into Flux.

Cass turned back to the gaping pair, stiffened, clicked her heels together and saluted. Then she turned and followed her daughter and grandson. She'd just been offered a very nice job, and this choice wasn't hard at all.

# WITCH'S SABBAT

"He's dead," Gifford Haldayne told the other five. "The-son-of-a-bitch is truly dead."

Romua Togloss, the former Queen of Heaven, President of the Council and Haldayne's half-brother, smiled and nodded.

There were smiles and nods all around. They were all there, in a rare gathering in a small, remote Fluxland all their own. Here was Chua Babaye, the beautiful self-styled Witch of the Southern Wastes, and Ming Ṭokiabi, the tiny, brilliant head of the technical department, and Vrishnikar Stomsk, the lean, gaunt, goateed mathematical wizard, and Zelligman Ivan, the huge, gruff military expert. Although now only six, they were the Seven Who Come Before, the Seven Who Wait, the most powerful wizards dedicated to opening the Hellgates.

"We must add a new member and select a new President," Ivan pointed out. "As much as we are relieved to be rid of that madman, we owe him a debt of thanks. In one series of strokes he demoralized the empire, eliminated Sister Kasdi as a symbol and a threat, sowed fear in enemy Anchor, and halted the relentless military progress. The empire is in discord, each little group and area preoccupied with its own selfish interests. It is exploitable discord!"

Haldayne nodded. "Indeed it is. And as the Political Affairs Minister here, I will take full advantage of it. We must, however, continue to encourage and fund scientific research and cooperation. Coydt knew more than any of us. We must locate and unify his research teams, know what he knew but withheld from us. With a knowledge and understanding of the Guardian's language, the Gates are open to us. Taking all seven Gates will not be easy, but I feel it will come. Licking the communications problem is the major obstacle."

"You underestimate the Nine if you think taking the Gates no problem," Gabaye commented. "To take and hold one Gate, two, even four or five, perhaps. But all seven at the same time will not be easy."

"I didn't say it was easy, just attainable," Haldayne snapped back irritably. "But the amplifiers don't work well around the Gates, and the Flux damps out any wireless signals, even if we could find some way to curve them around the whole of World's surface."

"Don't worry, we'll let *them* solve it," his sister soothed. "We have had to be patient for so long, so very long. What are a few more decades even, if we all live to see our dream come true?"

They murmured and nodded assent. An assistant came in and poured drinks all around. Haldayne rose and raised his glass. "To our certain victory and to a utopian world!"

"To *power!*" responded Zelligman Ivan.

*The Soul Rider saga continues with*
*Masters of Flux and Anchor*